PRAISE FOR THE WEBS WE WEAVE

"Expertly written, *The Webs We Weave* embodies a true fantasy adventure. Filled with tangled deception and questions of identity, there's an undercurrent that cuts through it all: truth holds more power than lies and one's lineage doesn't determine one's worth. Utterly gripping, heartfelt, and humorous."

—Alissa J. Zavalianos, author of *On the Edge of the Forgotten Sea*, *The Earth-Treader,* and *Endlewood*

"The world needs more books that can combine humor with heartfelt themes of belonging, identity, and standing up for what's right, and that's why it's a good thing that Cassandra Grace has written *The Webs We Weave*. The witty characters and sparkling dialogue will have you laughing, but this story goes deeper than chuckles and jokes. Adventure, plot twists, and a touch of romance combine to make this a truly captivating read that will have you hooked from the first zany chapter title."

—Elisabeth Aimee Brown, award-winning author of *What Comes of Attending the Commoners Ball*

"If you yearn for a story with humor, wit, and profound themes of value, then look no further than *The Webs We Weave*. Cassandra Grace, the Queen of Salty Banter, has knit together a stunning tale of hilarious accidental adventures and bravery despite status. You will be left laughing and weeping as our hero and heroine overcome every obstacle imaginable. Already, *Pirates & Politicians* promises the thrill of a lifetime."

— S.L. Klein, author of the *Liberation* duology

"Captivating right from the start, Cassandra's writing echoes of poetry and so much heart. Full of humor that will keep you gasping and smiling throughout, *The Webs We Weave* is deeply touching, profoundly healing, and impossible to forget. Full of intrigue and defiant survival, this story is an inspired lifeline to those who have ever felt alone and unworthy."

—Melissa Miyoko Scott, author of *Izabella*

The Webs we Weave

PIRATES & POLITICIANS
BOOK ONE

The Webs we Weave

CASSANDRA GRACE

Copyright © 2026 by Cassandra Grace

All rights reserved.

No portion of this publication may be reproduced, stored in a retrieval system, or transmitted in any form or by any means, electronic, mechanical, photocopying, recording, or otherwise, without written permission of the publisher. For information regarding permission, email cassandra.grace@cassandraspocket.net

No part of this book may be used or reproduced in any manner for the purpose of training artificial intelligence technologies or systems.

This book is a work of fiction. Names, characters, places, and incidents are products of the author's imagination or are used fictitiously. Any similarity to actual people, organizations, and/or events is purely coincidental.

ISBN: 979-8-9913126-2-2 (Paperback)

ISBN: 979-8-9913126-3-9 (Hardcover)

ISBN: 979-8-9913126-4-6 (ebook)

Cover Design by Emilie Haney, eahcreative.com

Map by Annika Crum

Editing by Olivia Jarmusch (The Glory Writers), Caitlin Miller, Teri Sammon

First Edition 2025

*For my mom,
who taught me to love stories and
encouraged me to write my own
from the very beginning.*

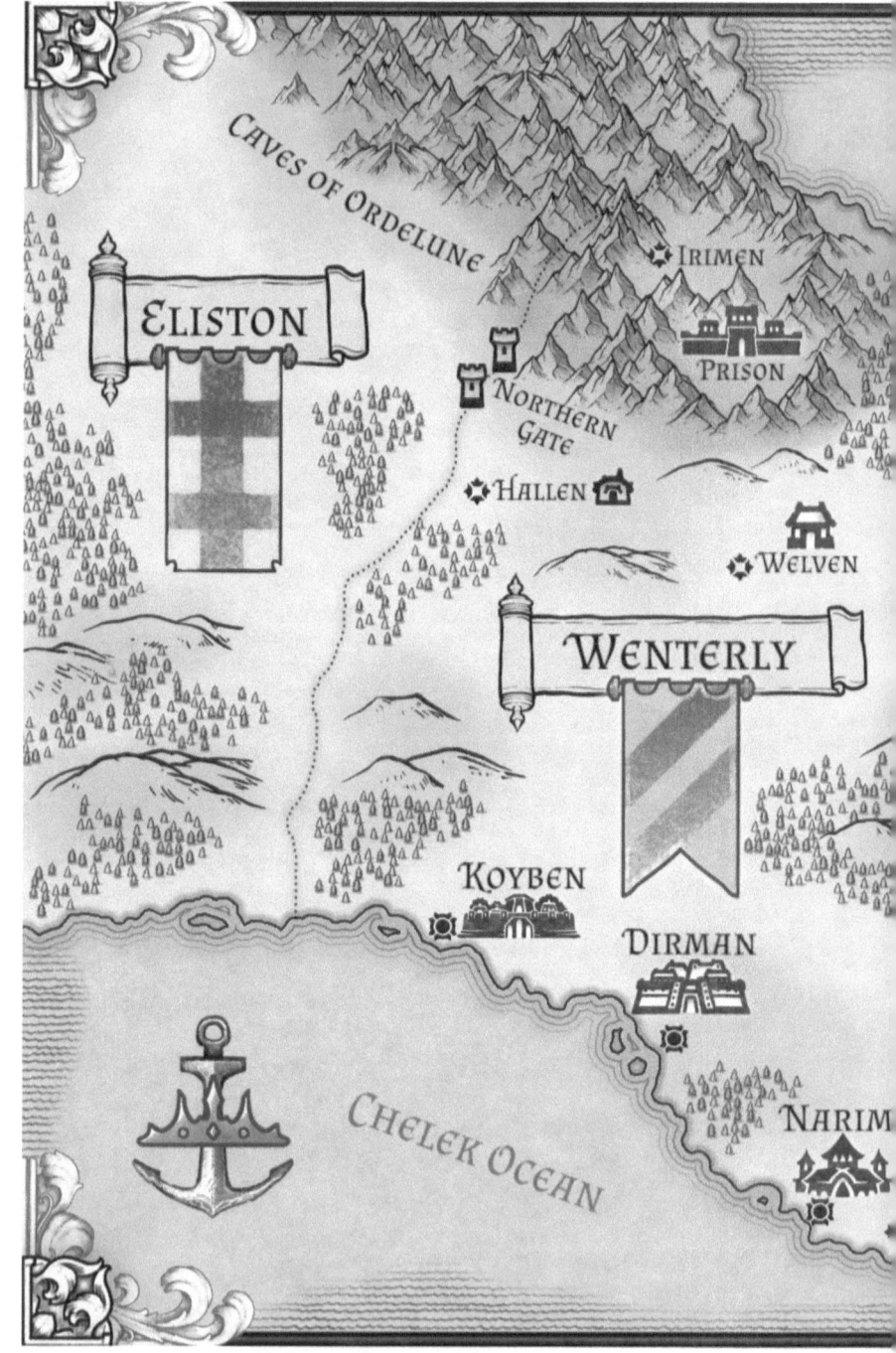

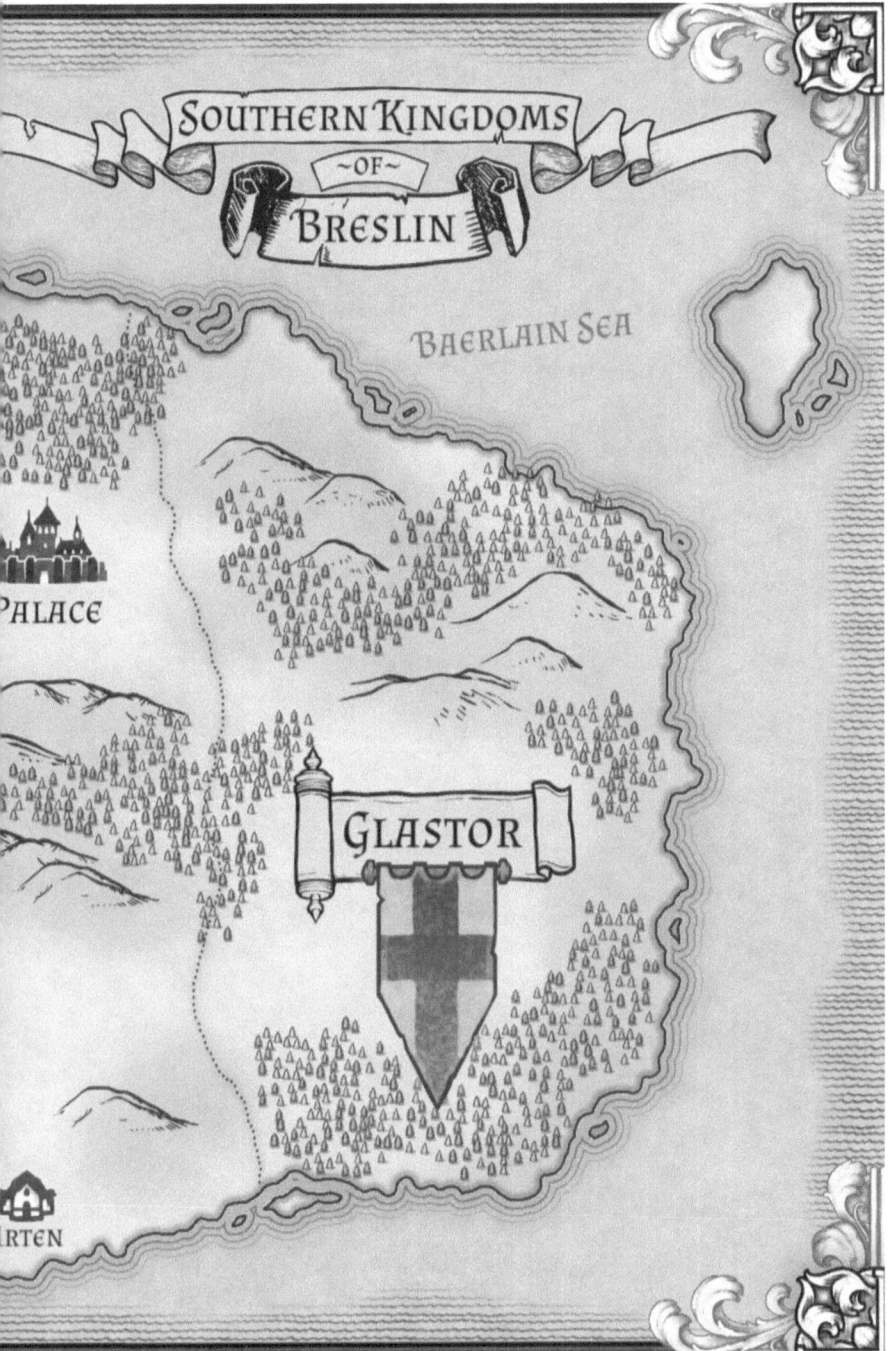

Prologue

Alastair

The door to my library burst open, causing me to jump and tip over my jar of glue.

"Stars," I muttered, hurrying to right the glass jar and contain the spill. "This had better be—"

After shutting the door with far more care than he'd opened it, Roland turned to face me, nearly out of breath, his eyes wide, and his tunic twisted around his body. Had he ... *run* here?

Most perplexingly, he clutched a sword in each hand. Roland taught me many things, but swordsmanship had *never* been one of them.

"We need to go." He spoke quietly, but with an urgency unlike any I'd heard from him before.

"Go? I thought I wasn't expected to meet with King Harland until dinner."

"You're in danger."

I froze. I had expected him to say "trouble." But *danger*?

He crossed the rest of the library, stopped on the other side of my desk, and placed one of the swords on the desktop for me to take. "Alastair, we have to go."

Footsteps pounded in the hall as servants—or guards—ran through the palace, further proving his point.

"What's happening?"

"I can explain later, but right now I need you to move your feet or I will carry you out of the palace myself."

"Out of the *palace*? I thought we were to go to the High Tower in case of attack."

"In case of an *outside* attack. This one is inside."

"Then why didn't you use the code? You should have asked what tea—"

"Do you think this is some test of wits, Alastair?" Roland walked around to my side of the table and grabbed my shoulders, trying to forcibly move me from where I stood. "Harland has placed your life in danger. Now will you move your blasted feet?"

"*King Harland* is the threat?"

"Yes. Let's *go*."

"Wait, my parents. Are they—"

"I don't know. I happened to walk by when I heard the commotion."

"What commotion?"

"Oy!" A voice called from the hall. "He's not down this wing. Has anyone tried the East yet?"

"Now do you believe me that we need to *move?*" Roland hissed.

"Okay." I glanced at my desk before grabbing the sword, abandoning the glue still in a puddle on the wood and the book I'd intended to bind.

Roland shoved me toward the back bookcase.

"Harland doesn't know of the tunnels?" I asked.

"Even if he does, it's still our best option."

We rolled the bookcase aside, its hidden wheels remaining mercifully quiet, considering how little use they got. I shoved the small door open, and off we went, down the steps, into the service hall.

These passages were originally for servants, back when the palace was first built, but were rarely used anymore, either believed to be blocked off or simply forgotten about over the years. But the Captain of the Guard demanded my family be familiar with them, if only so we could navigate the passages in such an emergency as this. Personally, I used them most often out of laziness. Sometimes it *was* a quicker route than the palace halls, if for no other reason than that it was a less sociable one.

But I'd never used them for something like this.

"Go to the stables," Roland whispered. "We'll take the horses out."

"Won't they see us?"

"It's at least faster than letting them see us run on foot."

"Fair enough."

I led the way through the corridor and down another set of steps. I kneeled before the small wooden door and realized for the first time that not only did I have a sword in my hand, but also a book. The one I'd set on my desk to reference its detailing for the new one I was binding. Why had I grabbed that? And when?

I shoved it under my tunic and crawled through, emerging outside behind a strategically placed hedgerow.

Roland appeared beside me a moment later, then took the lead to look for danger. "Clear."

We bolted across the path to the stable. Theoretically, there were to be three horses kept saddled at all times, just in case there was need for a hasty exit: one for each of the Royal Cathmoores.

Roland swung open the gate to the first stall and wasted no time swinging himself up into the saddle.

"What of my parents?"

"It's too late for them."

I froze. "What?"

"Fate's mercy," Roland cursed. "They aren't dead. Not as far as I know anyway. But he has them captured. Which is about to be your fate if you don't move."

"But you said—"

"I don't have time to explain everything right now, Alastair! *Move!*"

Somehow, my feet obeyed his command, though my mind hadn't budged an inch. *My parents were captured? How was that possible? Surely not* every *guard on duty had turned on us?*

Roland's horse shot forward, and I blinked, suddenly realizing I was no longer in the stable, but riding out on my own horse behind him. The book was still secure in my tunic, and my sword was now properly attached to my belt. *When had I done that?*

"There! He's getting away!"

I kicked and commanded my horse to run faster.

Roland and I flew across the palace lawn, beginning a chase I could hardly comprehend. Guards aimed arrows at us. Other guards took them down. Servants were everywhere. Some trying to stop the enemy guards from following us, and some merely running for their own escape. People shouted, blades clashed.

What in Fate's Design is transpiring?

Roland and I wove our horses through the field and the orchard, and then we charged at the East Gate—the only other entrance to palace grounds other than the Main Gate.

Thankfully, the East Gate was hardly used, and the guards watching it must have been loyal to my family, for they opened the gate as soon as they saw us approaching, letting us pass by without incident.

I realized I should say something—a warning, an explanation. But we passed them in a blur, and by the time I found my tongue, we were well past them.

I looked back to see they'd already shut the gate behind us and were drawing their swords to meet the other approaching guards and soldiers.

"Just ride, Alastair. Don't look back."

"But—"

"*Ride.*"

"Never is a man so at risk of discovering the heights of his stupidity or the depths of his intelligence as when he finds a wife, or finds his life is in danger."

Brigid, "Wildhearts in Wildfires"

I
Apparently Marriage Will Fix This

Evangeline

If becoming a criminal was my goal for the evening, then I suppose, I had succeeded. But if we looked at the specifics, *marriage* was not the crime I'd been looking to commit.

I wanted treason. Piracy.

All I got was a wedding.

But when had things gone my way over the last three weeks? In all honesty, I could probably count all the instances in my nineteen years on one hand.

I shouldn't have been surprised it ended up like this.

But the day had been shaping up quite nicely, so I let that convince me things were finally starting to turn in my favor. And, just as my mother had warned me years ago, that was exactly when it all went wrong.

I'd stolen my dinner while in the city. Koyben was the nicest city I'd ever seen, and the people there were surprisingly friendly. Perhaps it was my clothes—I'd stopped obeying sumptuary laws a few towns ago and had been elevating my wardrobe, and therefore my status, ever since. I snatched a green shirt in one town, a yellow skirt in another. The patterned corset was the hardest to find, but it had done wonders for improving my reputation.

I did feel bad about stealing from strangers, but what choice did I have? I didn't have money—not yet, anyway. And I'd never find a job without a reference or a guardian's permission if I was also dressed as... myself. A girl in solid brown and unbleached cotton was not the kind of girl anyone wanted to associate with.

But, while the new clothes made me look like a regular commoner and earned me much more polite conversations, getting someone to look past the fact that I had no letter of reference from *anyone* was still a lot to ask for.

So, if elevating my status couldn't earn me a living, there was only one other direction to go. Besides, Gratsis would expect me to try to raise my status. Lowering it might actually keep me safer.

I'd technically already become a criminal by stealing.

But pirates were even lower than that.

I spent the last few days out by the docks of Koyben looking for sailors who might know a thing or two on the whereabouts of pirates. They couldn't fathom why such a nice girl as myself would ask about such things, but a few smiles and well-placed laughs convinced them it was nothing more than morbid curiosity, and this morning, I finally heard that the *Gray Dagger* was moored just outside the city limits.

My stomach lurched as I walked toward the beach. This might have been the very beach where my life began. And my mother's, at least socially, ended.

I pushed away the grim thought. Her life had physically ended, too, years ago. So, I could hardly betray her by coming here. And even if I could, I was sure she'd rather see me turn pirate and live a decently comfortable life instead of die in the streets—or, worse, go back to Master Gratsis.

No one is goin' to look out for you but yourself, Evangeline, she would always say.

She had certainly been right about that, too.

I crested the dune and reached the overhang. Sure enough, a pirate ship was anchored out in the shimmering blue sea, and two dinghies were beached in the sand, exactly as the sailors had said. The sound of voices promised that the pirate camp would come into view below me in only a few steps, but I hesitated to take them, wondering if the fate my mother met at the hand of pirates might become mine too.

I took a deep breath. It was risky, yes. But at this point, everything I did and everywhere I went was risky. After all, *I* was my greatest liability.

I crouched and approached the edge of the overhang with caution. I didn't want them to see me yet. I needed to plan my entrance first.

The overhang was no more than ten feet above the beach. I was grateful I'd had the foresight to crouch down, otherwise the pirates below would have easily spotted me by now. And there were a lot of them. More than I had expected, anyway. Thirty? Forty? And I couldn't be sure there weren't more aboard the ship.

I searched for any women, but it was difficult to tell if there were any around. I saw no skirts, but I had also heard pirate women dressed the same as the men. Some claimed those kinds of rumors were proof enough that there was no such thing as female pirates.

But there had to be.

There wasn't an easy way to get down to the beach from here. Perhaps I should call out to them from up here. I had to make it clear from the beginning I was hoping to join them and not trying to sneak up on them. I started to stand—

"Get down!" a man hissed as a hand grabbed my arm and yanked me back.

I screamed and whirled to see who ambushed me.

A startled man held a finger to his lips, but didn't loosen his grip on my arm.

Did he follow me out here?

I tried to pull myself free from his grasp, but only managed to step right off the edge of the small cliff.

The man was either too stupid to let me go before I dragged him down with me, or he severely failed in an attempt to keep me from falling. Either way, he crashed to the sand right on top of me, crushing my lungs under his weight.

He quickly rolled off, and I was left spitting sand out of my mouth and gasping for air.

He scrambled to his feet much quicker than I, since he only had to recover from the fall and not a *giant* also crushing him. He offered a hand to help me up.

I did not take it.

I'd seen the man before, in Koyben. Was that just yesterday? He'd watched me closely in the market. Too closely. I thought I had evaded him.

But here he was, ruining everything.

As I glared at him, I realized he was hardly a man. He must have been near my age, and while I was hardly a child, I'd lived through quite a bit of life on my own, and judging by the boy's attire, he'd been pretty well off—at least for a commoner. His clothes, though sandy now, appeared new. A yellow shirt. Green trousers. Barely a stain on either of them. An artisan, perhaps? He was a commoner, but well paid.

Which meant he was naïve. *Hardly* a man.

"We have to go," he hissed, pushing his dark brown hair out of his eyes.

I opened my mouth to tell him I wouldn't go anywhere with him, but I never got the chance.

"Thieves!" a pirate called, and within seconds, the boy and I were surrounded.

"We're not thieves!" I spat, pushing myself up to my feet.

"Then what do ya be doin' approachin' a pirate camp?"

"We fell off the overhang," the boy pleaded. "This is all a misunderstandin'."

"Liars!" another pirate shouted. He was also a large man. As tall as the boy who fell on top of me, but far more muscular. "Search 'em, an' put 'em in the brig."

"Wait—listen, I just—" but my pleas were too late. The pirate surged forward and gagged me as another pulled the knife and pouch from my belt. The knife wasn't much of a loss. I'd stolen it from a butcher a week ago.

The pouch was far more difficult to part with. In terms of actual money, I only had two peb inside—like that was going to fill the pirates' chests—but my sewing needles and Missus Gratsis's necklace were also inside that pouch. Those were my livelihood.

The pirate who took my pouch immediately opened it and pulled out the necklace. I'd had little luck so far in finding someone I could sell it to without being accused of stealing. It was simple in comparison to the adornments of noble ladies, but it was the nicest thing Gratsis had ever bought for his wife. A gold chain with an opal pendant studded with rubies on each side. Not the kind of adornment a leech could wear.

"Ye've got a fine taste in fashion, eh, little lady?"

He reached for the necklace around my own neck, but was sorely disappointed to see it was only a brass pendant on a leather cord. He let go of it, and it thumped back against my chest. *Good.* Upon closer inspection, he would have seen that it wasn't simply a floral engraved brass pendant, but a thread cutter. The grooved edges of the pendant provided notches for my thread to meet the blade inside, while protecting my skin from doing the same.

But a small pin at the top of the pendant opened it, similar to a locket, allowing the blade to be taken out and changed when necessary. It was the only weapon I'd be taking with me now.

"She's clear. Get 'er out of 'ere."

I huffed through the gag as the large pirate—the captain, perhaps?—clamped a hand on my arm. He yanked the scarf off my head, ripping out a few strands of hair in the process. I blinked away the tears that sprang up from the sharp pain. My braid fell unheeded down my back, but I didn't protest. I was losing my dignity quickly enough as it was.

Meanwhile, the boy was taking a little more effort for the pirates to capture. He was taller and younger than most of them, but he only had a dagger to defend himself against multiple swords.

And the large pirate holding me was getting tired of waiting. "Drop yer weapon or I'll slide mine across yer little lady's throat."

I closed my eyes. *This is the end. This is—*

A soft thud reached my ears as the boy's dagger hit the sand. "Don't touch her," he demanded, but the slightest waver in his voice betrayed his nerves.

I opened my eyes as the pirates rushed in to gag and search the boy, and the large pirate laughed. "Oh, that's not fer me to decide, boy."

Apparently I was mistaken in assuming he was the captain. But he spoke with such authority to the others, I wasn't sure who else he could be. Perhaps there was more to pirate life than I knew.

The boy stared at me, and I glared right back. What was he playing at? He'd surrender for me? It couldn't be because of my clothes. No one was that nice for *anyone*. Except, perhaps, for the king or someone like that. But I was hardly royalty.

The pirates bound our wrists and led us to their boats. They rowed us to the ship, pulled us aboard, shoved us down to the brig below, then promptly tied our ankles and bound us together back to back before locking the cell and leaving us alone.

A proper institution would have at least given me some semblance of privacy, perhaps my own room.

But these were pirates. And they didn't see women and decency the same way the rest of the world did—which, ironically, was why I'd sought them out.

But it was not supposed to go like this.

The pirates hadn't bothered to so much as leave a lantern for us, so we were left in the near pitch-dark, alone. The boy shifted behind me, or tried to anyway. When he pulled against the ropes, he only succeeded in pulling them against me. I dug my hands into his back to let him know I didn't appreciate it. There was no freeing ourselves. It wasn't as if we could just wiggle our way out of knots tied by criminal sailors. Surely he knew that?

If my hands weren't tied behind me and smashed against some boy's back, I would be able to get the blade in my necklace and cut myself free. Then again, if my hands were free to get the blade, I suppose I wouldn't need it in the first place.

I tried to make the most of the time we were stuck there by planning what I might say to the pirates to right this situation. But the boy's involvement made things complicated. Clearly they assumed he and I were already acquainted, and the boy had only solidified that assumption by surrendering himself to save my life. Granted, the way he had watched me in the city yesterday suggested he *did* know me, but I hadn't a clue who he was—which only made me more unsettled about the whole matter.

Gratsis had posted a reward for my return—and the return of the necklace. This boy must be connected to that. But how did he know who

I was if we'd never previously met? He had no way to identify me. None of it made sense.

I supposed I should be grateful he surrendered to save my life, but as the ropes dug deeper into my ribs while he pulled against them again, I decided I was not.

And I would certainly not be making any similar sacrifices for him.

A loud thud sounded from the side of the hull as, I assumed, they pulled up the anchor. It felt as though an eternity had passed since they imprisoned us down here. Despite the activity on the ship, few pirates paid us any mind, more focused on setting sail than sorting out their captives.

At least another hour must have passed before anyone came to check on us.

"Alright now," a pirate finally called as light spilled into the brig, hurting my eyes. "What's a little lady and her little man doing with a crew of pirates?"

The boy fell eerily still behind me, perhaps surprised, as I was, at the tone of the pirate's voice. It wasn't gruff or accented like the other pirates', as if the sea salt stung at their throats and after a while all they could do was rasp. His voice was smooth as silk. It slid through the air like the voice of a poet. His vowels were short and round, similar to the accent of the upper class.

The pirate entered our cell. I was facing the door, so he naturally approached me first, bending down to get a good look at me. I could smell the rum on his breath as he asked, "Surely you weren't planning to steal our goods from us?"

He moved to the side of us, so the boy and I could both look at him if we turned our heads. My eyes finally adjusted to the light, and I could see that he was quite old for a pirate. His eyes crinkled in the corners, and his shoulder-length hair was almost entirely white. I was told the captain of this ship was an older man, but surely not someone old enough to be my grandfather.

Since he hadn't bothered to remove our gags, he continued on without an answer to his question. "Well, regardless of your motives, you're a long way from home now, with no loved ones around. The price for stealing from our camp is a hand each." He pulled his sword from its sheath and let it glint in the lamp light. "After justice is served, we'll discuss the details of getting your ransom."

My heart raced. This was exactly what I had been trying to *avoid*. And I probably would have succeeded if not for this insufferable boy. I had to explain, but this stupid gag kept any of my pleas from being comprehensible.

The boy also tried to say something. A *long* something. He went on and on, seemingly not planning on stopping.

The pirate chose the boy over me. He stepped over to face him, taking the lantern with him and leaving me looking into the darkness.

A few agonizing seconds passed as the pirate removed the boy's gag, but when he spoke, it was hardly the panicked plea I'd expected to hear. "Sir, if I may, my beloved and I were seekin' no harm or ill in approachin' your camp."

If the pirate's threat to cut off my hand quickened my pulse, this development stopped my heart altogether. His *beloved*? Surely he was joking. But he *had* been trailing me when we were caught. Was he an admirer of some sort? He couldn't be. Anyone coming after me would want to send me back to Gratsis, not keep me for himself. Right?

The pirate kicked him, which unfortunately, jolted me as well. "Am I to believe you stumbled in on accident? Or that you got curious and wanted to see what we were like? We saw the jewels in your lady's pouch. Only a thief wouldn't wear such a thing."

"We want to be married," he said plainly. "We were hopin' the necklace might be payment for your services."

Perhaps it was a good thing I was still gagged. Everything in me wanted to tell the pirate that this boy was nothing but a liar, that I had never seen him a day in my life.

"You've got bishops and lawmen for that in the towns."

I felt the boy shake his head. "No one is willin' to marry us. We are both illegitimate, you see, and as such, we've been deemed unfit for such a covenant."

My heart started racing again as the pirate swung the lantern to get a better look at both of us. "You aren't dressed like leeches."

"Looks can be deceivin', sir,"

My breath caught. Yes, this boy knew *exactly* who I was.

"We want to see the captain," he continued. "We want him to marry us."

The boy was firm in his request, but otherwise quite calm. It didn't sound like a desperate plan. It *sounded* like he was telling the truth. He was either crazy, or there was a method to his madness. Even I knew that legends claimed pirates' greatest weakness was love, though it was also their greatest strength. Many a town had been burned and reduced to rubble in the name of love. But would the pirates really let us go unharmed if they believed all we wanted was a wedding?

And if they did let us go, what was the boy planning next?

"A couple of lovebirds, eh?" The pirate circled back around to face me and ripped the gag from my mouth. "Is this true?"

I swallowed, and the boy grew still behind me. The pirate seemed too interested in the boy's story for me to be able to make my own case. If I denied the boy's claims, he probably wouldn't find *either* of our stories reliable, and where would that get me? At least this romance story might save me my hand, and that was the most immediate threat.

"Yes," I spat before I could convince myself this was a bad plan. I didn't know the boy's intentions at all, but there would be no salvaging *my* intentions for the evening. I had no choice but to take my chances with him. "I love him very much, sir," I added for good measure.

The pirate grunted and stood up straight. "Two illegitimate children grow up and fall in love? With no one to marry them but a pirate captain..." He considered this a moment and laughed. "It makes for a great story, I admit."

I would have laughed too, had it not been a story involving me.

"May we speak to the captain about this, sir?" the boy asked again.

"You just did. Captain Mothway of the *Gray Dagger*." The captain spread out his arms, though the gesture was not very impressive from below deck. "You've managed to humor me. But let's see how you do with the rest of the crew."

With that, he freed our ankles and hoisted us to our feet. He grabbed the rope tying me and the boy together and dragged us up to the main deck.

The sun had set since our capture. We emerged into the night, now surrounded by deep waters, with land only on the distant horizon. I felt as if I'd been transported to another world, like perhaps all of this was nothing more than a dream, and I'd wake up in an ally in Koyben any minute now.

Captain Mothway called the crew to gather on the main deck with us. Only after everyone arrived did he cut the rope binding me to the boy. Our wrists remained tied, but we'd be crazy to try anything with the pirates surrounding us like this.

The boy quickly positioned himself in front of me, too close for my taste.

Mercy, he was tall. I practically looked straight up at the sky to make eye contact with him. I searched for any reason to abandon this insane story: a smirk on his lips, a hungry glint in his blue eyes. His knowledge of my clothing hiding my illegitimate status was enough to convince me he was somehow involved with Gratsis, which was reason enough not to trust him. And I didn't. Not long term, at least. Even if I *did* trust him enough to tell me the truth, I couldn't ask what his intentions with this love story were, since Captain Mothway didn't move from our side.

But eyes didn't lie. And the only thing I saw in the boy's eyes was his attempt to search me much the same way.

Fine then. We'd pass this interrogation with the pirates, and then I would interrogate *him*.

Once we were all settled, the captain called out, "Two lovebirds emerge from the depths of the ship! Now, let us listen to their story and determine if their wish to be married shall be granted, or if their story is nothing more than a string of lies, and we should send them to the bottom of the Chelek!"

The pirates cheered, all manner of weapons glinting in the moonlight as they raised their arms.

The blood drained from my face. How had our punishment escalated from losing a hand to losing our lives?

2

My Only Chance to Marry for Love, and It's a Lie

Alastair

"Let us begin the questioning then," Count—er—*Captain* Mothway said.

My heart hammered in my chest as I quickly looked around at the crew of pirates surrounding me. Pirates captained by the former Count Reuben Mothway of all people.

Fate was turning out to be a sick and twisted thing. I had been running for my life the last three weeks because of one traitor, and now I was practically begging for it from another. I hoped he didn't recognize me. I hadn't seen Count Mothway since before he'd left his nobility for piracy a few years ago, and I'd changed a lot since then. With any luck, my dyed hair and commoner clothing would prevent him from recognizing me as the young blond prince in the background of every political dinner he'd shared with my father.

He hadn't let on to remembering me so far. I had to make sure it stayed that way.

I was grateful I had listened to Roland and kept my ring hidden in my pack at our campsite instead of on my person as I had wanted to. It was a risk to leave something so valuable unattended, but now I understood what Roland meant when he said it was far riskier for me to be caught with it. If my face or voice didn't immediately give me away to Mothway, the prince's ring certainly would have jogged his memory.

I looked down at the young woman before me. The breeze blew strands of her dark blonde hair into her face, but she didn't bother trying to fix it. With our hands tied, and her scarf taken, I supposed it was inevitable. After her attempt to size me up, she was now purposely avoiding my gaze, looking around the ship with her brow furrowed and lips pressed together.

Maybe this was a bad idea.

But it was too late to change course now.

She hadn't said much, but I needed to mimic her lower class accent. I'd already adopted the accent for weeks, vowels placed further back in my mouth, the pitch of my voice varying far more often throughout a single sentence than felt natural. If we were in love, then the woman and I would have come from the same region of Wenterly. Hopefully her dialect was similar to the one I had already used with Mothway. Or, if it wasn't, that she had enough sense to adapt her speech to mimic mine.

Assuming we convinced the pirates to marry us, we'd have until sunrise to escape before the wedding ceremony. And if they agreed to the wedding, we were bound to be in their good graces, and I could probably convince them to let us walk freely about the ship, which would be necessary for the escape.

If we didn't escape before the wedding, I'd be in a heap of trouble—even more than I already was in now. Judging by the young woman's dress, she was a typical commoner, which would be quite the scandal to take up while trying to reclaim the throne. But at least a commoner wasn't the *lowest* class in society. She could have been a criminal, or a leech, as we were pretending to be. Even so, marrying someone like her could certainly ruin me. Ruin my family. But all the more motivation to get off this ship in a timely manner.

I'd lied plenty of times at various dinners and balls. *"It was a pleasure to speak with you." "Yes, I would love to hear about the gardens at your estate."* But I'd never lied with my life on the line. I needed to sell this. I wasn't going to actually marry her. Not if this all went according to plan. But I had to make it seem as if I wanted to. With our hands still tied behind our backs, all I could do to communicate any fondness for her was to smile at her in adoration.

She barely kept a glare off her face.

When the pirates settled down again, Mothway asked the first question. "When did you two meet?"

"About two years ago, though it feels like only yesterday," I answered quickly. Given the way the woman was looking at me, I wasn't sure how convincing her storytelling would be. I planned on leading the conversation as much as possible. Besides, I knew Mothway. I could lead and mislead him more easily than she could.

The young woman squared her shoulders before some sort of decision finally softened her gaze. "For me, it was love at first sight," she cooed, then cracked a playful smile. "Gabriel took a bit more convincin'."

I blinked in surprise. It seemed the woman did have some theatrics in her after all.

I smiled back.

"So how did you convince him?" Mothway prompted.

"Well," she started softly, unsure of herself. "Gabriel and I were—"

"Loud enough for everyone to hear," Mothway said.

The woman surveyed the crew stretching all the way down the main deck. She cleared her throat and began again. "Gabriel and I were both lucky enough to fall into indentured servitude as children. A far better fate than many of our other illegitimate peers, as I'm sure you're aware."

She had the fortitude to still look at the pirates as she said that, though the percentage of them who were illegitimate was likely far higher than it was in civilized society.

She was connecting with them on their level. Gutsy, but smart.

She turned her attention to Mothway and continued, "I'm a seamstress. Though when I wasn't sewin' for my master's business, I ran his errands throughout the town."

"She met me at the bookshop," I cut in, wanting to quickly establish my own backstory before she stuck me with an occupation I knew nothing about. "I'd worked in the back, doing the actual work of bindin' the books nearly all my life, but I'd recently been promoted to handle customer relations as well. Lucinda came in one day." I noticed the woman's eyebrows furrow slightly at the name I'd given her, but I continued on. "And although I noticed she was pretty, I didn't think much of it. I couldn't allow myself to. I'd grown up knowin' I was illegitimate, so I'd resigned myself to never being able to marry."

"As had I," she agreed. "Though when I met Gabriel, that all changed for me in an instant," she said a little too pointedly, then cleared her throat. "I knew from the moment I ... saw his..."

My smile faded as her voice faltered.

She cleared her throat and quickly recovered, "I saw his smile, and when he smiled at me, I felt like I was the only girl in the world. I wanted someone to look at me like that for the rest of my life."

Had she really failed to finish that sentence on that first try? Or was that pause part of her act? I couldn't tell. Could the pirates?

"And so? What happened?" Mothway prodded.

She took a deep breath. "I described the book cover my master wanted and delivered the pages over to Gabriel. A few days later, I returned for the book. When I went to give him the payment, my handkerchief happened to fall to the shop floor."

"Of course, I didn't notice until after Lucinda had left," I added. "I didn't know where she lived, but I had the name of her master. I recognized his name from the name of his business, and I figured I could return the handkerchief to her there."

The woman's eyes widened slightly, but the pirates laughed.

"You dropped yer kerchief?" someone in the crowd hollered. "I didn't know women actu'ly did such a thing!"

"O' course *ya* wouldn't, Baxley!" another responded.

"Well, it's a good thing they do. It worked like a charm," I said, winking at her.

My mother would have fainted at seeing me behave with such indecency. But I wasn't a prince in this story. I was a love-struck, foolish leech.

And the pirates seemed to love it. They hollered, whistled, and roared in laughter at their own jests and our entertaining tale. It was a cacophony that should have filled me with fear. But if I was honest, it was exhilarating. They were playing right into my hand.

So, I continued, "I walked into the tailor shop, and the man was sittin' at his desk. I let him know that his servant had left her handkerchief at my shop the day before, and that I wanted to return it. He called for her, and she came to retrieve it from me, apologizin' that I had come all that way just to return it. But I could tell from the way she looked at me that she wasn't sorry at all. She was glad to see me again. It piqued my curiosity. No one had ever been glad at the sight of me before."

The woman picked up the story. "It was another month before my master acquired another book. But, to my luck, he is an avid reader, and spent nearly all his profits on new books whenever he could. Of course, I volunteered to take it to the bookshop. I had to see Gabriel again. Not a day had gone by since our last meeting that I hadn't thought of him."

She paused, and I found myself momentarily at a loss too, trying to think of what could possibly happen next in our story. Though this tale we were spinning certainly wasn't the traditional love story, I had no life experience to help me along in telling it. I'd never courted. How could I, when every individual conversation I held with a lady resulted in whispers and schemes and jealousy? But, I must have read something in the past that could be useful. What had Brigid written about love?

His passage "Wildhearts in Wildfires" came to mind. Yes, I could use that.

"She came back to the bookshop and once again described the bindin' her master desired. She started to hand the book over to me, and had the audacity to drop it on the floor instead. Of course, she had done it on purpose, all the more audacious, knowin' how expensive books are, how precious each copy is. We both bent down to pick it up, our hands brushin' as we both reached for it. I swear, a spark ignited in my bones at her touch." I lowered my voice, still loud enough that Mothway would hear, but quiet enough that he might think I only meant for the woman to hear what came next. "I still feel that spark every time we touch." I stooped down to kiss the woman on the cheek, the action far more awkward than I'd anticipated with my hands behind my back. I straightened, doing my best to maintain an air of romance.

The woman smiled up at me, but it didn't come close to reaching her eyes. I'd never seen a smile look so threatening.

I carried on, because I couldn't go back now. I would apologize when this was over. "Wantin' her to stay longer, I offered to show her the back of the shop, where I bound the books. To my relief, she agreed. I showed her the dyes, the leather, the glue. Dreadfully borin' things, but she listened and looked at me as though I was showin' her the world."

The woman rolled her shoulders back and locked eyes with me in a steely gaze—which was not quite the look I had just described. She wasn't smiling anymore either, but frighteningly deadpan. Perhaps I had gone too far with the kiss.

I opened my mouth to continue, but she beat me to it, saying, "Not long after that, Gabriel came back to the tailor shop. He'd never had an issue before, but suddenly he kept gettin' rips in his shirts, and needed a seamstress to fix them. Of course, our interactions were always short and polite, as we were under my master's watchful eye. But Gabriel soon discovered that our shop had a back door, and he would secretly pay me many visits there."

I nodded. That was good, surprisingly. The woman was certainly not the best actress, but her storytelling made up for what her facial expressions lacked.

We looked to Mothway. I hoped he'd be satisfied with that.

"But it all went wrong," he concluded. "Otherwise, you wouldn't be needing our help, would you?"

Mercy, he was thorough. I sighed before I could catch myself, and then had to hope it merely sounded like agreement of our misfortune. "When we were of age, I approached Lucinda's master, asking for her hand in marriage. Of course, he denied me. He knew the circumstances of her birth, and all it took was a conversation with my own master to learn of mine. They forbade us from seein' each other. We went two months without so much as a glimpse of the other." I paused, as if the pain of our distance was still fresh in my memory. "Then one mornin', I couldn't take it anymore. I opened the back door of the shop, and we rode away together on my master's horse."

"Stole the horse *and* the girl!" the same pirate as before, Baxley, called out.

A few pirates snickered, but my patience for entertaining them was wearing thin. I just wanted this to be over.

I turned to Mothway. "That was a month ago. We've been travelin' the towns since, lookin' for someone to marry us. But without anyone to vouch for us, and not nearly enough money to bribe a lawman, we're turned away."

"And why do you need to get married anyway?" Mothway asked. "Why not move to a distant town, claiming to be wed, and live out your days with no one the wiser?"

I raised my eyebrows at the woman. He had a good point. And I couldn't think of an answer more convincing than 'because it's the proper thing to do.'

The woman lifted her chin. "Despite our status, Captain, we are people of virtue, and don't want our children to have the same troubles as we have. If we only pretend to be married, the truth is bound to rear its ugly head sooner or later. It must be done properly."

I couldn't help but be impressed at her answer. That was good, to bring children into the equation. This was about more than a wedding; we wanted a future together. I could work with that. I struggled to my knees before Mothway, my balance off-kilter with my arms tied behind me. "Please, sir, er, Captain, you're our last hope. If you don't marry us, my beloved and I will throw ourselves overboard. If we cannot be united in life together, at least we will be united in death."

The woman cleared her throat, and I didn't dare look back at her. She couldn't be happy about that escalation.

But it worked exactly as I'd planned, because Mothway clapped me on the shoulder and helped me stand. He directed us to face the crew. "Two fools in love!" he cried. "Who are we to stand in the way?"

The pirates agreed with a hearty cheer. I turned to look at the woman, but she was looking at the crew.

"Congratulations, Lucinda and Gabriel! Let us begin the ceremony!"

I balked. "Right now? Aren't ceremonies meant to be done at sunrise?"

"Aren't ceremonies meant to be between two *legitimate* children?" Mothway countered. "I've found that when it comes to breaking the law, there is no time like the present, my boy."

I couldn't argue with that. Not without jeopardizing our safety.

Hang the moon.

I was going to regret this.

3

I Marry the Stupidest Boy in All of Breslin

Evangeline

Had I really been in love, it would have been a beautiful ceremony. The moon was full and glinted silver light across the water. There was a slight breeze in the summer air. Our wrists had been unbound, though not without threat to run us through if we tried anything. My concern had turned from surviving the pirates, to surviving the boy in front of me.

What *were* his intentions in our fake love story? Were they as innocent as my intentions in going along with it? Or was he planning something more malicious? Panic nearly choked me. But what was there to do, besides jump overboard? We were miles away from shore, and the pirates' weapons were still at their sides, although they seemed to be in good spirits now.

I forced my resolve. Whatever the boy's intentions were, there was no choice but to marry him. My chance to deny associating with him had long passed.

Conveniently, the ropes that had bound our wrists were also long enough for the hand-binding ceremony in our wedding. Baxley brought a third rope to the captain, who then called everyone to attention. "Our man Gabriel has been waiting for this night for quite some time, so we'll keep the ceremony brief." He winked at the boy, who nodded in appreciation.

I bit the inside of my cheek.

"The laws of man have kept these two apart for far too long," the captain continued. "Luckily, the laws of man don't apply on our ship."

This earned a cheer from the pirates, as if I needed to be reminded just how tricky of a spot I was in.

"As Captain of this ship, it is in my authority to wed those I deem worthy, and these two certainly are. So, before this company of witnesses, and according to the ways of a *proper* ceremony," the captain added, looking right at me, "please clasp arms for the laying of the threads."

With some guidance from the captain, the boy and I held each other's right forearm. Captain Mothway instructed the boy how to drape and wrap his rope around our arms and hands, then instructed me to do the same with the rope in my hand.

"You have entwined your lives with one another, and now Fate binds you together, should your own weaving ever begin to fray," he said as he wrapped a third rope around our hands. "Now, I ask you two to repeat your vows after me." The captain cleared his throat. "I solemnly swear before these witnesses."

"I solemnly swear before these witnesses," the boy and I said in unison.

The boy's hand trembled. I glanced down, and thankfully, I couldn't see the movement, but I could feel him shaking all the same. I looked back up into his eyes, and they were focused on me, wide and pleading.

Was he *afraid*? This was his idea!

Great, I was marrying an idiot.

The captain droned on as we repeated our vows after him, promising to honor and respect, cherish and obey, help and heal, love and adore, on and on and on.

So much for a short ceremony.

Finally, the captain instructed us to grab the ends of the ropes in our right hand and pull our hands back through to tie the knot. The coarse ropes scratched the back of my hand as I pulled, but we successfully knotted them, signaling Fate's approval of our union, and the end of the ceremony.

Brilliant.

Mothway smiled. "I am pleased to pronounce you man and wife!"

On cue, the pirates cheered, some enthusiastically waving their weapons in the air.

Taking the knotted ropes from us, the captain said, "Gabriel, you may kiss your bride."

My heart lurched as the boy took a slow step toward me, closing the already small distance between us. But that was the only visible hint of hesitation he showed. He cupped my chin while his other hand landed on my waist. I couldn't breathe. I closed my eyes, more out of fear than anything else. His lips pressed against mine, but I couldn't bring myself to kiss him back. He lingered a moment, then stood back.

When I opened my eyes, I could see the smile on the boy's face was forced.

"Well then." Captain Mothway placed his hands on each of our shoulders. "We'll let you two enjoy the rest of the night. But you will be put to work tomorrow," he warned.

To my dismay, we were escorted back down to the belly of the ship by none other than Baxley—the same pirate who'd ordered our capture on the beach. Despite having won over the pirates, we were still their captives.

The boy kept his hand anchored on my waist the whole way.

Baxley took us past the cell we were held in earlier and led us to a room where we would actually have privacy. It was surprisingly considerate. Or would have been, if our story was true. I touched my necklace, hoping it would look like nothing more than a nervous habit. As soon as the boy and I were alone, I would pull the pin at the top and pull out the blade. Baxley hung a lantern in the small room, then bade us a good night with a great deal of laughter and winking and locked us in.

I immediately took a quick step backward so the boy was in front of me. As I opened my pendant, I kicked at the backs of his knees. He wasn't prepared for it, and his knees buckled. With one hand, I pressed his right arm up behind his back and threw my other arm around his neck. "If you so much as lay a hand on me, I swear I'll kill you," I said as I pressed the small blade beneath his chin.

He stilled. "Woah, relax, will you? And lower your voice. The pirates think we're in love."

"I'd rather the pirates discover we lied than have you—"

"I'm not going to touch you. Have you ever heard of acting?" His voice was different. Not just because he was annoyingly calm in the face of my threats. It sounded as though he had Mothway's accent.

I tensed. "I don't know who you are, and I don't know where you came from. I have no reason to trust you."

To my surprise, the boy sighed. He grabbed my arm with his free hand, pulling the blade away from his skin. In one fluid motion, he freed his right arm, lifted me off the ground, and flipped me over so that I landed on the floor in front of him, flat on my back. For the second time in one night, I gasped for air while he stood over me, unamused.

"And *I* have no reason to trust you, especially since you just threatened to kill me." His accent returned to normal. Had I imagined the change? He watched while I struggled for breath, and didn't offer a hand to help me up this time. But he didn't further threaten me back, either. The strength he'd just displayed spoke loudly enough. I was no match for him.

I placed the blade back in my pendant. I pushed myself up and faced him, annoyed that he was still a good foot taller than me.

"Now I'm goin' to sleep over there." He pointed toward the door. "You'll sleep over there." He gestured to the other side of the room. "And when the pirates come for us in the mornin', we're goin' to pretend like we've never been more in love with each other. If you try to kill me in my sleep, you better believe you'll have a far more brutal questionin' from the pirates than we had tonight."

The room was nearly empty. A couple of sails were tossed to the far end of the room, not even folded. A long tear down the side of one of the sails revealed the reason for the lack of care. A few ropes were strewn about the room as well, too short or frayed to be of any use. There was no furniture. No windows. No decoration of any kind. It was a storage place for useless things.

How fitting for them to put the two of us down here.

I turned to the boy. "If I'm goin' to trust you enough to keep goin' along with this plan, I need answers. Don't think I don't know who you are. I saw you starin' at me in Koyben. What's your plan here?"

"Oh. That's..." He wiped a hand over his face, and his accent shifted again to sound like that of the upper class. "I thank you for not mentioning my identity to the pirates. I know the marriage thing was a bad idea, but I couldn't come up with any better reason two people like us would be passing through a pirate c—"

"Why would the *pirates* care who you are?"

"Why wouldn't they?" The confusion in his question matched mine. He tilted his head to the side. "Pardon, who do *you* think I am?"

"I know you're connected with Gratsis."

"Who?"

I crossed my arms. "Don't play dumb with me. Why else would you be followin' me?"

He furrowed his brow.

"How much is the reward? I'm surprised you thought marriage was better than offerin' for Gratsis to pay my ransom."

"Pardon, who's Gratsis?"

I scoffed. "You think you can drop all these hints and then pretend you don't know what *I'm* talkin' about?"

A blank stare.

"You said we're 'both illegitimate,' and 'looks can be deceivin',' and that the name of my master is the name of his shop—"

"That's just standard—"

"—the back door to the shop, calling me *Lucinda*. How stupid do you think I am?"

The boy gaped, opening and closing his mouth like a fish out of water.

"Aren't you worried this weddin' ceremony might make Gratsis look less fondly on you in his reward for findin' me?"

"A reward for finding—Pardon, who are *you*?"

I resisted the urge to shove him. "What game are you playin'?"

"What are *you* playing?"

We stood there a moment, sizing each other up. He seemed genuinely confused, but if he knew I was on to him, of course he would act that way. I'd never willingly go anywhere with him if I didn't trust him. He knew that.

He crossed his arms. "Ask me anythin' you want, plainly, and I assure you, I'll have no idea what you're talkin' about." Lower class accent again. Was I going mad? Or was he?

"Anyone can pretend *not* to know somethin'. That's the easiest lie there is."

"I don't know how else to convince you I have no idea what you're on about. Koyben was the first I ever saw you."

"So maybe you don't know Gratsis personally. But the only reason you'd come after me on the beach was if you were followin' me."

"Because you're a thief! Even if you only steal enough to survive."

"Why wouldn't you arrest me in the city, then? You didn't have to trail me all the way out to a pirate camp."

"I'm not an officer. I wanted to recruit you. But by the time I realized you were headed toward a pirate camp, we were practically in the middle of it. If I knew I'd get in this much trouble, I wouldn't have bothered, believe me. Did *you* know you were headed for pirates?"

I shrugged. Whether he was connected with Gratsis or not, my personal business didn't concern him. "Recruit me for what?"

"Well, that doesn't matter much now, does it? Not unless we can get off this boat before we're hundreds of miles away from the city!"

He was getting upset. Understandable. I wasn't happy with this situation either. But I didn't want to be locked in a room alone with an angry man. Especially not the kind of man who needed to recruit thieves. I decided to pretend a change of subject, hoping to catch him in some lie. "Did you really work at a bookshop?"

"No. Though I gather you were a seamstress," he said, eyeing my necklace.

I nodded. "The best lies are threaded with truth."

"Hmm, a sewin' pun. In times like these."

"It wasn't intended."

"A shame," the boy said flatly, turning toward the door. "I was hopin' my wife had a sense of humor."

I clenched my fists, anger burning in my chest. "What were your intentions with our marriage, anyway?"

He kicked a coil of rope further into the corner, clearing a spot for himself. "Nothin' more than to buy us some time. Save our hands, and our lives, as it was. You can't negotiate with pirates. You tell them what you want, and you say it in a way that makes them think it's what *they* want. I didn't think things were goin' to escalate that quickly with the weddin' ceremony. I thought they'd think it over a while longer. Or at least wait until sunrise for a traditional ceremony. Give us some time so we could escape before anythin' actually happened."

I waited for him to say more. To give any indication of our next steps. He merely shrugged.

"You idiot!" I blurted. I'd gone along with that insane plan, and *that* was the end of it?

He whirled around and glared at me. "You didn't have to go along with it if you didn't like it."

"Please," I scoffed. "It's not like I had much of a choice. As you said, the marriage saved our lives. Your plan might have ruined *everythin'* I'm tryin' to do here, but I'm not stupid. Of course I would risk bein' taken advantage of by one man than be left at the mercy of a crew of pirates." I kicked at a sail that had been thrown in a heap at the back of the room. "We can still try to escape now. What did you have in mind?"

"I thought we'd gain a little more favor and freedom to try to jump ship. I don't know how we're supposed to escape from down here."

"Oh, you're full of bright ideas then, aren't you?"

The boy blinked. "I don't see you comin' up with anythin' helpful either. We're alive and still in one piece. And you can rest assured I have no intention of harming you. So, if anything, you should be thankin' me, not insultin' me."

I was so appalled, I laughed. The absolute audacity of this boy seemed to have no end. "You have to be the stupidest person I've ever met."

"I was educated by the greatest mind in Wenterly."

I gave a dramatic gasp, as if that was supposed to impress me. "Is that so? Well, either you were a dreadful student, or your studies didn't include 'Common Sense'."

The boy took a few steps toward me, then abruptly turned on his heel and walked in the other direction. He stood there, facing the door a moment, and I thought that was the end of our discussion for the night.

Just as I was about to sit on my side of the room, the boy turned back to face me and spoke again. "Look, like it or not, our lives currently depend on each other. We might be on this ship for days. If I know Mothway, he won't be prone to violence. Tonight has confirmed that. But, if he finds out our story is a lie, that *will* be the end for us."

If he knows Mothway? He didn't know Mothway any better than I did. For all we knew, the captain was just toying with us.

"So, once again, I have no choice but to pretend to like you? To ignore everythin' *I* want for the sake of *your* plan, which seems to have no actual end goal?"

"My goal is to get out of here alive. Are you tellin' me you have somethin' else in mind?"

I crossed my arms.

"Look," he said, softening his tone, "I'm sorry whatever you expected to happen tonight didn't work out the way you wanted. Believe me, I'm quite disappointed with the night's events, too. But unfortunately, we've already committed to this story. So, no, you don't have to pretend to like me. You have to pretend you're in *love* with me. And I have to pretend I'm in love with you. Only until we get off this ship." Despite his apology, he spoke with authority, as though he was commanding me to continue with this charade, instead of begging me to.

"I will do what I need to in order to survive this catastrophe *you* created. For now, that means pretendin' I'm your wife. But we are *not* a team."

What I didn't tell him was that if I had the opportunity to escape—or join—the pirates, I didn't care if he did so with me. In fact, I hoped he didn't.

He nodded. "I suppose that will do. It seems alliances don't mean that much these days anyway." His tone was full of bitterness.

"Are you always so dramatic?"

"Just go to sleep, Lucinda."

I grimaced at the name. Although he *did* seem to be quite clueless about my life, I gave one more test of his coincidental story. "Lucinda is what we called the stray cat in our alley."

He laughed. *Laughed.* "Good, it suits you then."

I stomped over to my side of the room, annoyed that despite his unawareness of my situation, his words rang true. Lucinda was objectively the worst of all the stray cats in Welven. He wasn't the first person to say she and I were a suitable pair.

I laid one of the damaged sails across the floor, and used it as a partial bed mat, partial blanket.

"You want the lantern lit or snuffed, Lucinda?"

"It doesn't matter to me."

The boy—I supposed I was to think of him as Gabriel now—snuffed out the lantern. In the darkness, fear struck me again at being alone with this stranger. But his footsteps didn't come any closer. I heard him settle down on his side of the room, and then I lay awake until his breathing slowed and deepened.

I pulled the sail firmly around me, wondering how the day had strayed so far from how I had envisioned it. But the ship rocked to and fro, and before long, I fell asleep.

4

A Toast to the Newlyweds

Alastair

I woke before Lucinda. It was an unfortunate name I had given her, true, but based on how she had treated me so far, she deserved it. Nevermind the fact that she was my wife now.

No, I had time enough to worry about the implications of our wedding. For now, I needed to focus on getting through the day. If it even was day. Were the pirates going to let us sleep through the daylight and wake us when the sun set? It was darker than a dungeon down here, making it impossible to tell the time.

The ship suddenly rocked to the right. What was that, starboard? It had been a long time since I'd thought about ship terminology. I'd dreamed of being a pirate when I was younger, of course. What child didn't? But that was hardly appropriate, and when my mother asked if I was interested because I wanted to protect her from them, I gladly took the excuse to justify my obsession. Of course, as the years passed and I grew older, I learned to disdain them; they had a life of depravity more than a life of adventure. The occasions in which I had thought about pirates as of late was only with the question of how to be rid of them.

And that was quite a worthy question to consider at the present.

But perhaps they weren't as evil as I'd been taught. It had been shockingly easy to get the pirates to marry us. A little *too* easy, actually. Roland would have my head over my getting married, though at least I still had a head for him to have. But if the pirates had so easily believed our love story, maybe they could also be persuaded to let us go. Still, I couldn't help but wonder what it was that actually convinced Mothway and the rest of the crew to believe us.

Granted, we still had to see what the day brought us. But if they'd humored us this long, surely it couldn't be that bad, could it?

My stomach rumbled. I hadn't eaten since the morning before our capture. The night had been so chaotic, I hadn't noticed that I'd missed dinner. Now, though, I was ravenous.

Footsteps sounded outside our room. It could be someone come to get us, or hopefully, to bring us breakfast.

"Lucinda," I called quietly. If the pirates opened the door and we were on opposite sides of the room, it would arouse suspicion. I took six steps, putting me near the center of the room, if I remembered correctly. I was hesitant to come any closer. The young woman wasn't a real threat, even with a small blade in her necklace. But nevertheless, I wasn't keen on testing her fight or flight response. "Lucinda."

"What do you want?" she muttered, her words slurring together slightly from sleep.

"I think they're comin' for us."

"So?"

"So,"—I crawled toward her voice, not wanting to accidentally step on her—"it's supposed to be the mornin' after our wedding night."

She cursed, which, given the circumstances, was an understandable reaction. But it also led me to question—not for the first time—what kind of woman she truly was.

I bumped into her right as the lock clicked. It wasn't long before they'd see us. I quickly situated myself next to her on the sail. The hinges squeaked as the door opened, and light spilled into the room. I wrapped an arm around her shoulder and pulled her close, hoping the pirates would find the action protective.

"When we get off this ship, you're welcome to never see me again, but for now, we've got to work together to sell this thing." I whispered in her ear.

"When we get off this ship, the first thing I'm doin' is punchin' you in your stupid face."

I bit back a laugh. "Could you reach that high?"

She probably would have punched me right then had the pirates not interrupted.

"Alright, lovebirds," Baxley called. He must be the Quartermaster, or the First Mate. Why couldn't I remember these things? The titles worked differently for pirates than on our ships, didn't they? "Captain wants you on deck. Let's move."

I stood, then gave Lucinda a hand as she untangled herself from the sail. To my relief, she accepted the help and took my arm as we walked toward the pirates. Maybe we could pull this off after all.

Mothway met us on the main deck, where he'd married us the night before. Now, the sun blazed overhead; it was midday. I was thankful for the sea breeze as the sun mercilessly beat down on the ship.

"Ah, the lovebirds!" he greeted.

I got the feeling this was going to be our nickname, and I was not fond of it. I could only imagine how Lucinda must feel about it.

He ushered us into the cabin behind him. It was cluttered, but filled with finery. A large, ornately woven red rug covered half the floor, and a large tapestry hung on the wall behind a desk in the far corner. A bed was in the opposite corner, not lacking in pillows, although I hardly understood how such a thing made sense in a room that rocked from side to side. A large chest sat at the foot of the bed, and a cabinet with glass windows showcased porcelain cups and plates, and little trinkets that would be better suited for decor at a ladies' luncheon than a pirate's cabin. Another cabinet beside it was solid wood, betraying no indication of its contents. How much of this was how pirates normally showcased their wealth, and how much was Mothway's personal preference from his former life of nobility?

A square table in the middle of the room was dressed in a yellow and blue tablecloth with four chairs around it. Mothway directed us to take a seat as he shut and locked the door behind him.

My heart skipped a beat as I realized the tablecloth was not actually a tablecloth, but a Wenter flag. The last connection he had to his own kingdom, the place that had provided him with a life of luxury, was now reduced to catching crumbs from the meals that sustained his treasonous life.

Mothway slung an arm on my shoulder, startling me out of my thoughts. I realized that Lucinda had already seated herself, and I'd been standing here like an idiot.

"Is everything all right, Gabriel?"

"I'm merely admirin' the decor. You have fine taste, Captain."

He squeezed my shoulder before finally letting me go. "I'm glad you think so. Now have a seat. I believe we ought to celebrate your new matrimony. How about a drink on me?"

I sat adjacent to Lucinda as Mothway crossed the room to the wooden cabinet, swung open the door, and perused the bottles inside. He chose a small round container, pulled the cork, and poured three glasses. He returned to the table and set the glasses down in front of us.

"Oh, that is too kind, Captain," Lucinda said, eyeing me warily.

"Nonsense. It's not every day I get to officiate a wedding." He sat adjacent to me and lifted his glass. "But if it's poisoning you're worried about,"—he took a swig—"you can lay your fears to rest."

I nodded to Lucinda, and we raised our glasses.

"To our future," I toasted. "May it be as sweet as you are to me."

"Here, here!" The captain raised his glass. "May you two spend the rest of your lives at each other's side!"

"I'm happy to drink to that thought," Lucinda muttered, then added a smile for the sake of the captain watching us.

We all took a drink.

5

MY HUSBAND LOVES THE DEAD ROYALS MORE THAN ME

Evangeline

I sputtered as the alcohol burned my throat, and Gabriel choked on the sip he took.

"Perhaps some food, Captain?" he risked.

Captain Mothway laughed. "Scared you can't hold your liquor?"

Gabriel looked from the captain, to me, then to the drink before him. How long *had* it been since we'd eaten? I'd stolen some food right before I came to the pirate camp. That was what, seventeen hours ago? I'd gotten used to sparse meals over the last few weeks, but I hadn't been drinking on an empty stomach. And certainly, never anything this strong. Despite the captain's assurance, this certainly tasted like it was closer to poison than drink.

I wiped my mouth with the back of my hand. "Is this your own brew, Captain?"

"Certainly is. Finest brew on the five seas. So, bottoms up! You won't get drink like this again."

"It certainly is fine. Unfortunately, I'm not much of a drinker, and I'd hate for you to waste such—"

The captain pulled his dagger and plunged it into the table—piercing right through the tablecloth—mere centimeters away from my hand. "I said, drink."

Clearly, we wouldn't be moving on with the day until we had downed our glasses. He wanted us drunk, and my mind raced to figure out why. Wouldn't we be more useful to him sober? Able to help out on the ship?

I took a cautious sip, wincing as I swallowed.

He sat there, watching us, as we continued to choke down the "fine" brew. When we finally reached the bottom of our glasses, he spoke. "How did you find my ship?"

"We got lucky," Gabriel answered. I turned to look at him, and as I did so, the air seemed to shift around me. I closed my eyes a moment, acknowledging that the alcohol was already doing its job. "We'd been walkin' along the shore for a few weeks, hopin' to come across a captain willin' to marry us."

When I opened my eyes again, the captain was leaning back in his chair, considering this. I realized he was interrogating us. An unusual method, to get us drunk, and I hoped not very effective. But I certainly welcomed it if torture—what I had always believed was the pirate standard—was the alternative.

But Captain Mothway wasn't your standard pirate, was he? The man looked weathered, but by age, not by a hard life. Aside from the dagger still buried in the table, it was difficult to find the man intimidating.

"I thought pirates were young," I blurted.

Captain Mothway raised his eyebrows at me.

"I mean, younger than you, at least," I clarified. "I know pirates aren't *children*. But you're, well, an old man."

The captain frowned. "I joined the crew later in life. I was a nobleman once upon a time, and grew bored of the political realm. My children married, my wife died, and I set sail. Four years later, I'm Captain of my own ship. So, not bad for an *old man*."

"Four years already? Your time's up any day now, then," Gabriel said.

I nodded. The knowledge I'd gathered in Koyben had also told me it was rare for pirates to be in the occupation for more than five years—two or three were generally considered a full life on the criminal sea. Whether they died, got arrested, or were too injured to continue sailing, the dangers of the occupation kept them from going on for long.

"Maybe if I was just a crewman. But I've been promoted to Captain. That's going to give me some more time."

"Assumin' you don't die from old age first." I wasn't one to hold my tongue, but I was speaking before *I* even realized what I was saying. *Get a grip, Eva.*

The captain glared at me. "Doesn't matter much. It's not as though life in Wenterly would be going well for me at this point anyway. At least on the sea, I'm a free man." He leaned forward, resting an elbow on the table, turning his full attention to Gabriel. "How *are* things in Wenterly? Have things changed much under King Harland's rule?"

I laughed. "Not for people like us."

The men turned to me, and the captain raised his eyebrows.

"Sure, there were a few days of uncertainty where the towns grew tense. But with the Cathmoores dead, what are we goin' to do? Life goes on. Harland has been the King of Glastor for who knows how long before this, so he knows how to rule. He wants the kingdom to keep doin' what it does. He just wanted to be the one in control. Who cares?"

Gabriel frowned. "You could show a little respect to the royal family, Lucinda."

"Yes, may their souls be at peace," I mumbled as I ran my finger along the rim of my glass.

"You didn't approve of the royal family?" Captain Mothway asked, eyebrows raised, though his lips twisted into a smirk.

The boy was looking at me just as expectantly as the pirate.

I leaned back in my chair. "I didn't *care* about the royal family. What do they matter to me? They made sure we had trade routes so I had clothes to sew and food to eat. Good. Harland can do that too. I don't care much who's sittin' on the throne, so long as they're runnin' the kingdom. The throne was likely to be changin' hands soon anyway. We'd be adjustin' to life with the prince just as much as we are with Harland."

"That is utter nonsense, Lucinda! The prince would receive a peaceful transition of power from his own father, where his loyalty to Wenterly was clear. We have no idea what Harland's plans are for the kingdom. Did you know all Glastorian men are *required* to serve in the army from ages eighteen to twenty-five? They marry later there, when the men have completed their required service."

"If that's the worst of it, then again, what does that matter to me? We're on this ship, not in Wenterly *or* Glastor. So I doubt you'll be joinin' Harland's army any time soon. And we're already married. So"—I raised my empty glass in a mock toast—"lucky us."

He scoffed. "Harland is a liar and a murderer. For all we know, he's takin' things slow to win over the minds of the masses so he can ruin our lives down the road without us battin' an eye. You—"

"You know I'm not one for politics, Gabriel. Save the lecture for someone who cares."

He huffed, then held his glass out to the captain.

Mothway raised an eyebrow, but refilled it.

Yes, drown your frustrations, husband. Truly, it was one smart decision after another from him.

"And where, exactly," the captain began as Gabriel took a large swig, "does your political interest come from, given that you're nothing more than a book binder's servant, Gabriel?"

"I read a lot," he offered. "I like to know about things."

The captain turned to me, and I shrugged. "He doesn't retain the things he learns very well, if you ask me. But I've never had much of an education, so maybe that's just how learnin' is."

The captain waved away my commentary. "Tell me about your master, Lucinda. You ran away from him, but he's probably looking for you. Might be willing to pay a good amount to have you back."

Indeed. But it was better the captain didn't know about the ransom already on my head.

I rolled my eyes. "Whatever price you're askin' for isn't goin' to be worth the trouble he'll have to go through to make sure I don't run off again."

"But you owe him debts."

Did I? I thought I'd told him I'd paid everything off. No. He didn't know that part. Did he? It was hot in the captain's cabin. The afternoon sun must be working overtime. I needed some water. "Only because the interest rate changes by the day," I finally replied.

"And I suppose you have the same story, Gabriel?"

"Pretty much." He shrugged, then took another swig.

"You do realize if I can't return you for a ransom, I have no other option than to send you to the Pirate King, who is not likely to respect the relationship between you two as I have." He gave us a pointed look. "I myself only married you for some entertainment. It was good for the crew to have some livelihood. Boosts morale. And marrying two kids because they think it will save them a little trouble is the funniest thing I've done in a while." The captain laughed as if proving his point, then abruptly stopped with a sigh when we didn't join in. "Alright. That's enough for today, then."

He leaned across the table and took my hand before I could think to pull away. With his other hand, he pulled his dagger from the table.

I screamed.

"Let her go!" Gabriel yelled as the captain pulled me out of my chair.

Gabriel stood, but nearly fell backward as he did so. He caught the edge of the table and held on a moment, regaining his balance.

"Relax, I'm taking you two back to your hold," Mothway grumbled. He sheathed his dagger and grabbed Gabriel's arm. "It's the Pirate King for you two. Perhaps we'll find a way to make you useful in the meantime, but you've got to sober up first."

Captian Mothway dragged us out onto the main deck, the sea breeze a momentary blessing against my skin. I blinked in the sunlight, and before I knew it, we were already back in the belly of the ship.

Gabriel and I fell as we were shoved into our room, and the door slammed shut. A lantern was already lit inside. Gabriel struggled to his feet, but I remained on the floor.

"Oh, mercy," Gabriel said as he stumbled across the room.

"Hmm?"

"We got food."

I lifted my head to see Gabriel shove dried fruit in his mouth at an alarming rate.

"Save some for me."

"Then you better come claim it, Lucinda."

I scooted over and grabbed a fistful of food. The tray was empty in seconds.

I rolled onto my back. The rocking of the ship felt more dramatic than last night. I wondered if we were in rougher waters or if it was the alcohol swimming around my brain.

"Do you truly hate the royal family? Or were you only saying that?" Gabriel asked suddenly.

I sighed. I did not feel like talking anymore. "Who cares?"

"I do."

I closed my eyes.

"Lucinda, why do you hate them?"

"I don't hate them," I snapped, glaring at him. "They just don't matter much to me."

"Do you have no loyalty to your kingdom?" His accent had changed again, his question low in pitch, despite the obvious accusation in his tone. How long had he been talking like that?

"Really, Gabriel, I'm not a traitor simply because I wasn't dearest friends with King Esmond." If anything, I was a traitor because I'd planned to join the pirates. But he didn't need to know that.

"Will you not care when the royal family returns to their throne and defeats Harland?"

"They're dead, Gabriel."

Gabriel laughed, then went quiet. I closed my eyes again.

Perhaps a minute of blissful silence passed before I heard a sniffle. A few seconds later, a shaky breath followed by another sniffle. I opened one eye.

Gabriel was sitting with his head on his knees, arms wrapped around his legs. His shoulders shook.

I closed my eye. That was none of my business. Maybe he'd think I'd fallen asleep.

But the quiet sniffles didn't stop.

I wasn't obligated to see what his problem was, so I decided to ignore him. But I felt too guilty about it to fall asleep.

"Why are you cryin'?" The question was supposed to sound concerned, or at least curious, but it came out completely monotone.

Gabriel didn't look up. He didn't even try to answer me, just kept quietly crying.

I rolled away from him, thinking the conversation was over.

That was when he finally whispered, "I miss them."

"Who?" I rolled back to face him. He couldn't mean the pirates. "The royals?"

He nodded.

"Why? Did you know them or somethin'?"

To my surprise, the boy nodded again.

"What? You *knew* them? How?"

He sniffed, and part of me acknowledged I should leave him be. But now I was curious.

I sat up. "Are you rich? A noble?" I shook my head. What would he be doing out here if that was the case? Then again, he was demanding enough to convince me it was a possibility.

He didn't answer.

"Were you a servant in the castle? Or friends with the prince?" The prince was a year younger than me. The two would be close in age. If he was a noble, it was certainly a possibility.

He leaned back, lying on the floor as I had a moment ago.

"Gabriel?"

He didn't answer.

And although I didn't care about him, and I'd tried to talk to him about it anyway, guilt continued to nag at me as I closed my eyes and turned away from him.

6

MIND YOUR STATUS

Alastair

I awoke to complete darkness. The lantern had burned out. But it was just as well.

My head was pounding as I sat up. "Lucinda?"

She didn't answer, and I wasn't sure where she was in the darkness. I stayed put, rubbing my eyes as bits of the previous conversation came back to me.

I'd cried in front of her, which was embarrassing, but easily explained by the alcohol, I hoped. As long as I didn't cry in front of her again, I should be able to maintain my dignity.

I'd never been more than a little tipsy, and even that was purely accidental. But commoners didn't have the same worries of reputation as I, and I figured requesting a second glass from Mothway would help assure him I wasn't hiding anything.

Not my brightest idea.

My thoughts drifted to the situation at hand. If Fate decreed I had to be captured by pirates, it was lucky we were captured by *these* pirates. It was awful that the captain had to be Mothway of all people, but he was also our saving grace. Between our wedding and unusual interrogation, I was right that the man's upbringing as a noble made him less prone to violence than others. And while joining the pirates was an act of treason—and coming from a noble, it felt more personal—Mothway hadn't let on to nearly as much animosity toward the royals as Lucinda had.

Lucinda. I wiped a hand over my face. Somehow I'd married a girl who didn't care whether it was my family in power or Harland. Which meant she wasn't a good candidate for the mission anyway. Why would she risk her life to help restore a kingdom she cared nothing about?

It was best to rid myself of her as soon as we got off the ship. Then again, I'd *married* her. Could I really walk away from her as easily as that? If the marriage *was* legally valid, then that put her under my care. She was my responsibility. If she recognized me once I was restored to the throne, what would stop her from using the situation to her advantage? If the wedding *didn't* hold up legally, the very notion that we had the ceremony would still be quite the scandal, and that was the last thing my family needed. I'd have to keep the girl with me and talk to Roland about all this. He'd know the proper solution.

A groan sounded near my feet. Lucinda was waking up.

Perhaps if we paid her enough, she'd be willing to keep quiet about the whole matter.

"Are you up?" she softly called.

"Yes."

A soft shuffle told me she sat up. "I, er, I'm sorry about ... what I said earlier. I didn't know you knew them."

I grunted and decided it was no use trying to hide my accent from her anymore. "It's not like knowing would have changed your opinion."

"No, but I could have been more accommodatin' to the situation."

"Honestly, I'd rather know the truth of how you feel."

She took a deep breath, and for a moment, I thought she really might be about to lecture me on how she truly felt. "How did you know them?" she asked instead.

I clenched my jaw. While I was thankful I hadn't given away too much when I was drunk, the trouble now was coming up with a believable lie on the spot. Roland and I had agreed to tell any possible recruits that we were guards from the palace who had left after Harland overthrew the Cathmoores. And while that might convince her the royal family were good people from a servant's standpoint, I couldn't help but think Lucinda was right, and my lie should be closer to the truth.

"I'm a noble," I said slowly. "Alastair and I are—were—good friends."

"Friends with the prince," Lucinda mused. She paused briefly and then *hmphed* before continuing with much more suspicion in her voice.

"But if you're a noble, your family is rich. *You're* rich. Why didn't you tell the captain so you could get a ransom and go free?"

"Because then he'd know our entire story was a lie and kill us both. Or worse, he'd want to know my family's name. And my family's name is dangerous now that Harland is in power."

"And he'd know your family was close with the royals, being a noble himself once."

"Precisely." She was putting this lie together nicely for me. "He might decide to hand me over to Harland instead of the Pirate King for all I know. And whatever the Pirate King has in store for us, I know it will be better than what Harland would do to me."

"Did you know the captain, then? Before he became a pirate? You must have ran in similar circles?"

I still sensed a bit of suspicion in her tone, but I obliged her anyway. "My parents knew him more than I did, and we didn't see him very often to begin with, but I'd been to a few gatherings with him, yes." That much was true.

"But I don't understand. If you're a noble, why would your first solution to us gettin' caught be to marry me?"

"Trust me, marriage wasn't my first solution. I thought through a lot of excuses before I landed on that one. And as I said before, I wasn't planning on the wedding actually happening."

"But surely your family had arrangements for you already? You must be near twenty."

I laughed, surprised at how many of these questions I was able to answer with honesty. "I only turned eighteen a few months ago. I'm barely eligible for marriage. I have a good relationship with my parents, so there's no rush for me to start my own family and claim my inheritance. I have two years to enjoy my last bit of freedom before I would be expected to do so anyway. Besides, there's a lot that goes into finding a proper wife. We'd narrowed it down to a few options, but hadn't officially settled on anyone before Harland took over."

"But that's my point exactly. You're supposed to find a *proper* wife. And you marry a random girl without askin' about her lineage first?"

I shrugged. "We didn't have opportunity for you to inform me. But I sized you up well enough in Koyben. You're a commoner, middle standing, judging by your clothing, though it seems Harland may have put you on rougher times. That, or you just steal for the thrill of it."

She didn't respond to that assessment, so I continued. "Besides, people like me don't marry for love. The least I could do was marry you to save our lives." I realized this would be a good opportunity to try to dissuade her from using the wedding to blackmail me, now that I was trying to convince her I was a nobleman. "And who knows if such a wedding will hold up legally anyway? Certainly the circumstances are extraneous enough to make it invalid." I wasn't convinced that was true, but hopefully I could at least convince *her* it was.

"They better be. I figured you were some slimy townsboy. If you're really a noble, you're goin' to lose everythin' bein' married to me."

Her concern surprised me so much that I laughed it off. "I already lost everything because of Harland. I doubt marrying a poor girl can make my life any worse than he already has."

"That's *honestly* all you think I am? A poor girl? You're tellin' me that whole story you told Mothway ... you made that up? Pulled it out of the sky? You really have *no* idea who I am?"

My jaw tensed. "I thought we already went over this. It was the perfect cover story. It protected my identity and gave us an innocent reason to end up in the pirate camp. Being a couple leeches justified our needing the pirates to wed us. It made them the heroes of the romance *and* allowed them to defy the law—two of their favorite things."

"Careful how you talk about leeches, *noble*." Her tone went cold.

Dread crept up my spine, a physical manifestation of the terrible realization making its way to my brain. But she was dressed as a commoner, not an illegitimate child.

Then again, hadn't Mothway made the same observation? And what had I told him?

Looks can be deceiving.

Indeed. I, too, wasn't dressed according to my status. But it wasn't a crime to dress lower than your status, only to dress above it.

"Lucinda," I said slowly. I needed to be careful how I phrased this. It was clear I'd already offended her. "I promise I don't have a clue who you are or what you're running from, but are you telling me—"

"My father was a pirate," was all she said.

It was all she needed to say.

"I see," was all I could say in return.

The news certainly put a damper on what I had already known to be a poor decision. I knew it was a gamble to marry a stranger, but I didn't think I'd end up with the *worst* lot possible. Yet here I was, the second most powerful man in the kingdom—when Harland wasn't sitting on my father's throne, anyway—with one of the lowest women in the kingdom. This was a disaster. What would Roland say when he found out? Or my mother? No, it was best not to think that far ahead right now.

Still, Lucinda's feelings about the predicament didn't make sense. Why wasn't she taking advantage of the situation? From her perspective, this should be a miracle. The best thing that could have happened to her. So why was she so angry?

Before I had the opportunity to press further, the door opened.

I turned my head away as lantern light spilled into the room. Lucinda quickly swiped her hand over her cheeks and stood.

Baxley and two other pirates entered the room. Baxley hung the lantern and passed by me to go to Lucinda. By the time I got to my feet, the two other pirates had their swords drawn and pointed directly at me.

"We're just 'ere fer the girl," the shorter of the two said.

"Why only me?" Lucinda asked.

I was afraid I knew.

Baxley grabbed Lucinda roughly by the arm and pulled her away. A dagger at her back glinted in the lantern's light.

I tried to dodge past the two pirates guarding me, but they were skilled swordsmen. They blocked my path, their blades at my throat. If I'd had a sword of my own, I may have been able to take them, but I was defenseless.

"Gabriel!" Lucinda called over her shoulder as Baxley dragged her out the door.

My heart lurched at the fear in her voice. "Stop! Wait!" I yelled. "Stop!"

Of course, they didn't listen to me. Lucinda was dragged out of sight. The two pirates holding me off slowly backed toward the door.

She screamed for me again.

I rushed at the shorter one and managed to throw him out of my way. He fell to the floor, but the other pirate was ready for me. He yanked me off balance. The pommel of his sword smashed into the back of my head. I crumpled, crying out as stars filled my vision.

They were out the door before I could stagger to my feet.

"Don't hurt her," I pleaded.

The click of the lock was the only response I got.

I threw myself against the door and tugged on the handle with all my might. But the lock held fast. I yelled threats and promises of money for Lucinda's safe return. No one so much as yelled back for me to be quiet. I started to feel lightheaded, and sweat rolled down my temple. I bent over, trying to catch my breath.

The lantern was left behind, whether on purpose or on accident, I didn't know. But the light seemed to be getting brighter. I closed my eyes a moment, and when I opened them, I realized I was sweating so much that the beads dripped onto the floor, where they glistened red on the wood planks.

No. Not sweat.

Blood.

I raised a hand to my head where the pirate struck me, my hair startlingly wet to the touch. I pulled my hand away, somehow still surprised to see it coated in crimson.

The room spun. I cursed as my knees gave way beneath me.

7

Is This an Interview or an Interrogation?

Evangeline

Baxley delivered me kicking and screaming to Captain Mothway's cabin.

"That husband o' hers be causin' quite the scene below deck," he informed Mothway as we entered the room.

It was true. I could hear him shouting all the way up to the main deck, which was quite confusing. Was Gabriel actually worried about me? He'd barely said anything after I finally admitted my bloodline.

Leeches they called people like me, though usually only behind our backs. He'd said it to my face. Granted, he didn't realize I was included in that term at the time. Regardless, he couldn't be happy that he was now married to one. So, what did he care what happened to me? It must have been part of his life-preserving act.

The captain dismissed Baxley, but told him to stay outside the door, lest I try to escape.

I contemplated reaching for my pendant, but I wanted to keep its usefulness hidden from the pirates as long as possible, so I looked for something in the cabin to serve as a makeshift weapon. I wasn't about to suffer the same horrors as my mother. Not without a fight.

"At ease, Lucinda. I've brought you here to sew one of my shirts."

"You ... want me to sew for you?" I narrowed my eyes, my skepticism clear.

"Yes. Do you have a problem with that?"

"No, of course not! I just figured you'd have someone on your crew who normally does that."

"Yes, normally. But he met his end two weeks ago, and the man that's replaced him is certainly not as skilled as a *real* seamstress."

My head—and my heart—pounded. "This is a test, isn't it? You want to see if our story is true."

"Smart girl." He threw the shirt at me.

"I don't suppose you have a needle and thread? My needles were taken from me at the beach."

"On the table." He pointed to a set of needles, *my* needles, waiting for me in the middle of the room.

"If you have my needles, what need do you have to test me? Why would I carry these if I wasn't a seamstress?"

"For all I know, these could be a prop to help convince me of your tale. I don't make guesses as to *why* someone might choose the lie they do until after I determine whether or not they are, in fact, lying."

I narrowed my eyes. "Fair enough."

We both took a seat on opposite sides of the desk, and he watched me carefully as I threaded the needle. The shirt was ripped at the elbow. It was a simple fix. Hopefully, I'd be out of here in under two minutes. He let me make the first few stitches in silence, but his curiosity won over before long. "So Lucinda, you and Gabriel willingly decided to seek out a crew of pirates?"

I glanced up from my work. How many times were we going to have to rehash our story? "Yes."

"Knowing full well what the reputation of pirates is around women?"

"It seems to me there are two very opposite reputations that pirates have around women. But, *yes*," I hissed. "I'm *well* aware."

The captain chuckled. *Chuckled.* "Fortunately, you lucked out with my crew. We have quite the respect for women on this ship."

"Hmm."

"How are you doing with sea sickness? You had any trouble?"

"Between the fear of dyin' and the hangover you gave us, it's hard to pinpoint the exact cause for feelin' sick to my stomach."

The captain clapped his hands together. "Witty, too! Were you a man, you just might have the potential for a proper pirate."

I frowned. "Are there really no female pirates? I've heard rumors of some." I did my best to keep my voice level, only passively interested in the answer.

"There's a few." He frowned back. "But they aren't *proper* pirates."

"I thought you respected women." I raised my eyebrows.

"As the weaker sex, yes, of course."

"Of course." I knotted my thread, nearly cutting it on my pendant out of habit. I caught myself, and snapped the excess instead. "It's finished. May I be excused, Captain?"

He picked up the garment and examined my stitches, tugging at the fabric to see how they held. "Very good. You'll mend our sails tomorrow."

"Very well." I got up to leave.

"I did not say you were excused. Have a seat, please."

I clenched my jaw, but returned to the chair.

"There's something about you…" he mused. "Which of your parents were you most similar too?"

"I imagine my mother. I never knew my father." My words came out distant, cold.

"No? Most couples get married after their leech is born, from what I understand."

There was that word again. I straightened my spine, trying to sit a little taller, as if I could force the sting not to weigh me down. "My parents were not a couple." However disgraceful people deemed the truth, it was better to me than letting people think my mother had any fond association with my father. I crossed my arms. "My father was a pirate."

"Ah! That's what it is!" Captain Mothway's excitement at this news caught me quite off guard. No one had ever received my lineage with *delight*. "You're your father's daughter, I'd bet my ship on it."

I blinked. "You know my father?"

"No, I highly doubt that. If he was a pirate that long ago, he likely would have left the profession one way or another years before I came into it. But you've got the sea in your blood. Even I can see that."

"So, I remind you of … the sea?"

"Wild, reckless, and beautiful. If your father cared at all about his lineage, I imagine he'd be proud."

The idea stole the breath from my lungs, starting a whirlwind of emotion in my chest that I didn't have the slightest desire to sort out. I lifted my chin. "He ruined my mother's life."

"Not enough to make you scared to death of us, though, like most people. In fact, you sought out the very people who 'ruined your mother's life' for your own personal gain. And *that* is the pirate's way."

I shifted in my chair. Somehow this man was managing to simultaneously flatter and insult me.

Yes, my father was a pirate, but I was my *mother's* daughter. Seeking out the pirates was not to betray her. It was an act of desperation.

And still, he, a pirate captain, believed I *did* have the potential to be a good pirate, which is what I had originally come here to do, though I certainly couldn't admit that now.

Or could I?

"If you're lookin' for a more skilled tailor on your ship, perhaps Gabriel and I could serve you, instead of you turnin' us over to the Pirate King."

"And what good is your book-binding husband going to do on my ship? Half my crew is illiterate. We have no need for books here." He leaned forward, his eyes gleaming. "Unless you know of some other skill of his I may find useful?"

Was he suspicious of Gabriel being a noble? The look he gave me suggested he knew *something* that he assumed I also knew. But I wasn't fully convinced myself who Gabriel was.

I shrugged. "I'm sure he could learn whatever you require of him." I was also sure Gabriel would be quite unhappy that I'd volunteered him to serve a crew of pirates. But why should I care what he wanted?

"Mmm." The captain took a moment to consider my offer. "Let's see how you do on the sails."

I nodded, unsure if the flutter in my stomach was from hope or anxiety.

He called for Baxley, who immediately opened the door. "Yes, Captain?"

"Lucinda is dismissed. Escort her back down with dinner for her and her *beloved*."

"Gabriel?"

He was lying in a crumpled heap near the door, which Baxley closed and locked without any concern. I set the tray holding our next meal on the floor and turned to him, trying not to panic at the sight of blood on Gabriel's still form.

"Oh, mercy."

His head was bleeding, or had been. Blood coated his hair and the right side of his shirt, and red streaks dripped down his face.

"Gabriel," I said again.

When he didn't respond, I reached for my pendant. I sliced a notch into my petticoat and tore off a strip of the tattered hem, poured a bit of our water on the fabric, and returned my attention to him.

But when I tried to lean closer to examine him, my shadow covered exactly what I was trying to see.

"Stars above, nothing is simple," I muttered, retrieving the lantern from its hook on the ceiling and setting it beside him.

I cautiously wiped away some of the blood on the side of his face, not entirely sure where the wound was yet. "Gabriel, come on, wake up."

And finally, he did. It took a moment for his eyes to focus on me, and I noticed his pupils seemed far larger than normal before he gasped and scrambled to sit up.

"Lucinda!" He reached out as if he were going to take me by the shoulders. But he hesitated, afraid to touch me. "I'm so sorry, I tried to—" A jumble of curses and apologies fell from his lips, the words barely comprehensible.

"Woah, slow down. I'm okay," I assured him. "They didn't hurt me."

"What?"

"I'm fine. Much better off than you are, at least. What happened? I was only gone for fifteen minutes."

"I don't understand."

I handed him the wet cloth. "Wipe your face and let me see your head."

He glanced down at the cloth, then back at me.

"Does your head not hurt?" I asked. "You're covered in blood."

"Oh." He wiped the cloth over his face, and pressed it against the top of his head.

"Is it still bleedin'?"

He pulled the cloth away. "I don't know."

I grimaced and instructed him to tilt his head toward the light so I could take a look. "How did this happen?" I asked, hoping his explanation would help distract me from how gross it was to look through his bloodied scalp for the injury.

"One of the pirates hit me with the handle of his sword. I didn't realize how badly he injured me at first. And then I passed out."

"Took the whole actin' thing a little farther than you meant to again?"

"I wasn't acting," he snapped. "Even if I don't like you, you still don't deserve to be abused like that."

That made me pause, certainly a distraction. "Oh." I swallowed. "Thanks."

I took one last look at his head. "It looks like it's not bleedin' anymore," I concluded, quickly stepping back to put some space between us. "Try not to touch it."

He nodded slightly. "If you're alright, then what did the pirates want you for?"

I flopped to the floor. "Captain had me sew a shirt. A test on our story. Although he already had my sewin' needles, so I don't know why he had much reason to doubt me. But he said I did a good job, and he's goin' to have me work on some sails tomorrow."

Gabriel frowned. "Are you lying to me?"

"Believe it or not, I haven't lied to you once since I met you. I wouldn't lie about this."

"Then why did they come in armed and threatening? Why didn't they tell us that's all the captain wanted?"

"Probably because keepin' us frightened is amusin' to them. It keeps their power over us. And besides, if they had come in and said they just wanted me to sew a shirt, would we have believed them?" I shrugged. "I probably wouldn't have."

Gabriel's gaze passed over me again, clearly still not believing *me*.

"We have food," I remembered. I retrieved the tray, happy to leave the weight of his gaze, if only for a moment.

It was dried fruit again, but this time we'd each been given large cups of water too. Gabriel didn't reach for anything, but that didn't stop me from eating my share.

We sat in silence for a long while. The fact that Gabriel got hurt *did* comfort me a little. If he was willing to fight for me, maybe I should give him a chance for a second impression. But then again, when he saw me, he had hesitated to touch me. Was that because of who I was? Or because of what he thought had happened? Or was he merely obeying common decency? The boy was a mystery.

I finished eating my share and scooted the tray closer to Gabriel. He took the remaining cup of water and sipped at it.

"A peb for your thoughts?" I asked.

He paused, the cup half raised to his lips. "A peb? Standard idioms value my thoughts at a copper at *least*, sometimes two."

"Yes, but unfortunately, all I've got is two peb—if you don't mind the fact that they're currently in the captain's possession."

"Two pebs? That's one copper. So you *are* robbing me."

"Robbin' you? When I have two pebbles to my name, and you're supposedly a nobleman's son? No. You can have *one*. But I'm keepin' one for some other stranger's thoughts."

"That's seriously all the money you have?"

I glared at him. *Nobles.* "You're avoidin' the question."

"Well, for only a peb, I have to think of a pretty worthless thought."

"I was more interested in what you were thinkin' about just now."

He scoffed, though his blue eyes glinted with humor. "For a peb? Please, Lucinda. Those thoughts should earn me at least a gold."

"A *gold*?" I laughed. "You are not worth that much."

"*I'm* not worth *one* gold?"

"I suppose as a *person* you're worth that much. But I doubt even the king's thoughts are worth one whole gold. And the thoughts comin' from the same man who decided to marry a total stranger without askin' for her lineage first are certainly not that valuable."

"Jump ship, Lucinda."

I stood and walked the few steps to the other side of the room. "I'm afraid this is the best I can grant that request at the moment, *sire*."

"Actually," Gabriel started, and I braced myself for a diplomatic lesson, but instead, he asked, "Can you swim?"

"Of course. I haven't in years, but I don't think you can forget how."

He nodded. "Good."

I raised my eyebrows. "You're not thinkin' of *actually* jumpin' ship, are you? We're miles away from any shore. When I was up there, it was just the ocean in every direction."

"I just want to know what our options are."

Our options. So he wasn't so offput with me that he was going to try to escape alone. *Interesting*.

He softly tapped the floor with his knuckle a few times as he thought. "Do you think the pirates would give us any more favor if they knew your dad was one of them?"

"First of all, not my dad. He was my father. I will not allow any familiarity with that man."

"Fair enough." He shifted his legs. "But the question still stands."

I sighed. "I told the captain about that when I was up there."

"And?"

"He doesn't care. Not really." I fell back so I was lying on the floor. Certainly not appropriate manners for the company of a man, but at this point, decorum was the least of my worries. "He said my father would have died long before he got involved in piracy." I considered sharing more of my conversation with the captain, but decided against it. It would only raise more questions about my personal life, and Mothway had made my feelings about my parents complex enough already. I didn't need some entitled boy adding his opinion to the mix.

"Is that why you came to the camp? Were you hoping to find him or something?"

My stomach lurched at the thought. "No. I hope he's dead. I'm not sure what I'd do if I ever met him."

He took a long drink, then set the empty cup down with a clang and looked me in the eye. "I want to know about your life."

The notion caught me so off guard I couldn't help but laugh. "Why?"

"I'm curious. Is that not a good enough reason?"

I sat up. Now it was my turn to scrutinize him, trying to determine his motives, still wondering if he was lying to me as much as he was to the pirates.

"Fine," he muttered. "We need to discuss the implications of our marriage. A lot of those depend on who you are."

"You already know who I am."

"I know your social status. I know you're a seamstress. But *who* are you? You're not quite what I expected you to be, obviously. So what *kind* of person are you? If your father was a pirate, but you hate him, why would you go to a pirate camp? And why don't you care about Harland or the Cathmoores?"

"What does this have to do with our pirate weddin'?"

"The legalities of a marriage—"

"Please. It's an illegal weddin' by all accounts. Let it drop."

"And what happens when word gets out?"

"Why would word ever get out about such a thing? And who would actually *care* if rumors of it surfaced?"

"It matters for someone like me."

"Nobility, you mean?"

"Yes."

I squinted at him.

"You still don't believe me?"

"Can you blame me?"

"It wouldn't kill you to trust me a little, Lucinda."

"That's the thing, *Gabriel*. It just might."

He covered his eyes with his hand. "Maybe if you let me have one normal conversation without accusing me, you would see that I'm not whoever you've made me out to be."

I had been hoping to use the rest of the evening to sort out my feelings about my past and my current predicament with the pirates. But, at this point, what difference did it make if I did so while he listened?

I took a deep breath. "Where do you want me to start?"

8

WELL, THIS IS A NIGHTMARE

Alastair

"To understand my life, you first have to know about my mother." Lucinda paused and took a deep breath. "She grew up in one of the smaller towns outside of Koyben and liked to go to the beach. It was peaceful. She always said the waves seemed to wash away all her troubles."

"Was she a commoner?" I asked.

She nodded. "She didn't talk much about the life she had, but I think she was pretty well-off as far as commoners go. She was raised on more than one meal a day at least, which is more than I can say."

"Is that ... normal? For commoners not to eat every day?"

She shrugged. "I mean, usually you can find somethin'. But certainly not three square meals. Do you honestly not know that?"

I blinked. "All my servants always eat."

She tossed her braid over her shoulder. "Yes, well, the servants of nobility are higher up the ladder than regular common folk. And certainly higher than my mother and I."

"I suppose, but—"

"Do you want to know about my life, or do you want to argue with me about the reality I grew up in?"

I clenched my jaw. This woman was a real test of my patience.

She took my silence as permission to continue. "Anyway, my mother went to the beach one night alone. She couldn't sleep. She was too worried about somethin', though all those years later, she couldn't remember what about. She wasn't supposed to wander so far from home alone, let alone at night, but she figured, what was the worst that could happen?" She paused and shook her head. "She was strict about that. Me not wanderin' off without her knowin'. '*The worst can always happen. And it happens as soon as you think it won't.*'" She made her voice slightly deeper to mimic her mother scolding her. "She was right about that."

She sat there a moment, fiddling with the fabric of her skirt as she worked through how to go on with the rest of the story.

"I don't need the details. I'm gathering she ran into your father that night?"

She nodded. "*I* don't know the details. She didn't talk about that part. But there was a pirate camp, and she was defenseless and alone. Anyone can fill in those gaps."

"Lucinda, *you* approached a pirate camp alone."

"The difference being that *I* approached them. They didn't find me unaware. Well—" She glared at me. "They *did* end up findin' me, but that was your fault."

"And I said I was sorry! But how do you know any of that would have made a difference?"

"I don't. Between Gratsis and the pirates, I guess that would have been my inescapable fate," she mumbled. I wasn't sure if she had intended for me to hear it. "Regardless, they let my mother go, or she escaped—again, I don't know the details. She went home and didn't tell anyone. She was worried she'd get in trouble for sneakin' out, and that everyone would blame her for what happened. She blamed herself for a while."

My stomach twisted. This story was a nightmare.

"Obviously everyone found out soon enough because, lo and behold, she found herself pregnant with me. When she finally told her family, no one believed her that it came about the way she said it did. They assumed she was sneakin' out with some lover, and that this was the consequence of a long-kept secret.

"Her parents pressed her to confess who the man was so they could arrange the marriage. But she couldn't give them a name, and they assumed the man was *already* married. I don't know how long all the theories and disagreements lasted, but eventually, they came to accept that a pirate had fathered the child she carried." Lucinda wrapped her arms around her knees, the only sign of vulnerability she gave in this retelling. "They had to disown her. She would have been cast out anyway if she'd been sleepin' with some other man, but at least she'd have been married with someone to provide for her. And for me, I suppose. But as it was, there was nothin' they could do. She had no description of him other than that he was a pirate, and huntin' *him* down so they would marry was not only an impossible task, but arguably far crueler than just leavin' her on her own."

Although Lucinda could talk about such things with a level voice, this was completely new conversational territory for me. Perhaps I should have expected as much, but clearly I was mistaken in this being any kind of "normal" conversation. It wasn't appropriate for me to be discussing such things with a woman. Though, the way Lucinda regularly sprawled on the floor while we talked suggested she didn't care in the least about propriety to begin with.

I cleared my throat. "Can I ask a question?"

Lucinda blinked, as if she'd forgotten I was there. "I suppose."

"If your mother hadn't ended up ... with you, would she have carried on with her life as normal? If the news came out eventually of what happened to her, what would her family have done?"

"She didn't plan on ever tellin' anyone. It might lessen her chances of findin' a suitable husband, and even if it didn't, she didn't want to hear anyone say, '*You should have known better than to go out alone at night.*' It was the worst moment of her life. She didn't need any help regrettin' it."

"But she could have had a normal life still?"

"If not for me? Yes, it would have been a possibility."

"That poor woman."

Lucinda huffed and leaned back on her hands. "Yes, my mother lost everythin' because of me. My very existence is a curse."

"That's not what I meant—"

"Isn't it, though? Everyone thinks it, even if they don't say it directly. I know it's true. So there's no point denyin' it. My life ruined my mother's."

I swallowed. "Was it difficult, then, living with her?"

"Only in the sense that everyone thought I was the embodiment of some sort of evil. With most other illegitimate children, their parents at least loved each other. But mine didn't, and *worse*, my father was a *pirate*. So that's doubly bad. If normal illegitimate children can't marry for the fear that their birth out of immorality will make their bloodline inherently *more* immoral, then what in Fate's Design is to be done about someone like me?"

I was getting quite sick to my stomach, and my head was throbbing now, which didn't help at all. "I see."

"My mom, though," Lucinda continued, "she never blamed me for any of it. Not for ruinin' her reputation, her family, her future. She lost everythin' because of me, but she only blamed herself those first few years, and eventually, she only ever blamed my father. *He* was the one who ruined her life. *He* was the reason her daughter didn't have any hope for a future."

She brushed a few tears away and sniffed. "Her parents had hoped somethin' would go wrong with the pregnancy before she started showin', so no one besides them would ever find out what happened. But she always wanted to be a mother, and while the circumstances were not at all what she had wanted, she certainly wasn't goin' to be havin' any other kids now. Even if she lost her baby before she started showin', she knew the truth of what happened to her was bound to come out at some point, and there would be no chance of marriage after that.

"From then on, I was all she had. So she vowed to make the most of it. She loved me with every fiber in her bein' I think." She sniffed again. "She was all I had too." Another sniff. "Before I was born, she moved away from Koyben. It was too hard to live where everyone knew who she had been once. It was still shameful to be known as nothing more than the woman cursed to conceive by pirates, but she said it was an easier shame to bear than the people who knew her as a respectable girl once. She ended up outside of Welven, a month before I was born. We lived in a shed at the edge of a farm. Lookin' back, I don't think the arrangement was entirely legal, but the landowners at least took enough pity on us to let us have shelter. My mom worked on their farm, and eventually I did too. They didn't pay us, but they kept us alive, so what more could we ask for?"

I wasn't sure how to respond to that, but it seemed she was waiting for me to say something. "That's quite impressive."

"What is?"

"How your mother cared for you despite having every reason not to. After everything she went through, and everything everyone said or thought about you, she still made her own decisions."

"I know." She let out a short laugh. "I dragged her to the depths of society, and she was just happy to have me as her company."

I frowned. "It sounds as if you still blame yourself for everything, even though she doesn't."

Lucinda broke eye contact with me and gazed into the lantern light instead. "I hated my father and blamed him for everythin' too. But there was always a naggin' guilt. A knowin' that things might have turned out differently for her if I never existed. After she died, and I ended up livin' in Welven, I was around far more opinions about my life. The most positive of which was that I was worthy enough to be tolerated and put to some sort of use." She looked back at me with a challenge now glinting in her eyes. "*Maybe* it's not all my fault that my mother died alone in a shed hundreds of miles from her family without a peb to her name. But I also can't deny that it never would have happened if I just didn't exist."

Mercy.

"How old were you when she passed?"

"Twelve. She told me not to get a doctor. But I did. Because if she died, I wouldn't have anyone who cared a whit about me. I *couldn't* lose her. The doctor charged for the travel, for the care, for the travel back to town. She died anyway. And I had no way to pay him."

My head pounded so ferociously that I had to close my eyes and lie back down. But Lucinda was finally talking to me as if I was trustworthy, and I was loathe to end that over a headache.

"So when did you get involved with the fellow who's looking for you now?" I asked. "Gracely or something?"

"Gratsis." She let out a heavy sigh. "My mother's death was exactly when Master Gratsis came into my life. He paid my debts to the doctor, and in return, I became indebted to him. Since my mother was disowned, she had no guardian, and neither did I. But in becomin' an indentured servant, Gratsis became my guardian.

"I stayed with him and his wife while I was still young. He trained me in his tailor business durin' the day, and I cleaned their shop and home in the evenin's. I worked hard. I knew how to from our time on the farm. Any time I started to grow lazy, my mom would remind me, '*If you can't be wanted, at least you can be useful.*'" She laughed as she brushed fresh tears from her cheeks. "Well, my mother was the only one who ever wanted me, and she died. So, I've been tryin' to stay useful ever since."

I frowned. "What happened then for you to end up back in Koyben?"

Her face fell. "Missus Gratsis died a few months ago. By then, I'd paid off my debt to Master Gratsis, he'd hired me on, and I paid him rent for my own room above the shop. After Missus Gratsis passed, he was a wreck. I started workin' extra-long days to make up for him not bein' able to work. And I didn't mind, because I knew what it was like to lose the best person in your life. But ... after a few months, things changed.

"It wasn't anythin' really concernin' at first. He was a little extra nice. I figured it was because he'd raised me for a few years with her. Certainly not in the traditional sense, but still. He'd mention sometimes how lonely it got in the house. After five months or so, I asked him if he'd ever consider marryin' again." She scowled and then groaned, burying her face between her knees. "I came to find out there *was* someone he'd recently grown interested in, but *I* certainly wasn't someone he could marry."

My eyes widened. "He had affections for you?"

She lifted her head just enough to glare at me. "I don't think *affections* is really the right word, but yes. He brought it up very ... subtly at first, and so I denied him in the same manner. Clearly that was the wrong choice, because he then brought it up *very* directly the next day. I bolted. Ran right out of the shop. Sure, Gratsis may have let it drop after that, but I also know what my mother taught me: the worst can always happen. I wasn't goin' to let her fate become more of mine. So, I've been lookin' for a new life ever since."

"And how long has that been exactly?"

She exhaled slowly. "It feels like forever. But only a few weeks now. I left Welven right before Harland claimed the throne."

"And now you're stuck here with me."

She nodded.

"I thought my life was a nightmare lately," I mused. "But your life sounds as though it's only *ever* been a nightmare."

"Yes, thank you for noticin'." She clapped her hands together, and I winced at how the sound made my head pound harder. "On that note, I think I'll go to sleep. Try to escape to a different nightmare for a while." She offered a half-hearted smile before she turned away, like perhaps she was only joking. But I didn't think she was.

I woke to two pirates opening our door.

"Good mornin'," Lucinda said to them. She was already awake, standing and greeting the pirates as if they weren't our enemies.

"Time t' work," one of them responded. "Both o' you."

They instructed us to grab the sails that had been stored in our room and bring them up to the main deck.

It was morning, the sun still low in the sky. I surveyed the vast expanse of sea surrounding us. There was a strip of land on the horizon to port side. But it must have been a few miles away still.

We climbed the steps to the helm, where Lucinda got situated with the sails and her needle and thread. She set to work immediately, calm and focused.

The pirates then led me to the bow of the ship, where I was to untangle and cut frayed ropes. It was menial work, but what else was I good for? The crew believed I was nothing more than a bookbinder, and that was a useless skill here. I did know a little about sailing, though more in theory than in practice. So, it was better to play dumb. They'd want to know where I learned to theoretically sail, and I was not in the mood to come up with more lies today.

I examined the knife in my hands as I sawed away at the frayed ropes. The blade was short and dull. It would be useless as a weapon, never mind how outnumbered I was.

I turned toward Lucinda, still sewing at the stern. The wind whipped her hair around her face, but it didn't seem to distract her from her work. I noticed for the first time that her hair was unique in shade, dark blonde at first glance, but tinted orange in the direct sunlight.

I couldn't help but notice the pirates watching her too. It made me uneasy to see them staring at her, and I knew our—her—good fortune here wasn't bound to last. And even if it did, the Pirate King would bring a swift end to it for certain.

The day passed slowly. After I cut all the ropes, they had me tie the pieces together. I'd made a swab. And then I swabbed the deck with it. Truly a humiliating morning for me, while Lucinda simply sat and sewed the whole time. But the pirates paid me little mind. As the day went on, I noticed their attention was more and more focused on her.

Twice, pairs of pirates would talk while looking at her, and then turn to look disapprovingly at me. I wished I could hear what they were saying, but I doubted the context would make me feel better.

Around noon, we were given water and food, and allowed a few minutes to sit together on the main deck.

"You look terrible," was the first thing she said to me.

"We can't all sit around and sew," I mumbled.

"No, I mean you still have blood in your hair and on your shirt."

"Well, I'll be sure to request a bath when we get to the Pirate King." I looked out at the shoreline, wishing it were closer. A dot caught my eye, and I squinted, as though doing so would improve my vision. It was either a large rock or a small boat, still quite a ways away from the ship, but close enough that we might be able to swim for it if our lives depended on it. And taking another glance around our company, they certainly did. "Or maybe I could take that bath now."

"Hmm?" Lucinda turned to me, puzzled.

I lowered my voice to a whisper. "We're going to jump ship."

"I told you, I haven't swam in years. There's no way I'll make it all the way to the shore."

"We don't have to get to the shore. There's a boat or something not too far away. See it?"

She scanned the water.

"Eleven o'clock," I directed.

Her brow furrowed. "That's still quite a ways out, Gabriel."

"The pirates have been sizing you up all morning. I'm going to go for it, and you need to come with."

She glanced around the ship, calculating her options. "Captain Mothway is considerin' lettin' me join the crew. That's more of a future than I have on land at this point."

That raised my eyebrows. "He's *considering* offering you a job? Stars above, Lucinda, when were you going to tell me about that?"

"I don't care much for your opinion on the matter, and I knew you wouldn't approve, anyway."

She was insufferable. "Look, I'm happy to go on my own, but before I do, I think you should take a look around this ship. Regardless of what the captain has done or not done to and for us, there are men here with other ideas in mind. And if Mothway decides he doesn't want you here, are you willing to risk what the Pirate King has planned for you?"

She was quiet a moment, but after one final surveillance of the decks, she shoved the rest of her food in her mouth, her decision made. "Fine," she finally said. "If you're leavin', I suppose I have little chance of stayin' in their good graces." She paused as if I might change my mind, but I wasn't about to. "So, how do we do it?"

"Simple: run and jump over the railing. Jump as far out as you can. Too close to the ship, and you could get sucked underneath."

She clenched her jaw. "Alright."

"You can't hesitate," I warned.

"I won't."

"Alright, then." I stood up, casually brushing of my clothes. "You're ready?"

She nodded and stood with me.

"Now."

We bolted to the side of the ship, pirates turning and gaping in surprise. By the time they started moving again, my foot was on the rail, launching me into the sea.

9

AT LEAST I'M NOT LUCINDA ANYMORE

Evangeline

The water was cool, but not cold. I plunged below the surface, and for a moment I was ten years old again, jumping into the pond out in the country while my mother laughed on the bank. As I kicked to resurface, I was brought back to reality. The water weighed down my skirts, and the fabric tangled around my legs. When I broke through the surface, the commotion above was even more unpleasant.

The pirates shouted from the deck, trying to get the captain's attention.

"You fools!" Captain Mothway shouted. "The shore is miles away. You'll never make it!"

We didn't answer, just kept swimming.

"There's a boat!" someone aboard called. "Only a mile out."

"Should we go in after them, Captain?" Baxley shouted.

"I doubt they'll make it."

"Better make sure..." I didn't hear the rest of his sentence, and I glanced back up at the ship.

Baxley held a pistol in his hands.

"Are you mad?" Captain Mothway shouted.

"Dive!" Gabriel called before plunging his face down into the water.

I followed suit, not a moment too late. The *CRACK* of the gunshot reached me underwater, though, thankfully, the bullet did not.

My skirts tugged against me as I swam down, down, down. The salt water stung my eyes. How far beneath the surface did I have to go to be hidden from their sight? My lungs started to ache. It had been mere seconds since I was at the surface. But I needed to swim away from the boat, not just down. I reoriented myself and pushed forward, away from the ship. I had to rely on my arms to propel myself forward, since the fabric around my legs hindered my movements. I'd have to get rid of my petticoats if I was going to actually get anywhere. I released a bit of air from my mouth, offering some relief to my lungs.

I realized, too late, that the bubbles on the surface could allow them to track me under the water. The skirts would have to wait a moment more. I swam on, keeping my mouth sealed shut until I couldn't take it any longer. I kicked for the surface, feeling as though my chest was about to burst.

I broke the surface and sucked in a deep, greedy breath.

"Baxley!" a pirate yelled.

I didn't look back to see how far away I'd gotten before diving under the surface again. Down first, then forward.

CRACK!

A second shot. Once again, I felt no pain. Had he been aiming for me or Gabriel?

The last thing I wanted was to risk being seen, but my lungs already ached again. I kicked for the surface.

I gulped in air and glanced back at the ship as another gunshot pierced the air. The pirates shouted and ran around the decks, swords clashing. Were they fighting ... *each other*?

Whatever the chaos, they didn't seem to have their attention on us anymore. The ship was already sailing past us.

It was over.

We got away.

Which meant my chances of being a pirate were now nonexistent. What more was left for me?

Supposedly, Gabriel wanted to recruit me for something. Or *had* wanted to. I doubt he still had the same interest, assuming his story of recruitment was true. But despite my reservations, I'd trusted him enough to jump ship. With the pirates now out of the picture, it was finally time to sort out what *his* deal was.

I turned around in a circle, searching for him. "Gabriel!"

Movement caught my eye as he popped up from the depths, ten yards ahead of me. He wiped the water from his eyes and looked around.

"Behind you," I called.

He turned around as I swam toward him. He watched the ship for a moment, making sure it was going on without us, before looking over at me, a genuine smile on his face. "Are you alright?"

"Yeah. Are you?"

"Yes." He turned toward the small boat we were heading for, still quite a ways away. "We'd better get moving."

"Give me a second," I said before tugging off my petticoats. I left my outer skirt on. I certainly wasn't about to get out of the water only half dressed.

Gabriel raised his eyebrows but said nothing. We continued on. Now that we weren't swimming for our lives, it was rather pleasant to glide through the water—for the first few minutes anyway.

I soon grew tired, and all my thoughts turned to keeping myself afloat. If Gabriel was tired, he didn't show it.

I looked at the small boat ahead. "I don't think it's gettin' any closer," I said.

"It is." The words were clipped and matter of fact.

"How's your head?"

"Fine."

I frowned. He was shutting down any attempt at conversation. He hadn't been this quiet since the night we were captured together—because he'd been *gagged*.

"What are you so upset about?" I pressed. "We got away."

"I'm not upset, Lucinda. I'm thinking."

"Evangeline," I corrected.

He didn't even turn to look at me. "Evangeline," he repeated.

I pushed forward to get in front of him. "And you?"

He swam around me. "Silas."

"Okay, Silas, do you want to tell me what you're thinkin' about?"

He inhaled and dipped under the water, resurfacing in the same spot. "Using your second peb already?" he asked.

I splashed him in reply.

He swam ahead. "Any chance you can steal a horse?"

I wished I could see his face. He couldn't be serious, could he?

"Is that a no?" he asked.

"Look—" I had to take another breath before I could continue, more winded than I'd realized. "I know you saw me steal in the market, but I'm a *seamstress*, not a thief." I tried to disguise another few breaths as simply allowing myself a moment to swim up next to him. "Did it ever occur to you that the reason you caught me in the first place was because I'm *not* good at stealin'?"

"Hmm," he said as he disappeared under the water again, popping up a few feet away.

I was panting at this point, my shoulders and arms starting to burn. "I need a break," I said as I turned to float on my back.

Gabriel—no, *Silas*—didn't protest, and floated alongside me. The sky was clear, the sun shining directly above us. I closed my eyes for a few moments.

"What are we goin' to tell the people on the boat?" I asked.

"That we escaped from the pirate ship. They saw it. They'll know."

"They'll know ... what?"

"That we did!" he huffed. "You ask so many questions. How about you think about that little boat over there, and let me think about what happens *after* we get on the boat." He didn't seem tired in the least. Tired of *me*, perhaps. But not from the physical exertion.

"I think we should be on the same page when—"

"You're annoying me, Lucinda."

"Ev—" I started to correct, before realizing he called me that on purpose. To annoy *me*. And worse, it worked.

He started swimming away.

I hurried after him. "If you think you can order me around just because you're some *noble*, you're wrong."

That did the trick. He turned around to look at me. "I'm 'ordering you around' because I'm the one who knows what's at stake here. And you better not drop my status around anyone. It's dangerous. Not just for me. Your association with me is enough to get you put in prison, too. Do you understand?"

Could I trust a single word out of his mouth?

I glared at him. "Yes."

"Good." He turned back around. "Now be quiet and let me think."

We swam in silence almost the rest of the way. But when the boat finally started to draw nearer, I realized we really did need to be on the same page with our story. "Will you be goin' to a city after this?"

Truthfully, I was a little surprised when he answered me. "I have to get back to Koyben. Depending on how far we traveled, I'll probably go to the closest city and find transport there. Why? Do you want to go together?"

Any thoughts I'd had of working with him were long gone. I'd tried to give him the benefit of the doubt that his attitude was a result of being kidnapped. But we were free now, and he was still insufferable. "With you? Not a chance."

"Not all the way to Koyben. But it's probably safer if you at least travel to the next city with someone."

"You assume I trust you far more than I actually do."

His head jerked back. "I was alone with you for hours on that ship, and did I ever lay a hand on you? What threat do I pose?"

I remembered him flipping me over his shoulder and onto the ground the first night we were together. But, that was self-defense. He'd shown genuine concern for my well-being on multiple occasions, and I had to admit it was hard to convince myself it was only a continued part of his act.

Plus, he had been properly horrified at the story of my mother and Gratsis. Like he hadn't heard any of it before.

Maybe he was telling the truth about being a noble. I hated to admit how much I wanted to believe it. The moment I let down my guard was the moment he could betray me. It was safer not to trust him.

"Fine," I relented. "We'll go together. But *only* because I might have a better chance of gettin' a job if people see me arrive with a man."

"Deal."

We swam the last few minutes in silence. Silas had finally begun to breathe heavily when I realized the men were rowing their boat closer to us.

Fate's mercy. My muscles were burning. This swim couldn't be over soon enough.

Silas called out a "hello," to them, as if we were simply strolling by and not depending on them to keep us from drowning.

The four men were already looking at us or beyond us—likely to the pirate ship far in the distance now.

"We jumped off the pirate ship!" I confirmed for them.

One of the men cursed. Another said something I couldn't make out.

"Are *you* pirates?" the oldest looking one said.

"No. We were captured by them!" Silas yelled. "Can you help us?"

"Just get them in the boat, Linel. Are you really goin' to sit there and watch them drown?"

The old man—Linel, apparently—huffed and ordered us to swim to the right side of the boat where we wouldn't get tangled in his fishing net. But he did indeed just sit there while the other three men helped pull Silas and me into the boat.

There were benches on the bow and stern, with an open space in the middle for the fishermen to haul their catch. It was big enough to fit all six of us, but it was crowded.

Silas and I sat there in the middle, surrounded by the men and a few of their fish, no one sure what to say.

"Thank you," I finally said when I'd caught my breath.

"No, thank *you*," one of the men responded. "You're our biggest catch of the day."

"Barth," Linel scolded him.

"Are you injured?" another one asked, looking at Silas. His hair was clean now, but his shirt remained blood-stained.

"Nothin' that still requires attention," he said, in his lower class accent. "What city do you hail from?"

"City?" Linel snorted. "There's no cities around here. A few towns, though. Closest one is Arten."

"How far is that from Koyben?"

He lifted a brow. "That where you're from?"

We nodded. It was where we'd been captured, anyway.

Linel thought for a moment. "Three weeks walkin', I'd guess."

"Hang the moon," Silas swore under his breath.

The man who had asked if he was injured cleared his throat. "Or, you could walk half a day to the port city, Narim. If they have boats headed that way, it'd save you quite a bit of time, I'd think."

Silas and I looked at each other. It was probably our best bet.

"Narim it is," he muttered.

10

I Do Not Understand Poor People

Alastair

The fishermen fought with Linel over whether or not we were turning back to shore or waiting for the workday to end. Linel, of course, wanted to stay out on the water. The other men argued that there was no room for a catch now that Evangeline and I were there.

Time was of the essence for me, but luckily I didn't have to chime in. Linel realized soon enough that it was him against the rest of the boat, and we headed for shore.

As the men took up the oars, they introduced themselves. I smiled and nodded, but I was hardly listening.

I was familiar with Narim, as my family had made appearances there on several occasions. It was one of our main port cities, a major trading center. There *had* to be ships heading toward Koyben, or at least somewhere nearby it. But that was when things were right. Who knew how the ports operated under Harland's control. But the fishermen seemed to think the ships were still sailing. That was good.

It would be risky, of course. With Harland's men everywhere, I would have to tread carefully. I might have to fill Evangeline in on more of the situation, to make sure she understood the *seriousness* of it all.

But could I trust her? She didn't care about my family, or that Harland was in power. Nor did she seem convinced of my nobility claim. How would she feel if I suddenly told her my position was even higher than that?

No, I wouldn't tell her my true identity. Believing I was friends with the prince was good enough. But she needed to know that if we went separate ways, mentioning her time with me could endanger her—and my mission. It'd be easier if she came with, where Roland and I could keep an eye on her. But I wasn't sure I wanted her to.

A hand nudged my shoulder, breaking my concentration.

"What?" I snapped at Evangeline.

"I said your name at least three times." She cast an apologetic glance at the fishermen. "Gregory said we can stop by his home and get food before we head out, if we'd like."

We had eaten not long ago, but the swim gave me an appetite. And if it was a half day's journey to Narim, I wasn't going to turn down a meal.

"We don't have any way to repay you," I said to the red-headed man I hoped was Gregory.

He shook his head. "Not necessary. Just tryin' to help out some kids, that's all."

I was skeptical, but Evangeline seemed unfazed. "That's very generous. Thank you, Gregory."

We reached the shore not long after that. Gregory bid the other three men farewell as they put everything away. Linel attempted to convince them to head back out, and an argument ensued as we walked away.

"My wife will be glad to see you," Gregory told us. "She loves havin' company, and we don't get much of it in these parts."

"Do you live in Arten?" Evangeline asked.

"The outskirts of it. Linel isn't too fond of people outside the family. I'm sure you could tell. We all live in our own sort of community. Sell our fish in the town and buy what we need. But we mostly keep to ourselves."

"The four of you are all related?" I asked.

"Did you hear a word on that boat, Silas?" Evangeline scolded. "Stephen and Barth are Linel's sons. Gregory is his son-in-law."

"Oh, sorry." But the reprimand didn't help me pay attention to the rest of the present conversation. Despite what Gregory said about his wife appreciating company, it was clear that he was also a lonely man, one who seemed to be taking full advantage of company who hadn't heard all his stories before.

After about fifteen minutes, we came upon a cluster of cottages.

"Welcome to our humble home," Gregory said.

They were small houses, but well built. The women were out and about, farming, hanging laundry, and chatting with one another. A few children played off to our right.

"Gregory, who've you got there?" one of the women asked. She looked at him with softness in her eyes, despite the surprise in her tone. I assumed this was his wife.

"Two kids who jumped off a pirate ship. They swam all the way to our boat. I figured we could give them some food before they head back home."

"Pirates?" The woman was too stunned to move.

"Oh, you poor things," another woman murmured.

"It wasn't as bad as you would think," Evangeline said. "I think we got lucky."

"That's... good, I suppose," Gregory's wife said. "Well, come on in, and I'll fix you somethin'. How do you two know each other?"

"Newlyweds," I answered. Evangeline shot me a glare, and I shrugged it off. If she told them we had never met before our capture, they probably wouldn't let us travel alone together. And I needed to speak with her privately to either convince her to come with me to Koyben so Roland could sort out what to do about my association with her, or to make sure she kept her mouth shut about our history for the rest of her days.

"Oh, my. Well, if you can survive kidnappin' by pirates in the first few months together, I suppose the rest of your trials will seem quite manageable in comparison." She laughed dryly.

I was relieved Evangeline didn't tell her it had only been a matter of *days*.

"Greg, dear, find them some clothes to change into while I get some food together."

The inside of the home was indeed humble. Only two rooms, a living space and the bedroom. It was hardly furnished beyond the basic necessities. I couldn't possibly take clothes from people this poor.

"Oh no, that's not necessary. I think we're mostly dry by now."

The woman put her hands on her hips and gave me a look reminiscent of one my own mother often fixed me with. "You've got blood all over your clothes. And she's clearly missin' her petticoats. You can't go into a proper city lookin' like that. What will people think?"

It was clear there was no use in arguing with her. She had us put our shoes by the hearth, where she set to boiling a kettle.

I followed Gregory into the bedroom. He opened a chest and pulled out a tan cotton shirt.

"Try this. If it doesn't fit, we'll have to get one of Linel's."

I held the shirt up. It seemed promising. He turned his attention back to the chest as I changed.

"As for pants, I'm not sure what we can do. You're a tall fellow, and I don't think any of our things will fit you right."

"That's fine, Gregory. The shirt is more than enough."

The man eyed me warily, probably considering how his wife would respond to my only being half changed. "Alright," he relented. "Say, has anyone ever told you that you look a little like the late prince?"

I nearly choked. "No, sir, I can't say anyone has."

He hummed a moment. "It's not like I knew him personally, just seen him in portraits on the rare occasion. A shame what happened to the Cathmoores."

I swallowed and nodded in agreement. "Has Harland's rule changed much for you here?"

He shrugged. "Nothin' besides emptyin' our pockets whenever he gets the chance. Same as you, I'm sure."

I nodded again. If only money was all Harland had taken from me.

We returned to the main room, where Gregory's wife was slicing bread while Evangeline stood by the hearth.

Gregory's wife glanced up at me. "Ah, that's an improvement. Can you fetch my green dress for Evangeline, dear?" Gregory began to protest, but she insisted, "I haven't fit into it since the kids. And Kathryn won't fit into it for another few years. Better to put it to use now."

Evangeline cast me a sidelong glance, as though I might demand she be put back in brown and unbleached cotton instead of breaking more sumptuary laws. But I had already claimed we were married. I wasn't going to contradict that now.

"So the green dress, and ... what else, exactly?" Gregory asked.

His wife set her hands on her hips. "Two married men and we can't even openly discuss *petticoats*." She chuckled as she stepped away from the bread. "I'll sort you out, Evangeline."

The two women entered the bedroom, shutting the door behind them.

"Take a seat." Gregory motioned to the table. "I'm sure you're exhausted."

"Yes, thank you." As I slid into a chair, I realized I wasn't sure what kind of conversation commoners engaged in, and while Gregory had seemed open to discussing politics, it probably wasn't the safest topic for me to engage in at the moment.

Gregory seemed equally unsure of what to say to me. "You, er, it looked as though you may have been injured on the ship?"

"I was. But that was a few days ago." If yesterday could count as a few days ago. "I'm fine now. That was the worst of our trouble."

His wife emerged from the bedroom, shutting the door behind her while Evangeline changed.

"Were those your kids outside?" I asked, eager to turn the conversation away from myself.

"No, those are Stephen and Octavia's." She offered me a half-hearted smile that quickly fell.

"And your name? I'm sorry, I didn't catch it."

"Marna," she said softly, as though her mind was elsewhere. She took a deep breath, and then returned to gathering food for us with renewed enthusiasm. "Where are you headed after this?"

"Narim. We'll see if we can get a boat back to Koyben, where we're from."

"Your family must be worried sick."

She had no idea.

"Do you have any money to buy passage to Koyben?" she asked.

I considered lying, but I'd already told Gregory we couldn't pay for any of his kindness. "No, ma'am. The pirates took what little we had."

"I'll talk to the others and see if we can pull somethin' together for you," Gregory offered.

"Oh, no. You've already done more than enough. We couldn't possibly take any more from you, especially with all of Harland's—"

"You're not takin'. We're givin'."

"But—"

Marna dismissed me with a wave of her hand. "I don't know how they do things where you're from, but here, we take care of one another."

I didn't argue, but only because I was rendered speechless. Where I was from, every favor, every compliment, every kindness, had an expectation of being returned. Among nobles and the wealthiest men in the country, everything had a price. And yet, in this little cottage, where each copper was hard-earned, they gave freely. And we weren't even one of their own. Could that be true?

I was quite far out of my element here, and I had counted on Evangeline's help to navigate any conversations appropriately. But she was taking a while to get dressed. I supposed she had more layers involved, but I was going to start exposing myself as upper class if she took much longer.

It seemed Marna was starting to have the same line of thought—about Evangeline taking a while, at least. She stepped toward the bedroom door. "Evangeline, is there anythin' else you need? I can find you another dress if that one doesn't fit."

"No, I'm—" Her reply was cut short by a sob.

The couple turned to me, and I raised my eyebrows before remembering I was supposed to be her husband. Who'd known her for months.

Brilliant.

"I'm fine," Evangeline finally called. "I'll be out in a moment."

I hoped that would be that, but Marna and Gregory were still looking at me expectantly. I approached the door. "Evangeline, uh..." I cleared my throat. What was I meant to be asking? To go in the room? For her to take her time? "I know the last few days have been a lot for us. So if you want to talk about anythin' privately before—"

To my surprise, the door opened, and Evangeline's red-rimmed, puffy eyes greeted me.

"I'm fine," she insisted. "I just needed a moment."

I nodded and stepped aside so she could join us in the main room.

Marna crossed over to Evangeline and wrapped an arm around her shoulders. At her touch, Evangeline burst into tears.

"Oh, my dear," Marna cooed, bringing her into a hug.

"We survived, Evangeline. That's what matters," I offered. I didn't have much practice in comforting others, let alone someone who had done nothing but get on my nerves. But she was still one of my subjects, and I owed her my concern, even if most of it was a sham.

"I know." She sniffed. "I think the whole thing is finally catchin' up to me. Everythin' I thought was going to happen, and everythin' that did instead..." A sob interrupted her.

Marna continued to comfort her, while Gregory and I stood there uselessly.

I wondered what twisted whim of Fate had drawn me to her in the market at Koyben. Not only was she not a real thief, but if she wasn't able to handle stress well, she was a *terrible* fit for the mission. This had truly become the most infuriating delay in my timeline. Sure, Evangeline had been given a tough lot in life, and I felt sorry for her. But that didn't change the fact that she wouldn't be much help in *my* life.

Perhaps I ought to let us part ways in Narim and be done with it.

Evangeline calmed down enough, and Marna directed her to a chair at the small table in the middle of the room. Gregory and I also sat down, and Marna brought over jam and bread and hot tea.

"It's not much, I know," Marna apologized. "But you're welcome to stay for supper if you want a proper meal."

Evangeline and I assured her it was plenty.

"We'll have to get goin' after this, I'm afraid," I added. I'd already lost, what? Two or three days on the pirate ship? And who could say for sure how many more I'd have to waste before I found Roland again? At this rate, he might go on without me.

I ate quickly, drinking the tea with purpose, not pleasure. Evangeline conversed easily with the couple, saving me from further making a fool of myself, exactly as I'd hoped she would. As she sat there easily discussing the weather for their little farm and different types of teas, for the first time, I saw her as she was. No longer looking through the lens of worry for our safety or selling a lie.

While in the bedroom, she had rebraided her reddish-blonde hair, and a small white cloth covered the crown of her head—the first time she'd been properly modest since our capture. She was quite striking in Marna's green dress, the color making her hazel eyes shift to a matching hue. She still wore the floral-patterned corset, and her belt and pouch still hung around her waist. I knew she was pretty before, but now I really *noticed*.

Gregory excused himself, I assumed to get the money he'd talked about. I wanted to protest, but Marna's scolding still rang in my head.

Here, we take care of one another.

So be it. Besides, it was probably the least my people owed me. If they weren't going to revolt at Harland taking over, they could at least lend me some coins.

It's not their fault. They think you're all dead, I reminded myself.

For a moment, I considered revealing myself. Roland had said I couldn't do it because Harland's men would be after me in a heartbeat. But out here? With this family? Gregory seemed to like my family well enough. There was no danger. And maybe they would spread the word to Arten, and Arten to the other cities, and—

And then Harland's men would be on to me.

No. I had to cling to my anonymity for as long as it lasted. Roland and I were skeptical that dying my hair from blond to black would serve as an effective disguise, but it was the most we could do with such limited time, and I lacked the genes to grow a proper beard anyway. We blindly hoped no one would recognize me, the only child of the king and queen. And so far, no one had.

Which, honestly, was a little offensive.

Granted, I had remained in the background of public appearances whenever I could. But I was still in the portraits and at the public addresses. I was still the future king.

No one is going to be looking for a prince they think is dead, Roland had said. I don't know why I was so surprised he was correct.

"Silas? Are you alright?" Evangeline's voice cut through my thoughts.

I realized I'd been sitting still, staring into my now-empty cup. "Yes, fine." I straightened and stood. "We should get goin', though."

Evangeline held her gaze on me a moment more, then downed the rest of her tea and stood with me.

We thanked Marna earnestly for her hospitality and, at Evangeline's prompting, helped her clean up the best we could. Then we were out the door and heading down the road, when Gregory called after us to wait.

"This is what we can spare for you," he said as he handed me a small sack, coins clinking as they came to rest in my palm. "It's not much, but we hope it's enough to get you where you need to go."

"Gregory, I—"

Evangeline set a hand on my arm. "That's very generous, thank you."

Gregory smiled, so I followed her lead. "Yes, thank you. You've been far too kind to us."

He shook my hand, the friendly gesture taking me by surprise. "Take care of yourselves." He nodded to Evangeline, a sad smile on his lips. "Get on now, you can still make it before dark."

Evangeline thanked him again, and we turned back down the road. I pocketed the bag of coins and committed these people to memory. *Marna, Gregory, outside Arten.* Gift or not, if I made it through this, I would owe them a great debt.

"It is a delicate thing, to trust another."

Brigid, *Duty to My Fellow Man*

II

Only a Noble Would Be This Dramatic

Evangeline

Silas and I walked along the road in silence. It was clear he was deep in thought, and it was also clear that he hated to be interrupted when thinking. Which was fine with me. I had my own thoughts to worry about. Like, what in the world was I going to do once I got to Narim? It wasn't likely this city would be any different from the others I'd visited. Without a letter of reference or guardianship, no one would give me the time of day.

I just wanted to go home. But home was a place that didn't exist for me anymore.

I sighed.

To my surprise, Silas glanced over at me. "You need a break?"

I shook my head. I *was* tired. But emotionally, not physically. The respite at Marna's home had allowed time to recover from the swim, and walking was different enough for my muscles that I didn't mind it. But the fear and shock of the last few days was slowly ebbing away, and in its wake, I was drained.

I took another step and nearly toppled over as my foot got caught in my long skirts. Silas grabbed my arm and steadied me.

"Thanks," I muttered, quick to detach myself from him. "Marna's a bit taller than me." I tucked an edge of the skirt into my belt to keep it from humiliating me again.

Silas watched me with a frown, and then we resumed walking. "I think you should know some more about me, before we part ways."

I almost laughed. "And why is that?"

"Well, for one, you told me an awful lot about yourself, so it only seems fair." He paused. "But secondly, I told you that my family name is dangerous right now. I mean that. And if you go around telling people *anything* about me, it could endanger you."

Now I frowned. "So you convinced me to accompany you to Narim for the sake of my safety, just so that you could explain why associatin' with you is dangerous?"

"Don't keep trying to make me sound like an idiot. I needed time where I could explain this to you seriously."

"Were you not serious on the pirate ship?"

He wiped a hand over his face, looking up to the sky as if Fate itself might send him some relief from me. "It's the fact that you don't believe me," he finally said. "I'm worried you'll tell the wrong person you had a run-in with some insane man who tried to tell you he was a noble and friends with the Cathmoores, and the next thing you know, you'll be in an interrogation room, and I'll have soldiers on my tail."

"I do believe you."

He stopped in his tracks. "You do?"

"I do now."

"What changed your mind?"

I took a deep breath and released it with a sigh. "A bunch of little things, I suppose. But, in the end, it was the money."

"The money Gregory gave us?"

"What other money is there?" I shook my head. "If you *were* after me for my ransom, you wouldn't be the kind of person to turn down extra coins. So I don't think you're tryin' to return me to Gratsis."

"Ah, well, I'm glad to know you at least think I'm not a scoundrel."

"*And*, I've never heard any commoner so adamantly refuse money—especially in our situation. Clearly, you aren't accustomed to *need*."

He frowned.

"I'm sayin' you're obviously upper class."

"Yes, I gathered that much, thank you. I didn't expect it to feel like such an insult."

I laughed. "That's also very upper class of you."

He glared at me. "So you understand then, you can't breathe a word of me to anyone. No one can know you were with me, or you'll be in as much of a mess as I am."

"But that defeats the whole purpose of me goin' to Narim with you! I need the people to see me with a man so they'll think I have permission for employment. Obviously, I'll lie about who you are."

"People might recognize me. Even Gregory thought I looked familiar."

"You look like a thousand other boys. If anyone thinks you look familiar, it's because they've seen your face in half their neighbors."

"You are not good at compliments."

"I'm not givin' compliments. I'm statin' facts."

He mumbled something I couldn't decipher, then said, "If you need a letter of recommendation, you could write your own. It's not like the people in Narim are going to go all the way to your hometown to make sure it's legitimate."

Just when I thought he couldn't get any more clueless. "If I wasn't illiterate, that might have been a good idea."

"Oh. Right." He kicked a rock in the pathway, and it rolled ahead of us. "I could write you one, then, before I go. It wouldn't take long."

"You'd do that?" I couldn't keep the surprise out of my voice.

"I certainly can't parade you around town so people see us together."

"We'll have to buy paper. You want to use our coins on that?"

"Do we have to? I got into this whole mess because you're a thief."

"*Hardly* a thief." I rolled my eyes. "For a noble, you have quite a loose affinity for the law."

He laughed. "For a pirate's daughter, you have quite a concern for it."

I scoffed, but wasn't about to waste my breath justifying myself to him. "How much money do we have?"

"Whatever it is, we'll split it half and half." Silas took the little bag out of his pocket and handed it to me. The gesture surprised me as much as his words. He was nobility through and through, not realizing he'd probably need every coin to get himself across the Chelek. But on top of that, he was trusting *me,* the "thief," to count the money?

He was something else.

I poured the coins into my palm, all coppers.

"Enough to get you to Koyben, I'd think. And to get both of us dinner." I put the coins back and handed him the bag. "Not much more than that though."

"What about you?"

I shrugged. "I'll have your letter and find employment."

"What about Gratsis?"

"He can't hunt me forever."

"Why is he after you, anyway? Why not just let you go?"

"He decided to tell everyone I stole that necklace the pirates took from me." The words left a bitter taste in my mouth. "So now there's a warrant for my arrest and the return of the necklace."

"So you *are* a thief!"

"Hardly! He gave me the necklace before I ran away. Claiming I stole it is his excuse to keep anyone from questionin' why I left and hurtin' *his* reputation."

He didn't respond for a few steps, then kicked another rock. "I'm sorry."

Another apology?

I nodded in acknowledgment, and we continued in silence for a few minutes. This was going to be a long walk if we carried on with those as the last words to hang over us.

"So," I started, "since you know why I'm on the run from the law, why, exactly, do Harland's men care about *you* so much?"

Silas glared at me, then looked around to make sure we were alone on the road. "I told you," he whispered, "I'm friends with Alastair."

"And, what? Harland's scared you're goin' to avenge him for his death?"

"Something like that."

"But what threat could you possibly—"

"Trust me, the less you know about it all, the better. Besides, what do you care? The royal family doesn't matter to you anyway."

"I don't care about *politics*. That doesn't mean I think people deserve to be murdered."

Silas studied me for a long moment. "To be blunt, I still can't trust you with that kind of information."

I barked a laugh. "Do you mean to drop your commoner accent around me? Or do you just forget to use it when you're upset?"

His mouth opened slightly as his eyebrows lowered, looking the most confused I'd ever seen him. "What does that have to do with anything?"

"Because if you're droppin' it on purpose, then in some way, you do trust me. If you forget, then I shouldn't fault you so much for it."

"I've already told you who I am. What does it matter how I speak around you?"

I shrugged. "Like you said, you shouldn't trust me with such information."

"You're *agreeing* that I shouldn't trust you?"

"I'm sayin' that if your story is true, you're right, and you probably shouldn't be trustin' *anyone*."

He turned from me and continued down the road. After a moment or two, he *hmphed*, clearly having some internal dialogue without me.

"What?"

"Nothing. You just told me not to trust anyone."

I wasn't sure I cared enough to continue this game. But Narim was still hours away. Better to fill the time talking about nobility and political nonsense than suffer with him brooding in silence. "Yes. But even if I *were* to tell anyone your secrets—which I assure you I won't—who would believe me? I'm not exactly a woman of good repute."

"Your argument for telling you the most dangerous information in the kingdom is that ... you are not trustworthy?"

"My *reputation* isn't trustworthy. I, on the other hand, am the most trustworthy person you'll ever meet."

He scoffed. "You're sometimes a thief!"

"And only sometimes is pretty good, isn't it?"

He shook his head, but didn't say another word. I resigned myself to silence the rest of the walk.

After what must have been a half hour, he suddenly said, "Alright, I'll tell you," with enough annoyance you'd think I'd been pestering him the entire time instead of walking in silence. "But it's strictly confidential.

Breathe a word of this—especially to the wrong person, and your life will be in more danger than it already is for being associated with me. You're certain you want to know?"

"You're the one who wants to tell me!"

"And you've made me reconsider."

We both stopped walking, and stared the other down.

"Clearly you want to tell me."

He lightly pressed his lips together.

"Tell me, or don't," I said. "It doesn't matter to me. Either way, we're partin' ways soon, and I won't tell a soul. But it's a long walk to Narim, so I'd prefer to fill the time with *somethin'*."

He nodded and took another glance down the road before he spoke. "The royals are still alive. Harland faked their deaths so no one would rebel against him. My team and I are going to rescue the Cathmoores and restore them to the throne. But Harland and his men know we're looking for the royals. If they catch so much as a rumor about where I am or where I'm going, not only are *our* lives at stake, but so is the entire future of Wenterly. Is that clear?"

I gaped. "How do you know they're alive? There were reports of their bodies at—"

"He *faked* their bodies. I saw the king and queen alive with my own eyes *after* the reports of the royals' bodies hanging from the palace parapets came out."

"Where did you see them alive? Why wouldn't you have rescued them then?"

"It's all very complicated, Evangeline," he answered, his voice strained.

"Is that what you needed a thief for? To help with the rescue mission? You don't already have one on your team?"

He nodded. "Truthfully, I shouldn't call it a team. It's only Roland and me. I've known Roland practically my whole life, but that means that Roland is about as useless as I am for the more ... delicate aspects of the plan. I can fight, and he has some skill with weapons, but he's more of the planner. He spent his early years trying *not* to become a soldier, devoting himself to academics instead. Unfortunately, that's working against us now that we're trying to break into a prison."

"What do you need stolen? The keys to the cells?"

He eyed me. "Among other things."

"And this Roland, is he your age?"

"He has fifteen years on me."

"Does he have any idea what happened to you?"

"He knows I went after you. But I'm sure he's nearly lost his mind since I disappeared."

I scuffed my foot along the path as I turned his story over in my mind. "I hardly know what to think about all this. But I won't tell anyone about it."

"Good. Thank you. Also, I—" He cleared his throat, and when he spoke again, his tone was surprisingly gentle. "I'm sorry that I intervened on the beach. For a lot of reasons. But one of them is that you clearly have enough trouble in your own life. I'm sorry for adding to it."

I froze mid-stride. He just told me how he was trying to rescue a family the world thought was dead, and he was still apologizing to *me* for how hard *my* life was? Never in my life had anyone been that sincere and considerate of my own feelings. I wasn't sure what to say. I didn't have much practice in receiving apologies, let alone under such circumstances.

I forced myself to keep walking. "Thanks."

Eventually our little pathway merged onto a main road. After another half hour, we heard the clip-clop of hooves behind us. Silas and I stepped into the grass on the side of the road to get out of the way. I turned to see who was approaching.

A man on a cart was coming down the way, his horse walking at a leisurely pace.

"We might be able to get a ride," I told Silas.

"How much will he want for it?"

"Usually people do it for free. So long as you're goin' the same way."

"Oh."

I waved to the man as he approached. He stopped his horse and nodded at us. "You headed west?" he asked.

I nodded. "We're goin' to Narim."

"You want a lift?"

"Please, if you don't mind."

He tilted his head, inviting us onto the cart. Silas took a seat next to him. I climbed into the bed with his goods. Strawberries, mostly. He must be going into the city to trade.

He flicked the reins and the horse pulled us down the road.

"I'm not much for conversation," the man said.

I laughed. "Neither are we."

12

The Man I Married Is, Unfortunately, Very Thoughtful

Evangeline

Another hour passed in silence, the man true to his word. He didn't bother to ask so much as our names or where we hailed from.

Without conversation, I listened to the monotonous clop of the horse's hooves, and it wasn't long before I started to doze off in the back of the cart.

The cart bumped, jolting me awake. We'd traveled a long way from where I'd last opened my eyes. Buildings rose on either side of the road, replacing the trees I'd seen for miles.

"Here is great, sir," Silas said.

I sat up. This was Narim? It wasn't as nice as Koyben. I had figured they'd be about the same, considering they were both port cities. But this place was definitely dirtier. Louder. A breeze picked up, and I wrinkled my nose. Narim was smellier than Koyben, too. A lot more fishermen seemed to use these docks.

Silas walked to the back of the cart to help me down. I took his hand only so the man wouldn't find our behavior odd. But the man continued down the road without another word or glance in our direction.

Silas and I stood at a wide cross-road that sliced through the middle of the city. I could look all the way down to the docks on our left. To our right was the City Center: law office, inn, and a clock tower.

"First things first, to the Portmaster," Silas said, his commoner accent in full effect.

"What about my letter?" I asked.

"I haven't forgotten about that. But I think we should figure out exactly how much it will cost me to get to Koyben first."

We made our way to the docks, passing fewer people than I'd expect in such a large city. Silas was not nearly as taken aback by our surroundings as I was. In fact, he led the way as if he knew exactly where he was going. Had he been to Narim before?

I followed him into a small building to the left of the docks. Inside was a small office. Maps and clocks set to different times covered the walls.

A short, round man glanced up from the desk he was sitting at. "Can I help you?"

Silas stepped forward. "I'm lookin' for passage to Koyben."

"Just you?" he asked, opening a large book on the desk and perusing its contents.

"Yes, sir."

The Portmaster looked up at us for a moment, his eyes darting between us as though he was trying to figure out what I was doing there then, but he said nothing and returned his attention to his book.

"Got a cargo ship headed to Koyben in three days."

"That's too far from now. I'm in a hurry."

"That don't change the schedule."

Silas folded his arms and glared at the man. The man glared right back. They stayed like that for a good half a minute before the man sighed.

"Seven a.m. tomorrow I got a ship headed for Dirman." The Portmaster pointed to the city on the map of Wenterly behind him. "That would get you halfway there."

"I'll take it."

"*But*," the man continued, "it's at full capacity. You'll have to wait at the dock and hope someone doesn't show up in order to get on."

This time, Silas sighed. "And that's my best option?"

The man spread his hands. "Unless you're goin' to charter your own ship, that's the best I can offer you."

I tuned out their discussion of accommodation and payment for the trip to Dirman and studied the map above the Portmaster's head. I found Narim at the southern edge of the kingdom. At least I assumed I did. It was the only red-inked dot, and situated on the coast. If that was Narim, this was the farthest I'd ever traveled. Where should I go next? Aside from the issue of money, the world was mine to explore. I had no family ties or roots to hold me down. I could go anywhere in Wenterly. See the mountains in the Northwest. Or, why keep it to Wenterly? Maybe Eliston to the West held my future. Or Glastor to the East, King Harland's home kingdom. With him ruling Wenterly now, I doubted it made much difference whether I lived here or there.

I faintly realized the men had stopped talking. Silas was bent over the desk, writing on a piece of paper.

"Evangeline, remind me how long you worked for my, uh, uncle?"

I furrowed my brow, clueless as to what he was talking about.

"At his *tailor shop*," he added.

"Oh, right. Sorry. I was distracted..." I tucked a strand of hair behind my ear. "Seven years."

The Portmaster looked between us once more, but said nothing.

I realized Silas would need a name to sign the letter. "Leonard Gratsis was a good master. He taught me a lot."

"Everyone loves Uncle Leonard." Silas dipped the pen in the ink well and gave me a pointed look. "It was too bad when he moved so far away to that little town."

I caught his meaning. "He made a nice home for himself in Welven, though. Everyone respected our work at Gratsis' Threads and Fabrics."

Silas nodded. "Yes, I know," he said with a long sigh, as if he really did know. "Can't believe that's the name he went with though." He wrote some more and then asked, "Remind me, when was the last time you were there? Only a few weeks ago, right?"

"Yes. Three days before Harland became king."

"Right. How could I forget?"

"A lot has happened since then." I shrugged, but my mind was reeling. He was navigating this conversation quite effortlessly. He was clueless about many things, but how to lie in front of an audience was not one of them. What *did* nobles get up to in their free time?

Silas continued to be a mystery. A mystery that, much to my dismay, I was more and more interested in figuring out.

It took another minute or two for Silas to finish the letter. He pulled a copper coin from his pouch and gave it to the Portmaster, half-heartedly thanking him for his help. Then he folded the letter, tucked it in an envelope, and headed for the door. I followed him out.

After we walked a few paces away, Silas handed me the letter.

"What'd you write?"

"That you were an exemplary employee." He shrugged. "I put in what you told me, that you were orphaned and started out as an indentured servant before earning a permanent position. Then I added that you were always happy to learn new skills and that his children were old enough to apprentice, so he no longer needed your help, though he was sad to have to let you go. I don't know what his signature looked like, but more than likely, no one else you meet will know either."

"That's brilliant. Thank you."

"I also dated the letter more recently than the date you left. Enough time to get you from Welven to here, but recently enough that it won't look as though you've been getting rejected for weeks."

He was shockingly thorough with his details. "That's very kind of you. Thank you." I tucked the envelope under my belt.

"I also didn't specify your exact social rank. There's nothin' that says you *aren't* illegitimate, but there's nothin' that says you are either."

"You..." I didn't know what to say to that. "Why would you do that?"

"I figured you need all the help you can get. Besides you can't carry a letter that says you're illegitimate while dressed like that, can you?"

"But—" I stammered. "Why would you do that?"

He frowned ever-so-slightly. "Would it make you feel better if I told you it slipped my mind?"

I shook my head. "How much does the trip cost?"

He obliged my quick change in subject. "Fifteen copper."

"To *Dirman*? That's about what I thought it would be to get to Koyben."

"Apparently, Harland added a hefty tax to water transportation. Probably scared that people will board ships and flee the kingdom. Plus, there's an extra two copper for stand-by passengers."

"Why?" I scoffed. "You only get on board if someone doesn't show up. They're already prepared for a person in your place. That doesn't make sense."

Silas sighed. "If you can charge for it, you charge for it. That's business."

"Well, that doesn't leave you much. Between the trip and the paper, there's only three copper left, if I counted right. How will you get the rest of the way to Koyben?"

He shrugged. "I'll worry about that when I get there. Right now, we should see what we can eat. What do you say to one last meal together?"

I didn't answer right away. I had no reason to hesitate. Why should I want to keep company with such a man? But, aside from his poor decision-making and outlandish claims about the late royals, his demeanor had always been quite sane, poised even, and—most absurd of all—kind, at times. The thought of leaving him awakened the loneliness I'd learned to stuff down years ago.

Mercy, I didn't want to be all alone again.

"Yeah, I could eat."

As we continued down the road, a trio of officers made their way out of the law office ahead of us. They wore sashes of red and yellow, the colors of the Glastor flag.

Silas immediately turned left, down a side street.

I followed him as we wound our way through the city. We turned yet another corner, and I realized I had lost track of where we were in relation to the docks and city center. "Where are we goin'?"

"Summer Festival."

"Where?"

"Did you listen to anythin' the Portmaster said?"

"Not really."

"Every Saturday night durin' the summer, Narim has a gatherin' in the market. There'll be a ton of people there, so I can blend in a little easier. Plus, music, dancin', and, most importantly, food."

13

I Discover How Commoners Dance (and It's Incredible)

Alastair

The market was split into an east and west side. The east side had food and drinks. People milled about, chatting and eating.

On the west side, the remaining market stalls were butted against the buildings, providing more room on the already-wide street. A handful of musicians played a lively tune. But what really drew my attention was the people dancing.

Their feet were flying. They bounced around the marketplace, partners swinging each other out and then back in again. Some of the women had their skirts belted or tied up, so as not to trip, but it scandalously exposed their legs from the knee down.

I knew that town dances were different from the balls of nobility. But I had always assumed it was because the politics of who-dances-with-whom weren't involved. I'd heard my mother off-handedly remark that "the common people bring shame to good dancing," but I thought that meant they had bad technique. I never would have thought it was because they dance... Well, compared to how we danced, this seemed like it should be labeled as something entirely different.

And it was incredible.

"I thought you were tryin' to stay out of sight," Evangeline commented. "This is quite the crowd."

"We aren't from here," I answered, without looking away from the dancers. "It would be far more suspicious for us to be slinkin' around than blend in with the crowd."

A handful of the men suddenly spun while lifting their partner into the air. The moment the women's feet touched the ground again, they kicked and jumped back into their quick steps.

"Do you want to dance?" Evangeline asked.

I realized I'd been staring at the dancers with my mouth slightly agape. I quickly directed my attention to the food vendors. "No. Let's see what we can eat."

There were herbed rolls, cakes, and pies. A few varieties of fruit—including the strawberries the man who brought us here was selling. Evangeline waved to him, and he politely waved back, though he didn't offer any indication of recognition.

They were selling wine as well. But the thought of drinking anything alcoholic made my stomach turn.

Everything was being sold in small portions, which meant everything was within our price range.

Evangeline and I each got a herbed roll, and we also bought a half-dozen strawberries to share. It was the least we could do for the man who'd helped us get here.

We made our way to one of the pedestals set out in the road. There were no chairs, just a place to set your food. I faced the dancers as we ate, trying to recognize step patterns and failing to find any. It was almost as if they were just flailing about. And yet, their partners knew how to move with them. I couldn't make sense of it.

"This is the best bread I've eaten in my entire life," Evangeline raved, her mouth full.

I raised a brow. "I think you're just hungry."

She took another bite. "No, this is the best bread I've eaten in my entire life."

"You shouldn't talk with food in your mouth. Don't you know that?"

Evangeline looked me right in the eye as she took another bite. "Sorry, sir. I'm just some farm-raised leech. No one ever taught me any manners."

I scoffed. "Okay, Lucinda."

She scowled.

Another song ended, and the dancers stopped to applaud their partners. A few walked away to get refreshments, panting as they left the dancing space, but giddy smiles on their faces nonetheless. Others joined the dance as the next song began, similar expressions on their faces at the anticipation of it. I never knew dancing to be something so exhilarating.

"I can't believe they're doin' this every week of summer," I remarked.

Evangeline nodded. "Me neither. But, when I think about it, it is a relatively simple festival, confined to a small area of the city." She shrugged. "Plus it's nice to have somethin' to look forward to each week."

"Yes, but also..." I lowered my voice in case there was an eavesdropper nearby. "It's a little strange that everyone is celebratin' like this. After what just happened to my f—my friend." The Cathmoores were my *friends*, not my family.

Evangeline lifted her brow. "That's all the more reason to have the festival. It gives a sense of normalcy. It's something happy and familiar despite that whole mess."

I considered that for a moment. "It still feels insensitive."

"Well, believe it or not, not everythin' is about you."

I blinked and nearly took a step back. Evangeline reached for a strawberry as though what she said didn't have any weight to it at all. Was this how she regularly spoke to people? Even those she *knew* had higher social ranking than her?

Then again, of course she would think this had nothing to do with me. She didn't actually know who I was. If I was back in the palace, in finer clothes, with servants for my every beck and call, would she still talk to me this way?

"I beg your pardon?" I finally said.

She glanced at me. "What? Don't tell me you actually think a random city should be takin' your feelin's into consideration on whether they have a festival?"

I took in the market full of people enjoying their evening—people who were also completely unaware of who I was. I'd never been part of such a gathering. Not one so lively, nor one so impersonal. At every ball I'd attended, every person I spoke to, danced with, and entertained was measured and calculated.

But Evangeline was right. These people in this marketplace didn't care what I did here. And better yet, they danced or ate as they pleased, not looking to me or anyone else for what to do next. Did they know what a privilege that was?

Evangeline began humming to the music as she continued eating. She was the only one here with *any* concept of my true status, and even she didn't seem to care. Perhaps in this moment, I too had the privilege of anonymity.

Cheers rose from the west end of the market, winning over my attention. The men had lifted the women up above their heads again, but this time, the women kicked in rhythm before being set back down on the ground and moving right back into their quick, jittery steps like it was effortless.

"Oh, go join them already," Evangeline insisted.

"I don't know any—"

She rolled her eyes, "Fine, I'll be your partner."

I shook my head.

"Come on. Ever since we got here, you've been starin' like dancin' is your favorite thing in the world."

I ate a strawberry.

"Next song, we're goin'."

I swallowed. She was relentless. "I can't. I don't know how."

She paused, another strawberry halfway to her mouth, and her brows scrunched in disbelief. "Are you serious? You can't dance?"

A woman across the market spun out and back into her partner's arms. She jumped and he swung her into a dip, her legs up in the air, skirts hanging open a moment before she bounced back onto the ground.

"Not like that. Can you imagine the ladies of high society showin' their legs?" I couldn't help but laugh at the very notion of it.

"Wow." She popped the strawberry in her mouth and then added, with her mouth still full, "Nobles *are* borin'."

I ignored her comment, as two officers entered the market square. I took surveillance and cursed myself for not doing so sooner. There were already other officers posted and watching in each corner of the market.

"Do you think there are a lot of officers here? There's already four, and two more just came in."

She looked around, but didn't have the same vantage point as I did. She shrugged. "It makes sense that more officers might be added as the evenin' progresses to make sure people behave. Or they could have been walkin' their rounds and stopped by to see how things are goin'."

That made sense. No reason to panic when there were so many other plausible reasons for the officers' presence. I eyed the two new arrivals. They were conversing with one another, paying us no mind.

"How'd you learn to dance?" I asked, trying to push the worry from my mind.

"My mom taught me. It looks harder than it is. You just feel the music and move with it."

I watched the dancers' feet, still not recognizing any patterns to their movement. "I doubt that."

"I can teach you," she offered.

"I don't want to call any attention to myself. Even if it is just as the man who doesn't know how to dance."

"Okay," she said quietly, as if disappointed.

I glanced over at her. Her gaze fell to the table, the corners of her mouth turned down.

Oh. She *was* disappointed.

"Do *you* want to dance?" I asked.

"I'd like to." She eyed the dancers, then me. "Does that surprise you?"

"A few hours ago, you escaped a kidnappin' and cried from the fear of nearly dyin'. So, yes, I'm a little surprised that now you want to dance like none of that happened."

She laughed, but pity filled her eyes. "I don't know how things work where you come from, Silas. But where I come from, life is hard, and then we die. So, if Fate gives me an opportunity to dance in the meantime, I'm goin' to dance."

Her words rendered me speechless. The statement bordered on philosophical. Not what I'd expected from an uneducated woman.

She scowled. "Don't frown like that. Are you actually goin' to stop me?"

I hadn't realized I was frowning. "Why would I stop you?"

"Even at a town dance, I'm not really allowed to approach a partner."

"I've seen plenty of women ask men over to dance."

She pointed a finger at me. "Not a female rule—a leech rule."

"Oh."

She shrugged as though it didn't matter, but I noticed the light in her eyes dimmed.

"Then, lucky for you, no one besides me is any the wiser."

She looked at me out of the corner of her eye, trying to gauge if I was serious. "You, supposedly a high man of society, are suggestin' that *I* break the very rules our society is built on?"

I scoffed. "Give me a break, Evangeline. This isn't a ball where political alliances are made during a waltz. It's a *city festival*. Besides, if Fate is givin' you an opportunity to dance, even I can't stand in your way."

A sly smile lifted her lips, right as the song came to an end. "Alright. Just one song. But don't leave without me."

"I'll be right here."

I watched as she crossed the market, rebelting her skirt at a good dancing height. She approached a group of three young men as the next song and dance commenced. Whatever she said won them over and one of the men led her to the dance floor. The next song began, and the man spun her to his side as they jumped into a frenzy of steps. She smiled. Genuinely.

Perhaps I wasn't the only one discovering the relief anonymity could be.

It was a shame we met the way we did. Perhaps she wasn't half bad. Just weary of Fate, as I had been as of late. Perhaps I shouldn't have dismissed her so quickly for the mission. But then again, what was the use in reconsidering now? She clearly wanted to part ways.

Or did she? Why had she asked me not to leave without her?

"There aren't many who would let their lady dance with another man."

A hand clapped me on the shoulder, and I looked behind me.

My breath caught in my throat.

14

NOT EVEN A BABY WILL FIX THIS

Alastair

I quickly turned my head back to the dancers, hoping the officer hadn't gotten too good of a look at me. But he wasn't one of the new officers who'd recently entered, and if he was referring to Evangeline as 'my lady,' then he must have been watching us for a while.

"I'm useless for dancin'," I said.

"So you're willing to risk another man wooing her than make a fool of yourself?"

I shrugged. "There's no harm in lettin' her enjoy herself. I know I'm the one she goes home with at the end of the night. Better she comes home happy."

"A happy wife makes for a happy man."

I nodded as I attempted to casually put my left hand in my pocket. I didn't want him to notice I wore no wedding band.

"Where are you visiting from?" the officer continued. He stepped in front of me, blocking my view of Evangeline. I had no choice but to look at him. He was nearly my height, only an inch or two shorter. He appeared to be only a handful of years older than me, too. His features were all sharp angles, and his eyes cold steel.

"Arten. Small place southeast of here." I made sure to fully pronounce the *h*, knowing any slip in my accent may as well be a death sentence.

He narrowed his eyes slightly. "I've heard of it," he said flatly. "What brings you to Narim?"

"The festival." Evangeline's words from a moment ago came back to me. "We decided we could use some levity for a change."

"Naturally." The officer nodded and took a step back. "Enjoy your time, then."

I nodded to him, watching him in my periphery as he made his way back to the edge of the market.

My heart pounded in my ears as another officer made his way over to him, and they engaged in a brief conversation. How long had they been watching me?

And how many were still watching?

I resisted the urge to look around, and turned my focus to Evangeline.

She was a marvelous dancer, feet flying here and there as though it was second nature. Her partner swung her around, spun her in and out. But any previous enjoyment I'd had in watching her was long gone.

I needed to leave. But to do so without her would immediately arouse suspicion. And then they'd probably arrest both of us. Of course, the same could happen if we left together, but at least that gave us a chance of the officer believing my story.

Finally, the song reached its conclusion. Evangeline offered a small curtsy before she and the man parted. I nearly gritted my teeth with the effort to wait for her to return to my side. I couldn't look like I was in a hurry. I needed to blend in.

Evangeline trotted up to me, panting slightly as she readjusted the white fabric on top of her head. The officer was still watching us. I forced a smile.

"You're very good," I said.

"Thanks!" She smiled back. "Listen, I wanted to—"

She stopped short as I wrapped a hand around her waist, pulling her against me. "We're being watched," I mumbled against her hair. "We need to go."

I released her, and she quickly took a step back. "What do we do?"

I held out my arm to her, still smiling. "If you're not feeling well, we can call it a night."

She took my arm. "Married again? Or just betrothed?"

"Married."

I turned us toward the exit farthest from the officer I'd spoken to. I lost sight of him as we navigated the crowd, but hopefully that meant he'd lost sight of us too.

"You better be careful," she warned. "I might start to think you *want* to be married to me."

"The officer brought it up first. Wasn't my idea."

"You talked to an officer?"

I side-stepped another couple as I made my way to the exit. "Not by choice."

"Is he suspicious of me? Or you?"

"Me. But he noticed you too, so I suppose, he's wary of both of us."

"What did—"

"Heading out already? It's barely eight o'clock," the same officer interrupted as we approached the exit.

How did he get over here so quickly?

"Are we not free to come and go as we please?" Evangeline asked, the tone of curious innocence in her voice impressing me.

"Of course you can. But you came all the way from Arten for the festival. I'd think you'd want to make the most of your time here."

"I'm afraid my wife isn't feelin' very well. So unfortunately, we've decided to cut the night short."

The officer raised his eyebrows and turned his attention to Evangeline. "You certainly looked alright when you were dancing a moment ago."

"Oh, thank you. But that did me in, I'm afraid." Evangeline exhaled loudly. "I'm suddenly feelin' quite nauseous. All that spinnin' and hoppin'—"

"Why don't you sit down?" the officer offered. "I can find you a stool."

"Oh, no. I'll not risk gettin' sick here and causin' a scene. I'm sure we'll make it to the inn just fine. I'll rest there."

"I'll escort you." He gave a two-fingered wave to another officer to indicate he was leaving his post.

"There's no need, sir. We can handle ourselves. Thank you," I said as I stepped past the man.

"It's no trouble," he insisted, falling into step next to me. "I'm Officer Larson, by the way. You chose a lovely night to come for the festival."

Evangeline squeezed my arm while Larson droned on about the weather for a moment. I looked down at her.

"*Now what?*" she mouthed.

Perhaps if Officer Larson thought Evangeline had some real sickness, he would leave us alone. "You know, love, maybe it wasn't such a good idea to come to the festival today. You have been havin' these spells rather frequently as of late."

Evangeline narrowed her eyes and gave me the smallest shake of her head.

"Don't protest," I continued. "You know I'm right. If it's not nausea, it's fatigue or headaches. There's always somethin' ailin' you."

"Perhaps we can discuss this when we don't have company," she suggested, her voice slightly strained.

To my surprise, Officer Larson chuckled. "I have a wife and children, my lady, I'm no stranger to the symptoms of pregnancy."

"*Pardon*?" I stopped short. That was *not* the malady I had been hoping the officer would conclude.

Evangeline and Officer Larson stopped to gape at me, my own surprise reflected on both their faces, though Evangeline's shock was tinted with the subtle rage I was growing accustomed to from her.

"Forgive me, I had assumed—" he began, as Evangeline blurted, "I was goin' to tell you tonight!"

Now Officer Larson and I stared at Evangeline.

Why hadn't she denied it? She could have easily continued the narrative that she was simply ill. We could have sent the officer to get a doctor and ran once his back was turned. What was *this* plan? What good could a baby possibly add to this situation?

Evangeline sputtered under our attention, her cheeks turning pink. "I—I was just waitin' for ... the right time." She brought her hand to her forehead briefly, and I couldn't tell if it was for dramatic effect, or because she truly was that flustered. "And I'd figured after the festival, you'd be in a good mood, and—and I wanted it to be a special moment and—"

She was floundering, I could tell. But I had nothing to offer. This topic was well beyond my expertise.

She grabbed my hands, squeezing them harder than necessary. "Please, say somethin'. Tell me you're happy."

"Er," I started. She nearly crushed my fingers at my hesitation, flicking her eyes to the officer watching us. I had no choice but to play along. "Of *course*, I'm happy, Lucinda." I quickly pulled her into an embrace, more to free my fingers from her crushing grip than for the show. "Surprised, obviously. But happy all the same."

She pulled back a little to look up at me. "Good."

The town clock tower rang for eight o'clock, and the officer cleared his throat. "Again, I apologize for bringing the subject up…"

"No harm done," I said, hoping the quick dismissal of the subject would result in a similar dismissal of the officer.

"Unfortunately," Evangeline added, situating herself at my arm again. "I am still not feelin' well—"

Officer Larson nodded. "Yes, to the inn, right away."

My heart sank as he resumed walking. When he turned his back to us, Evangeline shot me an incredulous glare.

I shrugged. She couldn't blame me for the way this had turned.

We made our way to the main road in awkward silence. As we passed the law office, Officer Larson waved to the man posted there, using the same two-fingered wave he had in the market. I looked away, muscles tense until we'd passed the building.

When we were one building away from the inn, two men stepped out from its door. They turned to face us, the red and yellow sashes draped over their tunics instantly revealing their intentions.

I grabbed Evangeline's arm and turned to run the way we'd come, but the officer who had been standing at the law office was right behind us now, along with another man.

We were trapped with buildings on either side of us, the officers blocking the way down either end of the street.

Officer Larson spread his hands almost apologetically. "I'm afraid we need to ask each of you a few questions."

15

No, Really, I Love Being Interrogated, and I Love That It Always Involves Being Married to a Stupid, Stupid Noble

Evangeline

Any doubts that may have been lurking in my mind about Silas's story quickly evaporated. A runaway leech could be taken into custody right in the middle of the market. But to lead us away and trap us with four other officers? That reeked of a political affair. These officers clearly believed Silas was a threat. And unfortunately, exactly as he'd warned, I was clearly associated with him.

"On what account?" Silas asked. "Is it a crime to visit this city?"

"You are not under arrest," Larson clarified. "We are merely following up on a report of suspicious persons. However, should you not comply..."

The four other officers on either side of us drew their swords.

I decided to play dumb. "Oh, there's no need for that." I waved off the men and turned to Officer Larson. "My husband and I are only visitin' the city. What would we know about any suspicious persons here?"

"Miss, you and your husband are such the persons."

I gasped, as if this was shocking news. "That's absurd! There must be some mistake! We are good, law-abidin' citizens, loyal to the throne. How could anyone possibly find—"

"Loyal to whose throne?" Larson asked.

Idiot. My face flushed at my mistake. It was such a standard phrase, I hadn't thought anything of it, despite five men in Harland's colors surrounding me while, apparently, a friend to the original heir stood next to me. "I mean, sir, that we are loyal to the throne of Wenterly, regardless of who is on it."

Silas put a hand on my arm in warning. He probably wished I had said "Harland's throne, of course," but these officers seemed smarter than to receive such easy lip service.

"We are loyal to this land and its people," I continued. "And to the throne that lets us remain."

"I apologize for my wife—" Silas started.

"No, no," Larson replied, but fixed me in a firm stare. "The honesty is refreshing. But you'll be wise to note that Wenterly no longer exists. You live in New Glastor now."

Silas's grip tightened on my arm.

"Of course," I said. "I apologize, I haven't had much occasion to get used to the new name."

He made an amused sound, somewhere between a laugh and a grunt. "Nevertheless, we have a few questions for each of you. If you'll follow me, please."

"If we are bein' questioned, it's within our legal right to know what for," Silas demanded.

"I told you, you've been reported as suspicious persons."

"But suspicious of *what?*"

"That doesn't matter."

"It's our *right* to know—"

"In Wenterly, yes, it *was*. But not in New Glastor. Now walk with me to the law office, or you will be arrested for non-compliance."

Silas inhaled loudly, and this time, I squeezed his arm in warning. He held his breath a moment, then nodded, much to my relief.

We followed Officer Larson into the law office. If they knew who Silas was, who did they think *I* was? Surely not his secret, pregnant wife!

Regardless, we kept up the charade, with Silas holding my hand as we entered the building. They led us past the front desk, halfway down a narrow hallway, and into an empty room directly across from the holding cell.

"Wait here," Larson ordered. "We'll be with you momentarily."

He shut the thick wooden door and promptly locked us in.

I ripped my hand from Silas's and shoved him.

He turned to me, his eyes wide. "What's that for?"

"I thought you were goin' to get rid of him," I hissed, my voice barely above a whisper.

"I tried!"

"By makin' me *pregnant*?"

"I was trying to imply that you were sick and contagious!"

"Havin' a baby isn't contagious!"

"I know that! That's not what I—"

"How clueless are you?"

"*Excuse me?*"

"You barely passed as a man findin' out he's a father for the first time. There's no way that officer isn't suspicious."

His eyes widened, caught between bewilderment and defensiveness. "First of all, I'm pretty confident he *already* was suspicious of us. And secondly, how am I supposed to know how that scenario would go?"

"You've *never* thought about it?"

"You *have*?"

"Of course," I whispered coldly. "I've thought about all the conversations I'll never get to have."

His expression quickly morphed into a glare. "You're really playing that card right now?"

"I'm not *playin'* anything—"

"Good, because this isn't some game. The next conversation we have with those officers is going to determine how much longer we have to live."

That stilled me.

"Silas," I started, worry quickly overcoming any accusation in my tone.

"Gabriel," he corrected. "You're Lucinda. We're from Arten."

"How long have we been married?"

"Six months?"

"Works for me. What else?"

He didn't get a chance to answer. The lock clicked as the bolt slid into place and an older officer appeared in the doorway.

I instinctively grabbed Silas's arm.

"I'm the Chief Officer here," the man said, sounding quite bored already. "I'm going to ask you a few questions, and if everything is in order, you will be free to go. Is that understood?"

"Yes, sir."

"Names?" he asked.

"Gabriel and Lucinda," Silas replied.

The chief raised an eyebrow. "And last name?"

"Gratsis."

I bristled at the name. But it was a good choice, I had to admit. We told the Portmaster he was Silas's uncle, after all.

"Uh-huh." He looked us up and down. "You from around here?"

"Arten. Just outside of it, actually."

"Uh-huh," he said again. "I ask that you hand over any weapons or anything that could be used as a weapon at this time."

Silas and I glanced at each other. His eyes fell on my necklace a moment, but he knew better than to mention it. We looked back at the officer, and I shifted my weight, uncomfortable under the man's scrutinizing stare.

"I will not ask again."

"We're unarmed, sir," Silas said.

"You expect me to believe that you traveled here, all the way from Arten, with your pregnant wife, without so much as a knife on you?"

"If it helps, sir, I did not *know* she was pregnant until ten minutes ago."

The officer responded with an even less enthusiastic "uh-huh" than before. "And what's in the envelope?" He nodded to the letter under my belt.

"Oh." I pressed my hand against the paper. "It's nothin'."

The chief held out his hand.

I slowly pulled the envelope free and hoped that Silas didn't include any details that would contradict our story.

The chief snatched it from me. I held my breath as his eyes skimmed over the words. "A letter of recommendation ... from an employer with your same last name?" He raised his eyebrows at us.

"My uncle," Silas explained. "He's how we met."

"You met your wife through this Leonard Gratsis?"

"Yes, sir."

"Elaborate."

"I was visitin' Uncle Leonard and saw her workin' at his shop. I inquired about her, and now we are married."

The chief turned to me. "This is true, Lucinda?"

"Yes, sir."

"Well then," he continued, "why does this letter discuss the employment of a Miss Evangeline?"

I forced myself not to tighten my grip on Silas's arm. *Think. Think of anything.*

"Uh, she—" Silas started.

"She's my sister," I interrupted. "We both worked for Leonard Gratsis until I married Gabriel six months ago and moved with him to Arten."

Silas nodded, giving me a bit more confidence.

"My sister sent us a copy of the letter to see if we could scout for work for her over here. It would be nice for us sisters to be near each other again, but Evangeline doesn't want to waste the expenses of comin' all this way if there's no work to be had."

"Uh-huh." The chief read the letter again. "Wait here," he instructed before leaving the room, letter in hand, and locking us in once more.

16

Should I Hope This Is Goodbye?

Alastair

I nearly slumped to the floor in relief. Instead, I took Evangeline by the shoulders.

"That was brilliant!" I whispered.

She scowled. "That was way too close."

"True, but I think we have a good chance of getting out of here."

"Uh-huh," she deadpanned, perfectly mimicking the old officer's disbelieving tone.

The chief officer returned a moment later, accompanied by the one who lured us here.

"You've met Officer Larson," the chief stated, nodding to his counterpart. "Now, stand with your feet apart, arms out to the side."

Evangeline moved to obey, but I reached out a hand to stop her. "What threat do we pose, officer?"

"You've handed over no weapons. We are confirming your claim."

"We've told you our story. Do you honestly still believe us to be suspicious persons? What are these people you were alerted about guilty of? Perhaps if you were more forthright in your concerns, we may be able to better assist you in realizin' our innocence."

"I'm sure you would like to know more, but I'm afraid that information is confidential. For now, you may know that the people we are looking for are traitors to the throne. And as such, we cannot be too thorough in our examination of your claims."

"But on what grounds do you think we—"

"Gabriel," Evangeline interrupted. "Just do as they say. We have nothin' to hide." Her tone was calm, soothing even. So different from the accusatory one she'd had moments ago.

I took a deep breath, hating that she was right. If we had nothing to hide, there would be no need to be defensive until they outright accused us of something. And thankfully, with the prince's ring still not on my person, they would find nothing incriminating.

I adjusted my stance and held out my arms. The chief patted me down, while Officer Larson did the same to Evangeline.

Of course, they found nothing on us but our pouch of coins from Gregory. The chief handed the pouch to Officer Larson, with an off-hand comment that they'd "keep it safe" for now. Satisfied, though surprised that we really didn't have any weapons on us, the officers stood back.

"Just a few more questions," the chief said. "How long did you say you two have been married?"

"Six months," Evangeline and I said in unison.

I glanced at her. Did it sound rehearsed?

"Yet neither of you wears a wedding ring."

"We don't have much money, sir," I offered, bowing my head as if hiding my shame.

"And yet you can afford a trip to visit your uncle in..." He glanced at the letter he took from Evangeline. "Welven."

"That trip was over a year ago. Unfortunately, our financial situation has changed since then."

"So you expect us to believe that Lucinda's father allowed her to marry a man who lost so much financial constitution that he couldn't purchase a wedding ring six months after a trip across the kingdom?"

"My parents are dead, sir," Evangeline said. "Which, I believe is stated in the letter."

The chief turned to her. "Then who's care are you in?"

"*His.*" She indicated to me, and I couldn't help but wonder how much of the frustration she packed in that one word was directed at me instead of the officer. "But before that, it was Leonard Gratsis's."

"So your Master gave you up to a man who could by no means provide for a wife, let alone pay him the profits he'd lose without your labor?"

I cleared my throat. "You're forgettin', *sir*, that he's my uncle. *And*, as you can also see in the letter, his own children were about to begin apprenticeship. He'd be lettin' Lucinda and her sister go soon anyway. Better to see at least one married off than unemployed."

"Uh-huh." The chief officer folded up the letter and put it back in the envelope. "Very well. Prove your story, and then there's no possibility that you are the suspicious persons we're looking for. Officer Larson, the terms, please."

Officer Larson pulled a piece of paper from his vest and held it out to Evangeline. She stared at the paper, but didn't take it. A few seconds of silence passed before she said, without looking up, "I can't read, sir."

The chief nodded, and Officer Larson held the page out to me. Should I say I couldn't read either? Did most common men know how to read? Surely they did, didn't they? I tried to quickly skim the proposal to figure out which would be more to our advantage.

"Sir, I—"

"Don't lie. Your eye movements will betray you," Officer Larson warned.

I decided he was far too observant. "I was merely goin' to ask if I could hold the page myself." I took the paper from him and read it properly. As I did, I fought to keep my face neutral.

I couldn't believe our luck, or rather, our lack thereof. They were asking us to confirm the only part of our story that was technically true, and we still had no way to prove it.

I reached the end of the terms for our release and looked at Evangeline, clearing my throat so my tone wasn't tense. "Nothin' to worry about, love, they merely want proof of our marriage. One of us has to stay here, while the other retrieves our certificate of marriage from Arten. Once it's brought back here for review, we'll be free to go."

"Oh." She ran her thumb over her brow, stalling for however brief a moment she could, I imagined. "That's simple enough, though a bit unnecessary if you ask me." She sighed dramatically. "But whatever it takes to get this ridiculous ordeal settled. You remember where I put it?"

Good. Evangeline must have had the same line of thought as me. I could easily forge a marriage certificate and get us both in the clear. I took both her hands in mine, squeezing them in genuine gratitude. "Of course. I'll be back before you know it." I turned to the officers. "I assume you'll be payin' for her room at the inn while I'm gone, since it's you who is requirin' one of us to stay?"

"Wrong," the chief said. "She's going. You will stay here. In the law office."

"But—" Evangeline started. "But you must know better than most that it's not safe for women to travel alone. And my husband—"

"Your *husband* could forge a document or run off if he's not kept under careful watch. As for travel, Officer Larson would be happy to accompany you, if you wish."

Officer Larson's smirk turned to a frown. "Sir, wouldn't I be better used—"

The chief waved him off. "You can leave in the morning, Missus Gratsis." Evangeline's fingers tensed on my arm at the address. "We won't make you travel at night. That *would* be irresponsible of us. You can stay at your room in the inn tonight and leave first thing in the morning."

A beat passed, a million thoughts colliding in my head. Calculating the risk of doing exactly what they asked against the risk of fighting back, asking for different terms. *What would an innocent person do?*

"Alright," I relented. "Although your terms are hardly fair, we agree to them, as we have no quarrel with you, officers. But we haven't rented our room yet, so she'll need to take the money..."

The chief took the pouch, counted out five copper, and handed them to Officer Larson. "Escort the lady to the inn and pay for her room. She can have what's left over from that for her journey."

My heartbeat pounded in my ears. Never mind that I needed every coin left in the bag to get on the ship for Dirman tomorrow morning—it was clear I wouldn't be making that voyage now—but less than five copper was nowhere near enough for Evangeline to purchase a decent forgery.

It was over for me.

"Needless to say, this is *not* how I had envisioned this night going," Evangeline said, a hand drifting to her stomach, subtly reminding the officers of what they were allegedly putting at stake. "But your terms are simple enough. Officer Larson may take me to the inn, but I won't require his services on the road. I'm not willin' to travel with a man who thinks my husband and I are criminals."

The officers smiled at this. Larson's was one of relief, but the chief's was more ... sinister. As though he expected that to be Evangeline's choice.

"Lucinda, perhaps you should—"

Evangeline grabbed my hands and cut me off. "It's alright, Gabriel." She stared at me intently, but I couldn't for the life of me decipher what she was trying to say. She turned to the officers, her hands still gripping mine. "You'll treat my husband well while he's here. You have no evidence of any crimes against him, other than suspicious rumors, yes? I expect him to be treated as the innocent man he is until I return."

"Of course," the chief assured. "He will face no harm unless more concrete evidence arises, or you fail to produce the document by noon overmorrow."

A day and a half. If the officers were true to their word, my life was over in thirty-six hours. If they weren't, it would probably be over the moment Evangeline left the law office. My stomach dropped as possibilities filled my head. If they were able to confirm my identity, they could come up with false evidence and frame me for any crime they desired. Maybe they already had and were simply trying to get Evangeline out of the way. But Evangeline wouldn't abandon me here, would she? Skip town in the morning and never look back?

Sure, I was the rightful heir to the throne, and as such, she owed me her loyalty. But, once again, she didn't know that. Even as a noble, I supposed she owed me her help, but she'd made it clear where her loyalties lay. She just wanted to live her life. And now I had taken that from her. Twice. She had no chance of getting me out of this mess, but if she abandoned me and ran for it, the officers would track her down in a heartbeat.

"In the meantime," the chief continued, "we will send someone to Welven to verify all of this with Mister Leonard Gratsis."

Evangeline's grip on my hand went slack. *Mercy.* I tried to do *one* nice thing for this girl, and this was the outcome?

I kept holding her hand anyway, not wanting to alert the officers to her fear. "It will take you many days to get to Welven. Lucinda will be back well before then. There's no need to trouble yourself—"

"Don't tell *me* how to do my job, Mister Gratsis."

I bowed my head. "My apologies. I only meant to help, officer." I squeezed Evangeline's hand as I said it, hoping she'd know I meant the words for her.

Evangeline took a fortifying breath. "That's settled, then." She turned to me. "I'll be fine on the road. You know I've traveled alone before."

I pulled her into a hug, lowering my face against hers opposite the side of the officers, so they couldn't see me whisper to her. "I'm so sorry, Ev—"

"I'll see you soon," she said brightly, without giving me a chance to finish. She quickly kissed me on the cheek and added, "I promise."

My heart nearly split in two. Whether she meant it or not, there was no outcome that could possibly be in our favor.

Officer Larson grabbed her arm, yanking her away from me, as the chief secured both of my arms.

Evangeline parted easily from me—perhaps too easily, considering she was supposed to be pregnant with our child. But, as she had so kindly pointed out, what did I know about that? Hopefully, the officers wouldn't read too much into it.

The chief pushed me into the holding cell across from the room we'd come out of. I pressed against the bars, watching as Evangeline left, hoping for some signal or sign from her that she'd actually return for me. But she wasn't looking at me. Just scowling at the crowd of officers who'd helped arrest us.

I supposed I couldn't blame her if she wanted nothing more to do with me.

As soon as Officer Larson dragged Evangeline out the door, the chief turned to me. "That's quite the story the two of you came up with. Tell me, is the woman actually pregnant?"

I imagined the bars between us were locking him in a cell instead of me. But that didn't stop my heart from pounding wildly. I clothed my growing fear in a façade of anger, careful to watch my accent. "If you think everythin' I've told you is made up, enlighten me as to what you think the truth could possibly be. Who do you think we are?"

The chief laughed. "Once again, I'm afraid I can't disclose that information right now. But we are gathering evidence. You'll get your due accusation in time."

"What acts of treason, then? These people you think we are, what have they done?"

He paused, then nodded as he decided to tell me. "Conspired against the king. They plan to overthrow him."

"To what end? Who else could rule in Harland's place?"

He laughed. "Who, indeed? You think loyalty to the old throne isn't enough cause for people to riot against a new leader?"

"Apparently it's not. I haven't heard of one revolt against Harland in all of Went—" I clenched my fists. "New Glastor."

"Don't sound so bitter about it. You might betray yourself."

The chief had been far less intimidating in front of Evangeline. What kind of game was he playing here?

I swallowed. "You think our loyalties still lie with the murdered royals? What good would a revolt do if the people we want in power are dead?" How hard would I have to push for him to admit my family was still alive? Was it a secret so closely guarded that he wouldn't even admit it to *me*?

"You keep saying 'we' as if that woman is included in your statements." He stepped closer to my cell. "Perhaps you should notice that only *you* are behind bars, Gabriel."

He paused to dramatically hold up Evangeline's letter of recommendation. "Since you seem so intent on saving me time, what will my men find in Welven? I wasn't sure Leonard Gratsis was a real man until you were so defensive against us investigating the matter. What's his role in all this?"

I glared at him, but didn't dare say anything more.

"Don't fret. We'll figure it out." He tucked the paper into his vest. "We always do."

The chief walked away to converse with his other officers, but I hardly heard him. Whatever scheme Evangeline might come up with was my only chance of getting out of here. But she'd never beat them. Once they found out about Gratsis, they could use it as leverage to get her to admit any information she knew about me. Never mind the fact that they could actually return her to him.

For her sake, it would be better if she abandoned me altogether.

And if my time with Evangeline had taught me anything about her, I was certain she would do exactly that.

17

Oh Good, Another Man with a Plan

Evangeline

Officer Larson yanked me away from Silas. I let him, not keen on engaging in any more physical contact with him. Hopefully the kiss on the cheek was enough to convince the officers we really were married. I wasn't about to do anything more than that.

As we left the interrogation room, the other officers who had helped in our arrest stood at the front of the law office, murmuring to one another as we all watched the chief lock Silas in the holding cell. Well, *almost* all of us.

I felt eyes on me, and turned to the four men. One of them was watching me intently, amusement glinting in his gaze. He didn't have the decency to look away when we made eye contact. Instead, the corners of his mouth twitched, as though he thought about smiling, and then decided against it. As he should.

I glared at him in the moment I had before Larson pushed me out the door.

The salty night air blew in my face, taking away every thought with it, except one: *What in Fate's Design should I do?*

I decided to be the prime example of subordination as Officer Larson took me to the inn, demanded the clerk alert him when I left in the morning, paid three copper, and handed me the remaining two.

Brilliant.

But it was twice the amount I'd had when I met Mothway's crew. Not that that did much to comfort me.

I shut the door to my room and sat on the bed. This situation with Silas was ... complicated. But then again, had any of my time with Silas *not* been complicated? I had been looking forward to us going our separate ways—up until we'd reached Narim, anyway. Between Marna and Gregory's and our time at the festival, something had won me over to him, and my fears of being completely alone again got the best of me.

Well, I was certainly paying for it now. I was alone regardless, and the closest thing I'd ever had to a friend was locked up for being a noble loyal to the late Cathmoores—or the secretly living Cathmoores. I'd have to sort that detail out at another time.

I could just leave. Silas would likely spend the night worrying I would do just that. Theoretically, I *could* run away and get back to life as normal—but not while the officers still had my letter for employment. And *especially* not if they followed through on contacting Gratsis. I'd hoped his search for me would die off soon, if it hadn't already. But news of my whereabouts would start the whole mess up again. Between Gratsis and my association with Silas, there wasn't likely to be a single city in the kingdom where someone wouldn't know something about me.

Nowhere was safe.

But if I tried to rescue him, what then? I'd follow him back to Koyben? Who was to say the officers in that city wouldn't recognize him? What if prison *was* his fate? There was no point getting tangled up in that.

But I was already, wasn't I? The lies Silas and I told wove us together in a knotted web of deceit and desperation. At this point, how much worse could it get? There I was, alone and without a worthy future, just as I was before, just as I would be if I decided not to help him. And I wouldn't be able to live with myself if I abandoned him. I had to at least try.

I stood and walked to the window. I could see the law office from here. It wasn't a proper prison, so Silas wasn't bunking with criminals. But the thought of him there under careful watch, while I was here—more or less free—felt wrong on so many levels. He was a *nobleman*. And I was ... a leech.

With a groan, I turned away from the window and began pacing the floor. I needed to focus. I only had a day and a half to free Silas.

In the weeks since I'd left everything behind in Welven, I'd relied a lot on the free kindness of strangers—and a little bit of petty theft. Unfortunately, the people who offered kindness to strangers were not usually the same people who would be willing to break the law by forging legal documents. And I'd never stolen money before. How much would I even need to pay for a good forgery? Certainly more than two measly copper.

And to think Silas was originally following me so he could recruit me as a thief.

The night was an agonizing one. At midnight, it began to rain, and I hoped the pitter-patter on the roof would help me get some sleep. Rest might restore some order to my thoughts and give me fresh ideas. But I couldn't stop thinking long enough to drift off, and I soon returned to my pacing, and leaning, and staring, and thinking, and lying on the floor in defeat.

I'd need a disguise of some sort so the officers wouldn't recognize me in the city. I'd need to lie a lot more. And I'd have to search out some people with questionable morals. Or at least, a loose obligation to the law. Which meant, I also needed to find a knife, should the need for a weapon arise. I didn't have a complete plan, but hopefully the remaining steps would become clear as I reached them.

Eventually, the rain stopped and the world beyond my window began to lighten. About an hour and a half later, the clock struck seven. Silas's boat for Dirman was leaving.

And so was I.

I bid the innkeeper goodbye, telling him I was taking an early start to Arten, and that he could tell the officers I hoped to be back by sundown. I hadn't the slightest idea what my timing would be, but a loving wife would want her husband freed as soon as possible. And it meant no one would be looking for me in Narim all day. I left the inn, walked down the main road, and exited the city on the same street the strawberry merchant had brought us in on.

I continued down the road for another few minutes. I half expected to catch someone following me, but the only other sign of life on the road was the rustling of animals in the trees and brush.

Fortunately, it was a Sunday, so there weren't many people up and about yet. Nothing was open except Petitioning Houses, which I hadn't visited since my mother died. It was a waste of time to think Fate cared a whit about our desires. But if the Petitioning Houses encouraged people to put off their chores for the morning so I could slip through the city unseen, who was I to complain of the tradition?

I stepped off into the ditch, leaped over the soggy ground, and hurried into the woods to loop back into the city.

I shed my patterned corset while hidden in the trees. It nearly broke my heart to abandon it, but a garment like that was memorable, and I needed to make sure none of last night's lawmen would recognize me if we crossed paths today.

I made my way around to the east side of Narim, where, if the layout of the city was anything like Koyben, the majority of the people resided. To my luck, rows of houses came into view as I emerged from the treeline.

I walked the streets, looking for the poor family who had left their laundry out on the line in last night's rain. A cloak would have made the easiest disguise, but in the summer heat, it would only arouse suspicion. Since the scarf I had gotten from Marna hardly covered my hair, a larger one that did would have to suffice. Maybe a skirt or apron would help too.

As I was about to give up on my search, a line of fabric came into view on my right. No real articles of clothes, but a handful of shawls and wraps.

Brilliant.

I hurried to the line, careful to keep out of view of the windows on either side of me. I felt the fabrics for the driest one, landing on a brown linen square that would suit my needs well enough. I pulled it off the line and scurried back to the edge of the woods. I wrapped my braid into a bun and tied the fabric around my head. I could have taken something else, but stealing multiple items from the same family didn't sit well with me. Perhaps I'd find another—

"Don't tell me that's the best you've got for a disguise."

I jumped at the voice, turning to face a middle-aged man. "I beg your pardon?"

He was standing several yards away. A dagger was strapped to his belt, but he made no move to grab it. Nevertheless, I adjusted my footing so I could flee at a moment's notice.

"The chief and Larson and the lot are daft, but they're not blind. You'll be recognized in half a second."

At the mention of the officers, I recognized him. He wasn't in uniform today, and he spoke with a commoner accent—unlike the chief and Officer Larson. But he fixed me with the same stare as he had last night.

I took a step back, and the man held up his hands, as though I was an animal he was trying not to spook. "I want to help you. I may be an officer, but I assure you, my allegiance is not to Harland."

I didn't say anything, but I didn't retreat either. Whatever this man was playing at, I needed to gather as much information as I could. What he didn't say would tell me just as much as what he did.

I took a closer look at him. I realized the gleam in his eyes was curiosity, not amusement.

And eyes didn't lie.

"We all know the two of you aren't married," he continued. "And while I don't know who you are, I'd recognize him anywhere. If you're on his side, I'm on yours."

He'd recognize some noble's son *anywhere*? How invested were these officers in Wenter politics? I crossed my arms and stared at the man. "Prove it."

The man kept his right hand out toward me, but used his left to take the dagger off his belt—including the sheath—and tossed it low to my feet. "Take it. You can keep it, actually."

I slowly bent down, not taking my eyes off the man, and picked up the dagger. I removed it from the black sheath and held it at the ready.

"Chief wanted one of us to trail you and report back. I volunteered. Any other officer would have immediately reported that you didn't go to Arten after all, and it would have been over for you both. But I'm goin' to tell the chief that you went back. Buy you some time."

I narrowed my eyes. "Why would you do that?"

"Because—" The man glanced around to ensure we were still alone. "The throne doesn't belong to Harland."

"And who would you rather see it belong to?"

The man blinked, as though my question was a surprise. "The Cathmoores. Naturally."

"Even if that may be," I said slowly, "you and I both know the royals are dead."

The man nodded. "And you and I both know the *evidence* to the contrary." He grinned, as if we were sharing some private joke.

Stars above, maybe there was something to Silas's crazy story. I returned the man's nod, but I still didn't trust him as far as I could throw him. Better to play along until I could figure out this man's true intentions.

"My name's Reeves. I've been an officer in this city longer than any of the others—Chief included."

"Then why is he Chief instead of you?"

"Because I'm not a sell-out." He winked, which caught me quite off-guard. "I almost quit and ran the day Harland took over and made us swear our allegiance. But I didn't want to put my family in danger—not like that anyway. We decided it was better to stay here and do what little good we could." He shook his head. "After they told me the truth about the Cathmoores, I was glad I stayed. Still, I never expected an opportunity like this."

Brush rustled behind me, and I spun, dagger outstretched. A squirrel scampered up a nearby tree. I whirled back, but the man hadn't moved an inch.

"I'm not here to hurt you," he said.

"Why are you tellin' me all this?"

"I want to help you. You *are* goin' to try to free him, aren't you?"

I shifted my weight, my knuckles white as I gripped the dagger tighter.

"I get it. You have no reason to trust me. He made a smart choice in you as a companion."

I barely held back a snort. Silas hadn't made a smart choice since I met him. Associating with me was certainly the *worst* of them.

The man seemed to think my amusement was directed toward the first part of his statement, rather than the latter. "If you'll allow me to lay out your options, I think you'll see my help is a necessary part of his rescue."

I glanced around, realizing this all could be an elaborate trap. Another conversation meant to distract while the other officers surrounded me. I shifted my weight again, preparing to run if the man came any closer or anyone else showed up.

Reeves took my silence as a sign to continue. "Any marriage license you give the officers will be scrutinized to no end. They'll test how fresh the ink is. They'll find out what kind of paper was used. They will evaluate the handwritin'. They *need* to prove it's a forgery. Even if you somehow came up with a legitimate marriage license from Arten, from six months ago, with your fake names on it, they still would find fault in it."

"Why send me to get it, then? If it doesn't matter anyway?"

"They're testin' you. They want to know if you pose a threat. If you're aware of who you've gotten yourself involved with. But, obviously you do. Otherwise, why would you have gone along with your story once you were arrested?"

Yes, why else *would* I have gone along with it? Certainly not just because I was an idiot, and the only thing I'd known to do with Silas was lie under interrogation. Yet here I was, without him at my side, doing it again. Pretending I knew exactly what I was talking about and further entangling myself in this mess.

I sheathed the dagger, hoping Reeves would take it as a sign he had won my trust. "If it's so obvious, why bother sendin' me away then? Why not arrest both of us and be done with it?"

"Anything dealin' with … *him* is a delicate matter. Harland has managed to take over Wenterly with hardly a revolt because he does things carefully and quietly, always exercising caution. Then he springs his trap all at once, without any warnin'. If there's a network of rebels you are connected to, Harland will want to know that. He plays the long game."

"Fine, so I can't rely on a marriage certificate. That's well enough. I don't have money, and I can't write, anyway. What do you suggest, then?"

"He has to be broken out. A real escape. You can't try to reason your way out of this. They will *always* be smarter than you. And when you get him out, you have to flee. Far and quickly. You'll both be wanted criminals—perhaps publicly now, though for a false crime, of course.

He's been on the wanted list for weeks. But your name is goin' to be added right next to his."

"It doesn't sound like you're offerin' much help if that's the outcome you're proposin'."

"I can buy you time, and I can help ensure you escape. Without me, it's the short road to execution."

I gripped the dagger tighter. "I'm not lookin' to take the long road there either."

"And I pray you don't. I can't guarantee what road you take after this, so to speak, but I can help you *avoid* the short one."

A breeze ruffled the trees, birds breaking into renewed song, blissfully unaware of the life-altering decisions I was making below them.

But really, I had little choice in the matter. I'd pretend to trust him, but I had terms, same as the officers had given me. And my terms would be met, or I would have no part in this. "We'll need money to get away. Even if we get our money back from the officers, there isn't enough for both of us to get where we're headed."

"How much do you need?"

I hesitated. With Harland's new taxes, I had no idea. "A lot."

He laughed. "Still don't trust me, huh? Can't say I blame you. Look, I can get you the money. You're goin' by boat, otherwise I'm sure you wouldn't have risked comin' to a city this big. But I can create a set up for when you escape. Let the other officers think you ran for it instead."

Tears welled in my eyes. If this man could read our situation so easily, how did I have any hope of rescuing Silas? Desperation clawed at my throat, suffocating me. I wasn't cut out for this.

Reeves's demeanor softened, my distress clearly evident. He raised his hands again in that non-threatening way of his. "We will get through this. I will do everythin' I can to see you two succeed."

His eyes told me his sympathy was genuine. And it cracked the barricade I'd built around my rising fear. "He was supposed to leave this mornin'. Just him. Our next option leaves Tuesday, I think. I don't know when. It's a cargo ship to Koyben. I don't know exactly what it will cost with—"

"I'll look into it and get you the money by this afternoon. Then we'll discuss the details, alright?"

A tear slipped from my eye, and I quickly wiped it away. "Where do I meet you? Here?"

"No, there's a well a few blocks over." He told me exactly how to get there. "Wait there for a young woman, about your age. She's my daughter. You'll know it's her, because she'll give you the money as promised. Then, she'll bring you to me. Two o'clock. Listen for the town clock—and don't talk to anyone. Stay out of sight until you go to the well. Do you understand?"

"Yes."

"Good. Then it's agreed." He offered me a reassuring smile, "Long live our king," he added, then turned and walked into the city at a brisk pace.

Tears slid unheeded down my cheeks, and my breath shuddered as I tried to steady myself. If Silas and I got out of this mess, he had a lot more explaining to do.

18

Maybe This Is the Best Bread I've Ever Eaten

Alastair

I'd hardly slept. When my thoughts finally did quiet down enough that I had a chance of falling asleep, the officers seemed intent on making enough noise to keep me from finding a moment's peace.

Come morning, things settled down. I had nearly drifted off when the chief asked, "What's the status?"

"Lucinda has indeed gone to Arten," a new voice responded.

I walked to the front of my cell to see him. He wasn't in uniform, but his next words suggested he was an officer. "I trailed her for thirty minutes to make sure it wasn't a diversion. But she seems true to the course."

"Really?" Larson asked, not bothering to hide his surprise.

"Perhaps the girl is from Arten," the chief mused.

"And if she is, couldn't she get more money there and pay for a forgery?" Larson asked.

"She said she'd be here by sundown. That doesn't give her enough time to have one made. And if she somehow *does*, she'll just be wasting her money."

I, too, wondered what she was doing going back to Arten. I highly doubted Marna and Gregory or their family would be able to help us more than they already had.

The man cleared his throat. "I came back to get my horse. I'll catch up to her on the road and see where she goes from there."

Larson and the chief agreed with his course of action. I hoped that Evangeline would have enough sense to lose the man when he found her.

"What about *him*?" The man tossed his head in my direction, and I quickly stepped out of their line of sight. "Has he said anythin' useful?"

"He's sticking to his story," Larson complained.

"May I?"

"Be my guest."

I stepped forward as the man approached my cell. He wasn't as old as the chief, but he was certainly older than Larson.

"You realize you're causin' me quite the hassle?" he began, the smile on his face not matching his tone.

"I could say the same," I countered. "You saw my wife? How was she?"

"It's difficult to tell from a distance. She seemed to be focused, perhaps a bit stressed. She mutters to herself, I noticed."

"Yes, she does." I had noticed as much on our way to Narim. Even when she wasn't peppering me with questions, she couldn't seem to keep her mouth shut. "What was she sayin'?"

"Again, I couldn't tell"—the man glanced over toward Larson and the chief—"given the circumstances." He gave me a pointed look, then flicked his eyes back toward the officers again.

I straightened my spine. A double meaning?

"Have you received any food this mornin'?"

"No, sir."

The man sighed. "You have to still feed the man," he called to the chief and Larson.

"Do it yourself, Reeves, if you care so much. One day without food isn't going to kill him," the chief called back.

"Wish it would, though," Larson said. He likely only meant for the chief to hear it, but his voice carried down the hall to us anyway.

Reeves shook his head. "Give me a moment."

He walked to the back of the building and disappeared briefly before returning with a plate of two herbed rolls.

"Are these from the festival?" I asked as he slid them through the metal slot.

"Indeed. We always get some of the leftovers as thanks for the extra hours we put in for it."

"You don't have food specifically for your prisoners?"

"We do." He lowered his voice to a whisper. "But trust me, you don't want it."

I lowered my voice to match his. "What are you doin'?"

The man winked, but answered at his normal volume. "We promised your wife we'd look after you, which is why it is imperative you eat *everythin'* I've given you. You need to keep your strength up durin' your stay." His tone was casual, but his eyes bore into mine, unblinking. "We don't want her to come back and say we didn't hold up our end of the bargain."

"Give it a rest, Reeves," the chief barked. "He knows we aren't buying his little story."

Reeves winked at me one more time before heading back to the front of the building. "Oh, well, how am I supposed to know that? You've had me watchin' for the girl all mornin'."

I picked up the bread to examine it further. There was something *way* off about Reeves. Perhaps he had poisoned the rolls and couldn't act natural under pressure. I ripped the first roll in half, but it appeared normal. Smelled normal too. I picked up the second, quickly noticing it was sliced at the bottom. I ripped it apart, revealing a folded piece of paper inside. I quickly retreated to the far corner of the cell.

She will not return tonight. Do not lose hope.
Long Live Our King.

The first sentence made my stomach drop, but the second moved me from fear to curiosity. The third launched my heart into my throat.

Our king. Not *the* king. *The* king was Harland.

Reeves was on my side?

I quickly folded the paper back up and ate it with the rolls as the man instructed.

Perhaps Evangeline was right. This *was* the best bread I'd eaten in my entire life.

19

Maybe Thievery Is My Destiny After All

Evangeline

As the city bells rang for two o'clock, I stepped out of the woods and approached the well. Narim was particularly sleepy on Sundays, especially for a large city. Even at this point in the afternoon, there wasn't much activity. Perhaps it was due to the festival the night before. Who knew how long into the night it had gone? I should have paid better attention when the Portmaster and Silas were talking.

Less than a minute after I reached the well, a young woman emerged from the nearest house. She seemed a year or two younger than me. Was that Reeves's daughter?

"Gretchen!" she called, hurrying her pace to reach me. "You made it!"

I forced a smile. There was no one around. Were we performing for prying eyes? Or was she simply mistaken?

I fought the impulse to reach for the dagger at my waist.

She clasped my hands when she got to me, two coins transferring from her hand to mine. "I'm glad you came."

I frowned. Only two? That wasn't near enough. I didn't know exactly how much it would cost to get us to Koyben. But I was banking on at *least* thirty copper. Perhaps Reeves was holding on to the rest for now.

"Of course I came, what choice did I have?" I tried to keep my voice cheery for anyone who might be listening, but I wanted the girl to understand I was not completely sold on this scheme. *Especially* if Reeves's idea of payment was only two copper.

She laughed. "There's always a choice. Although, the majority of options are usually poor ones."

She released my hands, and I looked at the coins she left there. My breath nearly caught as I realized they were *silver*.

"The trip can't possibly cost this much."

The girl smiled. "It doesn't. The offer has improved. Come now." She linked arms with me as if we were old friends and led me to the house.

The whole family was in the main room, two boys a few years younger than the girl, Reeves, and a woman I could only assume was his wife.

Reeves's daughter hurried to latch the door shut, and before I had a chance to panic, the older woman was introducing everyone to me. "It's a pleasure to meet you, miss. I'm Helena." She gestured to the two boys looking at me with wide eyes. "This is Friedrick and Clement. You know Reeves, of course. And that's Willa who brought you in."

I nodded, but addressed Reeves. "I wasn't aware this was a family affair."

"It takes a village to save a kingdom. Besides, I thought you might find my home more comfortable than any other place we would truly be alone."

He was probably right about that, though I would also be more comfortable without his sons gaping at me like I was some kind of spectacle. Did this whole family have a staring problem? "Yes, thank you."

"Alright, then, everyone knows the drill. Children, rousin' conversation here in the main room. Helena and I are goin' to meet with our guest in your room."

Willa clapped her hands, finally taking the boys' attention off me.

"I'm thinkin' a boisterous game of Prince Philosopher," she announced.

One of the boys groaned, but the other lit up. "Good, I've got a good one I've been thinkin' up."

Reeves chuckled as he led me to his children's room. Helena shut the door behind us, muffling their voices.

A sheet hung near the middle of the room, I assumed to offer Willa some privacy from her brothers. We passed behind the sheet where one bed and three stools awaited us.

"You have secret meetin's a lot?" I asked as I sat down.

"Only within the last few weeks." Helena sat closest to me.

"You got the money from Willa?" Reeves asked.

I held up the two silver coins. "What's the catch? Surely one coin would have been generous enough?"

Helena laughed, and Reeves put a hand on her forearm, signaling that I was serious.

"There's no catch," he explained. "It's insurance. You may need to buy the silence of some of your travelin' companions."

"I'm not usually one to turn down money." Mercy, I'd just made fun of Silas for trying to do so yesterday. "But I'm not convinced I can trust you quite yet."

"If the money isn't enough to convince you my word is good, consider the fact that you're in the comfort of my home of your own free will." Reeves pointed out. "I told Chief you'd gone to Arten, as I promised I would. He believes I'm trailin' you there right now."

I surveyed the couple before me. Their clothes denoted commoner status, but were certainly nice enough. Their house was humble, but in good repair. I closed my fist around the coins and rested my hands in my lap. "I didn't realize bein' an officer paid so well."

Now Reeves laughed. "It doesn't. That's a communal effort." My eyes widened and he quickly added, "I didn't give any specific details. But The Guild trusts me. They know I wouldn't take a collection without good reason."

"The Guild?"

"Close friends of mine. Other sympathizers to the Cathmoore throne."

I frowned. "There's already sympathizers? It's hardly been three weeks."

"I've seen more happen in less time."

My own experiences from the last few days were quick to confirm the truth of that statement. "Fair enough. So, what are you thinkin' for our escape?"

My stomach growled, ruining any attempt I had made for a formal, business-only discussion.

"Have you not eaten either?" Reeves asked.

"You told me to make sure no one saw me. You think I store bread in my pockets?"

"If only my children listened to me half as well as you do," he muttered. "Helena, do you mind..."

She was already up. "You two carry on. I'll be right back with somethin' for you, Lucinda."

She opened the door, the muffled voices now clear enough for me to understand.

"And *henceforth*, I pronounce that you shall *evermore* endure my strident—"

She shut the door.

"What game *are* they playin'?" I asked.

"Prince Philosopher," Reeves responded, as though that explained everything. "Now, Miss Lucinda—"

"Lucinda isn't my real name."

He nodded. "Good. For your safety, I hoped it wasn't. But, to keep you safe, we'll continue referrin' to you two as Lucinda and Gabriel. Understood?"

How was that stupid cat still haunting me here in Narim? She would be so pleased with herself if she knew we once again shared a name. But I nodded my assent.

"Good. Before we get into the details of Gabriel's escape, I thought you should know that the chief has sent a man up to Welven to investigate. He took the letter with him."

I swallowed hard. "When did he leave?"

"Around an hour ago. He didn't send him until after I reported you'd gone to Arten. It will take about two weeks for him to return, so it shouldn't impact our plan here, but is there anything I ought to know about your situation there?"

I smoothed the fabric of my skirt while I decided how to answer. "I believe I'm wanted for theft."

"I am happy to help your cause, Lucinda, but I am still an officer of the law." I reached for the dagger at my waist, and he hurried to add, "I'm not arrestin' you. I'm tryin' to help you. Do you still have the item you stole?"

I nearly corrected him, but if he wasn't threatening to lock me up, it was easier to let him think I was a thief than explain what had actually happened. "No."

"Is that where your money came from? You sold it?"

I winced. "No. Someone stole the necklace from me." There was no use explaining that pirates took it. I wasn't about to open *that* jar of insanity. "The money was an honest gift from some people who helped us."

"Look, I'm happy to help innocent people, but I won't justify stealin' from other innocent people to do it. If it's too late for this Gratsis fellow's necklace, that's up to you to make right. But that scarf on your head will be returned to the Goldings. Helena and Willa can adjust your wardrobe if necessary."

Gratsis was hardly innocent, but so be it.

I untied the scarf and handed it over to him. "Anything else you'd like to criticize?"

"I'm not criticizin' you, Lucinda." The door opened, and we both glanced over at Helena entering the room with a tray of food. Reeves continued, "But a wrong thing done for the right reason doesn't make it a right thing done."

I frowned. "Are we not about to break a man out of jail?"

"A man wrongly accused. Freein' him is a right thing done for the right reasons."

"And the way we free him is entirely moral then, I suppose?"

Helena laughed as she handed me the tray. "Goodness, it sounds as though you two have started your own game of Prince Philosopher."

I stuffed a strip of dried meat in my mouth, while Reeves tried to explain he was only trying to help me.

"Let's get back to Gabriel," Helena directed, patting her husband's hand in a manner that suggested she understood his intentions but didn't necessarily agree with him.

Reeves sighed, but relented. "I have a few ideas for how we might go about the escape. I'll lay out the pros and cons of each, and you let me know what you're most comfortable with."

I crossed my arms. "What if I had some ideas of my own?"

He frowned. "You don't know the other officer's schedules, or what our orders are regardin' this kind of situation. But if you—"

I waved my hands for him to stop. "Only a joke, Reeves. Please, tell me what you've got."

Sitting in Reeves's house, waiting for his timing, was agony. My heart was going to beat right out of my chest.

Helena had given me clothes to help our charade, so it would look as if I'd walked to Arten and changed after the long walk. A white hair scarf, a brown corset, and even a pouch to store the silver coins in. She tried to give me a new dress, but I was loathe to part with the green one Marna had so generously gifted me. Helena's compromise was to spare me some thread, and I hemmed the length of the skirt while I hid in the house. In addition to the clothes, they had fed and housed me for the last day. *And Reeves had told me that while he wasn't privy to the location of the royal Cathmoores, he was quite confident they were all still alive.*

They'd treated me like one of their own children, without a clue as to who I was. Actually demanding I *not* tell them, for my own safety. The whole thing was absurd and foreign, and yet I knew I would sorely miss them when this was all over.

The door to the house opened. Reeves stepped inside and quickly shut the door.

"It's time," he said. "Remember, what happens in the law office is just as important as what happens after you leave this house. You remember exactly what I told you to say?"

I nodded. "Of course, I've been goin' over it all mornin'."

"Good. We have one shot at this. There isn't much room for error. If somethin' unexpected comes up, try to stick to the original plan as much as possible. *I'll* handle the improvisin' that gets us back on track. Understood?"

"Yes." I slipped the dagger he'd given me under the side of my corset, where it would remain hidden until our escape. My belt and pouch with the two silver coins were already tucked away beneath my dress. Helena had kindly provided an extra petticoat to help further conceal them.

"Remember, the people are passive these days. No one wants to get involved in legal affairs now that Harland is runnin' things. You have to cause a massive scene to pull any kind of crowd."

"I will."

He let out a slow breath. "Go on then."

"Best of luck," Helena said.

I climbed out the side window, walked behind a few houses, and then made my way to the well. There were far more people out today than the day before. I searched for Reeves's Guild Member assigned to get robbed by me.

Apparently, Fate was desperate to see me keep my reputation for thievery.

Finally, I spotted him leaning against the lamppost. He pocketed his watch with a heavy sigh. My signal to follow him.

As I trailed him around the street corner, I glanced behind me to see Reeves exit his house.

I picked up my pace, my adrenaline increasing with it. I didn't need to successfully pick-pocket the man. The whole point was that he'd catch me. But it had to at least look like I had a clue what I was doing.

When I was two steps away from the man, I looked over my shoulder at a passing shop—something in the window had caught my eye, perhaps—and crashed into him. The man whirled and caught my arm before I fell. He held me long enough to let me slip the watch chain around my fingers as I profusely apologized for my clumsiness. Then he let go, and I turned, hand behind my back, still begging his pardon.

As I hurried away, he mumbled something about me being witless. Then he was to check for his watch, and any moment now...

"Hey! Thief! Stop right there!"

I ran down the next side street, but despite there being plenty of witnesses to the chase, no one stopped me.

"Sir, what's happened?" Reeves called from somewhere behind me.

"That woman stole my watch!"

Reeves called for someone to catch me, but no one moved.

I had to help them catch up and, apparently, start causing a bigger scene. I faked a trip, but misjudged the timing of it. The dagger shoved under my new corset did not give me much flexibility in my fall, and I grunted as I hit the ground in a genuine face plant. A few people muttered reactions to my tumble, but still no one dared interfere. I groaned, letting myself wallow in my shame, and giving Reeves the few seconds he needed to catch up with me. He quickly tied my wrists behind my back and hoisted me to my feet.

Narim's salty air blew over us and, for a split second, I was on a beach, spitting sand out of my mouth and glaring at an insufferable boy who'd made me fall off a cliff.

"You're under arrest for attemptin' to steal private property." Reeves said, breaking the spell of the memory.

"Please, sir, you don't understand!" I pleaded.

"Save your excuses for the chief."

The people in the street murmured among themselves as they passed us by, but no one spoke up for me or the man I'd stolen from.

He had been right. Everyone was strangely uninterested in my arrest.

"I've done nothin' wrong!" I insisted.

"You stole a watch from a man." Reeves pulled it from my hand and handed it to his friend.

The law office came into view, and I felt like I could vomit. Phase one had gone exactly as planned. But what came next was the moment that counted the most.

I abruptly turned around and drove my knee into Reeves's thigh. Anyone watching closely would believe I'd poorly aimed.

Reeves cried out far more dramatically than I gave him reason to.

I faked making a run for it, but Reeves yanked me back.

"I'm innocent!" I cried, elbowing him in the chest.

"You're only making this worse for yourself!"

I searched the street, noting a few bystanders taking cautious steps toward us. It was working.

I took a deep breath and screamed.

20

Evangeline Threatens to Kill Me Again, and Is All-Around Very Annoying

Alastair

Evangeline didn't come back last night, just as Officer Reeves had said. His note had told me not to lose hope, but as the night wore on, I couldn't help but wonder if something terrible had happened to her. If *he* had done something terrible to her. How else would he know that she wouldn't arrive? Was he *really* lying to the other officers and telling me the truth? Or did he only want me to think that, and it was all part of their ruse?

I wished I could speak to him again, but he was either trailing Eva to Arten, or pretending to, and either way, wouldn't show up here again until it was too late.

It hurt my head—and my heart—to try to make sense of it all. Loyalty had seemed so much simpler before Harland betrayed my family. One good deed earned another. Reciprocity of favors was the currency of loyalty. Now, I was quickly learning loyalty couldn't be proven. You simply had to trust that it was genuine.

It made me nauseous.

Evangeline had an hour left to save my life. If she didn't come through, and I had a choice in the matter, I decided I would want to go to the prison my parents were at before Harland's men executed me. But I had a feeling these officers didn't have that in their plans. They seemed far too bloodthirsty to hand me over to someone else. I wondered if they'd accuse me of a fake crime so they could execute me publicly, or if they'd keep it a private affair, which would allow them to kill me more slowly.

That line of thinking made me sick with dread, and I retched, though by now, my stomach was empty. All I had eaten since being locked up were the two rolls Reeves had given me the day before.

I lay on the bench, trying to resign myself to whatever Fate had planned.

A scream pierced through my darkening thoughts. It came from someone in the street. No, not someone. I'd heard that scream before, on a beach four days ago.

Evangeline was outside.

The chief shot up from his chair. He reached the door as Officer Reeves shoved it open, dragging Evangeline in with him.

"Get your hands off of me! I've done nothin' wrong!" she yelled.

I gripped the bars that trapped me. This was not good. Reeves had betrayed me after all.

The officers ignored her pleas.

"She reached town about twenty minutes ago," Reeves reported. "Walked around the city a bit, stopped at the well. Stupid girl tried to steal a pocket watch in broad daylight. I searched her already. Took this dagger." Reeves pulled a small blade from his belt, in a brown leather sheath. She must have stolen it off someone. *Some good that did her.*

"Nothin' else on her, marriage license or otherwise," Reeves concluded.

"Surprise, surprise," the chief said, clearly not surprised at all.

"I had it!" Evangeline insisted. "If you would just listen! I had it with me, and then—"

Larson entered the building, cutting her off. He wasn't on duty this morning, but I could have predicted he'd stay close by. "There's quite a crowd gathering out there," he said. "Girl's got some lungs on her."

"Tell them to clear out," the chief ordered. "Then gather the others. Reeves, lock her up with the boy for now."

"No!" Evangeline screamed. "Listen to me! I'm tellin' you—"

"That's enough of that, you little brat." Reeves grabbed the back of her neck and shoved her toward my cell.

"Hey!" I shouted over them all. Everyone went quiet for a moment, as though they forgot I was still there. "Let her talk! She has a right to explain what happened. This is all some horrible misunderstandin'."

"Oh, she'll talk alright," Reeves sneered. "And so will you, if you want to meet judgment quickly."

Larson left the building, and the chief merely watched Reeves drag her down the hallway toward me. Her wrists were bound behind her, but she didn't appear to have any further restraints. I shifted my feet, readying to run through the door when Reeves unlocked it.

"Gabriel! Are you alright?" she asked when she was in front of the holding cell.

What kind of question was that? We were about to die. To be tortured and *die*.

"I've been better, Lucinda," I snapped. "What happened?"

"Move to the corner, boy!" Reeves ordered. "With your back toward me."

I clenched my fists. Of course he would anticipate me running. But I didn't move, trying to weigh our options for escape. Were there even any left?

"Move!" Reeves withdrew his sword and placed the blade under Evangeline's chin. "Or she dies right now."

Evangeline mouthed something, the movement so small I couldn't understand it.

"I'm not bluffin'." Reeves touched the blade to her skin.

Evangeline's eyes widened. "Gabriel, please do what he asks."

I took a step backward, and she mouthed the words again.

Trust me.

This was the pirate ship all over again. I didn't have much choice *but* to trust her. Though I couldn't for the life of me see how us *both* being locked up was going to improve the situation.

"Alright, alright, relax. Don't hurt her."

I moved to the corner, facing the wall.

"Hands on the wall until I say so. One move toward me and it's over for your girl, understand?"

"Yes, sir." I pressed my palms against the wall as hard as I could, the rough stone on my skin helping to nurse my anger.

I heard Reeves's key in the lock, the iron squeaking as the door opened. Evangeline reached me as the door clanged shut.

I turned to look at her, but Reeves called out, "I didn't say you could move yet!"

I stayed put. Eva wasn't looking at me. Her eyes were trained on Reeves, who I could barely see in my peripheral. He placed the key in the lock.

"Hey, Chief, how many people are out there right now, anyway?" he asked.

The chief *hmmphed* from down the hall. "Too many. Nearly fifty. And more coming."

"At ease, Gabe," Reeves said as he took the key from the lock. "We're all set now."

He winked at Evangeline, and she nodded.

I immediately set to untying her wrists, and Reeves walked away.

The knot was not well tied. Truthfully, I could hardly call it a knot. I pulled one end, and the rope fell from her wrists.

"Get ready," Evangeline whispered, unfazed by how easily the rope dropped. She turned to face me. "You have to trust me, no matter what."

I lowered my voice as I replied, "I'd like to. I really would. But if your idea of a rescue mission is getting locked up with me, I think that's the worst plan ever."

She glanced behind her for any watching officers, then grabbed my arms and took a step forward, pushing me back into the far corner. The fierceness in her eyes surprised me. "The door isn't locked. He never turned the key." She whispered even quieter, "Reeves is on our side."

I swatted her hands away and took a step to see for myself, but she moved to block me.

"Not yet," she hissed, her eyes still gleaming. "If we go too early, it's over."

"If we stay here, it's over!" I hissed back, easily pushing past her.

I took one step, two, three. But Evangeline's full weight crashed against my shoulders and back before I could reach for the door. Her hands flashed in front of me as she wrapped her arms around my neck and shoulders. "If you touch that door," she whispered right in my ear, "*I'll* be the one to kill you." She emphasized her point by touching metal to my skin. A blade much bigger—and sharper—than the one hidden in her necklace.

Stars above, this girl gave mixed messages.

"So what do you want me to do?" I whispered.

"Let me explain. A second ago, you yelled at those officers for not lettin' me talk, and now you're doin' the exact same thing."

I clenched my jaw. "Fine. I'm sorry."

She pulled the dagger away and released her hold, dropping to the floor. I turned around to face her, and placed my hands on my knees so I was at her eye level.

"Alright, Lucinda. I'm listening. You have my *full* attention."

She glared at me, but quickly filled me in, her voice barely audible. "There's goin' to be an explosion outside. Any second now. Reeves and Chief will go outside to settle everyone down, and *then* we escape out the back. There are two barrels outside the back door. We each get in one. The Guild is goin' to load us on the cargo ship to Koyben. They'll knock twice on the barrels to let us know it's them."

An *explosion?* The *Guild?*

I stood up straight. "Are you out of your mind?"

"I put my life in your hands the whole time we were on that ship. I'm askin' for a little reciprocity."

I let out a slow breath. Did it never occur to her that my life was also in her hands on that ship? "Fine. But you have to stop threatening me. You don't get to ask me to trust you and then put a blade to my throat in the same minute."

She had the audacity to smile as she sheathed the dagger and tucked it under the side of her corset. "I accept your terms."

I scoffed. "Assuming your brilliant plan does work out, you have a *lot* more to explain when we're on that boat."

"As do you." That fierceness lit up her eyes again. What happened to her the last day and a half?

There was a shout outside as something shattered against the front of the building. People yelled, and a few screams rang out.

"Homebrew explosives?" the chief exclaimed. "The railing's caught fire! What is the meaning of this?"

"Your guess is as good as mine," Reeves replied. "I'll secure the back door. You want to see what the matter is?"

"Hmm," was all the chief said before he hurried out the front door, shouting at the crowd the moment he crossed the threshold.

Reeves hurried down the hall, pausing a moment to look at each of us.

"Good luck," he said to Evangeline. "And long live the king," he said to me.

Evangeline nodded. "Thank you for everythin'."

"You haven't escaped yet. Follow me in fifteen." Then he ran for the back of the building.

Evangeline exhaled slowly.

"He thinks this is going to distract the officers for fifteen minutes?" I asked, finally at a regular volume now that we were alone.

"Fifteen *seconds*, idiot." Evangeline stepped toward the door. "I *knew* nobles were daft." She swung the door open easily, unlocked just as she'd said. "After you, *sire*."

21

Barrel, Singular, as in, Only One

Evangeline

Silas stepped past me, glancing to the front of the building to make sure the chief wasn't about to return.

"The last room on the right. There's a back door," I directed him.

We ran into a small storage room—not for records, but for general supplies. Some extra uniforms and tools. Weapons.

Silas reached for a sword from the wall. "You want one?" he asked.

I nearly laughed. "You think I can use a sword?"

"You *can't*?"

"Silas! Can we go?"

He tried to pull the sword off the wall mount, but it was locked in place. He swore.

"Here." I tossed him a dagger. It seemed only the swords were locked up.

He caught it with a defeated sigh. Then we were out the door.

The barrels were to our right, Reeves to our left.

"Looks like there was a bit of a miscommunication on this end," Reeves hurried to explain. "You'll have to make do."

I turned to the barrels—no, *barrel*; only one. I supposed it was technically large enough to fit us both. But it was going to be a tight fit. "Beggars can't be choosers, it seems."

Something caught Reeves's eye down the alleyway. "Larson!" he called, quickly turning the corner to meet the other officer and buy us some time. "What in Breslin's seven kingdoms is going on up there?"

Silas pulled off the barrel lid and handed it to me. "You're sure this isn't just another way to kidnap me?"

"If it was, I wouldn't be gettin' in there with you!"

He glanced down at the barrel, then back at me, as though it was only now hitting *him* what our escape was going to entail. *Nobles.*

I held the barrel steady as he climbed in. As soon as he was mostly settled, I hoisted myself into the barrel too. He kept his legs off to one side as best he could, and I squatted next to his feet, setting the lid in place as I squeezed into the remaining space. It smelled strongly of wine.

"This is horribly indecent," I muttered.

"Well, it's a good thing we're married, then."

Reeves returned and shut the lid the rest of the way, enveloping us in darkness almost in time to hide Silas's stupid smirk and my quickly reddening face.

"Where's this barrel from? The festival?" Silas asked quietly.

"The officers always provide the wine. On Monday, they send the empty barrels back to the winery. No one will find it suspicious that this is here."

"That's ... convenient."

"You still don't trust me."

"I don't trust Reeves," he countered.

"*I* trust Reeves. So if you trust me, then you trust him."

"Alternatively, my distrust in him leads me to no longer trust you."

"Don't make me regret my decision to rescue you," I huffed.

We sat in silence for several seconds, listening to the chaos ensue in the streets around us. Even so, now that I was sitting still and outside of the law office, my nerves began to settle.

Silas took a deep breath, and his hand touched mine. We both recoiled at the touch, but then he set his hand down on my knee. I jerked my leg back as he whispered an apology, but when I set my foot back down, I did so on his thigh.

Silas grabbed my foot and set it down firmly in the small space next to him.

Blast this barrel! The enclosed space was bad enough. Not being able to see one another was quickly making this a nightmare. And to think I had complained about the arrangements on the pirate ship!

We reached an unspoken agreement to simply not move again.

Someone shouted Reeves's name, thankfully pulling my attention to what was happening *outside* the barrel.

"Tun's in the back, as usual. All ready for you," Reeves called. "Just one today."

"What's all the commotion about?" a male voice asked.

"We're figurin' that out. It should be cleared up here soon."

In other words, the diversion was not going to hold their attention much longer. We needed to get out of here quickly.

The distinct crunch of wheels on cobblestone drew near.

"I have to say, these are always good barrels. Sturdy. Well crafted," a second man said before two knocks sounded on the top of the barrel. Our signal that the right men were picking us up.

The men's feet shuffled on the ground as they prepared to lift us. They counted down, and my breath caught as they hoisted us into the air. The movement was jerky. They continued to bump and tilt the barrel as they carried us to the wagon.

"Hang on, I'm losin' my grip," the first voice said, sounding much more strained than before.

"It's two more steps to the wagon," the second argued.

"And I'm *losin'* my grip."

Sure enough, I started tipping to my left.

But the second voice insisted he hold on for three more seconds.

I tried not to grunt as Silas's end of the barrel made abrupt contact with the wagon.

The second voice said, "Ready, push," as the first one said, "Let me adjust—"

We tipped over, my stomach dropping as I fell backward. Silas fell on top of me, his left knee digging into my shoulder, my knee pressing against his chest. Our heads collided as the barrel hit the ground, and I couldn't help but yelp at the sudden impact.

I half expected the barrel to splinter and break, but it held firm.

Sturdy indeed.

The first voice cursed as the second voice reprimanded him.

"Are you *tryin'* to kill them?"

"I *told* you I had a bad grip."

They continued blaming each other as they picked us back up.

Silas whispered another apology as he untangled himself from me as best he could. I was too mortified to even attempt to form words.

The men got us situated on the wagon finally, and then we were moving, bumping down the road to freedom.

We couldn't get there soon enough.

22

I Have a Lot of Questions About This

Alastair

I was terrified the entire trip to the harbor that the men would simply ride off with us to Fate-knew-where, abandoning the plan Evangeline was so confident in and kidnapping us for themselves. But the sounds of the harbor were distinct, and hearing the clang of harbor bells, seagull caws, and sailor's voices helped ease my fears.

Except the one where we drowned in a barrel. After they dropped us in the street, I couldn't help but worry that these men were also going to drop us off the dock as they transferred us onto the boat.

Luckily, we didn't fall into the sea, and the men delivered us—albeit with much tipping, jolting, and arguing—onto the ship and down to the lower deck. There was a third man with them now, who I gathered was the captain.

"There, in the back is good," he directed.

The men walked a few more steps and then set us down, still more roughly than I preferred.

The captain thanked the two men and dismissed them. Their footsteps faded, and then the captain knocked twice on the barrel. "Once I leave, you can come out. I want to be able to honestly tell the law officers I haven't seen you if I'm questioned.

"My name's Bentley. This ship's got a light crew. We'll be loadin' the ship around four-thirty tomorrow mornin' and leavin' at sunrise. Feel free to move about the lower deck until then, but keep quiet and out of sight. If anyone comes on the ship before then, it's none of us, so stay hidden. You'll have to hide in here again when the crew comes. Don't come up to the deck until we're out of the harbor. We don't want anyone tryin' to go back to report you." He shuffled his feet. "It's an honor to do this, I have to say. Never thought I'd have the privilege. Oh, and there's food in the galley for you." He paused again. "Well, anyway, I suppose that's about it. I'll be pleased to meet you properly tomorrow." He knocked twice again and then walked away.

Once I couldn't hear his footsteps anymore, I reached up and popped off the lid, letting in lantern light and fresh, cool air.

"Ladies first," I said, though Evangeline was already working her way out, nearly kicking me in the face as she did so. "Don't get me wrong, Evangeline. I'm grateful." I climbed out after her. "But at the same time, that is the worst method of travel I've ever endured."

She tucked her loose hair behind her ear, looking at the barrel—and not me—as she laughed. "Definitely not ideal. There *was* supposed to be one for each of us."

I surveyed the space. We were inside the hold, naturally. It was far larger than the room we'd been in on the pirate ship, though it was equally empty, since they weren't loading the cargo for a while yet.

Seeing as we were alone, I dropped the commoner accent. "I have a lot of questions about this, Evangeline."

"I have a lot of questions for you, too."

I turned and realized she'd taken the moment to study me, not the room. *What did Reeves tell her?*

"We should check the deck, make sure we're safe before we talk things over."

She nodded, and we crept toward the door. I eased it open, but didn't hear anything that would give reason for alarm.

I drew the dagger Evangeline had tossed me in the law office. Evangeline pulled hers from under her corset and grabbed the lantern. There was little else to explore on the deck, just the galley and two rooms for sleeping quarters. The accommodations were nothing fancy, only hammocks hung from the beams.

Content we were safe for the time being, we returned to the galley to have a proper conversation. I opened a cabinet and found a handful of dried fruit to satiate my stomach until I could focus on a proper meal. Right now, my priority needed to be figuring out what to do with Evangeline.

I held out the jar of dried fruit to her.

She crossed her arms. "I need an understandin' of what your deal is before I agree to another meal with you."

I paused mid-bite. Apparently she was having similar thoughts to me, though I hardly understood how we were in the same position. "I assure you, my meals don't usually end in disaster."

"All the same, I'd like a moment of peace after that, so I'm not riskin' it."

I wanted to laugh, but she said it so casually I wasn't sure if she intended it as a joke or not.

"I'd suggest we flip a coin for who goes first, but I think we left all our money in the law office."

"Oh! I'd nearly forgotten!" Evangeline grinned and lifted the top two layers of her skirts, revealing just enough of her petticoats to undo the belt she'd been wearing last I saw her.

I averted my gaze—it was far too late for decency, but better late than never.

"Reeves runs a little underground band of sympathizers to the original throne, apparently. Took up a collection and—Silas, you can look at me, it's alright."

I turned to look at her, and my cheeks flushed, though I wasn't sure why. Surely it would have been worse if she had called me out for looking *at* her. Her belt was now on the outside of her dress, as it should be, and she slid the dagger and its black sheath into place on it, on the opposite side of a brown pouch. She'd hidden those under her skirts?

I blinked, realizing the plain brown corset she wore wasn't the same one she'd left Gregory and Marna's house in. I supposed this corset *did* change the way the dress fell, causing it to poof out more at her hips so anything underneath—

I blinked, deliberately pulling my gaze up to her face. That line of thought was *certainly* indecent to ponder.

"Reeves took up a collection for our safe passage." She opened the pouch, held up a coin, and tossed it to me. I caught it—a *silver* coin.

"Wow." I could hardly believe I had already reached a point where a single silver coin was impressive to me. "That's more than we had from Gregory."

"Way more." She held up another silver coin as she sat down at the table. "Instead of payin' for our passage ahead of time and givin' the officers an easy way to track us down, we were supposed to wait until after we left port and then pay extra to the captain and hope he forgave us. Though, now it seems our captain already knows we're here, so I don't think we'll need to bribe him."

I turned the coin over, Harland's ugly face now where the portrait of my father was supposed to be. Harland could have only recently started replacing our currency, but I was not surprised Narim would already have access to the new coins.

A wave of sadness crept up like the tide, and I quickly spoke to keep it from rising higher. "Alright. Heads, I ask first. Tails, you ask first."

She nodded, and I flipped the coin. It landed in my palm, face up.

"Sorry, Evangeline, but patience is a virtue." I showed her the coin. "By the way, you ever have a nickname? Eve?"

"If I answer that, it counts as your question, and then I get my turn."

I shrugged. "This boat doesn't leave for another half a day. It's not like we're short on time."

She smiled, crossing her arms as she leaned back in her chair. It was nice to see her look so relaxed, a sharp contrast to how she'd been mere minutes ago at the law office. She looked more as she had at the Festival. "Eva, actually. But I haven't been called that in years. Not since my mom died."

"Oh. Sorry." I instantly regretted bringing it up. I handed the coin back to her. "So that's a thing you've kept between you and her?"

"No, no." She sighed. "I think it's just that no one else ever said my name enough to want to shorten it." She laughed, but there was no happiness in it.

"Well, I like Eva." I took a seat across from her at the table.

She smiled again. "And what about you? You have any nicknames?"

"Oh, of course. But only my parents and Roland ever use them. That level of familiarity is scarce when you're at my level." I winced at the last few words. It sounded so ... pretentious. But how else was I to say it?

Luckily, she didn't seem bothered by it. "Makes sense. So what'd they call you?"

"Sorry, that's confidential."

She raised an eyebrow. "So Silas isn't your real name, after all." There was far less surprise in her voice than I would have expected. "I broke you out of jail and am now a wanted criminal *and* an accomplice in"—she waved in my direction—"*whatever* your deal is, and you're still afraid of tellin' me your real name? I should have found a way to make Reeves tell me, but it was hardly important—" She stopped, as though realizing she actually had a good point. She sat up straight. "Do you seriously still not trust me?"

I shook my head, trying not to show my relief that Reeves hadn't revealed my real identity to her, though I was not comforted that I'd fallen into her trap to pry information out of me. "It's not just about trust. This is more complicated than that. It's safer if you don't know."

"Safer for you. Because you think I'll betray you."

"No, it's for *your* safety, not mine. It provides you an opportunity to plead ignorance if things go poorly. Like Captain Bentley wanting to be able to tell the officers he hasn't seen us if they question him."

"I'm pretty sure knowin' your real name is the least important detail of all. You think it would qualify me for an ignorance plea?"

"You'd still have to lie a bit. But like you said, the best lies are threaded with truth. I can't tell you. I'm sorry." And I was. She'd earned the right to know, but it was a risk I wasn't willing to take for either of us.

She shrugged and looked over to the door. "Don't be. I get it."

I wasn't sure how she possibly could, but her tone sounded sincere. And that alone was enough to make me reconsider.

"Eva," I started, but as she turned to look at me, her hazel eyes wide, I knew I couldn't risk it yet. But if she guessed it on her own... "All those officers in Narim could recognize me. You honestly don't recognize me at all?"

She looked me over, her concentration on my face making me self-conscious. Finally she answered, "As I said, if you look familiar it's because you look like half the people in this kingdom. Not because I remember you specifically."

I tried not to frown. "I shouldn't have asked."

Her smile returned, but her eyes were mischievous. "Welcome to commoner life, noble. We aren't individuals. We are seen only as the masses."

"So, is that what you really think of me, or are you only trying to teach me a lesson?"

"Can't it be both?"

I scowled.

She raised her eyebrows. "*Should* I remember you?"

"No," I said with a heavy sigh. "It's not like we ran in the same circles."

"Definitely not."

"But there *are* family portraits in most of the cities and towns..."

She laughed. "Please. I barely know what the prince looked like, let alone the noble families."

I laughed with her, because that much was obvious. "Right. You and politics don't get along."

"Politics seem to be even more of a mess than I thought."

And she'd only seen a glimpse of it all.

"How did you get Reeves to help us?" I asked.

"Nuh-uh. It's my turn for a question."

"It is not! You asked me at least three." I held up my fingers to count for her. "One, if I had any nicknames. Two, if I trust you. And three, if you should recognize me."

"Nuh-uh," she repeated, the commoner phrase sounding quite amusing in her serious tone. "You *also* asked a bunch of follow-up questions."

"Fine, then we'll forget about taking turns. So, how did you convince Reeves to help us?"

She scoffed, but relented. "It wasn't me convincin' him to help so much as it was him convincin' me to let him. Reeves said he recognized you and would do anythin' to get the proper royals back on the throne. I thought it was a trap, so I told him the royals were dead. He said, 'But you and I both know that's not the case.' Which I did *not* know, not really, but what choice did I have but to see what he could offer us?"

"I told you the Cathmoores lived on our way to Narim."

She glared at me. "Yes, and you'd certainly proven yourself to be trustworthy by that point in time." The sentence was dripping in sarcasm.

"But now? What do you think of my trustworthiness?"

She crossed her arms again. "I'm givin' you a second chance."

I shook my head, but smiled nonetheless as my stomach rumbled. "Hopefully you're giving a proper meal with me a second chance too, because I need to eat."

23

I Guess I'm Now Involved in Politics and... Friendship?

Evangeline

Silas found a plate and began filling it, eating a little of everything while he did so.

"Did they not feed you?"

"Reeves did once. I doubt anyone would have otherwise." He shoved a handful of nuts into his mouth, chewing fully before he spoke again. *Such* a noble. "Thank goodness you actually showed up or I would have starved to death before they got a chance to kill me properly."

I realized this was the opening I was looking for. We hadn't established whether I'd be joining him once we got to Koyben, but I didn't see any other option. "Yes, all this time tryin' to get rid of me, but I've turned out to be quite useful, don't you think?"

He scoffed. "I'm pretty sure you were the one desperate to get rid of me."

"Either way, it's a good thing I stuck around, isn't it?"

He narrowed his eyes at me. "Are you leading up to ask for a reward?"

"A re—" I balked. "I'm sayin' I think I've proved my usefulness."

He squinted more, then turned his back to me to dig through more of the cabinets. "Yes, thank you. Again, I'm grateful."

I cleared my throat. "And so, I want to make sure we're on the same page that my life is now on the line just as much as yours." *If not more so*, I nearly added, seeing as I had Gratsis *and* the lawmen now looking for me. But I didn't think he would take kindly to that claim.

He turned back. "This *is* a lead-up to a reward. Look, I don't have access to any money right now. But yes, when things go back to the way they're supposed to be, I give you my word that—"

"Would you listen to me?" I slapped my hand on the table, startling him. "I'm sayin' that I want to join your cause. Save the Cathmoores and all that."

"Oh." He closed the cabinet and sat in the chair nearest him. "Do you want to join because you feel you have no other option, or because you're actually loyal to the cause?"

"Can't it be both?"

He glared at me. "You can't say that every time you don't want to answer a question honestly."

"Maybe I say it because I don't want to lie."

He shook his head, and I got the sense he was disappointed with me. "The mission would ask a *lot* of you. You don't even know how to use a sword properly. I'm not going to risk your life unnecessarily if you aren't sold out on it yourself."

"You've *already* risked my life unnecessarily!"

"And I'm trying not to make that mistake again!" He shut his mouth forcefully, like his raised volume caught him by surprise. "Forgive me," he muttered, then ran a hand over his face.

"Look, I'm sorry for the trouble I've caused you," he continued. "I truly am. I think we got off on the wrong foot. Despite the fact you've hardly said a kind word to me, I've seen how you talk to other commoners, and in spite of your disdain for my being a noble, I like that my status doesn't prevent you from speaking your mind. You're clever and resourceful, and as such, I could certainly grow to value your company. But I don't want you to join us if you don't want to keep risking your life for me. You can't honestly want to cross the kingdom with the man who ruined your life."

I opened my mouth. Closed it. Repeated the motions.

There was an awful lot to unpack there. *Another* apology? Taking responsibility for how his actions affected me? He *valued* my company—or thought he might, eventually? Had I really not said a *single* kind word to him?

I couldn't begin to address those things. But the last statement I might be able to handle.

"Gratsis is the man who ruined my life. Not you." I exhaled slowly. "At the festival, I wanted to ask. I just didn't get the chance."

"Ask me what?"

I dropped my gaze to the table. "If I could go with you."

"But why?"

"You keep ... surprisin' me, I guess."

"I thought everything I did was predictably noble."

"In some ways." I shifted in my chair. "But you also have done some very nice things for me. And I—" I clenched my fist under the table. "I don't understand why you would bother tryin' to help me."

He pushed his plate aside, only half empty. "Do you mean, why I'd help *you* specifically? Or someone *like* you?"

The fact he was giving this his full attention only made it more uncomfortable. "If I say both, are you goin' to get mad at me again?"

He laughed, which was the last reaction I expected. "I cannot figure you out," he said.

That makes two of us.

"Here's the thing." I cleared my thoat, wishing I could sink through the floor and to the bottom of the ocean instead of have this conversation. "What you saw with Marna and Gregory—that was all pretend. I don't know how to do... *this*." I covered my face with my hands. "But I'd rather risk my life with you than be alone again."

There was no response. I inhaled sharply and lowered my hands, preparing to make a hasty exit. But when I glanced at him, there was a softness in his eyes so foreign and unexpected, I couldn't bring myself to move.

"When you say you don't know how to do 'this,' what exactly do you mean?"

I hadn't the slightest idea how to explain.

"Trusting people?" he suggested. "Being honest with them? Caring about them?"

I swallowed. "I suppose so."

"If you come with me, you'll have to do those things."

I pushed my chair back. "Point taken. Forget I said anythin'."

"Eva, no. I—" He ran a hand through his hair. "Despite all the reasons I shouldn't think so, something about you is ... compelling."

"Is that supposed to be a compliment?"

"Now you know how it feels." He grinned. "I'm trying to say that maybe you're right. We ought to give each other another chance."

"Okay." I nodded. "Good. Thank—"

A shout from outside cut me off. Silas leaped to his feet, then froze. My heartbeat pounded as if it was trying to drown out the sounds on the dock.

Another voice yelled in answer, but I couldn't make out what he said. The harbor bells clanged, and a moment later, the commotion ended as abruptly as it had started.

I held my breath a moment longer, and Silas waited at least another minute before he sat back down.

"You do understand that coming with me puts your life in more danger, not less?" he whispered.

"The officers have already sent someone to find out what my relationship is with Gratsis. At least you seem to have *some* sort of plan with your friend to protect yourselves."

"We're planning on rescuing the Cathmoores and overthrowing Harland. We're running into danger. Not away from it."

"Are you sayin' we should stick together, or are you tryin' to talk me out of it?"

"I don't want you here for the wrong reasons. If you come with me, you're part of the team."

"I'll be plenty useful. I'm not lookin' for a vacation, Silas. Just the chance to live my life again."

He shifted in his chair. "That's fair. But the more you know about Roland and I and what we're doing, the more that puts you at risk."

I rolled my eyes. "Yes, you've made your point. Everythin' with you is very high stakes."

He nodded, either missing or ignoring the annoyance in my tone. "What do you know about Harland taking over?"

"You mean how he did it?"

"Anything about it."

I frowned. Was he still trying to talk me out of coming with him? "I'm not the most up-to-date on politics, obviously, and the fact that I've been wanderin' the kingdom since he took over hasn't helped me learn much. But I know Harland is the King of Glastor, and was an ally to Wenterly. The story goes that he came to Wenterly to meet with King Esmond, and they had a meeting about ... somethin'. King Harland didn't like whatever King Esmond had to say, thought he was a danger to the people, and it escalated into a fight. He had to kill King Esmond, and the rest of the Cathmoores' deaths were close behind. The whole family was corrupt, and he was savin' the kingdom from their rule."

Silas sat there quietly for a moment, though his hand was so tense, it looked like he was trying not to claw through the table. "Do you believe his story?"

"I don't think anyone fully does," I said slowly. "Callin' the Cathmoores corrupt makes sense as a cover story, since he swapped out a lot of officers in the towns and hunted down all the nobles loyal to the throne. But he obviously killed the Cathmoores, since there were reports of him hangin' their bodies from the palace parapets—or, it was easy to believe he had anyway, since *someone's* bodies were hung there." I grimaced at the realization. "You're *sure* that wasn't the Cathmoores?"

"I'm quite positive."

"Mercy." I swallowed. "Well, I managed to hear some general talk about Harland, too, though I didn't think much of it at the time. It seems people here are suspicious of him since he never married, and he's well into his forties now. I didn't realize he had never married. I thought that was a requirement for takin' the throne."

Silas nodded. "It is under normal circumstances. But Harland gained the throne when he was sixteen. His father died in a shipwreck. He *should* have married as soon as he was eligible. It's tradition, because it's symbolic. How can you pledge yourself to be loyal in leading and providing for an entire kingdom of people if you can't do that for one woman? But for whatever reason, he decided not to marry, and since he was already king, no one could coerce him into choosing a wife."

Surprisingly, perhaps the tradition was right. "I've also heard that Glastor has a lot of ports friendly to pirates. People were worried what it would mean for the future of Wenterly."

"Is that what gave you the idea to steal from a crew of pirates?"

I shifted in my chair again. I hadn't realized he still thought I only meant to steal from them. "It might have been."

"What else did you hear about him?"

I struggled to recall anything useful. "It was hard to tell what was true about his rule and what was fearful speculation. I had previously heard what you mentioned in front of Mothway, about him requirin' service in his army. Some people said he was goin' to enact a curfew, though I don't understand what the point of that would be. He's raisin' taxes, but on top of that, he also required a 'gift of gratitude' from everyone for freein' them from the Cathmoore's rule. Some sort of extra tax to help him 'rebuild the kingdom' or somethin'—"

"He *what*?"

I shrugged. "That's what I've heard."

Silas swore. "That snake."

"I don't understand why he'd go to all this trouble if he wasn't goin' to actually kill the Cathmoores, though."

"That is the question, isn't it?" Silas's gaze met mine. I hadn't realized how blue his eyes were. Quite striking in contrast to his dark hair. "I saw Harland haul the Cathmoores away in chains. Roland and I followed their carriage for a while before we lost them, but the reports of their deaths came out *before* we lost track of them. We managed to overhear enough of the soldiers' conversations to know they were being taken to some secret prison. We assume Harland was planning to torture them to uncover kingdom and family secrets, though as far as I know, there isn't much for him to discover. But why else would he keep them alive like that?" He tapped the table a few times, then took a deep breath and continued. "Harland told Wenterly the Cathmoores were dead to crush any hope the citizens might have in revolt. The whole plan was frighteningly thorough. He must have had loyalists infiltrating our kingdom for years to pull off what he did. Taking over with no warning of his intentions meant no war. No casualties except the ones he caused. It was brilliant."

His gaze dropped to the table and trailed his fingers over the grain of the wood. I didn't dare interrupt him now. He took another deep breath. "Recently, Roland was able to find out the general location of where they're being held. We've been making our way to them ever since. We're their only hope. If we try to spread the word about our cause, even secretly, Harland and his officers will be sure to get wind of it and stop us. Either by tracking us down to capture and kill us, or by relocating the royals, or killing them or—" His voice cracked, and he paused again to compose himself.

"This detour has cost all of us a lot of time. By the time we get to Koyben, Roland and I will have lost a week's time. That's one more week the royals are trapped, suffering only Fate-knows-what. And I try not to think about it because it kills me to think about it. Saying it out loud means it's real. And I think part of me keeps hoping I'll suddenly wake up and this will all be nothing more than a nightmare."

He finally looked up at me again. "So that's my deal. Roland and I were hoping to recruit a thief to help us out. Obviously we'll probably need to steal the keys to the prison cells, but the other skills thieves possess were really what we were looking for: stealth, lock-picking, deception. That kind of thing. That's how I ended up with you. In hindsight, I know I was horribly mistaken in thinking your thieving had any skill to it, but you have turned out to be quite the liar anyway. If you still want to come with us, I'm sure we'll be able to use your help in other ways. As you said, you've proved yourself useful." He cleared his throat. "You've already noticed, but I don't really understand commoner life." He laughed, but there was a bitter tone to it. Like he resented that fact. "I don't know when people are being kind and when they're bluffing to gain an upper hand. I don't know when to trust people. But, it seems, you know all that, though you're not the best at the follow-through. But every day I've been out here, it's become clearer to me that my upbringing was worlds apart from the Common Man's."

We sat in silence a moment. I didn't have a clue how to respond to any of that.

"You still want to join me?" he asked.

"I can't tell if you actually think I'm qualified. I'm hardly the Cathmoore's most loyal subject."

He grinned. "You're loyal to me. That's enough."

I blinked. Was I loyal to him? I had no loyalty to anyone but myself. I saved his life because it saved mine.

Didn't I?

"Are you in?" he asked.

I looked at him, his eyes sincere—hopeful even. No one had ever looked at me that way before. "Yeah, I'm in."

24

The Stress of Being Stowaways

Alastair

With the matter of Evangeline joining me settled, she finally agreed to eat something. She sat down with her plate and once again started talking with her mouth full. *Unbelievable.*

"So, now that that's all settled, what's our story until we get to Koyben?" she asked.

It was a good question. We could never say we were friends, though I supposed it was probably the closest to the truth. A man and woman traveling alone as *friends*? Forget it.

Marriage was the easiest solution, but I was afraid that if I brought it up *again* Eva was going to start thinking I actually wanted to be married to her—and I'd much rather forget about it altogether.

"Think we could pass as siblings?" I asked.

Eva wrinkled her nose. "Even cousins would be stretchin' it."

I shrugged. "This could be a good place to try it out. We'll need a long-term cover story when we're traveling with Roland, so it would be good to know what our options are."

We worked out the details of the rest of our relationship—what side of the family we shared, why we were traveling, and whatnot.

I yawned.

"You can go sleep for a while. I'll keep watch."

I hesitated. "Are you sure?"

She took my plate and started cleaning up. "Call it an exercise of trust."

"For me or for you?"

She bowed her head, trying to hide a smile. "I'll wake you when it's my turn."

I retired to the first of the sleeping rooms without further resistance, suddenly feeling the full weight of exhaustion from the last few days. There were a million things to still sort through—like how to convince Roland she was a worthwhile addition to our team—but that could wait. After everything she and I had talked our way out of, Roland was the least of our troubles. With any luck, we'd reconvene with him in a few more days and be back on track to save my parents.

I woke Evangeline when the crew arrived at the dock. We hurried to the hold, and while I was not eager to get in the barrel again, it wasn't as awful as it was the first time.

Before long, we could hear people moving about the ship. We weren't able to completely close the lid on ourselves from the inside, so the crack between the lid and barrel allowed a halo of light to filter down around us as the crew came into the hold and hung lanterns from the ceiling. Then they left to get the cargo.

Eva sat there with her eyes closed, looking quite serene in the dim light.

After a few moments, she opened her eyes, and I quickly shut mine, feeling, for some reason, as if I was caught doing something I shouldn't have.

The sounds of the crew returned to us, and a man addressed Captain Bentley. "Sir, do you know anythin' about this barrel?"

"Ah yes, the merchant was quite limited on his drop-off availability. I supervised as he brought it in yesterday. Nothing to worry about."

"Yes, but don't you think we should secure it with the other barrels?"

"Oh. I don't think that's necessary. I'd hate to mix up the merchants."

"We won't mix them up. The wood on that one is much darker than the ones for Chambren."

"I suppose I can't argue with that then."

Stars above. More of the crew was filling the room now, and it was increasingly difficult to overhear any conversation. But if they were moving us, they'd realize very quickly that this barrel's contents were quite irregular.

"Sure thing," Captain Bentley said, much closer now. "Say, Branson, give me a hand with this one, will you?"

He pressed the lid shut, thankfully, but it further muffled their voices.

Two knocks on the side of the barrel. I hoped that meant Branson was either someone Bentley trusted, or someone already in on this absurd plan. There was a long pause while we waited for them to lift us.

But they didn't lift.

We started tipping to the side.

"Slow, slow!" Bentley called.

We rolled at bit as we went down, so Eva would be falling on top of me this time.

The fact that we couldn't see was only beneficial for adding to the inconvenience of the entire situation. I felt her wrist touch my shoulder as she tried to keep herself off me.

Fortunately, with our slow descent, and the way Eva positioned her legs, she somehow managed not to fall *directly* on top of me when the barrel suddenly tipped the remainder of the way.

She fell onto my legs and right arm, which I'd also been bracing against the side of the barrel. My left arm was momentarily pinned between our chests, which *certainly* would not do, so as she pulled her right arm away from my face, I quickly lifted my arm from between us. But then there was the matter of where to set my arm. Her legs were against my side, so the only other place I could put my arm was across *her* side. That wouldn't do either.

I decided to press my hand against the other side of the barrel.

Eva whispered, "If they start rollin' us, I swear I'll—"

"Hush," I ordered. Though I quite agreed. Never mind what my mother would say about the pirate wedding. If she could see me *now*, I'd...

I'd rather die, honestly.

I could hear Bentley's voice, but couldn't make the words out over the muffled cacophony of the crewmen packing the ship.

Luckily, we did not roll. They lifted us and walked a few steps ahead. And then they set us down quite gently, for once.

Eva started to move to put a bit more distance between us, and I dropped my arm to stop her.

"Don't." I whispered it so quietly I wasn't sure she'd hear. And then I realized if she *did* hear, how easily she could misinterpret the reason for my words. "They might hear."

She didn't respond. But she didn't move either. I let go of her, drawing my hand back as much as I could. I had no idea how much longer they'd be loading the ship, but I doubted I'd be able to hold my arm up for that long.

The minutes stretched on, and I decided to pass the time figuring out how I'd find Roland when we got to Koyben, lest I start thinking too much about Eva's proximity. If Roland and I were separated, we had a week to rendezvous at our last campsite. If we didn't find each other by then, we'd both make our way to the Caves, and hopefully cross paths there. If I had kept track of time correctly on the pirate ship, we were scheduled to arrive in Koyben the day before Roland was supposed to start for the Caves. Hopefully he'd still be at our camp and I'd—

I suddenly realized it was quiet outside the barrel.

"Do you think they're gone?" I whispered.

"I think so. But Bentley told us not to come out until we left the harbor."

"He said not to come up to the deck."

"He did not," she insisted.

"Are you telling me you *want* to stay in here?"

"Surprisingly, I do think I prefer it over goin' back to jail, yes."

She made a good point.

"Two more minutes," I compromised.

She seemed to relax with those words. Whether from the exhaustion of waiting with tense muscles for so long, or from the relief of almost getting out of here, I wasn't sure. But somehow that made this feel worse than before. The situation was no longer just awkward, but also ... intimate.

Forget two more minutes.

I pushed off the lid. It clattered to the floor.

The room was dark. But no one appeared to see what had made the sound.

"I think you have a very loose grasp on the passage of time, noble."

I huffed. "Just get out, Lucinda."

25

Who Knew a Cargo Ship Could Be Paradise?

Alastair

We sat in the hold, waiting for the boat to finally set sail. Then we waited a while longer, making sure we were out of the harbor before we went up to the deck.

We emerged from the storage room and, thankfully, didn't run into anyone below deck. Not all that surprising, considering we just got on the open water, and Captain Bentley said it was a lighter crew. But the moment we reached the main deck, a crewman spotted us.

"When did you two arrive? I don't remember seeing you on the dock."

"We boarded early with the captain's permission," I answered.

His gaze narrowed on us. "He never said anythin' about two passengers."

"We were a bit last-minute."

"But you boarded early?"

I shrugged. "You're welcome to ask him."

"I will. Come with me." The crewman took us to the helm. "A moment, Captain?"

He barely glanced in our direction. "What's the matter, Corden?"

"You have two passengers board the ship early?"

Captain Bentley glanced at us again. "Ah yes. Did I not mention that? My apologies, it must have slipped my mind. Now please resume your duties, Corden."

Corden *harrumphed*, but left us.

When it was only the three of us, Captain Bentley turned to face us properly. He regarded Eva first and smiled. "It is a pleasure to meet you, finally. I have to say—" He stopped short as his gaze moved to me. "Stars above, I didn't realize—"

He stammered, shuffled his feet, and flapped his arms as though he wasn't quite sure what to do with his body all of a sudden. He almost looked to be imitating a bird in a mating dance, and it would have been humorous had I not feared he was about to end his performance with a genuflection.

I smiled and gave a slight shake of my head. "Happy to be humble passengers on such a ship, Captain."

Thankfully, he was alert enough to catch my cue and compose himself. "It's, ah, what was I sayin'? Oh yes, it's a pleasure to meet you, and just as any other passenger on my ship, sire—sir—I will shake your hand and welcome you aboard."

The exchange was far from natural, but as handshaking was a sign of equality, I could understand why the poor man felt the need to preface the action. I extended my hand, and for a moment, I worried he wasn't actually going to take it.

But after a moment's hesitation, he did.

Evangeline's brow furrowed. She glanced at me, as though I might give her an explanation for the captain's reaction.

Captain Bentley turned back to the helm. "So, what should I call you?"

"Lucinda and Gabriel."

He shook his head. "After the trouble those two caused in Narim? I don't think so. Unless you already told Corden those are your names."

I grimaced. "No. I guess we can go with... James and..." I turned to Evangeline for fear that I'd name her after another stray animal.

"Sylvia," she offered.

"James and Sylvia," he repeated. "Married?"

"Cousins," I corrected.

He nodded. "Happy to have you aboard. More than I can say. Make yourselves at home. We should arrive in Koyben around noon tomorrow."

"When would you like to discuss payment?"

He laughed. "Seeing you here is enough compensation. Save your money for a crueler time." His tone grew somber. "I'm sure it won't take long to find one."

I looked to Eva to help me gauge if the man was serious or bluffing. She gave me a nod to confirm that he was, indeed, sincere. These commonpeople were proving more generous than any wealthy man I'd ever met.

"Thank you." I dipped my head. "That's very gracious of you."

"It's my pleasure. Now go on down to the deck; the crew will think we're conspirin' up here."

As we made our way down the stairs, Eva whispered, "What was his deal?"

"I guess he's a good man."

"Not about the *money*, Silas."

"James."

"Not about the money, *James*. About *you*. Am I missin' somethin'? Are you really such a prominent—"

"You were charged not to speak of that." I waved her off. "I think he was just flustered that he *did* recognize me, and that we weren't anonymous sympathizers. Don't read into it too much." My stomach twisted at the lie.

She studied me a moment but finally let the issue go. "Fine. If you say so."

The trip back to Koyben was blissfully and, at our rate, *surprisingly* uneventful. They fed us regularly, we slept at night, and no one tried to arrest or kill us.

It was practically paradise.

But as the shore came into view, I thought the anticipation of continuing the mission was going to kill me.

I waved Eva over to me on the deck. "So, where exactly did we land on the whole 'marriage' thing?"

"We decided we're cousins, idiot. How did you already forget that?" I glared at her.

"Oh, *that* marriage." She shrugged. "It served its purpose. Like water off a duck's back."

"It ... doesn't matter at all? You're not worried about—" *how it might affect your real marriage?* I had to stop myself as I realized that was something Eva would never have the opportunity to worry about.

I had considered it though. Would a bishop marry me off to another woman if I were still *technically* married to Eva? But no one would agree to marry me if I divorced her, either. I'd decided to ask Roland for his advice, but the closer I got to that conversation happening, the more I worried the dilemma would nearly kill him—or cause him to kill *me*. I was starting to think it would be better if *no one* ever knew.

"I'm not worried about what?" she asked. "How me being married is technically illegal, and how I could face real legal consequences if someone were to find out about it? Even if the weddin' was little more than a sham? Or how you bein' married to me could ruin you and your family's legacy? How my entire life continues to be a curse to the people I'm close to?"

I frowned. "I believe the fact that you had that answer ready shows you are a little bit worried about it."

"Not as much as you clearly are." She leaned her forearms on the railing and turned to look at me, the sunlight highlighting the golden brown in her hazel eyes. "The way I see it, there's nothin' to validate it as a real marriage. The weddin' was illegal in every sense, and we have no proof of it happenin'." She smiled. "But if you're still worried, I'm happy to let you pay for my silence on the matter."

I laughed. "I think I've learned that I can trust your word."

"Pity," she muttered, then added, "even though my word is only as good as the man whose care I'm under?"

"Well, last I checked, that man was actually *me*, and I think he's pretty trustworthy, too."

"I'm only under your care accordin' to the marriage we're agreein' to void!"

"Don't get caught up in the details, Eva."

She scoffed. "So be it. You have my word that I won't tell anyone you were stupid enough to marry me."

I rolled my eyes. "Thanks."

She laughed. "Even if I did, you could easily convince everyone I was tryin' to blackmail you, if that sets your mind at ease. And if someone *did* believe me, then I'd be the one facin' the consequences of the law, and I have no interest in that. Believe me, there is no set of circumstances where sharin' that information would benefit me."

"I'm not sure it's right for me to find comfort in that."

"But you do."

I sighed. "A little. So truthfully, thank you. I think Roland would skin me alive if he found out, never mind the numerous other complications I'd have to deal with from my family *and* the law."

"Skin you alive?"

"You're right. He'd pick something worse."

Her eyes widened, and she seemed unsure if I was exaggerating. "This Roland sounds intense."

"He's strict, but only because he cares about me."

"How long have you known him?"

"Practically my whole life."

"And how long have you known the prince?"

I shrugged. "Practically my whole life," I repeated.

"You're pretty close to him in age. Are you older?"

I glanced at Eva before looking back out across the water. I couldn't bring myself to lie to her any more than necessary. "We're both eighteen." It would be best to turn the attention off myself. "I've been assuming you're about the same?"

"Nineteen."

"Ah, that's why you think I'm an idiot. You have a whole year of wisdom on me."

"Must be," she mused.

A whistle blew, calling us all to attention. Captain Bentley informed us that we'd be preparing to dock soon and requested that we go below deck and out of the way.

The better part of an hour passed before we could disembark.

Captain Bentley shook my hand, without hesitation this time, as Eva and I stepped foot on the dock. "You take care of yourselves. Stay out of the city as much as you can. And best of luck to you."

"I can't thank you enough," I said.

"The pleasure's all mine. And while your last experience in Narim may make you think otherwise, when the time comes, you'll have our support."

"Much appreciated."

Eva and I made our way to the street, careful to keep our heads down.

"Where to?" she asked.

"Are you hungry?"

"Not particularly. Though I probably will be soon."

"I agree with Bentley—we shouldn't linger in the city. Roland should have some food at the camp if you're alright with waiting a little while."

"That's fine with me. You know where Roland is?"

I turned to the west road leading out of the city. "I hope so."

"Every unexpected moment is ripe with unexpected fruit: some sweet, some bitter. Such a moment presents the opportunity to reach out and discover which fruit it will offer."

Brigid, *The Meaning of Shadows*

26

SO THIS IS ROLAND

Evangeline

It turned out that Silas and this Roland fellow weren't actually staying *in* Koyben. They were staying about an hour's walk outside the city—in the middle of the woods.

"How do you know we're going to the right place?" I asked Silas after we'd been traipsing through the woods for what felt like forever.

"Because we stayed here for a week before I found you."

"And you've been *gone* for a week."

"That doesn't change the position of the trees, Evangeline."

I surveyed the landscape. It all looked the same. Woods. Trees. Rocks and brush. Birds chirping and critters scurrying along the ground.

We walked a little farther, and sure enough, a campsite finally came into view. Silas laughed when he saw it, like he couldn't believe it himself, even though we came all this way because he *insisted* Roland would still be there.

It wasn't much. Canvas stretched across some branches for shelter. A few blankets and cookware near the ash of last night's campfire. But Roland was nowhere to be seen.

Silas called out his name a few times, in case he was nearby. But when we didn't hear a response, he didn't seem too bothered. He rummaged around the bags, stopping to look through the contents of one: a book; a yellow tunic, which he immediately put on over his shirt; and something small I couldn't make out, but his shoulders dropped in relief while he held it a moment, then immediately replaced it.

Satisfied with the bag's contents, he said, "We may as well make our waiting productive." Silas crossed over to a pile of brush and sticks and kicked them aside, then swiped at the dirt until he revealed a patch of burlap. He pulled back the fabric to reveal two sheathed swords. He picked one of them up and unsheathed it. The sun glinted off the steel blade.

"Wow." I stepped closer. "That's beautiful."

"You're going to learn how to use one."

I raised my eyebrows.

"If you're part of the team now, you should learn," he insisted as he sheathed the sword and reburied it. "I'll teach you."

He grabbed one of the sticks off the pile and held it out to me.

He couldn't be serious.

"Come on," he said, nudging my hand with the stick. "Roland will probably be in town the rest of the day. We should do something useful while we wait."

I crossed my arms. "After all that time we spent together, you really think sword fightin' is the most useful thing for me to learn?"

He frowned. "Yes? You said in Narim that you don't know how to use one."

"I've also said *several* times that I don't know how to read! Or write! If you want to teach me somethin', maybe we could start with literacy."

Silas copied my pose in an effort to mock me. "Perhaps you already forgot, but you're here to help me break the royals out of a *secret prison*. So unless, you plan on doing that by reading the guards a bedtime story, I think being able to handle a weapon is going to serve everyone better than knowing the alphabet."

I glared at him. He was right. Of course he was. But I didn't have to like it.

"There'll be plenty of time for literacy when our mission is complete." He held the stick out to me once more. "But *only* if you're able to stay alive that long."

I took the stick.

Silas spent the next several minutes showing me the proper grip and a few basic stances. He made me repeat the movements over and over again, like I was learning the steps to a very slow dance. I'd hoped learning to use a sword would be a lot more exciting. Surely it would have had I learned from a crew of pirates. But Silas was very concerned about form and precision.

Which made the whole thing *terribly* boring.

"Don't nobles have rifles nowadays?" I asked after what must have been the hundredth time through all the stances.

"Roland has a pistol. Keeps it on him all the time. But firearms aren't always accurate. And *are* always loud. Not ideal for a stealth mission."

"Well, I'm tired. My arms are startin' to ache."

"Imagine how much more tired you'd be with the weight of an actual sword in your hands."

I tossed the stick on the pile. "Whatever. I'm done for today."

Silas sighed dramatically, but his performance was cut short. Twigs snapped and rocks were knocked loose as something big made its way toward us. We both turned to see a man emerge from between the trees several yards away.

"Mercy." The man swore and broke into a run, shouting, "Where on the face of Breslin's seven kingdoms have you *been*?" He tackled Silas in a hug.

Roland, I assumed.

He appeared to be in his early thirties. His hair was dark, like Silas's, but that was where the similarities stopped. His face was long and thin, where Silas's was softer. Roland was also quite pale, though I couldn't be sure if that was natural or a result of his last few days, as his eyes were also bloodshot, and he hadn't shaved in a while. It seemed he'd been under just as much distress as Silas and I, and the whole combination, unfortunately, made me think he looked a bit like a rat.

He finally pulled back from Silas, but still held onto his shoulders. He swore again. "What happened to you?"

"I spent a few days on a pirate ship. Had to come all the way back here." Silas shrugged. "Nothing serious."

"Pirates?" He gaped. "You're not serious?"

"I wish I wasn't." Silas laughed. "And you'll never guess who the captain was."

Hearing the two of them talk in their upper-class accents made me feel *quite* out of place. Up until now, Silas had still been in my lower-class world. But here in the woods, I was the one outnumbered.

Roland didn't guess, so after a beat, Silas told him, "Ruben Mothway."

Roland gave him a playful shove. "Now I know you're lying!"

"It's true! Ask Evangeline."

Roland turned to me, as if noticing me for the first time. "This is the thief we saw?"

"I'm not a thief."

Roland raised an eyebrow at Silas.

"She's really not, it turns out." Silas admitted. "Steals when she needs to, but she's not particularly skilled at it."

"Then why'd you bring her here?"

"I want to help," I answered. Outnumbered or not, if I was committing the next phase of my life to traveling with these two, I wasn't about to let them get in the habit of talking over me.

Roland crossed his arms, but addressed me this time. "Why?"

"Because Silas saved my life, though his methods leave *much* to be desired." Silas widened his eyes, reminding me that he didn't want Roland to find out about our pirate wedding. "And he tried to help me get a job, which was also rather nice of him. And I'm on the run from the law too." I cleared my throat. Perhaps I should have left that part out. "Seeing as I'm associated with him now and everythin'... So I might as well join the team."

"I trust her, Roland. We've been through a lot together," Silas added. "I know we'll still need a thief, but I think she can help us get information. She understands commoners, seeing as she is one and—"

"One issue at a time." Roland held up a hand. "You aren't the only one who's had a busy week. I made some connections and gathered more information. As Fate would have it, we don't need a thief anymore."

Silas gaped. "You're serious?"

"Quite."

"Well, elaborate!"

"Momentarily. How much does, uh—" He turned to me and squinted. "What was your name?"

"Evangeline."

"And how much do you know of our circumstances, Miss Evangeline?"

"I know that Silas is a noble close to the royal family. I confess, I'm not sure your relation to the situation."

"I'm his uncle."

"Uncle?" My eyebrows shot up. "Huh. I hope you haven't been usin' that one for long, because I do not see the family resemblance."

Roland blinked and looked to Silas, unspoken questions evident on his face. "I married into the family," he said after a moment.

I glanced between the two of them. "That works, I suppose. But if I'm goin' to be Silas's cousin, what's my relation to you? *We* certainly can't be related."

"We'll work that out in a moment," Roland said. "What else do you know?"

"You're goin' to rescue the Cathmoores from Harland and restore them to the throne."

Roland nodded. "*Silas*, might I have a word in private?"

Silas gave me a long look, and for a moment, I thought he was going to refuse. But then he agreed, and told me to make myself comfortable while they talked.

I sat on a blanket, but I could hardly get comfortable knowing the two of them were deciding if I was truly worthy of their mission.

27

Roland Refuses to Believe That There's Nothing Nefarious About My Illegal Wedding

Alastair

As we walked away from the camp, I gave Roland a brief overview on the last week. How we got captured by the pirates, how Mothway interrogated us, how we jumped ship and the fishermen and their families helped us. But I left out the part where Eva and I got married, obviously.

We got far enough away from the camp that Roland was satisfied Eva wouldn't overhear us, but she was still within our line of sight.

"And after you escaped the pirates and found out she wasn't a thief, why didn't you leave the girl behind?" he asked.

"That was the original plan. I was going to find you, and she would stay in Narim and find new employment. But then the city officers recognized me and arrested us. They had me stay behind and sent Evangeline on an impossible mission to prove my innocence. But she managed to break me out, and at that point, we had to escape together. She's associated with me now. Harland's officers will be hunting her down just as much as you and me. We discussed it on our way here. Evangeline says she wants to help us. She's not great with politics, but it turns out, I'm not great with common life. Which means we're a good team. So, here she is."

Roland shot me a stern look. "The story you told her is not the one we agreed on. What happened to being soldiers from the palace?"

"Circumstances demanded a different story. I trust her, Roland. That has to count for something."

"Your parents trusted Harland, and look where that got us."

I bristled at his words. As if it should have been obvious Harland would betray us. As if Evangeline was the same as the traitorous king.

"I may have saved Evangeline's life. But she also saved mine—twice." She'd also threatened it twice, but that was irrelevant. "She could have left me to whatever fate those officers intended. But she didn't."

"If you saved the girl's life, she simply returned the favor, not wanting to be indebted to you."

"If that was the case, why would she still be here, *continuing* to risk her life to help us rescue my parents?"

"That's what I'm asking you to consider."

I scoffed. "Don't turn this into another one of your lessons."

"*Everything* is a lesson, Al."

I glared at him.

"And another thing," Roland continued.

"When is there not another thing?" I muttered.

He ignored me. "*How* exactly did you two survive the pirate ship? You can't expect me to believe they let you and the girl live without a compelling reason."

I crossed my arms, wishing I had put some thought into this ahead of time. "I fought them."

"You said you spent a *few days* on their ship. So you fought a crew of pirates to protect a girl you don't know and they just ... what, surrendered? Let you stay on their ship on your own terms? Didn't punish you or her at all for resisting them?"

"First of all, the *girl* is a year older than me, so at the very least, you can call her by her name. Secondly, the captain was *Mothway*. He's not a typical pirate. He interrogated us by getting us drunk! Not very effective, by the way. We lied our way straight through the whole thing."

"But *how* did you and the girl—"

"Roland."

"How did you and *Angelina*—"

"Evangeline. Are you doing this just to spite me?"

"I could ask you the same. Now, *how* did you two come out unscathed?"

I brought a hand up to my head. I wouldn't say unscathed, but I had also left that injury out of the story. "We were lucky."

Roland scowled. "I'm sure Mothway isn't a typical pirate. He had always been a spineless man. I'm surprised he made it to captain. But even if that much is true, I still don't believe you. What are you not telling me?"

"Nothing! I don't understand why you're so suspicious. You knew I was going to recruit her. Why weren't you against the idea then?"

"You weren't hiding things from me then." He glared at me. "I'm going to ask you one more time."

"Look, a lot of crazy things have happened the last few days, but I've told you everything that matters!"

"I've taught you for fifteen years. You think I can't tell when you're lying?"

I shut my mouth.

He headed for the camp. "Evangeline will tell me."

"Roland! Seriously?" I grabbed his sleeve and pulled him back. "Fine. I'll tell you. But when I do, there's no need to shout at me. Evangeline already made it abundantly clear that I was an idiot for it, and even without her reprimanding, I have a lot of regrets myself."

He didn't make any promises. Just stood there, waiting.

I glanced at Eva, and my stomach dropped. She was sitting with her arms wrapped around her legs, chin resting on her knees, looking more worried than I'd ever seen her on the pirate ship. Better Roland took his wrath out on me for this than her. I didn't dare meet his eyes as I spoke. "I told Mothway we were in love. Specifically that we were illegitimate children and needed someone to illegally marry us. It was supposed to do nothing more than buy us time, but..." I faltered as I watched him put the pieces together.

He clenched his jaw, then pinched the bridge of his nose. Not a good sign. "Tell me this isn't going where I think it is."

"He married us."

"*Mothway* married you to a *commoner*?"

I started to nod, but realized there was more to it than that. "Actually…"

"What more could there possibly be?"

"She's not really a commoner."

"No? Well, that's a little better then. I don't recognize her, but the women are less prominent. Although," he continued over my attempts to interject, "if *she's* nobility, then how does she not recognize you?"

"No, Roland." I wiped a hand down my face. "She's illegitimate. I didn't know it when I told the pirates as much, but as we know, Fate seems to have a sick sense of humor."

"Hang the moon, Alastair! You married *a leech*?"

"Shush, she can't hear you call either of us those names. She's Evangeline, and I'm Silas now."

"Indeed." He frowned, then sighed. "You truly trust her, though?"

"With my life." *Have I not made that clear already?*

"And the marriage? Is she holding you to that?"

"We agreed to void the marriage," I explained. "It was a wedding by pirates, under false pretenses, for a life-saving end. Surely that doesn't hold up legally."

"Perhaps. But, you also can't just *void* a marriage." Roland shook his head and walked in a small circle as he pondered the issue. "She must be trying to take advantage of the situation. Perhaps *that's* why she wants to help us. If the Cathmoores are restored, you can reclaim your inheritance as an alleged nobleman, and *she* can hold you to your pirate wedding for all it's worth."

"She was as concerned about the wedding ruining her life as I was about it ruining mine. It *is* illegal for her to marry."

"She could have been lying to gain your trust."

I crossed my arms. "She wasn't. But if she *was*, her status would make it quite easy to dismiss her claims as nothing more than an attempt to blackmail me on false accounts."

Roland raised his eyebrows.

"But I know she isn't going to do that!" I huffed. "Can we move on, please?"

"One of us has to think this all the way through." He shook his head. "Her parents ... are they at least respected now? I assume they married after she was born."

"Her parents both died when she was young. She was an indentured servant for a while, then gained a paid position as a seamstress." It didn't feel right for me to be the one to divulge Eva's story, but I also didn't want to make her explain the circumstances of her life again. I hoped my answer was sufficient for Roland.

He gave a low whistle. "This is all far less than ideal. But it's too late to change anything now. We'll keep her with us, and in our good graces. But I'll be keeping an eye on her. Understood?" He started walking back to the camp, not waiting for an answer. "Now we've lost a lot of time, and I have to fill you in on the details with Adeena and Esmond. I know where they are."

I hurried to catch up with him. "I thought we already knew where they were."

"Generally, yes. But now I have directions to the exact cave."

My heart beat faster. "You're serious?"

"Completely."

"That's incredible! How'd you come by that?"

"I told you, I've been here for a long time. Made some connections."

"Apparently so. Should we pack up while you fill us in?"

"No. We'll stay here overnight and head out in the morning. No offense, Silas, but you look something awful. You should get some rest before we travel anywhere else."

As anxious as I was to rescue my parents, Roland was right: I was still exhausted. And he looked as though he'd been losing quite a lot of sleep, too.

"Deal. Fill us in, and then we'll call it a night."

Eva stood as we approached, and I hurried to reach her before Roland. "I told him about our pirate wedding, so there's no need to dance around that issue anymore."

"Oh. Well, seein' as you still have your skin, I take it it went over alright?"

I laughed. "Better than I expected, at least."

"So, do I get to stay?"

Roland answered before I could. "Yes, Miss Evangeline. I apologize for the less-than-polite introduction, but Silas and I have a long history together, and in light of recent events, you must forgive me for being wary about his safety."

Eva nodded. "I understand. I'm sure his disappearance was quite distressin' for you."

"Yes. Exceedingly." He cleared his throat. "Which brings us to the remaining issue. I'm sure your guardian is worried about what happened to you. Silas told me you were employed. Was your Master also your guardian?"

Eva's eyes shifted to me before she answered. "Yes, I suppose my Master is still legally my guardian."

"You suppose?"

"Sure, assumin' you don't count Silas bein' my husband." She cracked a smile, but Roland was not amused. Perhaps I should have been more clear that not having to dance around the issue didn't mean she should bring it up unnecessarily.

She cleared her throat, realizing the mistake. "But my guardian is not a concern. There's no need to contact him."

"His name?"

Eva looked at me again, and I nodded for her to tell him. "Leonard Gratsis. In Welven."

"Welven? That's quite far North, isn't it?"

"I've been travelin' and lookin' for work for the last few weeks."

"And why is that?"

She shifted her weight. "His wife died, and after a couple of months he ... took an interest in me."

His jaw ticked. "Even though you're illegitimate? Why would he want to marry you?"

I groaned. This whole conversation was painful to witness. "He wasn't interested in *marriage*, Roland!"

His eyes widened. "I see." He cleared his throat and turned back to Eva. "Well, Evangeline, you may join us. You will, of course, be paid for your services rendered during our trip, and for your silence about any information you gather throughout your time with us. Unfortunately, we cannot offer you much in advance given the circumstances, but our word is good, and by the end of this adventure, you will never have want for anything so long as you may live. Do you agree to these terms?"

Eva gave me the briefest glance before answering, and I nodded at her once more. "Yes, sir. That sounds like a fair arrangement."

She spoke slowly, clearly measuring her words before speaking them. Something I hadn't seen her do before—even when we were lying with our lives at stake. Was she having second thoughts now?

"Good," Roland said. "Now that that's settled, we have some planning to do."

28

Welcome (and Unwelcome) Gifts

Evangeline

We all sat down, and Roland pulled a map of Wenterly out of a satchel.

"Silas and I previously discovered from our time in Koyben that the royals are being kept in the Caves of Ordelune." Roland pointed them out for me at the northwest corner of the map. "Ordelune is the mountainous region at the border of Wenterly and Eliston, so there aren't many large populations over there."

"I know what Ordelune is, thank you, Roland."

He glared at me to make it clear he hadn't finished his statement when I'd interrupted him. "*Which* makes it the ideal place to have a secret prison. I recently found out exactly which cave is being used for that prison." He set another piece of paper on top of the map. This one was also a map, but not professionally crafted. It seemed to only show the mountains and caves, one of them circled, and a whole host of scribbled writing on the left side of the page.

"But why wouldn't Harland take the royals back to his own kingdom?" I asked. "Doesn't it seem risky to keep the Cathmoores in their homeland? And close to an ally kingdom at that?"

"I'm surprised you know who Wenterly's allies are," Silas teased.

I bristled. "I'm a commoner, not a foreigner. I know the basics of the kingdom I live in, Silas."

He found that very amusing for some reason.

"As far as Harland is concerned," Roland said, "Wenterly *is* his own kingdom. And no one outside of Harland's men know the royals are alive except Silas and I, and now you, so there's no risk in their eyes. Afterall, Eliston's alliance with Wenterly dies with King Esmond."

"Except," Silas interjected, "word is spreading. We escaped Narim because of a group of people who knew the royals were still alive."

Roland's eyes widened. "Elaborate."

"There's an officer loyal to the original throne," I offered, since I spent the most time with Reeves. "He pledged loyalty to Harland because he had no alternative. And then when Harland revealed to the officers that the royals were still alive, he told some people he knew he could trust. They're continuin' to spread the word, though most people don't believe it."

"I'm sure they don't. But even so, this is ... serious news."

"Isn't it good, though?" Silas asked. "If there are people who want to help us, maybe we could get more support to—"

"No. You getting arrested in Narim is problem enough. Harland's men nearly had you—and they know it. That's only going to make them double their efforts to track you down. *And* multiply their efforts to stifle any wind of rebellion—so much as a breeze of it will be too much. It's more important than ever that we maintain a low profile. Harland's full army hasn't invaded Wenterly yet—as far as we know, anyway. But if word about the royals surviving gets passed around enough, that could change—and with it, the truth of the rumor."

"You're sayin' Harland would have the royals killed just like that, after the lengths he's gone to secretly keep them alive?" I shook my head. "That doesn't make any sense to me."

"Who can understand evil?" Roland asked. "We have to prepare for every possible outcome when it comes to Harland."

The three of us looked down at the map.

"Which, hopefully, your helpful officer in Narim knows," Roland continued after a moment. "Did the other officers seem suspicious of him?"

I turned to face Silas. "You saw how he was with the other officers more than I did."

"Hardly." He shrugged. "As far as I know, no one suspects him of anything. But after we escaped, I'm sure there will be a lot more suspicious eyes around."

Roland nodded. "I'm sure the Cathmoores will want to properly thank him when this is all over, assuming he doesn't get caught between now and then. What was his name?"

"Reeves Hills."

He repeated the name under his breath, committing it to memory. "Good. I'm glad he found you."

"Me too," Silas agreed.

"But back to *our* mission." Roland folded the maps back up. "We'll leave first thing in the morning. I'll leave at sunrise to head into Koyben. I'll have to get some more provisions for the journey, and I should let my connections know that we're leaving. You two can pack up the camp and head out an hour later. We'll rendezvous at the second-mile marker on the west road."

Silas and I nodded.

"Good. Then let's eat and get to sleep. I'll take last watch, since I'm getting up the earliest anyway. You two can fight over first watch."

With that, Roland started a fire for dinner.

"You can have first watch," Silas said quietly.

"Sure." I fiddled with the fastener on my belt, the reality of this adventure beginning to set in. A week ago, I hadn't had much of an idea what my future held, but I certainly never would have dreamed up anything like this. I kept my voice soft, mimicking Silas, though I wasn't sure why we were being quiet. "Is that a good thing or a bad thing?"

He laughed. A warm sound that set me at ease after such a strange afternoon. "For you? Good. First and last watch are generally the best because you don't have to interrupt your sleep. I prefer first because you don't have to wake up while everyone else is asleep."

"Oh. Well, you can have it then."

"I'll have my turn. Think of this as your 'welcome to the team' gift. It's the best you're going to get from us, I'm afraid."

I leaned toward him and whispered, "Except for that money Roland promised. I was only jokin' about you buyin' my silence."

"No one does favors for free in upper society. Let alone risk their life. I don't know how much of the generosity we've seen in our time together is normal for you, but it's all very foreign to me. And despite how much I've decided to trust you, I still don't quite get what makes you tick, Eva. It's certainly not the same stuff everyone else I know runs on. Truthfully, Roland is suspicious enough of you as it is. If you had refused the money, he'd never agree to let you join."

"So, he's bribin' me to keep my word? That's how politics works?"

He shrugged. "Pretty much."

"What if Harland offered me a bigger reward to betray you both?"

"Then I guess you'd be a bad politician to turn it down."

I smiled. "Good thing for you, I've never been one for politics."

"Would you two stop your whispering?" Roland snapped. "I'm here to lead a rescue mission, not chaperone. Keep that up, and I won't trust you two alone."

Silas stood and joined Roland at the fire. "Nothing to worry about, Roland. She and I have been alone for a week already."

Roland paused what he was doing to fix us with a stern glare. "That is *exactly* why I'm worried."

After the fire ignited and Roland got busy cooking, he removed his outer tunic. It was then that I saw the pistol tucked into his waistband. I had forgotten that Silas told me he carried one. The sight of it made me uneasy.

Though, why should the fact that he had it make him more of a threat? Silas had shown me the swords stashed here. I could be killed just as easily with one of those, I had no doubt.

I sat on a rock nearby and waited for the food to be ready. Of course I'd asked to help, but to my surprise, Roland refused. Another "welcome to the team" gift, perhaps? But watching Roland throw the carefully cut raw chicken and whole potatoes into his pot at the same time made me doubt how good of a gift this was going to be.

Silas sat closer to Roland, filling him in on the rest of the details of our misadventure while our food cooked. They mocked Captain Mothway for getting us drunk in order to interrogate us, though I was nothing but thankful for his aversion to violence. By the time we started eating,

Silas was telling Roland about our arrest in Narim. He skipped our walk with Officer Larson and the pregnancy mishap, and spun it as if we were surrounded right outside the market square. When he informed Roland that we escaped the prison by each of us hiding in our own barrel, I laughed to myself, though I could hardly blame him for changing those details—and was quite relieved that he had.

When Roland decided it was time to eat, I was unfortunately right about the state of our meal. The food was terrible, blander than what even I cooked with my small wages, and the potatoes were still firm while the chicken was horribly overcooked. But I choked it down without voicing a complaint. Silas certainly didn't mention how inedible it was, and I guessed he was used to far better meals than I. Hopefully, they would let me help cook tomorrow, and I could remedy the situation.

I ate only what was in my bowl, but the two men ate until all the food was gone. The sun had nearly set, and Silas finally wrapped up his summary of the past week.

"You forgot a detail, Silas," I said as I stood up and brushed stray leaves from my dress.

He flashed me a worried look, giving me all the confirmation I needed to know that he did *not* want Roland to know about how well-acquainted the two of us had gotten, regardless of our choice in the matter.

I pulled the two silver coins from the pouch on my belt. "We still have the money from Reeves."

"Oh, right," Silas breathed. "Two silver. Too bad we can't buy a horse with that."

"Every bit helps," Roland said. "I'll add it to what we've got."

I dropped the coins into Roland's outstretched hand. "I've never ridden a horse before."

"Seriously?" Silas asked.

"I rode the sheep sometimes when I was little. Is it similar?"

He laughed. "I wouldn't know."

"Enough talk." Roland stood and deliberately walked between me and Silas to get to his bedroll under the stretched canvas. "Time to sleep. We've got a big day of travel tomorrow. Did you decide who's on first watch?"

"Me."

Roland simply grunted in acknowledgment and handed me a pocket watch before he plopped onto his bedroll. "You hear or see *anyone* out here, Evangeline, you wake us up immediately. *No exceptions*, understood?"

"Yes, sir."

"Good. Goodnight to you both. Silas, it's good to have you back."

"Glad to be back, Roland."

Roland closed his eyes and rolled over so his back was facing us.

"We only have two bed rolls, as you can see," Silas said, not bothering to lower his voice. "Maybe *Roland* can buy another one when he goes into the city tomorrow morning?"

Roland grunted in acknowledgment.

"You can sleep on mine for tonight," Silas offered.

Roland turned back around. "What are you doing?"

"Offering Eva a more comfortable bed—if you can call it that. We're only using two at a time anyway."

Roland blinked.

"I'm being polite," Silas added.

"Why?"

"Because..." Silas gave me a long glance, searching for another reason that would satisfy him. "She's a woman?"

"It's improper."

"This whole ordeal is already improper!"

"So why should you increase that unnecessarily?"

"Are you serious? This is hardly—"

"She's a leech. She can survive on a blanket for a night."

"Roland!"

"I mean no offense, I'm only saying that she's probably used to conditions like this. You gave her first watch, that's charity enough. Your sleep is just as important—dare I say *more* important—than hers."

I cleared my throat. "That is still offensive, Roland, but for the sake of tonight, I'll dare to agree with you. I'll be fine on the blanket. But thank you, Silas."

Roland grunted again and rolled over once more.

Sorry, Silas mouthed.

I shrugged. Roland acted far more like what I had expected from nobility. I couldn't say I was surprised. "So, I let you two know right away if I see anyone. Anything else I need to do while I'm on watch?"

"Keep the fire going. It helps keep animals away. That's all really. Wake me up for my shift in three hours."

"I assume that's what the pocket watch is for?"

He nodded. "You can read a clock, right?"

I laughed. "Yes. That is one skill I do possess."

He raised his hands. "Just making sure."

"Alright." I stood up. "I guess I'll wake you in a bit."

Silas sensed my nervousness. "We haven't had any trouble the entire time we've been out here. You'll be fine. But if for any reason you get a bad feeling, don't hesitate to alert us. Better safe than sorry."

"Alright," I repeated.

Silas made his way to his bedroll. "Roland likes to sit against a tree where he can look over our camp. I pace around more to help me stay awake. You'll figure out what works best for you. Just don't fall asleep on the job."

29

Silas Tells Me Confusing Stuff About the Moon and Grief

Evangeline

It turned out, staying awake was more difficult than I thought it would be.

The first hour passed easily. It took Silas much longer to fall sleep than it did Roland.

The second hour was quiet—aside from the regular noise of the woods. The crickets chirping and fire crackling reminded me of my childhood and the shed my mother and I shared out in the country. Life had its own share of difficulties then, but it seemed simpler, too. Though, maybe that was only because I was young and hadn't grasped the weight of reality yet. Regardless, I missed it. And I missed her.

I realized Silas might be going through something similar to what I had experienced then. Granted, his friend, Alastair, was still alive—as far as we knew, anyway. But the stress of knowing that could change at any moment must have been eating him alive. And where was the rest of his family? His parents? Did Harland already capture and execute them? Why wouldn't they be here? Why wouldn't he have told me about them when he told me everything else?

The idea that he was hiding something nagged at me. But I'd decided to trust him. That was part of the agreement in joining him here. I would ask him about his family tomorrow. Surely he had a reasonable explanation for everything.

By the start of the third hour, I caught myself nodding off a few times. I took Silas's advice and walked several laps around the perimeter of our camp. I stoked the fire, walked around a bit more, and finally reached the end of my three hours. I approached Silas's bedroll and hesitated, realizing I wasn't sure how to go about waking him.

"Silas," I whispered, hoping I wouldn't wake Roland. I didn't, but I didn't wake Silas either. I nudged his shoulder with my shoe.

He woke up so quickly, he practically spasmed. He was already sitting up by the time he registered that it was only me.

"Shift over?" he whispered as he rubbed his eyes.

"Yes, sorry. Nothin' to report."

"Good." He stood up. "I know Roland threw a fit earlier, but you can still sleep on my mat if you want. It doesn't make sense for you to sleep on the ground when it's going to be unused for the next few hours."

I handed him the watch. "And when you wake up Roland, how do you think that's going to go?"

He shrugged. "It's up to you. *I* won't be offended either way."

"Thanks. I'll be fine on the ground, though." I was already crossing to the other side of the camp, where I'd folded a blanket for myself to lie on. Though I would never admit it out loud, Roland was right. I'd slept in worse accommodations after fleeing Welven. "Goodnight, Silas."

"Today's the big day! Rise and shine, everybody."

I opened my eyes, surprised to see how light it was already.

"Big day? I thought we were just traveling," Silas mumbled from his mat.

"And it's a big day of travel. Our first day heading to the Caves post-kidnapping. That qualifies."

"Fair enough."

"I'm heading out to Koyben now. You two pack up camp and head out in an hour to—"

"The second-mile marker. We know. Make sure you buy another bedroll while you're in the city."

"Yes, yes, I know."

It was a short exchange, but Roland was in a far better mood this morning. I was hopeful that he'd be kinder to me today. Silas and I appearing yesterday must have been a shock, let alone all the news we brought with us. Perhaps now that he'd had some more time to take it all in...

But just in case, I kept quiet until he was gone.

I looked around the campsite. "What do we pack up first?"

"First, we have breakfast." He tossed me an apricot. "How'd you sleep?" He sat on a rock across from me.

"Better than I have the last seven nights."

"I suppose that's positive."

I looked from him to my breakfast. Now was as good a time as any. "There's somethin' I was thinkin' about last night, that I wanted to ask you."

"What's that?"

"On the pirate ship, you said that you aren't betrothed yet because you have a good relationship with your parents and there was no rush for you to take over as the head of the family."

He nodded, but his expression was blank. I got the sense this topic was one I should tread lightly with.

"I was wonderin', if that's all true, where are your parents now? Are they in hidin' somewhere else, or..."

Silas shifted so he was sitting with his legs crossed. "That's a difficult question to answer."

"I don't mean to pry. If it's none of my business—"

"No, it's not that I don't want you to know. It's that..." He lifted his gaze to the sky, as though he might find the words he was looking for in the clouds. "I don't quite know the answer myself."

I wanted to ask "why" or "how" but bit my tongue. It was clear he was already wrestling with how to tell me more.

He shifted his position again and leaned forward. "Harland's coup involved an attack on my family. Given the nature of our relationship with the royals, he wasn't going to give us the same offer of changing allegiance he granted the rest of the nobles. Roland and I took two of the horses and ran for it as soon as we heard the commotion. If my parents are alive, I assume they're facing the same fate as the Cathmoores right now."

"Mercy, that's ... awful." I had no idea what to say. I had anticipated some sort of tragedy kept them from being here, but not one where so much was unknown. So much uncertainty surrounding so many lives... How did someone deal with that?

"I hope you don't take this the wrong way," I said. "I only want to understand what's happenin' here—but why are you and Roland lookin' for the Cathmoores instead of your family? Wouldn't it be easier to rescue the royals with all of you to help?"

He nodded, a bitter laugh escaping his lips. "It could be. But we would lose time trying to find them first. The longer it takes us to get to the royals, the riskier everything becomes. Besides, it's easier for us to blend in if we aren't all together. People would recognize me or my mom when they see us with my dad, but might not realize who we are individually. I know my parents are doing what they can, and we're doing what we can. And when we get the royals back on the throne, it will be safe for us to be together again."

He was staring into space, his face void of expression. I had taken him to a far more difficult place than I had anticipated.

"I'm sorry. That's a lot to deal with. How are you still standin'?"

Silas gestured to his folded legs and gave me a small smile. "I'm not."

I rolled my eyes. "You know what I mean. What you're dealin' with right now would be enough to kill me."

"You say that like you haven't dealt with loss yourself."

I shook my head. "At least I *know* my parents are dead. There's grief, but not worry. I'm not tryin' to balance havin' hope *and* preparin' for the worst, while every legal authority is also out to kill me. It's—"

"Pain isn't relative, Evangeline."

I paused, the strange phrase catching me so off guard I had to repeat it a few times in my head to try to grasp its meaning. "What?"

"You're trying to compare your experience to mine, but it's not the same. We're different people in different situations, experiencing different kinds of grief. They aren't comparable. Think of how night is dark, but a night with a new moon is objectively darker than a night with a full moon. Meaning, the darkness of night is relative. Pain isn't like that."

I frowned. "You're losin' me."

He sighed. "Looking at the pain I'm in doesn't make your past suffering hurt any less. You can *say* one kind of grief is worse than another, but it doesn't matter. The grief consumes us both the same. The pain is absolute."

I sat quietly for a moment, trying to process his words. "That's very philosophical," I finally settled on, though I still wasn't confident I fully grasped his meaning.

He shrugged. "I enjoy philosophy."

"Was all that from a philosopher you've studied?"

"Brigid. Though, the way he phrases it is more elegant."

"Oh."

He took a bite from his apricot and swallowed. "On that note." He stood. "I suppose we better pack up and meet Roland."

Silas and Roland had massive packs to hold their cookware, blankets, and bedrolls. I wondered how much they had bought after they ran, and how much they brought with them. The haul would cost a considerable amount of money in one go, though I was sure it wasn't as significant a purchase for noblemen. Still, they seemed oddly prepared to be running for their lives.

"What happened to the two horses you escaped on?" I asked as I hefted bags onto my shoulders.

"We had to sell them after we made some distance. They were great horses, but recognizable. We wouldn't be able to remain hidden from the right people if we kept them. Besides, we needed the money to get supplies and food. It's not like we had time to pack in advance."

Silas strapped his sword and stolen dagger to his waist, and I strapped Roland's sword to mine. Reeves's dagger rested on my opposite hip.

We started walking toward the road, and I hadn't the slightest idea if Silas was leading us along the same route we'd taken to Roland's camp, or if it was different. I adjusted the straps of the bags on my shoulder, already feeling weighed down. I'd never carried so much stuff at once, let alone for as long as this journey was going to be. It was strange how they were the ones traveling for speed and stealth, and yet they were far more burdened than I was when I fled Welven. But, I supposed a life on the run was bound to look different for the upper class.

"Forgive me for my ignorance again, but why did you stay in Koyben for a week before we got captured by the pirates?" I asked as we finally reached the road.

"We weren't sure of the exact location of the royals. After a lot of wasted time going south, we found out Harland took them west, but not specifically where. We spent some time here so Roland could try to get some more information, and so I could look for anyone who might be able to aid our cause."

"Well, it sounds like Roland was successful, at least."

"I think I did okay, too."

I nearly snorted. "All you got was me."

"I know," he said, his voice softer in his reply than it should have been.

I stopped walking. "You recruited me to be a thief, remember? And I'm not good at ... anythin'."

"Are you kidding? You can sew. You can dance. You can—"

"Things that *matter*, Silas! Who cares about dancin' and sewin' on a journey like this? That's not goin' to help us save the royals, is it?"

He shrugged, as though my argument hardly had any merit to it. "I stand by what I said. You understand ordinary people better than Roland and I do. That's how you broke me out of jail."

"*Reeves* broke you out of jail. I just trusted him to do it."

"And you know the common people well enough to know he was someone you *could* trust. That's my point."

I frowned. "So I'm helpful until we get to Ordelune. And then we'll be fully in your political sphere on the verge of ... what? *War*? I'm not a soldier by any means, and that's what you two need."

"Maybe. But think about what you said earlier. The stress of all this is enough to cripple me—maybe even kill me. Perhaps it's equally valuable to have a friend along so I don't lose it before we reach Ordelune."

"Ah yes, the power of friendship is goin' to save the throne. And ours is *definitely* one that's strong enough to do it—exactly like in the fairytales."

"Shut up, I was serious."

I re-adjusted Roland's pack on my shoulders. "I know," I said quietly. "Thanks."

We got to the mile marker before Roland. About fifteen minutes passed before we saw him heading toward us.

And he did not look happy.

30

Roland Is Stressed and That's Making Me Stressed

Alastair

"Did you get another bedroll?"

Roland didn't answer. He stared at Eva as he approached, looking her up and down. His jaw was clenched, and when he fixed his gaze on me, it was obvious I was about to get yelled at.

"Word from Narim has already spread about you two. A young man traveling with a woman, masquerading as a young married couple. These two are *violent* criminals, and the woman may be *pregnant*." He glared at Eva. "Are ... you?"

"No," she said, and while she managed not to roll her eyes, her tone made it evident she wanted to. "And even if I *was*, you don't have to be so upset about it. As I've had to remind *both* of you now, pregnancy is not contagious."

"What is she talking about?" Roland asked me.

"I'd rather not answer that," I said, but it was clear by Roland's glower that he wasn't going to let any of this go. "It was a misunderstanding with one of the Narim officers. It was embarrassing. That's all."

"It was *mortifyin'*," Eva added. "You should have seen him, Roland. He decided to get me pregnant, and then didn't know how to act like a father."

"*What?*" Roland yelled.

"Mercy, Evangeline, it wasn't like *that*." I turned to Roland, who looked as if he was on the verge of fainting. "It was *not* like that."

Whether Evangeline truly just realized the implications of her statement, or was only pretending to, she shouted, "Mercy, Roland, you don't actually think—"

"Silence!" Roland yelled. "I want a simple answer to the following two questions: yes or no. And I want the truth. Understood?"

We nodded.

"Is Evangeline pregnant?"

"No," she said.

"Good." He closed his eyes, the next question seeming to physically pain him. "Have you two done anything that might ... change that fact?"

"No!" we both answered, horrified at the thought.

"Do you seriously think that little of me, Roland?"

"All I'm saying, Silas, is that you are full of surprises. And Evangeline has shown little regard for propriety in the short time I've known her. So seeing as you did *marry* her, new information and *whatever* you two were just discussing required a confirmation. Now," he dropped the new pack he had bought for Eva onto the ground. "Let's get going. And so long as the answers to my previous two questions remain the same, we will never discuss this topic again."

"An excellent idea," Eva said, handing over Roland's pack and sword.

Roland took off down the road without checking that she was settled and ready to go. I waited for her to gather her things, and she glanced up at me as she situated herself.

"I'm surprised you're hangin' back after the mess that conversation was."

"As Roland said, I'm full of surprises."

She rolled her eyes. "Not my favorite trait of yours."

"I think most of my traits aren't your favorite."

She raised her eyebrows, so I provided the most recent example. *"Ah, Silas, why are you travelin' with so much stuff if you're tryin' to be stealthy and quick? Are nobles so incapable of a life free of materialism?"*

Her eyebrows immediately furrowed. "How did you know that? Surprise, you also hear my thoughts?"

I laughed. "Only when you say them out loud."

"But I didn't say that out loud."

"Not directly to me. But Reeves was right—you mutter a lot."

She bit her lip, probably holding herself back from muttering something right now. "Let's go. I don't want to give Roland reason to question us again." She shouldered her pack and took off, but not before I caught her cheeks turning a few shades pinker.

We took a short break for lunch a few hours later, and while Evangeline wandered off to relieve herself, Roland interrogated me *again*.

"I've been thinking, Evangeline could fetch a doctor for us after we get to Ordelune. No doubt your parents will be in need of one. Do you think she could be trusted with such a task?"

"Of course. I think she can be trusted with anything we ask of her. I wouldn't have let her come otherwise."

"Remind me, why do you have so much faith in her? She's a stranger."

"Who risked everything for me! She's loyal to me."

"There are many loyal to the throne. We can find someone else—"

"Not loyal to the throne. Loyal to *me*."

"So?"

"*So?* That's not something I've seen before. Everyone I've encountered in my life only offers me favors because of what I might offer them in return. Sometimes I feel like I only matter when there's a crown on my head. But..." I sighed. "Eva's the opposite. She thinks I'm a stupid noble, and she's helping despite that—not because of it. She cares about me for who I am." *I think.* Truthfully, she didn't know who I was. But I couldn't let Roland know I had *any* uncertainties about her. Not if I wanted her to stay.

Roland raised a brow. "Are you suggesting *I* don't care about you aside from your title?"

"Obviously not! But you're different. I mean, it's your job to care about me."

"It's my job to care about your *education*," he corrected. "I can assure you, trekking across the kingdom and breaking your parents out of prison was not on the job description."

"But still. You have long-standing loyalty. Eva doesn't."

"That's exactly why I'm concerned about her. If Evangeline is going to give you her loyalty that easily, what's preventing her from giving her loyalty to someone else just as easily?"

"You didn't seem this worried when I told you I was going to recruit her."

"That was before you two married and gallivanted around the kingdom together! I didn't think you falling in love with a leech was going to be another thing I had to worry about!"

I nearly choked. "Roland! That's what you're worried about? I do not have feelings for her."

"The way you talk about her suggests otherwise," he countered.

"I thought we weren't going to discuss this topic anymore."

"This is a different topic."

"Is it?" I muttered.

"A pretty girl about your age saves your life? It's only natural such a thing would spark *some* interest, regardless of her social status."

"Do *you* fancy her, Roland?"

"Don't be absurd. When have I ever expressed interest in courtship?"

"You could have a secret life."

"I don't."

"Great. Is this conversation over now?"

"I'm just saying, perhaps you're a bit biased in your assessment of her. Besides," he continued, clearly far from done, "how do you know she isn't 'loyal to you' so that she can get close to the *royals*? She may be thinking that becoming part of the Royal Rescue Team is her ticket off the streets. The king and queen will be so pleased, they'll give her rewards beyond her wildest dreams."

"Isn't that what you've offered her anyway? We'll *'pay her well'* so she'll *'never want for anything.'* Besides, *you're* the one who taught me that no one does anything for free. So why do you care what her motives are?"

"Because you're trying to tell me that she *is* doing this for free, just for you, because she's nice. There's no such thing. She has motives. Are they in our favor or not? On the off chance your assessment of her is correct, hopefully the money is enough motivation when her desire to 'do a good deed' wears off."

The brush rustled to our right as Eva neared us.

"Think on it," Roland said. "After the rumors from your time in Narim, I need a real reason to trust her by tonight, or she's out."

"So, I was thinkin'," Eva said, "if we're doin' any more cookin' of our food, I'd like to volunteer today."

Roland and I turned to face her.

"That's very kind of you to offer, Miss Evangeline," Roland said.

Eva smiled, then shot me a wide-eyes look that pulled a laugh out of me before I could stop myself.

"What's so funny?" Roland asked.

"I have a feeling Eva's offer has less to do with kindness and more to do with wanting to eat something decent."

"What's wrong with my cooking?"

"I mean no offense, Roland." Eva smiled, but her eyes glinted with mischief. "I just don't think high society has prepared you well for cookin' your own meals, let alone doin' so in the woods."

"I know how to cook!"

"But when was the last time you actually did?"

"Last night!"

She glared at him and I laughed, suddenly interested in the real answer myself. "When was the last time *before* Harland usurped the throne?"

"I—" he paused. "It's been a number of years, I admit."

"I rest my case," Eva said. "In fact, how about I cook from here on out?"

"We can take turns," I offered.

She scoffed. "We will *not*. If Roland can barely cook, I'm not goin' anywhere near whatever *you* put together."

"Hurtful, Evangeline."

Roland crossed his arms. "She's right. Why do you think *I* haven't let you cook since we've been out here?"

"Mercy, no one has any kindness when it comes to the kitchen I see."

"Food is one of the few reliable delights in this world, Silas. I will not be robbed of it for the sake of either of your egos."

That was clear. But even Roland was chuckling slightly, and I hoped that meant I wouldn't have to work so hard to win him over at the end of the day.

31

I Teach a Noble How to Sew

Evangeline

By mid afternoon, I had grown tired of carrying my pack. I adjusted it on my shoulders for the hundredth time that day, clenching my jaw so as not to mumble my complaints about my aching muscles. If a couple of nobles could make this trip without whining, I certainly could. If someone had told me a few months ago that I'd be going on a walking tour of Wenterly with *nobles*, I never would have expected that I would be the weakest link.

"What's on your mind, Eva?"

Silas's question pulled me from my thoughts, and I realized I was smiling a bit at the absurdity of it all.

I dropped my grin. "I don't know if I should say."

"How come?"

"It might be offensive."

He laughed. "When has that ever stopped you before?"

I glared at him and tilted my head in Roland's direction.

"Fair enough. So just tell me."

I gave him one more wary glance before caving. "I was thinkin' about how I'm hardly in shape for a journey like this. I spend most of the work day sittin' and sewin'. But I still walk all over town, and had that stretch before we met that I was travelin' from city to city, but still, this is exhaustin'. And I'm a little surprised that you and Roland aren't any more tired than I am."

"Why would you expect us to be?"

"Because you're nobles! Don't you stay in your houses and parade around on horses? You have servants to go and fetch everythin' you could need. It's not like you're doin' manual labor."

"Offensive indeed, Eva." He laughed. "Though, I suppose that's *partially* true. But we're still active. Well, most of us. But a lot of us are trained in swordsmanship—I had daily drills. Plus, on days when we don't leave our houses, it's not like we aren't going anywhere. Our houses are enormous. Your entire house could probably fit in one room of many noble's homes."

"My house *was* one room."

"Oh." His face reddened slightly, and he glanced down at the road for a few seconds. "Well, that only emphasizes my point," he said, although his tone was almost apologetic.

I smiled to assure him not to pity me, and pulled at the straps on my pack again.

"We can take a break if you need one."

I shook my head. "Nuh-uh. I'm not about to give Roland the satisfaction that I'm not cut out for this. And time is of the utmost importance, is it not? I'll be fine. I'm not sufferin', I'm just not comfortable."

Silas laughed. "You sound like me on Throne Room days."

"What do you mean?"

"You know how—uh—that's not what they're officially called. Just what Alastair and I called them. It's Holding Court, where everyone comes in and complains to the king and queen. Sometimes it's about real issues, but most of the time it's petty feuds that they should have handled on their own."

"You're not amused by drama?"

He shrugged. "It's just politics. But yes, I admit I don't particularly enjoy it."

"Wait. Hold on. Are you tellin' me that you gave me a hard time about not carin' about politics, and all this time, you hate it yourself?"

"Just because I don't enjoy every aspect of my political duties, doesn't mean I hate politics. Politics is my *life*. I hadn't known anything different until these past few weeks. But yes, seeing people live their lives without worrying about what everyone else thinks about every little decision they make is quite appealing to me."

I kept forgetting how much the threads of the political and personal were tangled together in Silas's life. I couldn't imagine living that way.

"Would you ever give it up? Once the royals are back on the throne and your family is back together and all that?"

"What, like *Captain* Mothway did?" he spat.

"No, you don't have to commit *treason*. Just don't take your inheritance. Go live in the country and lead a simple life. Surely someone else can carry on for your family's name?"

Silas jaw twitched. "It doesn't work like that. I have a responsibility to carry out the things my parents have started. And my children will have to do the same. To stray from that *is* treason."

So the threads had been tangled for a long time, even before Silas. The parents passing down a knotted rope generation after generation. An old idiom came to mind, and I spoke it aloud, "Heavier is the crown than scales can weigh."

Silas nodded and recited the second half, "On poorer men, a crushing fate."

"I never liked that last bit."

"How come?"

"Well, just because a man is poor doesn't mean he lacks ability. You can have a lot of skill and be born on the wrong end of society."

"It's not about financial poverty, Eva. It's about being poor in spirit and convictions."

"Oh." I hefted my pack again. "I'm not sure a lot of people know that."

"That's probably true." Silas muttered. "There's a lot of misconceptions about what we really do. Even among the upper class. Everyone aspires to be one rung higher on the social ladder, but no one actually wants all the hidden responsibilities that come with it. Even a simple edict is layered with countless decisions. People might disagree with the edict and say they would never make a decision like that, but they don't know about the indirect influences that made it necessary to begin with."

I nodded. "I get that."

Silas gave me a glance, his eyebrow raised. "Do you?"

"Don't sound so surprised, you just said it's not about poor people. Unless you think me incapable, too?"

He raised his hands. "I'm trying to figure you out as much as you are me. Please, enlighten me."

I huffed, but couldn't keep from smiling anyway. "People would come into the shop all the time, and it was always the wealthier people who had never made clothin' before that put up the biggest fight about our completion time. They think we cut the fabric out and sew it together, and then it's done! Why's it goin' to take weeks? Why can't you make me an entire dress by the end of the day? The people who had done it themselves and knew the work it took were often surprised how quickly we completed things and with such high quality. Sometimes it takes an amateur to appreciate a professional."

"That sounds philosophical."

"It was just somethin' Master Gratsis would say." I frowned as I said his name. It was still strange to think about how quickly our relationship had turned.

"So what *does* making clothes entail?" Silas asked, pulling me back to the present.

"Oh, well, first you have to figure out the shape of the pieces. Most of what we made was rather simple, so we already had a basis for every project. Then there's the measurements. You have to adjust the measurements of the body to allow for the hems and stitchin'. It's called the seam allowance." I flipped the edge of my sleeve inside out to show Silas the seam. "So, if I measure around my arm and cut the fabric to that exact same measurement, it would be too small, because this extra bit in the seam wouldn't be accounted for. And usually there's a handful of pieces involved, which means multiple seams to account for, which isn't *that* difficult, but it *is* math."

"How can you do math if you can't read?"

"Because they're not the same thing."

"But don't you write out the calculations?"

"No, I do it in my head or use the abacus if I need to."

He frowned. "Is it just addition and subtraction you're doing?"

"Usually." I shrugged. "But not always."

"And you don't write any of it out? How did you learn?"

"I don't know. It's countin'. Master Gratsis would occasionally write things down for me if I needed to remember them." I shrugged.

Silas's brows furrowed as his confusion grew. "I feel like you may be smarter than me."

The notion caught me so off guard, I couldn't help but laugh. "Not a chance!"

Roland looked back at us. "What's going on back there?"

"Eva's telling me how to make a dress."

"Oh? Are you planning on wearing one soon?"

Silas rolled his eyes and turned back to me. "So, you do a lot of calculations to get the measurements right. Then you sew it all together?"

"Not yet. Once we calculate the size of the pieces, sometimes we have to order the fabric. It's dreadfully expensive, and so you have to buy as little as possible, but that means you also can't afford to make a mistake. If we weren't confident how something would come together, we'd practice with parchment sometimes..." I cut myself off, realizing I was getting too caught up in the details. "But yes, then you cut out the fabric and sew, although that's also more complicated than some people think."

"Why is that?"

"Depending on the fabric—" I stopped short to gauge his reactions. Was he *actually* interested in all this, or was he only humoring me?

"What? Is it too complicated for my stupid noble brain to understand?" He cracked a smile.

"No—I just—er." I had to look away from him before I could remember what I had been saying. "You can't just attach the pieces with a straight stitch, you also have to go around the edges of the fabric, to protect it from fraying' and fallin' apart. Here." I showed him the stitches on the seam in my sleeve. "It's the worst part of the whole thing, if you ask me, because it can make the project take twice as long, and no one even sees all that work you put into it. But it's necessary for the longevity of the fabric."

Silas flipped the edge of his own sleeve inside out and studied it for a moment. "Huh. I never noticed that before."

"That's exactly what I mean. No one cares about it. But it's necessary."

He nodded. "So, then the dress is done?"

"Sometimes. I should note that the order you sew the pieces together matters, of course. Like buildin' a house. You can't start with the roof. Everythin' fits together a certain way. But yes, once the pieces are put together, it might be done, or if it's for a wealthy lady, you have to add the trim and embroidery. Sometimes I got to weave the trims, but Master Gratsis always applied the finishin' details."

"Do you enjoy the work, though? Overall, I mean."

"Of course. It *is* rewardin' to see it all come together. And I definitely prefer it to farmin'."

"Maybe, when this is all over, my family could hire you. You could become the personal seamstress of Wenterly's finest."

"That's very kind, Silas, but most nobility don't want someone like me makin' their clothes. Even some of the wealthy in Welven who don't have any grand titles requested I not take part in their order. I'm not sure I have the skillset to dress *real* nobles. You haven't even seen anythin' I've made."

"Hopefully someday I will. What's your favorite thing to make?"

"My word, you were serious," Roland interrupted. "I cannot keep listening to this conversation. It's dreadfully boring."

"Then stop eavesdropping, Roland!" Silas snapped. "We're not talking to you."

32

Trust, Swords, and, Hopefully, Horses

Alastair

We veered off the road about an hour before sunset to find camp for the night. There was a town only about a mile ahead, but it was too dangerous to stay in a civilized area—especially now that word had spread about Eva and I escaping jail in Narim. Of course, the real reason for our arrest hadn't been given. An arrest notice for the prince that Harland already claimed was dead wouldn't bode well for him.

We found an area in the woods that offered enough space and coverage for us to sleep. Roland handed Eva a hatchet from his pack and told her to get firewood while he and I set up camp.

The moment she was out of earshot, Roland asked the question I'd been dreading all day. "So, can you convince me she's trustworthy?"

I sighed. "No."

Roland paused, the rock he was about to toss out of the way still in his hand. "No?"

"Any reason I give you—regardless of how good an argument—you'll find a reason to refute it. You've already decided you want to get rid of her simply because you're afraid that I can't handle having a woman around. So, instead of telling you why you should trust her, I'm going to tell you why you should trust *me*."

Roland finally tossed the rock. He folded his arms across his chest, giving me his full attention.

"You've known me since I was three, right? So in the last fifteen years, have I ever droned on about a woman?"

"Well ... no."

"Exactly, because I am quite aware that I will be marrying for the benefit of Wenterly, not for my own whims of affection. Besides that, I have far greater priorities than getting married right now. Even before all *this* happened,"—I gestured generally to our camp—"it wasn't a priority. We both know I'm not ready to take over my father's rule yet."

"Yes, I agree, but—and I can't believe I have to be the one to tell you this—the rational decision to not marry yet has very little control over your desire to be with someone."

"Then it's a good thing there isn't anyone I *desire* to be with."

Roland glared at me out of the corner of his eye as he moved all the rocks he gathered into a circle for our fire pit. "As long as you promise it stays that way—"

"I promise. There's nothing to worry about."

"Fine. But I'm holding you to that."

"As long as you don't keep bringing this up *every* time we're alone, go right ahead. You're my tutor. Not a chaperone."

"I couldn't agree more. So don't give me a reason to bring it up."

"I haven't!"

"You *married* her, Al."

"*Roland.*"

He raised his hands in surrender. "Alright, fine. But when your mother finds out, don't expect me to come to your defense."

"If things go my way, my mother will never find out."

Roland laughed—genuinely. He wasn't scoffing. He was actually, genuinely laughing.

"Why is that so funny?"

"When it comes to you, your mother knows everything."

"She does not."

Roland raised his eyebrows.

"Do you *tattle* on me?" I gasped. "How many of my misfortunes are you responsible for?"

Roland's smile was full of guilt.

"You *traitor*! All this time I've confided in you, you've been going and telling my *mom*?"

"Not *everything*."

Eva reappeared then, which abruptly ended our conversation, to my dismay.

"Well, you two seem to be in a better mood." She plopped down her armful of wood and brushed her hands off. "Is that enough for the night?"

"I'll get more," Roland offered. He took the hatchet back from Eva and, after passing her, gestured to her and I with his eyebrows raised. I couldn't tell if it was meant to be a warning or a see-how-I-am-trusting-you-right-now look.

It better have been the latter.

It was dusk now, so Eva and I hurried to get the fire started. Once it was burning nicely, I instructed Eva to pick out a stick.

She groaned. "I'm so tired, Silas. I just want to rest."

"You can rest when you're dead—which if you don't practice, might be a lot sooner than you think."

"*Fine.*" She picked up a stick and I walked her through a few drills before she stopped again. "Hold on, if we only have two swords, which obviously you and Roland are going to use, shouldn't I be learnin' how to use my dagger properly?"

"We can go over that, too. But all of Harland's soldiers will have swords. You don't want to try to stop a sword blade with a dagger if you can help it. The second a sword becomes available, it's yours."

"And we're confident it's the soldier's sword that will be available before it's my dagger?"

I shrugged. "Only if you practice."

She did not find that funny.

"Roland and I will help cover you," I added, but it didn't help convince her.

"Fightin' requires a lot of blind confidence."

I sighed. "Again, Eva."

"Fightin' requires a lot of—"

"No, the *drill* again."

She huffed, but lifted the stick to low stance as Roland returned. "Watch your elbows, Evangeline. You're a leech, not a chicken."

Eva tossed her stick away at that. "What's the use? I'm not going to learn enough in a week to do any good."

"Come on, Eva."

Roland eyed me. "She's right. Which is why"—he turned to her—"you aren't coming into the caves with us."

I gaped. "What? I thought you agreed to let her stay!"

"And that hasn't changed. Do you not remember our conversation from this morning? I said that she should get a doctor for the royals. While she does that, we will go and break them out."

"Oh. I didn't realize those events were simultaneous."

"Not that I think my presence at the prison would make much of a difference," Eva prefaced, "but are the two of you going to be enough? I mean, the prison is bound to have a whole slew of guards for three royals, and what if the three of them aren't well enough to get out on their own? What exactly *is* your plan?"

I gave Roland a look. *Should we tell her?*

"Let Silas and I worry about that, Evangeline. I should be getting more information on our journey, which will reveal more details of what we'll be facing at the caves."

"From whom?" I asked.

"My connections in Koyben."

I frowned. "And why haven't you told me who those are yet?"

He waved a hand. "It's not for you to worry about. You have enough weighing on your mind. This is one burden I can bear for you."

I crossed my arms. "I deserve to know as much as I can about what's going on."

"And you do."

"Roland." It was my turn not to let the issue drop.

"Fine."

He sat, and Eva and I wasted no time in joining him on the ground. It had been a long day.

"One of my contacts is a man named Graven Reynolds. He told me of a horse breeder in Bayben. It would be about eight miles out of our way, so sixteen to add the distance back to our road. But if we mention his name, we'll get a deal."

"That being said, it would still take nearly all of our money for three horses, and, again, it's out of the way. But the time it would save us in the long run may be worth it. I initially thought it wasn't, but the more I think about it, the more I doubt that original decision. Time is of the essence. So, I'm putting it out to you."

"Of course we do it!" I blurted. "Horses could cut our travel time in half! Besides, what else will we need the money for?"

"Food. Bribes. The doctor. A number of expenses could come up."

"But if we cut our travel time, that's less food we need to buy. Every day that goes by increases our risks. If we can shorten that time at all, we need to do so."

"Yes, but there's another thing. If I remember correctly, Evangeline has never ridden before."

"That's true," she confirmed.

"We'll be trotting, not maneuvering around a battlefield. She'll be fine." I turned to her and reiterated, "You'll be fine. It's not that difficult."

"Then I agree, the horses would be worth it," she said.

"Alright, it's settled, then. There's only one more thing."

"What?"

"Evangeline has to get them by herself."

I cocked my head. "And why is that?"

"Because I'm not letting you go into town. Every officer in the kingdom is on high alert for you."

"Are you forgetting that she's *also* wanted by all of Harland's men?"

"All Harland's men have on her is a brief written description. They won't recognize her as they will you. She's lived a life of ambiguity up until now."

"Okay, so I'll wait while you and Eva go together. You can't send one person to fetch three horses."

Eva glared at me at the suggestion, but Roland was the one to outright refuse it.

"Absolutely not. The last time I let you out of my sight, you were missing for a *week*, and before you ask why I don't go myself, I'll remind you of the countless inane shenanigans you two got involved in during that same week. I'm sure I haven't heard the half of them."

"But—"

"I'm fine goin' alone," Eva interjected. "I know how to barter. I've been doin' it all my life. Besides, I'd love the chance to do somethin' useful for the group."

"Hear that, Silas? Eva would love to do something useful for the group."

The way he said it suggested that letting Eva go alone wasn't necessarily for safety so much as it was a test for me. Did *I* trust her enough to let her wander off with all our money?

"I can keep my hair fully covered when I go," Eva added. "That tends to be my most definin' feature."

I wanted to push back further, but if sending Eva out meant Roland would finally start trusting her, or at least start trusting me about her, then it was worthwhile. And if Eva was willing to do it, what reason did I have to stop her?

"Fine. We'll go to Bayben."

33

What Does It Take for a Girl to Get a Decent Horse These Days?

Evangeline

Roland took first watch, I took second, and Silas third. It wasn't as bad as Silas made it out to be. A bit annoying, but I wasn't any more tired when morning came than I was the day before. Although sleeping on an actual bedroll definitely improved the experience for me.

Silas woke us up for breakfast, and then we were off again, headed for Bayben.

The day passed similarly to yesterday, with Silas bouncing between conversations with Roland and with me. Though Roland tolerated me well enough—for a noble, anyway—we, unsurprisingly, had few common interests.

Fortunately, my pack didn't bother me as much as it did yesterday. It seemed I was already acclimating to life on the road.

As we had neared Bayben, Roland all but threatened to skin me alive if I ran off with all their money, and I informed him that if I didn't return, I hoped they would be willing to rescue me from another kidnapping, because that would be the only reason I wouldn't come back. Silas promised he would return the favor and break me out of jail, and then they both lectured me about horse qualities for the better part of an hour. Apparently that were *quite* a lot of things I should look for, to know I wasn't being lied to about the value of the animal.

Unfortunately, as it turned out, the man at the stables wasn't much of a liar at all. Instead, it was his honesty that nearly sent me over the edge.

"I have it on good authority from Graven Reynolds that you can cut me a deal," I repeated. "Three horses for three gold."

"An' I don't know a Graven Reynolds!" The man's accent was thick, his words all pinched up in the front of his mouth. It sounded very Glastorian, which was slightly concerning. What if he knew Harland? What if he was a spy?

No, that was a foolish thought. That would be like me traveling to Eliston, and someone assuming I had enough connections to report to King Esmond. Besides, a spy would be smart enough to change his accent.

I huffed and opened the money bag, still surprised at how much Roland and Silas had been carrying around. They said they sold their horses for quite a large amount of money. But then they made a few bribes and bought enough traveling supplies to stock a household. The coins in the pouch equated about four gold, maybe a few silver over that. I couldn't believe there was still that much leftover. But it meant I certainly couldn't offer the stablehand much more than I already was.

"Well, then, how much do you want for three horses?"

"Depends on the quali'y you're looking fer."

"The best you have."

"Twen'y-four gold fer three of them."

I nearly choked. "That's absurd!"

"That's the price."

I stared him down as best I could. "Let me speak to the owner of the stable."

"That's me today. Owner's gone out of town fer a bit."

"Well, the owner knows Graven Reynolds! And he'll be very upset that you didn't honor his deal."

"You don't know the owner at all! If you're a lying lit'le brat, Master'll have my head. I ain't risking thir'y gold an' three horses on the likes of you."

Unfortunately, I could understand the man's plight. I probably wouldn't risk that much on me either.

My nobles would have to lower their standards.

"What's the price of the worst horse you got?"

"Worst one?" The man looked across the stalls. "Two silver. He's old. Prob'ly make it through harvest and then pass on."

"And the worst one that isn't halfway through death's door?"

"Two gold."

Mercy. Roland's man really was getting us a deal. Or he *would* be, had the deal been any good. "When does the owner return?"

"Five days."

"Hang the moon," I muttered. It was plain as day that Roland sent me to get these horses to test me. I doubted he would accept difficulty with the stablehand as a valid excuse for failure.

To my surprise, the man had no real reaction to my word choice other than, "Business is business, ma'am."

"Yes, it is." I steeled myself. "And *my* business says I'm not to go back empty-handed." I stepped forward, invading the man's personal space. "Which of these animals is worth two gold?"

He gestured to a stall. "Starboard or Port."

"Show them to me."

The man eyed me warily, but led me over to the pair. I eyed the horses, but couldn't recall a single thing I was supposed to be looking for. They looked like horses. They'd do. They had to.

"I'll take these. Do you have another of similar quality?"

"Not unless you got six gold for the lot."

"How about this,"—I withdrew my dagger—"you give me these two horses and their saddles for three gold, and you don't suffer any harm by my hand."

The man laughed. "An' I'll suffer plenty from Master to make up fer it. You're thinking I'm threatened by a lit'le girl?"

"I have also spent considerable time answerin' to a Master. So, here's my full and final proposal." I grabbed the man's collar and shoved him against the stall gate, only able to do so because I caught him off guard. I placed my dagger under his chin and hoped he wouldn't call my bluff. "You tell your master that three men showed up and threatened you, askin' for your finest horses. You were scared, but weren't about to give away your master's best, so you lied and told them to take Starboard and Port, and one more. Two of the men gathered and saddled the horses, while the third continued to threaten your life should you intervene. You get to tell your master you saved him a greater financial loss, *and* you get to pocket my three gold, no one the wiser."

"You telling me to lie to the man who employs me?"

"Business is business. Your master can't be all that great."

The man had the audacity to mull it over. "Eh, I don't know…"

I pressed the flat of the blade a little harder against his skin. "Final. Offer."

"I'll give you Port an' Starboard, saddled. Not a third."

My jaw dropped. I had a knife to his throat and he was *still* making demands?

"I need a third!"

"Final. Offer." The man stared me down. He was calling my bluff.

"Fine." I sheathed the dagger. It was my fault for making that my first offer, anyway. "It's a deal."

I walked the horses along the edge of town, cursing myself as I made my way back to Roland and Silas.

They stood when they saw me.

"Are you going back for the third?" Roland asked.

I tried not to glare at him. "No."

"Is… someone else bringing it?" Silas asked.

"There isn't another one."

Roland grunted. "Even without an education, Evangeline, I trusted you knew three was one more than two."

"Yes, Evangeline's an idiot," I spat. "I'll have you know that whatever 'good word' your man gave you was absolutely worthless. The owner is out of town for the next few days, and the stablehand I had to deal with didn't know anythin' about a Graven Reynolds, nor did he find his life more valuable than a few horses, it seems! It's a miracle I walked out of there with these two. So you're welcome. You two can continue on your way, and I'll figure out my next plan."

I handed Silas the reins.

"You can't leave!" Silas sputtered. "We can figure something out."

"You two can figure out whatever you want. I just haggled like my life depended on it, because I'm pretty sure at least one of you would have killed me if I came back with nothing. Now if you'll excuse me, I need a moment."

Silas handed the reins off to Roland and followed after me. "What exactly happened with the stablehand?"

I scowled. Didn't I tell him I wanted to be alone? He of all people should have understood needing to think in peace.

"I had to threaten to kill the man *and* bribe him to lie to his master in order to get these."

Silas blinked, failing to hide a smile.

"What's so funny about that?" I snapped.

"In the time I've known you, you've lied dozens of times and threatened to kill me at least twice. I'm not sure why you're acting as though these grievances are new for you."

"She *what*?" Roland asked, a few feet behind us.

I ignored him. "That stablehand was an innocent man doin' his job!"

"So what was I?" Silas asked.

"An idiot!" I pushed past him. "Now leave me alone for *at least* ten minutes, or I'll threaten your life again, noble."

I stalked into the brush, hot tears already stinging my eyes. Guilt and shame squeezed my lungs, suffocating me.

If I couldn't be wanted, the best I could be was useful. I'd learned that long ago.

But if I failed to be useful? What was left for me to be then?

34

I'm Surrounded by Traitors

Alastair

"Are you *serious*? The girl tried to kill you, and you still brought her back with you?"

I turned back to Roland, regretting having made that point for a multitude of reasons. "The circumstances made her actions understandable."

Apparently, that was not a good excuse for Roland. "Saddle up. We're leaving her as soon as possible."

"I can't abandon her!"

He glared at me. "Why not?"

"Because she didn't abandon me when she had the chance."

"And for that we are grateful. But how many chances are you going to give her?"

Roland started packing our bags onto the saddles, but I didn't budge.

"I'm not leaving her behind."

Roland threw out his hands. "If she came along, we still only have two horses, and no more money. How do you propose rectifying the situation?"

I sighed and looked over the two horses. The saddle on the gray one caught my eye. It was an Eylian saddle, named after the northern kingdom, and designed to fit two riders. *Fate's mercy*. What were the odds of that?

"With that." I indicated the saddle. "I'm the one who wants her along, so you can have your own horse, and Eva and I will share the other."

He gaped. "I will not allow it. It's indecent."

"Well, I know *you're* not willing to ride with her. And even if you were, I'm pretty sure *she'll* abandon us if that's her only option."

"But you think she'd be willing to ride with you? After the way she just yelled at you?"

I shrugged. When we first met, Eva's yelling at me was part of the reason I found her company worth-while. She was honest, although she wasn't particularly nice about it. I doubted this instance meant the end of the strange friendship we'd formed. But there was no chance that Roland would understand that.

"We'll ask her and see. But I think it's the best option."

Roland crossed his arms and scowled. "I'm still concerned about this 'threatening your life' business."

"That was different—from before she got to know me! We have an understanding now."

His glare only intensified. "I stand by my point that I don't think you two should be riding together. You and I—"

"*You and I* could ride together? Yes, of course, Roland! The passerby won't question that at all! We'll *really* blend in on the road that way."

"If you could restrain your attitude for a moment, I was going to say that you and I made an agreement about your conduct on this trip. And riding with a woman you are not married to is highly improper. How do you think your future betrothed will feel about you riding with another woman, and a leech at that?"

"Stars, Roland, I didn't realize my future betrothed was keeping record of my moral failings. In that case, I think it will hardly matter to her that Eva and I rode a horse together, considering she would have already noted that I crawled into a barrel with her back in Narim." Never mind that I'd also kissed her at our pirate wedding. *Stars above.* Maybe I was a scoundrel, after all.

Roland's jaw ticked. "I beg your pardon?"

I had forgotten I had changed that detail when I recounted our barrel escape to him. "Well, keep begging, Roland. It seems only my future betrothed can grant pardons, and according to you, she's stingy about it."

"Once again, Al, lose the attitude."

"First, don't use my name. Eva could come back any moment. Second, *no*. You're being so unfair! I get that you're my tutor, but this isn't one of your lessons. Ever since I've come back to you, you haven't trusted me with one thing! Why are you being so difficult all of a sudden?"

He inhaled sharply. "I'm dealing with a *lot* right now, *Silas*—"

"And I'm not?"

"There are things in motion that you know nothing about!" Roland pinched the bridge of his nose and closed his eyes, unable to even look at me as he continued talking. "After you disappeared in Koyben, I was afraid the worst had happened. I needed to know if Harland's men had found you, so I asked around. I had no choice in the matter! I had to let Harland's men know who I was—make them think I was on their side—in order to find out if they knew anything about you!"

It was a punch to the gut. "You pledged loyalty to Harland?"

"Just words! You know where my loyalties lie."

"The pledge is legally binding!"

"Like a *wedding ceremony* is legally binding?"

Another punch. I had to breathe a moment.

"This contact who recommended the horse breeder, is *he* loyal to Harland? Are they *tracking* us?"

He shook his head. "That was a different contact. Unaffiliated with Harland."

"How do you know?"

Roland began to speak, but then abruptly closed his mouth.

"How do you *know*, Roland?"

"I can't prove another man's loyalties."

"Can you prove yours?" I yelled. All this time spent begging me to prove Eva was trustworthy, and he wanted to tell *me* he couldn't prove another man's loyalties?

"Seriously? Pretending to support Harland has proved to be worth more than I could have asked for. They gave me the map to the prison so that I could take you there if I found you. They think I'm about to betray you, and because of that, we'll be able to walk right into that prison. All we have to worry about is walking out."

"So they *are* tracking us. They know we're going to save the king and queen. Because *you're* updating them. That's worse! Don't you understand how that's worse? Are you out of your mind?"

"No. *They* think that *you* think we're going to save the royals. They aren't preparing for a prison break. They're preparing to make room for another prisoner."

"That does not make me feel better, Roland!" I pulled my hand down my face. "And why didn't you tell me this right away? You've been giving me all these lectures about *my* poor decisions and questioning my judgments, when all the while, *you've* been the one betraying me!"

"I have been *lying* to Harland's men in order to save your life and get us to the caves so we can save the royals' lives. This has been for our benefit—"

"You're such a hypocrite—"

"He's right, Silas."

We both jumped at the sound of Eva's voice.

"Roland's right," she continued. "This could prove to be good for us. Remember Officer Reeves? We only escaped from Narim's officers because he's faking loyalty to their cause. There's no reason Roland can't do the same."

"Exactly, thank you, Evangeline." He nodded to her before fixing me with a glare. "And, might I add, I actually know you, Silas, which should allow you *more* confidence in me to have your best interests at heart."

I groaned. They both made valid points. "Okay, *fine*. But you still should have told me."

"Well, don't hold a grudge, or I'll ask you what this barrel business in Narim is all about."

I cleared my throat. "Water under the bridge. Eva, if you still want to come with, you and I can ride together and—"

"We never agreed on that," Roland interrupted.

"We don't need to. I'm deciding it."

"You forget yourself, *Silas*."

"No, you forgot *yourself*, Roland. My word is superior over yours, is it not?"

He gasped. Actually gasped. Like a lady at Court. "You are walking a *fine* line with me."

"And you've already crossed it!"

He and I stared at each other a moment, but, to my surprise, Roland refused to continue the argument. "Let's just pack up and go."

The air was thick with tension as we readied for travel. We decided that Roland's horse would carry most of our packs, to help distribute the weight. Not that a pack weighed near as much as Eva or I, but it was the thought that counted, I supposed.

"What are the horses' names?" I asked after a few minutes, hoping to lighten the mood.

"Starboard and Port."

I glanced at Eva to see if she was joking, but her back was to me. "Are you serious?"

"I know." Eva half-supressed a laugh, then lifted a pack to her shoulder and walked it over to the horse we'd be riding together. "You and I seem to be destined for boat travel."

"Those are terrible names for horses. They should have grand names, for a grand animal."

She shrugged. "Maybe the breeder thinks boats are grand."

I was surprised how much calmer she was now than she had been a few minutes ago. Perhaps my fight with Roland had helped put things in perspective for her. These were dire times; her drastic measures were excusable. That was how I'd lessened the guilt of my actions over the last few weeks, anyway.

Roland straightened from organizing his things. "Speaking of boats, Eva, how did you end up at the pirate camp that day?"

She shrugged. "It was an accident."

I laughed before I could stop myself. "It definitely was not."

She scowled. "It's irrelevant now."

"Is it?" Roland glared at her the way he looked at me whenever I tried to derail his lessons.

"Okay, fine. But let the record show that, since then, I have saved Silas's life at the risk of mine, and given up my foreseeable future for the sake of your cause."

We nodded, and she took a deep breath. "I was goin' to ask to join them."

"*What?*" I had thought she intended to steal from them. Given her history with pirates and the way she talked about her mother, how could she even *consider* becoming—

"You're a traitor to the throne!" Roland cried.

"Says the man who *actually* pledged loyalty to Harland!" she threw back at him. "Technically, I only *planned* on bein' a traitor to the throne. I didn't actually become one. *And* I planned it under Harland's rule—not the Cathmoores'. So I didn't betray them, I betrayed Harland, and therefore I believe that shows I'm quite loyal to the original crown."

Yes, we were all busy justifying our crimes.

"That last part is definitely false, Eva, because in our first few days together, you told me *many* times that you didn't care a whit who was on the throne."

"True," she said slowly, "but time and circumstance have changed my opinion."

"That may be, but you still can't use it to defend yourself, since it isn't the view you held at the time."

"Either way, it's not like my betrayal was personal to the Cathmoores! Because you just said that *I* said that I didn't care a whit who was on the throne."

I shook my head. She had wits beyond many nobles I'd heard in Court. An insufferable trait. And yet, admirable.

"Fair enough. So why were you going to become a pirate?"

She crossed her arms, her hazel eyes glinting. "I can't be employed without a reference, and I can't be a wife with my lineage. The only thing left I could be was a criminal, and from what I'd gathered, pirates have the most fun."

Mercy, and she thought my ideas were bad?

Roland spoke up before I could. "You know what pirates *do* to women, don't you?"

She fixed him with that dead-pan glare of hers. "I'm the *result* of what pirates do to women, so, yes, Roland, I'm quite familiar."

Roland took a step back, the horror on his face making me realize that he wasn't aware of Eva's full lineage. He sputtered a moment, then turned to me. "Did you know about this?"

"Yes. She told me right away, actually."

"And you didn't think it was important to tell *me* that not only is she a leech, but pirate *scum*!"

"You entitled—" Eva started, but I jumped between her and Roland

"Everyone, calm down! We're all a team here. Roland, Eva is correct in that you have very little room to accuse her of treachery right now, when you didn't tell me that you *literally* pledged allegiance to Harland." I quickly turned my head to address Eva before she could gloat. "Eva, that does not mean I'm particularly thrilled about your news. However, you have proven your loyalty since, so I still trust you." I continued to turn my head from one to the other. "Just as I'm deciding to still trust you, Roland. Eva, you get to stay, because Roland gets to stay. You both get to mind your manners, and the plan continues as usual. End of discussion."

Roland clenched his jaw so forcefully, it was a wonder he didn't crack his teeth. He balled his hands into fists a few times, as though he was deciding which one of us he wanted to hit more. He finally pointed a finger at Eva, though his eyes were locked on me. "It was one thing to allow a leech on this adventure, but a girl with piracy in her blood is bound to betray us! What would your parents say about this?"

"I don't know, Roland, but you can tell my mother all about it and find out for yourself when you're reunited."

He turned and stalked away, and I couldn't help but sigh. This trip could not be over soon enough.

"I'm very confused about your relationship with Roland," Eva said.

"Honestly, so am I." I sighed. "He wasn't like this before Harland. I mean, he was difficult at times, but not … so reactive." Perhaps the stress of all this was getting to him, too.

"What do you think has him the most upset right now? You not trustin' him, or me still bein' here?"

"I imagine a combination of both."

"Because you're choosin' me over him?"

"I am not picking sides between you two."

She raised her eyebrows. "I'm pretty sure you already have."

"What makes you think that?"

"Everythin' you said in the last five minutes. Gettin' mad at Roland for his treachery, but fairly easily dismissin' mine."

"Those were different situations. The fact that he and I have known each other so long—"

"Means that you should trust him easier than you trust me. But you don't."

"I—" I wanted to deny it, but realized she might be right. "Do you think he interpreted it that way?"

"Based on the way he left? Absolutely."

I groaned. "I'll go talk to him when he's cooled off."

She bit her lip. "Maybe I should talk to him."

"I don't think that's a good idea."

"I appreciate the concern, but if Roland and I are going to last the rest of this adventure together, I probably should address some things with him anyway."

I nodded. "Alright. But watch your tongue. He won't appreciate your candor the way I do."

"We'll see."

She's impossible.

"If it doesn't go well, don't let him run you off. I like having you here. I know I say the wrong things sometimes. A *lot* of the time. But—"

"Don't get all emotional, Silas. I'm used to people speakin' harshly to me. At least you only intend to hurt my feelin's half the time."

"If I was the worst of your traveling companions, I might accept that answer a bit easier. But Roland is worse than I am."

She nodded. "He's the most arrogant person I've met. Although I've always imagined much of the upper class acts the same way." She took a deep breath. "But, if you really mean what you said, about likin' havin' me here—"

"I do."

She swallowed. "Then you're also the nicest person I've ever met. And I'm not ready to lose that quite yet."

It was as if a knife stabbed me right in the heart. After all the fights we'd been in, *I* was the nicest person she'd met? She deserved so much better than that.

"Good," was all I said. It was all I could say.

She nodded and started walking in the direction Roland had disappeared. But after only a few steps, she stopped and turned around. "You're certain we can't ditch him?"

"*Eva!*"

"Sorry! It was just a joke."

I crossed my arms. I would not pick her over Roland. I was choosing them both. That was that.

She walked into the trees, muttering away. I couldn't hear what she was saying, but her voice echoed in my head nonetheless.

You're the nicest person I've ever met.

Surely she wasn't serious?

At least you only intend to hurt my feelin's half the time.

Was that what the standard really was for her? Not whether someone offended her or not, but if they did so *intentionally*? Mercy, our lives were worlds apart.

Here I'd been finding relief that she could be so honest with me, that she was unconcerned about how I might reprimand her for speaking to a superior with such gall. I thought I had been returning the favor.

But she'd been hearing enough harsh words for a lifetime. Perhaps the best way to appreciate Evangeline was to be kind. I had to laugh at the realization, so simple and obvious, yet hitting me with the overwhelming clarity of divine revelation. How could it possibly have taken me so long to reach that conclusion?

Perhaps I really was an idiot.

35

Roland Is Such a Noble

Evangeline

Roland started speaking before he even turned around to see me approach. "I don't want to hear anymore from y—" He stopped short, narrowing his eyes. "I thought you were Silas."

"He wanted to speak with you, but I'd rather fight my own battles."

"Is that so?"

I crossed my arms and decided to get right to the point. "I don't know what kind of relationship you have with Silas, or how it's changed since you've been on the run, but I know that he trusts you. He would not stop talking about how he had to get back to you. So, I assume, you can't be ... like *this* all the time. You hate me, right? And so, by association, you're mad at him for lettin' me join you."

He didn't respond. Just stared at me. Which I took as confirmation of my theory.

"You don't like me because I'm a leech, and that of a pirate. Is that the *only* reason you dislike me, or is there somethin' actually in my control that bothers you?"

I waited a good while for Roland to respond, but he still didn't say a word.

"My apologies, was that too direct for someone of your status? Would you rather I danced around the issue over dinner?"

That finally goaded him into speaking. "Do you know your father? Have you had contact with him?"

"I never knew the man! Neither did my mother! I assure you, there is nothin' of his morality that I carry with me."

"Your only association with pirates is from when you were captured with Silas? Truthfully?"

"I swear."

He slowly exhaled, his eyes on the ground.

"Are we good here, then?"

He snapped his head up, and I realized we were still far from good. "My problem with you, is that you are treating us as though we are equals, but we are not. For the safety of our mission, safety from *you*, I can't tell you how wide the chasm is between us, but I assure you, at the end of this, you will find yourself falling."

I rolled my eyes. "I *know* you're nobles. I'm aware of the gap. And I would have minded it, had Silas not decided to treat *me* as an equal. Do you know how many people have ever apologized to me? That's a kindness I don't get, even from those of lower class. I assure you, despite my informality, I have nothin' but respect for him. It's because I respect him that I've tolerated *you* this long. He believes you're a good man, though right now I can hardly see why."

He scoffed. "What authority do you have to judge me?"

"I believe I'm posin' the same question to you." I walked around Roland. "You know why I've always hated the upper class? Because they are all hypocrites. I'm condemned because of my parents' status, but you are practically a god because of yours. Tell me, how did you choose the people who would conceive you? When did you weave centuries of family lines together so that you could be born into the perfect family? Or does spittin' in the faces of people poorer than you purify your blood?"

"How *dare* you speak to me this way—"

"And yet, you let me finish." I planted myself in front of Roland and looked him straight in the eyes. "You see, somethin' I've learned, Roland, is that people crave honesty. Yet the higher one climbs the societal ladder, the less there is to find. Because people get nervous about fallin' when they get so high up. You speak of a chasm I'll fall into if I don't mind my status, but here's the secret: I can't fall any lower. And because of that, I have the mighty privilege of bein' able to say what everyone else only wishes they could. You aren't better than me, Roland. You've just been a little luckier."

"My life has nothing to do with luck."

"Fate smiles on those it wills. From where I'm standin', you didn't do a thing to earn your place in the world. Fate wove you here. And Fate's woven me here too. Nothin' you do can change that. Get over yourself."

"A lesser man would strike you for speaking to him in such a way."

"Oh? Well, aren't I fortunate to be in such noble company, then?"

"Did you come over here to apologize, or to dig your grave?" Rage flickered in his eyes, but just as quickly as I saw the change in his expression, it was gone.

I took a step back for good measure. "Neither. I came over here to find out what your problem is with me."

"And I've told you. So, is this delightful conversation over?"

"No. I want to know why Silas likes you. Why he trusts you. There has to be somethin' that makes you a good man—besides having the self-control not to hit a woman."

"I don't have to justify myself to the likes of you! I can't fathom why Silas thinks you're worth the time of day with a mouth like that. You are a liability to our mission, and I'm growing more concerned about his judgment with each new detail of your life."

"Yes, I've felt the same concern for you."

"Are you implying that *I* would betray him? When I'm out here risking life and limb with an insufferable brat?"

"Again, I could say the same." I was going to strain my eyes with all the eye-rolling this conversation deserved. "But, no, I don't think you would betray him. However, you are in contact with an awful lot of *liabilities,* these days. I know you're usin' Harland's men for our benefit, but I will remind you that the only thing you can trust a traitor to do, is betray you."

He stared at me, and I could practically see the wheels turning in his mind. He clenched his jaw, relaxed, clenched it again. Suddenly, his expression softened, though the edge in his voice remained. "Not to worry, Evangeline. I keep a much more effective guard on my tongue than you do. So, I thank you for the insights you've provided today. I hope to hear far less of them in the future."

"If you stop yellin' at me for simply existin', you just might."

"Very well." He extended a hand to me. "Do you agree to a truce?"

I took a step forward, but didn't extend my hand yet. "I reserve the right to my own opinions about you, until proven otherwise. But yes, for the sake of Silas, I will agree to your truce and keep those opinions to myself."

"Then I am entitled to the same terms."

"That only seems fair." I gave him my hand and we shook.

I was genuinely surprised he didn't try to break my fingers in his grip. Perhaps he did have a better guard on himself than I did.

Roland and I walked back to the camp in silence.

Silas stood and looked from Roland to me. When neither of us said anything, he finally asked, "So, how did it go?"

I crossed to my pack, pretending I had to sort through my things. "Roland didn't strike me."

"That's..." He looked back over at Roland. "That's what happened? You *didn't* hit a woman?"

"Of course. I would never hit a woman." Roland said, quite matter-of-fact, while checking the saddle on his horse.

"So, that's where the bar's at for you two? The floor? I mean honestly, refraining from violence is the bare minimum."

"Yes," Roland and I said in unison. Which was annoying.

"But we've also agreed to a truce in terms of verbal attacks," I added.

Silas sighed loudly. "Well, at least that's a start." He picked up his pack. "And you'd better add to the terms of this truce that you won't speak ill of each other to me. I'm not taking sides in this. You *both* should be treating each other with respect. The three of us are a team. We're all working for the same thing. Understood?"

"Yes," Roland and I said in unison again.

I glared at him. "On that heart-warmin' note, let's stop wastin' daylight and get goin'."

They nodded in agreement and followed my lead in picking up the last of our packs.

"So, which is Starboard and which is Port?" Silas asked.

"Oh, er..." I looked from one horse to the other. "I don't actually know."

36

I Lower My Expectations That Everyone Will Get Along

Alastair

By evening, we had decided that the gray horse Eva and I rode was Port, and the black one was Starboard. Those were the names they seemed to respond to most, anyway. But even so, it was a bit hit or miss.

Not the best horses, but Eva did her best—or worst, considering she had threatened to kill the stablehand.

Regardless, it was still faster travel than it would have been on foot. So, at least there was that.

Riding with Eva was about what I expected. A little uncertainty at first with how she would straddle the horse in her dress. A little awkward exchange as we decided where to put our hands (I was strictly to hold the reins). And then as we settled into the movement of the horse's gait, we were fine.

Roland wasn't. He shot us glares every few minutes. But he and Eva managed to hold their peace.

What more could I ask for?

Well, a lot actually. A third horse for starters. But things could be worse, so I tried to be grateful.

We passed few others on the road. As the sun began to set and cast the world in golden light, we decided to find a place to camp.

We ate quietly. Although the tension from earlier this afternoon had eased, I was nervous one wrong comment might bring it back. It seemed the others felt the same.

I had considered continuing Eva's sword training, but after remembering how upset she had been after her run-in with the stablehand, I thought better of it. I'd only train her if she brought it up.

She didn't.

Roland confirmed our watch schedule, and then we called it a night. I hoped the morning would bring a new mood with it.

After breakfast, I helped Eva on Port, and then went to my pack on Roland's horse. I took out the book Roland had made fun of me for packing in a time of crisis. In my defense, it was right next to me at the time we fled the palace, and I didn't intentionally grab it. But I was glad I had. The thought of Harland having my *entire* library at his disposal did not sit well with me. At least this was one book I could ensure the safety of.

And hopefully, it was about to prove more beneficial that I ever would have expected.

"Hold this a second." I handed Eva the book while I situated myself on the saddle.

"This is beautiful."

"Thank you, I bound it myself."

She turned to look up at me. "Are you serious? You *actually* know how to bind books?"

"Everyone needs a hobby."

Roland mounted his horse, and we set off down the road.

"I thought nobles went huntin' as a hobby. Or, I don't know, somethin' else that most people do for survival, and they do for fun just to rub it in all our faces."

"Hmm, that doesn't sound like my idea of fun."

"But book-bindin' is?"

"As I've mentioned, I quite enjoy reading philosophy. And practicing my craft is a good excuse to expand my library."

"So, what book is this?"

"Brigid. *The Meaning of Shadows.*"

"Sounds poetic."

"I find most philosophy is."

"Are you goin' to read while we ride?"

"No, I'm going to teach *you* to read."

"Seriously?" Roland chimed in. "You're going to teach the girl to read and you're starting her with the densest book in your collection?"

"Well, if you haven't noticed, my options are somewhat limited at the moment. And besides, we aren't reading words yet, just learning the alphabet."

"And what happens when you get to one of the scarce letters? Does Brigid use the letter 'x' very often?"

One of my favorite quotes surfaced in a matter of seconds. "*The opportunity alone is enough to pour excitement into the heart of the adventurer,*" I recited. "Section Three. I have it underlined."

Roland scoffed. "Of course you do."

"If you have a problem with my teaching methods, you can take over."

"No, I'm sure you'll be sufficient."

"He better be. I'd rather stay illiterate than learn from you, Roland."

"Eva," I said. "He's a prodigy."

"Roland? A prodigy? In what? Being a—"

"He graduated from Iridescence at fifteen years old," I informed her.

Eva hummed a moment. "Remind me how old the average graduate is?"

"Twenty," Roland replied.

"Then what are you doin' *here*? Shouldn't you be off researchin' or inventin' somethin'?"

"I did for a few years, and then I was asked to be the royal tutor, though I'm afraid most of my brilliance has been lost on Alastair."

I cleared my throat. Roland's pride was going to end up giving us away.

"Oh." She was quiet a moment. "Then how do you and Silas know each other?"

"I ... taught both of them. Occasionally. Silas's family is quite close with the Cathmoores, and with them both only having one child nearly the same age, there was no harm in them spending some time together in the classroom."

"Except that it harmed our ability to learn anything."

"Yes, troublemakers anytime mathematics was brought up. This one wanted to talk philosophy and history all the time."

I huffed. "I think they're very valuable."

"I didn't say they weren't. But there are other valuable subjects that demand attention as well."

"Oh," Eva spoke up again, "this explains *so* much about the weird relationship between you two."

Roland and I glanced at each other.

"Weird?" I repeated.

"Absolutely. You both have been fightin' for authority this whole trip. In your eyes, Roland's a glorified servant, and in Roland's eyes, he's the mature, wise mentor who's too good for everybody."

"Roland, I'd like the record to show that I have never in my life referred to you as a 'glorified servant.' Not even in thought."

He grunted. "You better not have."

"Regardless," Eva said. "You get my point."

Roland glared at me.

But I did understand her point, so all I could do was shrug and hope it was enough to keep the peace.

37

Maybe Nobles Aren't So Bad

Evangeline

The book was fascinating, and not just because it was the first real book I'd had the privilege of rummaging through. It was full of Silas's markings and notes. Although I couldn't tell what any of it said, it was clear this book meant a lot to him.

Silas showed me what each letter of the alphabet looked like in his book, then said we would start by focusing on the letters called "vowels" because they were the most commonly used.

"This is an 'E.' It makes an *ee* sound. It's the first letter of your name. *Eva*. Do you hear it?"

"Yes."

"Sometimes, it's silent. Like at the end of your full name. But we won't worry about that yet."

I thought about my full name. "What do you mean, it's silent? At the end, there's an *ee* sound too."

He muttered my name, testing it out himself. "Er, yes. The sound is there. But it's the letter 'I' that makes the sound, not an 'E'. But your name ends with the letters 'I,' 'N,' 'E.' The 'N' is the last sound, and the 'E' is silent." He said my name again, slowly, as though that was going to help anything he said make sense.

"So, there are letters that don't make sound sometimes. And multiple letters that make the same sound?"

"Yes, sometimes. But it's not as confusing as it sounds."

I shrugged. "If you say so."

He pointed to another letter in the book. "This is 'A,' which is also used quite frequently. This is the first letter and last letter in Queen

Adeena's name. And the first in 'Alastair.' You also have one at the end of 'Eva.'"

"So it's..." I muttered the names, trying to separate the sounds. "I want to say it's an *uh* sound, but the first bit of 'Alastair' isn't quite right."

"Um." He paused, then muttered *mercy* under his breath. "Yes. It makes more than one sound. *Uh* like in your and Queen Adeena's names. And *a* like in Alastair. There's a lot of 'A's in Alastair actually."

"So, you're telling me that sometimes letters don't make a sound. Sometimes they do. Sometimes different letters have the same sound. *And* sometimes one letter makes more than one sound?"

"Yes." He grimaced. "Again, it's not as confusing as it sounds."

I sighed. "Do you have any easier letters we can start with?"

"Sure." He pointed to another spot on the page. "This is an 'S.' Like in the beginning and end of Silas. It always makes a *sss* sound. Like a snake's hiss."

"*Sure* it does, Silas," Roland drawled.

"Hang the moon," he groaned. "How did I ever learn how to read?"

"You had a good teacher," Roland gloated. "And you were four. You're teaching her as though she's an adult, so everything is complex and overwhelming. Teach the basics first and the exceptions later."

"I'm gatherin' that 'S' does *not* always make the hiss sound?" I asked.

Silas huffed. "Technically, no. But I'm going to teach you like you're four, so we're pretending that it does for now."

"Are you sure pretendin' I'm a child is actually a good idea and not Roland tryin' to sabotage me?"

"Please, Evangeline. If I wanted to sabotage your learning, I'd let Silas continue as he is. But I have a higher respect for education than to let such a disastrous lesson continue."

"Ah, for *education*. Not for me. I see."

"Be nice, you two." Silas reprimanded. "Eva, forget about the sounds for a moment. Let's just make sure you can identify the letters, okay?"

Silas showed them all to me again, asking me to find one on my own after each one. It was tedious, and I felt silly. But I was grateful he was at least trying.

I'm not sure how long we did that for, but after a while, the ink started to blur in my vision. "Alright, I need a break from this," I finally said. "What's the plan once we get to the caves?"

Silas closed the book and tucked it into my pack, since his was attached to Roland's horse. "Excellent question. Considering Harland's men *know* we're heading for the caves, what's our entrance supposed to look like now, Roland?"

"According to Harland's men, I'm to go to the Caves first, leaving you with the idea that I'm scouting things out, while I'm secretly locking down the final details with Harland's guards. But, in reality, I'll let them have the idea I'm locking down final details while I'm actually scouting things out."

I felt the muscles in Silas's arms tighten at my sides. I glanced down, and sure enough, his knuckles were white on the reins. When he spoke, I was surprised at how casual his tone appeared. "You love the complexity of your lying, don't you?"

He laughed. "It does provide some intellectual exercise, yes. But mostly, it's highly advantageous for us."

Who even talked like that? "If I doubted Roland was a prodigy before, I definitely believe it now."

"Thank you, Evangeline."

"I didn't intend it as a compliment, but you're welcome."

Silas whispered my name in warning.

Roland grunted. "Back to the important issue. Without the deal with Harland, my initial scouting of the Caves would be on the outside only: Where is the prison, and how many guards are posted at the entrance? But this way, I'll get to actually go inside. Take a look around and have a much better idea of what we're up against. After we rescue Queen Adeena and King Esmond, we can flee to Eliston. It shouldn't be too far to reach their border. That part of the plan will continue as we had originally discussed."

"*Just* the king and queen? Is Prince Alastair being kept somewhere different?"

Roland stumbled over his words. "Who? No. He's—"

"Alastair isn't significant in terms of us being able to approach Eliston," Silas explained. "Our alliance with them exists between King Heston and King Esmond. Not King Heston and Prince Alastair."

Roland cleared his throat. "Yes. Exactly. As I was saying, we will flee to Eliston, but I think Evangeline should fetch a doctor for us from Irimen, in case the three royals have needs that must be attended to sooner than Eliston can aid us."

"So, it really is going to be only the two of you going into the prison? With who knows how many guards?"

"From what I've gathered, there aren't that many guards. It is a secret prison, after all. I have no doubt that Silas and I can handle them."

"So what, you walk in and just start fightin'? This does not sound like a good plan."

"There's nothing else we can do," Silas said. "If we reveal that the royals are alive in order to recruit more help, Harland could have them killed before we get there."

"Then don't tell them what you're recruitin' for! Not until we get there."

"It's too risky. We'd have to secretly make sure any recruits aren't loyal to Harland, and we don't have any more time to spare."

"Besides," Roland added, "I'll be in the prison before we begin the rescue. If I find the risk is too great, we can change our course of action."

I shook my head. "Shouldn't you go to Eliston first and ask King Heston for help? If he has an alliance with King Esmond, isn't he required to come to his aid?"

"Unfortunately, it isn't quite that simple," Silas said. "Harland has the whole world thinking the Cathmoores are dead. And with Harland now bordering Eliston, King Heston will be toeing a thin political line. I doubt he'll renew an alliance with Harland, but they won't be eager to start a war with him either, especially if they haven't seen King Esmond alive for themselves."

I took a deep breath and let it out slowly. This shouldn't be such big news to me. Hadn't they already said as much? But the weight of what we were trying to do finally hit me, and a wave of fear came with it. This wasn't just a convenient way for me to hide from Gratsis. This was *actually* the most dangerous and insane mission I could have gotten myself involved in.

"So this whole 'being on the brink of war' deal is more of a question of *when* it starts, than *if* it starts."

"Yes," Silas confirmed. "Unless of course, we all die in the Caves. Then there will be no need for war."

I slapped one of his hands.

"Hey—what was that for?"

"I'll have none of that talk, noble."

"Nor will I," Roland agreed.

"I thought you had decided to a non-violent truce," Silas muttered.

"A truce with *Roland*. I have made no such agreements with you."

"I didn't know I should still anticipate being attacked."

I scoffed. "You and I have different definitions of the word 'attacked.'"

"Don't you know who I am?"

I swallowed my laughter at Silas's indignant tone, but being so close to him, he must have been able to tell I was laughing anyway, and he leaned into the melodramatic speech.

"A woman striking a man like me is enough to send her to prison."

"*Prison*? Well, then I suppose it's convenient we're already goin' to one."

"I still demand a formal apology."

"Jump ship, Silas."

He burst into laughter, and Roland gave us a curious glance. "What are you two on about?"

Neither of us answered. We just kept laughing. I couldn't remember the last time I'd laughed so hard. And at a time like this? Planning a rescue mission that would start a war?

Roland or not, I supposed there was worse company to be in at such a time as this.

NARIM, WENTERLY

The city clock rang out, eight long tolls, and Reeves Hills breathed a sigh of relief. His shift was over for the day, and there had been no news of the girl and the prince. His friend, Captain Bentley, would return to Narim tomorrow, assuming all went according to schedule. His report would hopefully be the last Reeves heard about the pair until they called for a revolution. When would that be? Days or weeks? Months, maybe? At least he was able to verify the rumors of the royals from a source other than Harland. He had finally seen it with his own eyes.

The Cathmoores lived yet.

He was about to walk out of the law office when a young man barged in, nearly slamming the door into Reeves's face as he entered.

"Sorry, man. I have an urgent letter for the Chief of Narim from the Chief of Koyben."

Not Koyben. News from Koyben so soon could not be good news. Had the prince been arrested the moment he set foot on the dock?

Reeves reached out to take it. "I'll see that he gets it."

The young man shook his head. "I have strict orders to hand it directly to the Chief Officer, and you don't wear that badge."

In less than a second, Reeves weighed the risk of letting the man deliver the letter unheeded to the Chief, or pushing the issue so that he might get a glimpse of what the message was about. "But, I wear the sash. I'm a man of Harland's law. Is there no trust among fellow officers?"

The blank look on the young man's face told Reeves everything he needed to know. The Koyben officers knew there was a rat. But did they know it was him?

"Very well, then," Reeves said. "Chief is currently in the back room, sortin' inventory for the week."

The young man nodded and hurried to the back of the building. Reeves hurried out, glad the other officer taking over the night shift already set out to walk the city.

He assumed a brisk, but natural-enough pace to get through town without drawing unwanted attention. He'd stayed to protect the people of Narim as long as he could, but now his duty was to protect his family. The moment he was through the door of his house, he ripped the Fate-cursed red sash from his chest. "Helena, get our things. It's time."

His wife's eyes widened, but she retreated into the bedroom without hesitation. Reeves entered his children's bedroom, not pausing to knock. His sons were in the middle of an arm wrestle, his daughter officiating the match.

But the atmosphere shifted entirely as their father entered the room.
"Children. We're leavin'."
"When?" *Willa asked.*
"Right now. Grab your things."
His boys stood, for once not protesting.
But Willa stayed seated. "What happened?"
"A letter from Koyben's Chief Officer. The messenger wouldn't trust me with it."
"What did the letter say?"
So many questions, so little time to answer them all. "If we wait to find out exactly, we won't have a chance to escape."

Thankfully, that was enough to get her moving. His children retreated to their beds to pull out their pre-packed bags. Nothing much. Some money and a change of clothes.

Reeves went to the stables to saddle their two horses. Helena and Clement would take one. Willa and Friedrick would share the other.

He led the horses out of the stable right as his family exited their home. The children mounted, but Helena approached her husband.

"How far behind us will you be?"

"Twenty minutes at the most. I need to stop at Bentley's. Let his wife know they may need to flee too. Then I'll get Conrad's horse and meet you there."

"Be safe," *Helena said.*

"You too." He kissed her quickly. There was no time now for tenderness.

The moment the horses took their first steps toward the road, Reeves turned to go to Bentley's house. He made it as far as his street before the Chief reached him.

"Surrender, Reeves Hills."

Reeves lifted his hands, turning to face the Chief. "Surrender what, exactly?"

The Chief had his pistol pointed at him, but he held up a letter in his left hand. Reeves couldn't read it from there, but he knew it was the letter from Koyben. "You are under arrest for treason and assisting in the prevention of justice through the escape of two dangerous criminals."

"Nonsense! Who has accused me of such crimes?"

"An informant in Koyben."

"What could a man in Koyben possibly know about my life here in Narim?"

The Chief didn't answer.

"Who has accused me of this?"

"That is not knowledge privy to a traitor." The Chief tucked the letter into his vest. "If you accompany me to the law office with no resistance, I will ensure that your execution is swift."

"And if I resist?"

The Chief cocked his pistol. "Then it will be even swifter."

People began to gather, though they gave the two officers a wide berth. Reeves contemplated pulling his own pistol, but too many citizens had gathered behind the Chief. If the Chief anticipated his shot and dodged, or—Fate forbid—his gun misfired, there was sure to be a bystander injured, if not killed.

Leave it to a situation like this for the citizens to finally take interest in an arrest.

"I know my rights. I am to receive a public trial."

"Yes, of course. Just as the young man Gabriel would have."

Meaning there would be no trial. No public execution. This was the biggest crowd Reeves was going to see for the rest of his short life.

And he would make the most of it.

"Very good. No need for threats, Chief. I'm an honorable man." He kept his hands held aloft.

The Chief began to lower the gun. Reeves took the opportunity to turn and run in the opposite direction, yelling at the top of his lungs, *"Prince Alastair lives! The Cathmoores live!"*

A gunshot rang out, and the bystanders screamed. But the shot missed Reeves, and the commotion caused the people to scatter so he could flee down the street.

"Down with Harland, the King of Lies! Long live the true—"

The Chief's second bullet found its mark. Reeves tumbled to the ground as a fresh wave of the onlookers' screams pierced the night.

The Chief sighed and approached the fallen officer he had been so foolish to trust. *"Told you it would be swift, Reeves."*

But already, Reeves could no longer hear him.

"The problem with the mind, is it can find rationale for the most irrational ideas when it is tangled too closely with the heart."

Brigid, in a letter to his son

38

EVA THINKS SHE'S A THIEF AFTER ALL

Alastair

I woke with a start, the stars above reminding me that I was not trapped in a cave, buried in the earth with my parents, and left to die. This was the third dream about them now. Never identical, but variations of the same thing. My parents, the prison, inevitable death.

I rolled to the right and saw Roland sleeping a few feet away, his watch over. Eva was up now.

My heart was finally beginning to beat at a regular pace. I sat up and looked for her.

She was already watching me.

"Is somethin' wrong?" she asked in a low voice.

I shrugged as I walked over to her. "I just can't sleep."

"I haven't been sleepin' well either the last few nights."

"Nervous about what's coming?"

She shifted her weight. "Are you not?"

"I'm terrified."

She nodded, and I realized she was holding a stick in her hand. But she wasn't near enough to the fire to have been stoking it.

"Are you practicing your stances?"

"Yes," she said, brushing a thumb across her eyebrow. "It keeps me awake."

"Do you want more lessons before we get to the Caves?"

She glanced away a moment. "Only if you want. It's not like I'm goin' in with you two."

I raised a brow. "Don't tell me you wish you were."

She quickly shook her head. "I'm not crazy, Silas. I know I'd never make it out of there. I'm just sayin' you don't have to waste your time teachin' me skills I don't need." She shuffled her feet. "Are you stayin' up for a while?"

I sat down on the ground. "I think so."

"Oh, okay." She shuffled again.

"Is that alright?"

"Of course," she sat down facing me, putting the stick down behind her.

"Are you nervous about something?" I asked.

She frowned. "I just told you I was."

"I mean right at this moment."

"No." Her thumb ran along her eyebrow again. "Why?"

I fought back a smile. "You seem like it."

She bit her lip, reached behind her, and then handed over my book.

I took it, unable to hide my surprise. I wasn't sure what I'd expected, but certainly not this.

"Where did you pull that from?"

"I slipped it under the back of my corset when I saw you stirrin'." She must have seen my brow furrow with my unasked question, because she added, "I don't tie it up properly to sit here on watch."

I attempted not to blush. Commoners had much looser boundaries for decent conversation than nobility. "But why do you have this in the first place?"

"I'm sorry," she said. "I know it's yours, and I'm sure it's expensive, but I've been very careful with it."

"I'm not mad, Eva. I'm just a little confused."

"I've been practicin'." Was it the flickering light from the fire, or was she blushing, too?

"How do you practice? Do you—" As I looked down to open the book, I saw the reason for her shuffled feet.

She'd been writing letters in the dirt. And I had sat in the middle of her parchment. "You're practicing *writing*?" I eyed the stick she'd set down. "Not swordsmanship?"

"I've been doin' both."

"Why did you try to hide that?"

"Because I need the book to help me remember all the letters correctly. And I figured you'd be mad if you found out I was usin' it without you knowin'."

"Then why didn't you ask me to use it?"

She was quiet a moment. "Wouldn't you have said no?"

"Why would I say that?"

"Because it's precious to you."

I blinked. This woman was never going to stop surprising me. Sometimes she read me as easily as I could read the book in my lap. And yet, she occasionally came to the wrong conclusions on what it all meant. "How do you know that?"

"Look at the pages." She pointed. "You've written on practically every single one. Circles, and lines, and words. But some of your letters look quite different from the letters printed in the book, so perhaps you can explain why that is at some point, because it's a bit puzzlin' to me."

"Eva—"

"Besides, who in their right mind packs a book when they are runnin' for their life except someone who really values—"

I reached out and touched her forearm. "You've made your point, thank you." I pulled my hand back. "I'm not mad. I'm actually a little proud of you."

"Why? Because I'm turnin' into a thief, after all?"

"I don't think it counts as stealing if you always return the item when you're done using it." I handed the book back to her. "Have you done this the last three nights? Since we started the lessons?"

"Only last night and tonight." She set the book down in the dirt.

I resented the twinge of panic the sight gave me. It hadn't rained recently. It wouldn't get ruined from being set on the ground for a moment.

"See, I knew it." She picked the book back up and brushed off the cover. "Just take it back."

I flinched to grab it, but didn't allow myself to take it from her. "It's true, I prefer my books well-kept. But I'm not going to stop you from learning. Just be careful with it. It *is* one of my favorites."

She smiled and set it in her lap. "What's it about?"

"Suffering. Specifically, suffering well. And the purpose of it."

"Has it always been your favorite? Or only in light of recent events?"

"Always has been."

She nodded as she unsuccessfully fought back a smile.

"What? You think I can't appreciate a book on suffering because I'm a noble and my life is so easy?"

"I wasn't goin' to say that."

"Hmm."

She sighed. "But yes, the thought did cross my mind."

"I knew it."

"But I think that's a thought from old Eva, when we first met. I think I have some new opinions now."

"On nobility, or suffering?"

"On you."

I stilled. "What do you mean?"

"Roland is what I've expected nobility to act like. You... are nothin' I expected."

"Because of my poor decisions?"

She *hmmed* a short laugh. "Because you seem to actually care about what hap—" Her voice caught, and she paused a second. "About what happens to me."

Is she emotional about that? The knife from when she'd gone to confront Roland stabbed me again. "That's what friends do, Eva."

She nodded, no longer looking at me, but off into the dark woods. "I know. That's why I didn't expect it from someone like you."

I swallowed. "Well, I am full of surprises. Even Roland agrees to that."

"Shouldn't Roland be used to your surprises by now?"

"Probably, but if anything, this trip has left him more surprised than ever."

She slowly exhaled. "Enough about Roland. I don't want to think about him any more than I have to."

"I thought you two were getting along again."

"Are we gettin' along, or are we just not speakin' to each other?"

I had to think about it, but she made a good point. I didn't think they'd said more than five sentences to each other in the last three days. "If it's too difficult with Roland... I understand if you want to go."

She furrowed her brow. "I never said anythin' about leavin'."

"I know, but if I were you, I'd be thinking about it."

"Well, I'm not. I'm too involved to give up on this whole thing now."

"Oh? Are you starting to care about politics, Eva?"

"Politics? Goodness, no. I care about what happens to you."

I smiled, far happier to hear the admission than I would have expected. "I'm afraid the two are tied together."

"Not tied. Just tangled."

"Is there a difference?"

She smiled back. "There is to me."

I couldn't begin to understand what she meant by that. Which probably meant it was high time I went back to sleep.

I stood up. "How much time do I have until breakfast?"

She checked Roland's watch. "Two hours."

"Well, then, I'll see you again in two hours."

"And I'll continue to see you for the next two hours."

"That's weird, Eva. You're just watching me sleep?"

She tilted her head, eyebrows furrowed. "Is that not the job? *Watch*?"

"You're supposed to be watching for *danger*. Not watching *us*."

She laughed. "I know. Just go to sleep, Silas. This is supposed to be your night of uninterrupted sleep. I don't want to hear you complainin' about how tired you are in the mornin'."

"When have I ever complained about that?"

"I didn't say you have. I'm sayin' I don't want you to start."

I rolled my eyes. "Goodnight, Eva."

I went back to my bedroll, knowing the next two hours would pass far too quickly.

But when she woke me, I found I was happier to see her than I was tired.

39

These Late Night Conversation Are Getting Dangerous

Evangeline

After nearly a week of travel, the days blurred together. Roland or I would stop at the small towns we passed by when we needed more food, but for the most part, we rode all day. Talking about my past around Roland was a volatile topic, and talking about Silas and Roland's past was clearly a touchy subject as well. Anytime I asked about it they only gave me vague answers. As if the minute details of their lives remaining secret made a difference anymore.

So, we didn't talk much about personal matters. Which meant we didn't talk much at all. Unless Silas was trying to teach me to read—*trying* being the key word.

Despite being taught by a prodigy, Silas was not much of a natural teacher himself. But even with limited opportunity for lessons and Silas's frequent backtracking and use of the phrase, "forget everything I just said," I could now identify all the letters and knew the main sounds from A through H. Plus, I hardly had to reference the book when I practiced writing the alphabet at night.

But regardless of the difficulties of the lessons and the lack of conversation, Silas still somehow managed to make me laugh. Whether his jokes were getting better or the weariness of travel was affecting my sense of humor, I couldn't say. But either way, it was nice to have those moments.

Between my lessons and the knowledge that the war we were facing was inevitable, I had plenty to keep me awake during my watch shifts. Silas had gone over a few more sword drills for me to practice, but not with the same intensity as before. I didn't mind, though. I was mostly interested in literacy.

When I was tired of practicing letters or practicing fighting, I'd toss the stick away and let my worries occupy me. Which usually led to me picking up the stick and practicing once more.

So, the trick was no longer trying to stay awake during watch, it was falling asleep when I was supposed to.

I'd been lying on my bedroll for quite a while after waking up Silas for his watch, turning this way and that, unable to find sleep. I finally decided to join him, as he had done with me a few nights ago.

He was pacing around the camp, as he usually did, but he stopped when he realized I was coming over to him. "Something wrong?"

"I can't sleep."

He smiled, and we sat, hopefully at a far enough distance from Roland that he wouldn't hear us talk.

We watched the fire crackle, little sparks rising to the sky every so often.

"I don't think I ever said thank you for teaching me how to read. I know I ask a lot of questions, so it probably isn't easy. But I do appreciate it. So ... thank you."

He smiled, the firelight making his blue eyes gleam. "Asking questions makes you a good student. It shows you care. The only reason it isn't easy to teach you is because I'm not a very good teacher."

"Lucky for you, I don't have anyone to compare you to. Any teacher is good enough for me."

He let out the slightest laugh before his smile faded. After so many hours on the horse together, the distance between us suddenly felt vast. Yet, we were less than a foot apart, still far too close for decent company.

Then again, when had Silas and I ever kept decent company? Our wedding replayed in my mind, the arrest, the barrel escape, the last few days on Port. It seemed distance and decency were not designed for us.

We sat there in silence for a few minutes while my mind continued to wander, for some reason always coming back to the wedding ceremony—particularly the things Silas had said to get us there. Looking back, his words had sounded genuine, and I couldn't help but think he must have truly felt that way about someone. But he'd said he wasn't betrothed.

I took a breath, and it shuddered, betraying nerves I hadn't realized were there. "Can I ask you a question I have no business askin'?"

"I expect nothing less from you."

I smiled at his teasing but turned my eyes from him to the fire. "Have you ever been in love before?"

He took a moment before answering. A log in the fire fell with a pop, releasing a flurry of sparks that quickly died out.

"No," he finally said. "Why do you ask?"

"I was just thinkin' about how all of this started and how I ended up here. Which, of course, got me rememberin' our ceremony." I glanced at him, and he was looking at me so intently I had to look away again. "The way you spoke about us and... me, to the captain, I thought you must have felt that way for someone once."

"No." He took a deep breath. "I've *read* about people who felt that way once."

"Philosophers?" I smirked.

"Naturally."

"Brigid?"

"Of course." The way he said it, it sounded like he was smiling. I turned back to him, and sure enough, he was.

"Did you quote *Brigid* at our weddin'?"

"Don't be absurd, Eva." He leaned toward me. "I *paraphrased* Brigid at our wedding."

I shook my head, but smiled nonetheless. "You're ridiculous."

"Probably." He leaned back on his hands, the movement causing our shoulders to brush. Had he moved closer just now?

But it didn't feel strange, to be so close when we didn't have to be. It felt natural. Comfortable. I didn't pull back from him, and neither did he readjust.

I didn't know what to make of that.

We sat there for a while, not speaking. Just sitting in each other's company.

"Eva, can I ask you a question I don't have any business asking?"

I rolled my eyes. "How would I have ever been in love?"

"That's not what I was going to ask."

"Hmm." I eyed him warily. "Then, I suppose."

"Do you miss your friends in Welven? I mean, if Gratsis wasn't a problem, would you want to go back?"

I sighed. "I don't know. Welven was home for years, but at the same time, there isn't really anythin' there for me to go back to."

"Your friends?"

I shook my head. "I barely had friends, Silas. People like me get polite acquaintances at best. People who will tolerate us. Besides, as I got older, all the girls my age started talkin' about marriage and romance, and I resented them for it. So, that didn't help my case either. I think my mother was probably the closest thing I'd had to a real friend." I found myself leaning slightly into his shoulder. When had that happened? I straightened my spine.

"Really? You've never had *anyone* you would call a friend?"

I turned to look at him. "Not until you."

His face immediately softened. "Eva."

"Don't pity me, Silas. It's just life."

"No, I—" He stuttered a moment. "You're my dearest friend, Eva."

I almost laughed. "Me?"

He nodded.

"What about your friend, *the prince,* who we've trekked all the way across Wenterly for?"

"Yeah, he's great," he said flatly. "But you're better."

"If Roland heard you say that—"

"Roland can jump ship when it comes to his opinion of you."

I blinked.

"What?"

"Nothin'." I turned back to the fire. "It's just nice to know that you tolerate me so much."

He sat up, angling himself toward me and taking my hand in both of his. "I don't tolerate you, Eva. Believe it or not, I actually enjoy having you around."

I looked at our hands, then up at him, his expression nothing but earnest. The kindness in his blue eyes made my stomach flutter. Had he always been so handsome? I turned toward the fire, blinking quickly. I was not about to cry over something like this. At least, not in front of some noble.

"I confess, I enjoy being here too, though, this whole thing is a lot more intense than I expected it to be." I pulled my hand away to tuck a strand of hair behind my ear. "Rescuin' the Cathmoores and all, I mean. But I suppose it's better than piracy."

He laughed. "I think it was Fate that I ruined all your plans that day. I don't think a life of crime suits you."

I turned back to him to lightly smack his arm. "You followed me to the beach because you thought I *was* a criminal and you wanted to hire me."

He smiled, nudging my shoulder with his, "And after getting to know you, I'm glad I was wrong."

A small voice in the back of my mind reminded me that this kind of intimacy was wrong. Certainly not for someone like me. With someone like him.

"You don't think maybe we're defyin' Fate?"

He raised his eyebrows. "If you can defy Fate, then I don't think it was ever Fate in the first place. Whatever happens is what Fate has decided. Even if it doesn't seem like it at first."

I smiled. "You're gettin' philosophical on me again."

"Sorry. I can't really help it."

Despite the warnings in my mind, I nudged his shoulder back. "You'd probably win Prince Philosopher pretty easily."

"Prince ... Philosopher?"

I laughed quietly. "I don't know, honestly. It's a game Officer Reeves's kids were playin'. I thought maybe it was a common game."

"Mercy, I hope not."

"Why is that?"

"No reason. Just that, uh—" He dropped his voice to an overly serious tone. "Philosophy is serious business. Not a game."

I laughed again. "Did Roland tell you that?"

"No, Roland never liked philosophy. He prefers mathematics and science. Calculating things."

That sounded about right.

"Does Prince Alastair like it?"

He gazed at me, a strange emotion on his face I couldn't quite place. Amusement? Puzzlement? He blinked and turned to the fire. "He likes it as much as I do."

"Maybe that's where the game comes from!" I realized.

He nodded, clearly already assuming that connection. "It probably is, which is embarrassing."

"Why?"

"Because then every child in the kingdom is growing up mocking the future king of Wenterly."

"*Ah*, nobles." I nodded. "Always taking things so personally."

"Isn't it personal, though? You said the game is literally called Prince Philosopher."

I raised my eyebrows. "Who cares, even if it is? You and the prince are smart and passionate about *life*. I can think of far worse qualities in a leader."

"Hmm. Me too."

It was clear his thoughts had instantly gone to Harland. It wasn't my intention, but I was foolish not to realize the obvious connection *before* I said such a thing.

"Tell me more about Alastair. What kind of king do you think he'll be?"

Silas took a long, deep breath. "I hope he's a good one," he said softly. I waited for him to say more. But that was it.

"If he's anythin' like you"—I leaned into him briefly, still trying to pull him from whatever kind of grief was capturing his attention—"I think he will be."

He blinked, and a tear rolled down his cheek. *Oh.* Apparently, it was a very *real* kind of grief.

"Is everythin' okay, Silas?"

Obviously not, idiot. Everything in Silas's life was as wrong as could be. Same as mine. *Worse* than mine, probably. I needed to shut up and stop making things worse.

"Sorry, bad question. Everythin' is obviously the worst."

He brushed his sleeve against his cheek and laughed, soft enough that it wouldn't wake Roland, but it seemed genuine nonetheless.

"It is the worst," he agreed, then leaned ever-so-slightly into me again. "But maybe not everything."

My stomach flipped. My first instinct was to brush the moment off. Tell him he was right, because I was pretty great. But this was the most honest I'd ever seen him. I needed to reciprocate that, not shut it down.

"I should go to sleep," I said instead.

He nodded and stayed seated while I walked to my bedroll. I expected to hear him get up and walk around again, but I didn't. Just the crackle of the fire and the breeze rustling the leaves overhead. A few birds began chirping, although the sun wouldn't rise for another few hours.

I lay awake, still unable to sleep. Worry rattled around my skull, but not about the Caves and the war this time.

This worry was a different kind entirely.

40

Oh No

Alastair

Have you ever been in love before?

Those words echoed through my mind the rest of the night and all the next day as we rode closer and closer to Ordelune. I tried to think of the mission, of anything but those words, but with Eva sitting right in front of me, my chest against her back, and my arms around her sides while I held the reins, it was difficult not to also hear her voice in my head.

Have you ever been in love before?

The answer I had given her was true. I'd told Roland the same thing a few days ago. In the past tense, I'd never been in love before.

But I worried it was becoming less true in the present.

Eva had no pretenses. She didn't need to. She was who she was, take it or leave it. And while I knew that kind of attitude came from a difficult past, I couldn't help but be drawn to it.

Had I ever had a conversation with someone where they said exactly what they wanted, unbothered with how their words may affect my opinion of them?

But that wasn't entirely true for Eva either. People's opinions of her bothered her. I'd seen her deflate and shrink back a few times with Roland's comments—and mine, if I was honest. Not that I blamed her. Fake nobles or otherwise, we were arrogant.

But we hadn't driven her away. She stayed.

I still couldn't quite understand that. How could she put up with so much? Pity and admiration were hand in hand when I thought of how strong she was to endure it all.

And speaking of hand in hand... I'd held *her* hand last night, taken it unprompted, with no audience we were hoping to convince of a lie.

It was genuine, which probably made it *more* indecent. Mercy, I hoped Roland was incorrect about my future betrothed ever hearing the details of this journey.

Now that Eva and I had gotten closer, it was getting harder not to tell her I was Alastair. But what good would it do to tell her? It was dangerous to reveal my identity, and therefore, selfish of me to want to. Why *did* I want to? Just because I was tired of hiding and pretending I was someone I wasn't, or because she deserved to know?

The clop of additional hooves on the road pulled me from my thoughts. I looked up as Eva leaned back into me.

"Officers up ahead," she whispered.

Four of them. Red and yellow sashed officers on horses bred for running—not farming, as ours were. They could easily take us.

"Keep moving," Roland instructed. "Stopping will invite conversation."

"Do they know you up here, Roland?" I asked.

"We'll find out."

"Hold my hand or somethin'." Eva whispered.

"What?"

"We need to look more natural. Comfortably married."

"I thought we weren't using the marriage idea anymore."

"On a horse, I think we have to."

She took my hand, no longer waiting for me, and wrapped my arm around her waist.

My heart pounded. We'd had an agreement. I was strictly to hold the *reins*.

The officers had nearly reached us. Too much was happening all at once.

Roland glanced from our hands to me, then moved in front of us. Hopefully the officers would see him first, and barely spare me and Eva a glance.

My breaths came shallow and quick. I lowered my head and swallowed. *I think I'm going to be sick.*

She gripped my hand tighter. "You had better not."

I hadn't meant to say it out loud.

I glanced up as Roland nodded to the officers. I lowered my head more, hoping it would pass for a deep nod.

The men rode on, barely giving us a second glance.

I closed my eyes, head still bowed as the officers continued down the road behind us. I let go of Eva's hand and pulled on the reins the moment the sound of the horses' hooves faded.

"What are you—"

I'd already dismounted. "Give me a second."

"Mercy, you were serious?"

I didn't answer her, just stepped off the road and into the woods. I heard her say to Roland, "After everythin' we've been through, I'm surprised a little ride past some officers is what got to him."

It was fine if they thought it was the officers that had rattled me. Let them bond at my expense, I could work with that. What I couldn't work with was falling in love with a commoner when I was supposed to be focused on rescuing my family and restoring the throne.

I didn't wander far—perhaps a dozen yards—and slumped against a large tree.

No. I wasn't falling in *love* with her. That was so dramatic. So serious. Tensions were high, and we'd been through so much together. My emotions were a mess. I didn't know what to feel about anything. Everything was so awful that I was searching for some shred of goodness or happiness. Romance was a new solution for me, but these were new stressors. So, that made sense.

I didn't fancy Eva. I was just stressed.

Besides, she didn't see me that way. She'd called me a friend only last night. So, it wouldn't work out even if I *did* feel that way about her.

Which I didn't.

So, there was no problem.

Brilliant.

I stood up and turned to go back to the group. But Roland was approaching me, alone.

Not brilliant.

"What's the matter with you?" he asked. I couldn't decide if he sounded concerned or annoyed. Probably both.

"Those officers. My last encounter wasn't exactly pleasant, in case you forgot, and *oh yes*, you're pretending to be one of them! Why'd they let us go, Roland? Because they *didn't* recognize me? Or because they *did* recognize you?"

"See, this is why I didn't want to tell you about that until we reached the Caves. The stress is getting to you."

"Yes, it is."

"Honestly, it doesn't matter *why* they didn't stop. They didn't stop. We can continue on. That's all that matters."

Yes. That was all that mattered. The only thing that mattered was continuing the mission.

"Yes, okay. Sorry. Let's go." I took a few steps, but Roland reached out to stop me.

"While we have a moment alone, might I offer some advice?"

"That depends what it's about."

"Evangeline."

I *was* going to be sick. I wiped a hand over my face. "What about her?"

"I have tried to give you the benefit of the doubt these last few days, but you need to make it clear to her that you don't return her affections."

"I don't—" I stopped short. "Pardon? Did you say 'return'? What world are you living in where she cares about me romantically?"

"Are you trying to play dumb with me, or are you actually that naïve?"

"I'm telling you the truth. There's nothing between us."

"Yes. There practically *was* nothing between you a moment ago."

My heart was in my throat. "Roland. It was a charade."

He raised a brow. "You think the move she made was necessary?"

"She panicked."

"Or did she take advantage of the situation?"

I scoffed. "Not a chance. Last night she called me her *friend*."

He blinked. "Last night? When did that happen?"

I clamped my mouth shut.

"*Silas.*"

"Between our watches."

Roland pressed his palms into his eyes.

"It wasn't a whole *moment*, Roland. Just a passing comment." Which was true. And then I made it a whole moment. But he didn't need to know that.

He was only pinching the bridge of his nose now. An improvement. "Tell me what she said *exactly*."

"Well... She, uh. Let me think what started it." I *knew* what started it. *Have you ever been in love before?* But I certainly couldn't tell Roland she'd asked that, could I? I quickly tried to calculate how much of the conversation I should edit out.

"I asked if she missed her friends in Welven, and she said she didn't have any friends until me. That's all."

"How did she say it?"

"Seriously?"

"*How* did she say it, Silas?"

I was momentarily torn between wanting to hide the extent of our conversation from him and wanting to know what insight he might have. Not that I *needed* insight. It would just be interesting to know.

"She said her mother was probably the closest thing she'd had to a friend. And I said, 'So you've never had anyone you'd call a friend?' and she said, 'Not until you.'"

"Her tone of voice. Was she resentful, playful?"

"I don't know! We were being quiet so we wouldn't wake you up."

"Did she smile when she said it?"

"Uh..."

"She did, didn't she?"

"Kind of. It was, like, a half smile."

"Stars," Roland cursed. "That's *worse*."

I took a step back. Could she *really* feel that way about me?

"How would you know, Roland? What authority do you have to lecture me about this when you've never courted someone yourself?"

"Maybe you shouldn't assume you know what I have and haven't experienced."

That raised my eyebrows. "You *courted*? When? *Who*?"

He simply stared at me, but I waited. He had to be bluffing. He shook his head, but finally relented. "I was seventeen, and so was she. She would turn eighteen a week after I did, and we were to marry the next Sunday."

"You were *betrothed*? And you never told me?"

"Why should I have?"

"I don't know, why *not*?"

"It was irrelevant."

I gaped at him. "You think you know someone."

Roland rolled his eyes, a gesture that belonged to Eva. It was foreign to see it from him.

"Still, that was a long time ago, with probably a very different woman," I insisted. "And you think that makes you an expert on Eva now?"

"I'm nearly twice your age, Al. I've spoken to *many* more women than you have. And they are *odd* when it comes to romance. They aren't supposed to make the first move, so they say things or do things to try to tell you that they are interested and open to *you* making the first move."

"And you're telling me that Eva wants me to make a romantic gesture, and the way she did that was by telling me she sees me … *as a friend*?"

"Yes."

I threw my hands in the air. "That doesn't make any sense!"

"It's in the *way* she said the word, not the word itself. It's the same as your little fights."

"What are you *talking* about?"

"You're telling me that when you two are arguing and having your little tiffs, you're not flirting?"

"I think you answered that question yourself when you called it 'arguing.' If you think she's interested in me because she fights with me, then she must be *madly* in love with you."

"That is not the same. She argues with me because she dislikes me. She argues with you because she cares about you."

"That still doesn't make *any* sense, Roland!"

"After every quarrel you two have, the both of you are smiling as though you were telling jokes instead. That's *odd*, Al. But fine, here's another angle. She has twice now offered to take second watch when it isn't her turn. Both times were on the nights *you* were on second watch. Why do you think that is?"

I shrugged. "She knows it's my least favorite. And that this is primarily your and my mission. She's here to help and doesn't think she's very helpful. Taking second watch is one of the ways she can be."

He pressed his lips together. "I don't like how well thought-out that answer was."

"Why? Because I'm right?"

"*No*. Because it means you've been thinking about it. Thinking about *her* and how much she cares about you. Now you have me worried you're trying to justify her actions as platonic in order to convince yourself not to—" He paused. "*Oh*. Oh, *no*. You *do* return her affections, and the only reason you deny it is because you think your feelings are unrequited."

Now I was the one pressing my hands to my eyes. "You came over here warning me that Eva has feelings for me, and now you're worried about me falling in love with her as soon as I realize that's the case?"

Roland sputtered. "I didn't realize you had already lost all your sense when I first brought it up!"

"I haven't. So let me emphasize to you *again*, there is nothing romantic between me and Eva. Besides, Roland, you and I both know this is not the time for romance."

"Yes, that's why I brought up the issue. Because it *cannot* be an issue."

"It's not an issue."

Roland glared at me.

"I swear! Even *if*—emphasis on 'if'—I felt that way about her, it would never work out. We're trying to reclaim the throne, and me marrying someone with her status would surely cause us to lose it again. I know that. So relax. Even *if* Eva feels that way about me, I'll never feel that way about her. Trust me a little."

Finally, Roland conceded, and we walked back to the road, where Eva was talking gently to the horses. But when she looked over at me with concern in her eyes and a reassuring smile on her lips, I knew Roland would be right not to trust me in this regard.

41

Silas Is Stressed and That's Making Me Stressed

Evangeline

I had been tempted to follow Roland, but didn't want to be too overbearing. Besides, if Silas really was going to be sick, I didn't need to be a witness. But perhaps I should have gone, because shortly after Roland left, I heard their voices rise in another argument. *Brilliant.* I highly doubted a good scolding was what Silas needed right now. They weren't loud enough for me to understand them from the road, but the way things went last time I eavesdropped on one of their conversations was enough to keep me waiting with the horses.

I wasn't sure what to say as the two returned to the road. But I didn't want to push Silas as Roland had. Something had been on his mind all morning, that much was obvious. The officers seemed to have been the last straw. Whatever he was working through, if Silas wanted to talk to me about it, he would.

"Feelin' better?" I simply asked.

"Yes," he replied. His one-word response was clipped, and he avoided looking at me.

He was lying.

As if he could sense my assessment, he added, "Sorry for the interruption. Everything seemed to suddenly catch up to me just then."

I lowered my voice as Roland passed us to get to his own horse. "You don't have to apologize for bein' human, Silas,"

"Where I'm from, it's called weakness."

I mounted our horse, for once looking down at him as I spoke. "Maybe it is. But it's a universal weakness. So hardly somethin' you should be faulted for."

He pushed his dark hair out of his face. "If you say so." His hand fell heavily back to his side, and his hair was now a ruffled mess.

I reached out to fix it, but caught myself. "Silas, you've messed up your—"

I stopped short. What *was* wrong with his hair? It was light brown in strange patches, not at all aligning with the strands of his hair. Toward his scalp, his hair almost appeared transparent, but that couldn't be right. Was it ... blond?

"I think your hair is changin' color."

"It's what?" He put a hand to his head. "What do you mean?"

Roland directed Starboard over to us. He grabbed Silas's head, tilting him like he needed every angle of sunlight to get a proper diagnosis.

"Hands off, Roland. I'm not a doll."

"No, a doll wouldn't have this problem," Roland said, unamused. But he did let him go. "Your hair has grown. Some of your natural color is showing, and the dye is beginning to fade. I'd suggest we redo it, but one way or another, by overmorrow you won't have to hide like this anymore. We'll be in Ordelune by then."

I nearly laughed. "You *dyed* your hair?"

Silas ignored me. "We reach Ordelune *in two days*?"

"Indeed," Roland answered, though I wasn't sure which of us he was responding to.

"I thought we had four more days."

"We took a shortcut."

"Why didn't you tell me?"

"Look at you, Silas. Look at what just happened. You're a wreck. The anticipation is killing you."

"And so you don't think I need time to prepare for this?"

"Have you not been preparing these last few weeks? You have all afternoon and all of tomorrow. Then you and Evangeline will wait while I scout things out. We won't make our move till the day after that. That's plenty of time to prepare."

He took a few deep breaths. "Okay. Yes. The sooner the better."

Roland clapped him on the shoulder. "Exactly. They're waiting for you."

He nodded. "Let's go, then."

Silas mounted our horse, grabbed the reins, and started us down the road again.

The day passed slower than the others. Where I had been able to rely on Silas for some conversation before, he now only gave me one- or two-word answers. And the times he did try to say more, he ended up trailing off mid-sentence and never picked the thought back up again. Whatever had gotten into him this morning was clearly not going to leave him alone.

I could understand his silence. Once we got to Ordelune, he and Roland wouldn't only be fighting for their lives in that cave, but they would also finally see the royals again—assuming they were still alive—and the future Silas had placed his hope on would be determined. It was a lot to weigh on the mind, and Silas didn't like to talk when he had a lot to ponder.

But as the hours passed and I listened to his practiced, deep breaths, I started to wonder if it might be better for him to spend a little less time in his head.

We made camp earlier than usual, and Roland immediately went to sleep after our meal. Though I also welcomed the idea of an early night, I stayed up, looking over Silas's book and practicing my letters, hoping to allow an opportunity for him to open up about everything.

But he didn't.

The night grew dark, and I put the book away and approached him. "Silas, are you alright?"

He looked over at me like the question surprised him. "I'm as good as I can be, given the circumstances."

"It's certainly a lot to deal with."

"It is."

I sighed. "I'm worried—"

"Don't be. It will all work out just fine."

More of the same. Shutting down any real conversation before it could even begin. Fine. If that was how he wanted to cope, I had to trust that was what was right for him.

I nodded, bid him goodnight, and went to my bedroll.

When Roland woke me for third watch, I actually did spend a considerable amount of time watching Silas. His sleep was fitful. He woke up twice during my shift, but didn't come over to talk with me.

The following day was more of the same. Silence. No eye contact. The concern I'd had yesterday grew into a tremendous ball of worry bouncing around my chest. Something was very wrong with Silas. And I worried that what I had laughed off on our first day on the road was turning out to be some sort of prophecy.

Silas had said it might be just as valuable to have a friend along, if only so that he didn't lose it before we reached Ordelune.

Now, barely over a week since he'd spoken it, I was officially worried he *was* at risk of losing it. And if I was going to be a valuable friend, I had to do something by the end of tomorrow.

42

I Am Pathetic

Alastair

I rubbed my eyes as Eva woke me for second watch.

"Sleep well," I told her. "Last night before Ordelune."

"Actually, I was hopin' to talk to you a moment."

I had managed to avoid another late-night conversation with Eva last night. I should have known I wouldn't be fortunate enough to do it again. "Of course."

I got up and she sat, not facing the fire, but facing me. I prepared to guard myself against any and all feelings. I wouldn't let the conversation feel intimate. I would not let my feelings for her distract me from what mattered.

I sat mirroring her.

"Are you sure you're alright?"

"I'm fine, Eva."

She shook her head. "You haven't been actin' like it. Even before the officers showed up yesterday, you were quiet, and when you were talkin', it was as if you were only half there, your mind somewhere else. And I can't believe I'm sayin' this, but Roland's right. You're a wreck."

"I'm fine," I repeated.

"Are you lyin' to me or to yourself?"

Mercy, she was persistent. I ran a hand down my face, trying to think of what I could possibly tell her that would set her mind at ease.

"How do you want me to act, Eva? My parents are gone. I've been hiding the last few weeks so I don't get murdered. And I'm about to walk into a prison where I very well could be murdered anyway. Do you expect me to smile and carry on as if nothing is wrong *every* day? I—"

"No, I don't. That's the opposite of what I expect. I told you on our first day with Roland, I don't know how you're still standin'. Even then, I didn't realize how dire all of this really was. But you did."

Ironically, she still didn't know how dire it was. "And I told you not to compare grief."

"I'm not. I'm makin' observations. You're barely keepin' it together, Silas."

I wanted to be mad, to argue with her. But I was exhausted. All I really wanted was for all of this to be over. I sighed. "I'll be fine."

"I know." She took my hands. "But it's okay if right now you're not."

My chest ached at her touch. I desperately wanted to tell her everything. *Everything.* But I couldn't. I tried to refuse her prompting, to pull my hands away, but the tears were already welling up in my eyes.

"I have to be, Eva." My voice broke on her name.

"You can't afford to keep pretendin' you're fine. I think it's eatin' you alive."

She was right, and I knew it. And I hated it. I hated that I couldn't handle this pressure. I hated that she could tell I couldn't handle it.

A sob hit me before I could stop it.

I pulled one of my hands free to cover my mouth, stifling the sound so Roland wouldn't wake.

Another sob wracked me.

She gently squeezed my other hand.

Tears streamed down my face. My shoulders shook. And then my whole body trembled with each silent sob. I wanted to cry loudly. I'd wanted to scream for days now. But if I was going to have an actual breakdown, no one was going to hear about it. Who would want a king who couldn't handle a few trying weeks? No one could see me like this.

But Eva did.

"Do you want me to sit with you or give you some space?" she softly asked.

The question was such a bizarre response, I couldn't help but cry harder. I wasn't entirely sure what I was crying about at this point. Everything, I supposed, all at once, crashing down on me.

I held her hand tighter in answer to her question, as if she was the only one who might be able to pull me out from under the rubble. Like she was the only thing keeping me from losing my mind along with everything else I'd lost: my parents, the only way of life I'd known, my future, even my library. What a stupid thing to cry about. But *I* was stupid. So, so stupid.

I laid back, unable to face Eva any longer. The movement pulled my hand from hers, but that was just as well. One way or another, I was bound to lose her too.

The thought of it ripped another sob through my body. I covered my face with my arms, curling in on myself. I wanted to scream. I wanted to die. No, I wanted to live—but not like this. I just wanted it all to stop. Stop. *Stop.*

But all I could do was keep crying.

A hand on my shoulder, the touch feeling a million miles away.

Her thumb brushed back and forth, the smallest movement. I focused on it, dodging the falling pieces of my life to do so.

Slowly, I began to calm. Silent sobs no longer claimed control of my body, only an unsteady breath.

She shifted behind me. I grabbed her hand on my shoulder.

"Please stay," I managed to whisper. Eyes still closed. A prayer.

She didn't lift her hand, but I felt her move even so.

"Stay," I pleaded once more. The request couldn't make me look much more pathetic than I already had proven myself to be.

She stilled. "I'm not goin' anywhere," she whispered. "Breathe. Take your time."

I listened to her breathe, quietly whispering for me to inhale and exhale. I tried to follow her instruction, but my own breath shuddered in my chest, as though my lungs were afraid to lose the air I put in them. "I can't."

"Take your time," she repeated, and squeezed my hand reassuringly. "I'm not goin' anywhere."

43

ROLAND SAYS I'M NOT ALLOWED TO BE IMPRESSED BY THE CAVES OF ORDELUNE

Evangeline

Eventually, Silas's breathing returned to normal, and he fell asleep. I wasn't surprised. I'd had many dramatic cries myself, and he clearly had a *lot* he'd been holding in.

It was unsettling to see someone cry like that. In such visible agony, and yet not making a sound. His mouth agape, jaw locked in a soundless scream. As if his crying was so sacred, I wasn't allowed to hear it.

A few tears of my own rolled down my face. The way he begged me to stay when I was only readjusting how I was sitting was enough to keep me frozen at his side until the fire began to die. How had I gone from the girl in the ship who listened to him cry and did nothing for him, to the girl who held his hand and promised she'd stay?

That ship felt like a lifetime ago. That girl too.

A lot had changed in the last two weeks, my feelings for him being the greatest. He was no longer a stranger who'd ruined my life. For better or worse, I cared about him now. Deeply. More than I had cared about anyone in a long time. Maybe ever.

It terrified me.

I slowly broke away from him, pausing a moment to make sure he didn't wake, and stoked the fire.

For a moment, I considered returning to Silas and sitting next to him again. But he was calm, sleeping peacefully. There was no reason for me to sit so close. No explanation for why I wanted to regardless.

I sat a few yards away, so I'd be right there if he were to wake up and need me. Though, who was I to think he would?

When the fire died down again, I revived it. And then I sat there until it died a third time.

I checked Roland's watch. Silas's shift was nearly over.

I hesitated to wake him. But it would be better if Roland didn't know about any of this. Silas would probably want it that way, too.

I kneeled and shook his shoulder. "Silas."

He woke more calmly than I'd ever seen him wake. "I fell asleep?"

I nodded.

"Sorry. You should go to sleep. How long was I out for?"

"Your shift's over. I'll lie down and you can wake up Roland."

He sat up. "You stayed up my whole watch?"

I nodded again.

"Why didn't you wake me sooner?"

"I didn't mind."

"Eva." My name fell heavy from his lips, like what I did was something remarkable.

"Silas," I said back, not wanting to lecture him about how much he needed what had happened. Hoping his name would say as much as mine had.

The fire crackled, dying light flickering across his features.

He reached out and slowly brushed my hair out of my face, his fingers pausing at my jawline. My breath caught, sure he was going to lean in and kiss me.

He put his hand on the back of my head and pulled me to his chest instead.

"I'm glad you're here, Eva. I mean that."

A hoard of emotions welled up in my chest. I closed my eyes a moment, because despite the confusion in my heart, I realized I felt safe here, with him.

"I'm glad I'm here too." I took a deep breath, the scent of the woods and the campfire smoke on his tunic a strange comfort. But I let myself stay there only a few seconds longer. "I should go to sleep."

"You should." He let me go. "I'll let you get settled a moment before I wake Roland."

"Thanks."

"And Eva," he added before I could turn away. "I..." He hesitated. "I feel as though I need to apologize, but I also think you'll tell me not to."

"You're right. Nothing happened that you need to apologize for."

"But—"

"And even if there was somethin'—which there *isn't*—I was asleep the last three hours, and you had an uneventful shift. Why would you need to apologize for that?"

"Because that's not the truth."

I smiled. "What's the harm in one more lie?"

As soon as I sat on my bedroll, Silas called my name again.

"Thank you," he whispered across the fire.

"You're welcome."

I lay down and closed my eyes, hoping sleep would claim me in a moment. Instead, I listened to Silas revive the fire, wake Roland, and lie on his own bedroll. I listened to Roland circle the camp and find a spot to sit and keep watch. I listened as the birds started chirping, ushering in the sunrise. I listened for any more silent tears from the kindest person I'd ever met. But, of course, how could I hear any, even if they were there?

I managed to fall asleep, but it felt like it was only two minutes before Roland woke us for the last day of our journey.

The day that would change everything, for better or worse.

Roland had a nervous energy about him as he packed up camp. His movements a little quicker than normal, his sentences a bit too chipper. But I couldn't blame him. He was going to witness firsthand the horrors the Cathmoores had faced these last few weeks. That we, in a sick way, *hoped* the Cathmoores had faced these last few weeks.

Because if they hadn't, then they were dead.

Silas was far more somber. He still wouldn't meet my gaze. He moved slowly. But he did manage to eat, which was an improvement.

Though I hardly slept a wink, I was surprisingly awake. Perhaps my own nerves were at play, keeping me more alert than I should have been.

I tried to bridge the mood between Roland and Silas. This was their adventure, afterall. Who knew what I would do when this was over? But that was something to worry about overmorrow. Today we reached Ordelune. Tomorrow we started a war. After that, it would be one day at a time.

We packed and loaded the horses. As Silas situated himself behind me in the saddle, I had to fight the urge to instantly lean against him. There was so much unknown ahead of us. But right now, here, with him, I was safe.

Ten minutes into the ride, my eyelids grew heavy, and I couldn't help but lean back. Silas adjusted how he held the reins, his arms wrapped tighter around me than usual.

"If you're able to sleep, you should," he whispered.

"I'll be fine," I assured. But he was so warm, and I was so tired, and I leaned further against him, closed my eyes for just a moment...

I woke to an entirely new landscape. The mountains I'd last seen on the horizon were now here, surrounding us. We were passing through a valley now, but the road ahead began climbing the slopes.

I sat up, and Silas loosened his hold on me, only letting go when I was resettled in the saddle.

"Welcome to Ordelune," he said.

There wasn't much of a road here. Trampled grass and exposed dirt every so often. Hummel grew in large yellow patches along the path. I'd seen hummel before, when my mother and I would wander the countryside or go to the pond and swim. But we only had a few stray flowers here and there. This looked like a farm for it. You could gather the deadly plant in basket-fulls. Thankfully, it wasn't dangerous to the touch, only poisonous if ingested. I hoped its sudden appearance wasn't a bad omen.

Perhaps it was a good one: Despite the possibility of death looming over the next several hours, we would pass by, unharmed.

Roland pulled the map of the caves from his pocket. "Not much longer. I'll leave you two in a different place than they instructed me to."

Silas tensed. "Do they know we're here already?"

"If they do, it's not because I told them. That's why I took the shortcut. It gave us an advantage in that they aren't expecting us yet."

"But we passed those officers two days ago. They may have passed word on that we were on a different road."

"That's exactly why I'm leaving you somewhere else."

"You don't think they'll suspect you for that? Not sticking to their plan?"

"I can tell them it was your idea, and I wasn't able to deny you or alert them to the change without raising suspicions."

"Do you spend most of the day plannin' out all the layers of your lies?" I asked.

"Yes, I do. Believe it or not, a good plan requires careful planning. A lesson you two could stand to learn, it seems."

I rolled my eyes. Could he get *any* more annoying?

We continued on, letting Roland lead the way up the mountain slopes. When we came upon our first visible cave, I excitedly pointed it out.

"Yes, thank you, Evangeline. That's such an astute observation considering we're in the *Caves* of Ordelune," Roland was quick to retort.

Silas didn't say anything. In fact, he had been quite still since Roland had informed us of his plan. As Port took his next few strides, I couldn't even feel him breathing. I reached out and touched his hand.

He immediately let go of the reins and intertwined his fingers in mine.

"Breathe," I whispered to him.

I couldn't tell if he did, only that he clutched my hand tighter. He didn't let go until Roland stopped outside of another cave. This one wasn't deep. More of an alcove, really. We could see the back of it from the mouth.

Roland unloaded his horse, but Silas didn't move to get off of ours.

"This is where you'll wait for me," Roland instructed. "It may take a while. I'm not going to rush the meeting with them. I'll find out as much as I can. You stay out of sight. I anticipate returning in a few hours."

That finally broke Silas's silence. "*Hours?*"

"I'm leaving you a ways out from the cave. We'll still have plenty of time after I get back to strategize accordingly. We're still ahead of schedule."

Roland remounted his horse, though Silas and I still hadn't moved off ours yet. "Use this time to rest. You both clearly need it." He prodded Starboard to start moving, then turned back, one last time. "And Silas, don't forget yourself and why we're here, please."

Port stomped, nervously lifting his front feet up and down, wanting to follow.

"What was that about?" I asked.

"Roland saw you sleeping as we traveled. He said he noticed because it had been 'blissfully quiet' for more than ten minutes."

"I don't talk that much."

"He exaggerated a little, yes."

I leaned back against him. "Speakin' of quiet, how are you holdin' up?"

"If I thought I felt sick yesterday, then I think I must be dying today."

I squeezed his hand. "Well, we can't have that."

"I know Roland knows what he's doing with this plan, but it's killing me that we're so close. That he'll be there with them and we still have to wait here."

"I know. And I definitely think we should discuss this more, but do you think we could do it off the horse?"

Silas sighed and dismounted. "If I can't keep my focus now, how am I supposed to do it once we get to the prison?" He stepped away, looking off in the direction Roland had gone.

I climbed down from the saddle and secured Port. I had been worried about the same thing. But I had also seen him get through numerous situations that would have caused plenty of other people to freeze up. "You're great in a crisis. With the pirates. With the officers. You know how to handle yourself when it counts. The difference is that this time, you're anticipatin' the crisis. But once the time comes, I have full confidence that you'll know what to do."

"A week ago, you said that I was an idiot for the way I handled those situations."

"Eh." I nudged his arm with my shoulder. "Maybe I just didn't have the wisdom at the time to see the brilliance in your ideas."

"Jump ship, Lucinda," he said, but he was smiling.

"I'm goin' to sit down. Think you can keep me company?"

Another long sigh. "Yes. I can do that."

44

Brigid Really Has a Way with Words

Alastair

I did try to sit with Eva. But my thoughts kept racing, and I hoped some pacing would slow them down. I paced for so long that I cleared a path in the grass by the time Eva demanded I rejoin her in the cave.

She patted the space next to her on the blanket she'd laid out. "Sit. You're goin' to wear yourself out."

"I'm just walking."

"Fine, you'll wear out your shoes. Come over here."

I begrudgingly plopped next to her. "If you're taking away my walking privileges, I hope you have another suggestion for how to pass the time."

"I do." She handed me my book. I hadn't noticed she'd gone through my pack to find it. I needed to *focus*.

"Eva, I'm sorry, but I don't think I have the capacity for a reading lesson right now."

"I don't want a readin' lesson, I want you to read."

"You think I can focus on something like this right now?"

Her features softened, and the genuine concern in her eyes stilled me. "You said this book is called *The Meanin' of Shadows*, right? And it's about sufferin' or somethin'?"

"Yes."

She nodded as though I'd made her point.

"I've read the book cover to cover a dozen times, Eva. I know what it says."

"I know you do. But maybe you need to read it again. That's what you packed it for, isn't it?"

I stared at the book, but didn't open it.

Eva briefly leaned into my side as she spoke again, and it took everything in me not to wrap my arm around her shoulders and keep her there. "When I was little, my mom would tell me stories before I went to sleep. There was one she always told me when I woke up from a nightmare to help me calm down. After she died, I thought about that story a lot. Because I kept wishin' the whole thing was only a bad dream. At night, before I fell sleep, I would tell it to myself out loud. I *knew* the story, but hearin' it again was what helped." She reached across and pointed at the book. "Maybe this is your mom story."

"How do you know I don't have a real mom story?"

She raised her eyebrows. "Do you?"

I dipped my chin. "No. Not anything like that anyway. Maybe you should tell me yours."

She shook her head. "It wouldn't mean the same to you. But I think Brigid does."

I set the book down a moment and turned to her. "How do you know all this, Eva? What I need and how to convince me I need it?"

She blinked. "I have eyes, Silas."

"Not normal ones. Sure, maybe I'm a big enough mess right now that both you and Roland know I'm a breath away from losing my mind, but *you* were the one who knew what I needed last night. Not Roland, who's known me my whole life. How is that?"

She straightened, but lowered her gaze and set her hands in her lap. She was quiet for a moment, fiddling with the hem of her dress, then laughed under her breath. "It's probably some sort of crime to say this..." She glanced at me, then back down at her hands. "But I see a bit of myself in you. And I know you said not to compare grief, but..." She inhaled deeply and finally met my eyes.

"I can't help thinkin' about what you've lost and how you've been ripped away from the only life you knew. And I know it's different and on a much bigger scale for you, but I thought about what I wanted when my world came crashin' down. My mother was able to shield me from a lot out in the countryside, but I always knew who I was, and why I was so lonely. I had always wanted to live in town with other people, but not the way it happened.

"Once she was gone, I didn't want the doctor to promise me he did everythin' he could. I didn't want Master Gratsis to tell me I had done the right thing. Or have Missus Gratsis assure me that everythin' would be alright eventually. I just wanted to be able to grieve and be angry, and I didn't want to feel so alone anymore. So, I thought, maybe that's what you wanted, too."

I blinked back tears, my heart simultaneously growing heavier and lighter with her every word. "I don't know anyone like you, Eva."

She laughed—a nervous laugh. "I'm not sure if you mean that as a compliment or not."

"Definitely a compliment. You're brilliant." I had nothing to say to her but praise. She must have been the wisest person I'd met. And she was so beautiful, sitting there, speaking to me so honestly, so freely. The way she seemed to know me, to read me so easily, was the most comforting and most terrifying thing in the world. I was about to say as much, to tell her what she meant to me, when she reached for the book and placed it back in my hands.

"Then, read, noble. Doctor's orders."

I sighed, but how could I refuse her?

"Look, I'll give it a try, but I don't think I'll be able to focus for very long."

"Then read out loud, to me."

"Then you're picking the section we read." I handed her the book.

"What are the sections?"

"Not telling. Just flip through and pick a page that looks interesting."

She gave me the book again, without so much as opening it. "I want the one you quoted the other day. About an excitin' opportunity or somethin'."

"*'The opportunity alone is enough to pour excitement into the heart of the adventurer.'* That's Section Three. Good choice." I thumbed through the pages. "We'll start at the beginning of the section so you get the context, if that's alright."

She nodded.

I cleared my throat and began reading. "*If we presume the sun to still be shining even during the darkest night, then we come to the conclusion that the absence of light does not equate its extinction. Conversely, on the fairest summer day, we still know that night will fall once its time has come, just as it always does. It is also true, then, that the absence of darkness does not equate its extinction, for even in the daylight, we see shadows.*"

I glanced over at Eva. She propped her head on her hands, looking far more content than I was.

"*Since the dawn of Man, we have striven to elongate the bliss and pleasure of our lives in the hopes that we may one day eradicate our suffering. But I will remind Man that even on the summer solstice, night falls.*

"*As day and night passed, Man learned to appreciate its passing with the invention of Time. Because of the clock, night and day have their place. We no longer fear the darkness, so long as it appears during its assigned hour.*"

I swallowed. "Eva, are you sure—"

"Shh, don't interrupt, this is fascinatin'."

I smiled, genuinely surprised. "You like Brigid?"

She sat up and shrugged. "I guess so." She pointed to the pages. "But I also like watchin' you make that nonsense turn into somethin' real."

I laughed. "It isn't nonsense. Look, I'll show you." I set the book between us so she could see. I pointed to the words as I read them. "*My hypothesis, then—*"

"His hypothesis? We're nearly halfway through the book. He's just *now* tellin' us his hypothesis? Mercy, it's a good thing we started in this section."

I laughed again. "Who's interrupting now?"

She scoffed. "Nevermind. Keep goin'."

I took a moment to answer her question anyway, explaining that each section of the book posed a new hypothesis that built from the previous one.

"*My hypothesis, then, is that the good and bad we face on the earth are much like the rhythms of the day and night. The presence of one experience does not negate the reality and possibility of another. The problem is that many men believe they can dictate when the good happens and when the bad happens. And then they grow bitter that the bad must happen at all.*

"*But Man did not set the moon and the sun in correspondence with his clock. Rather, he set his clock in correspondence to the heavens.*"

Eva leaned over and rested her head on my shoulder. Somehow, I kept reading, though I lost all comprehension of the words for a few sentences.

She set her hand on my arm to get my attention—as though she didn't already have it—and said, "Keep reading. But I'm going to close my eyes, so you don't have to point at the words anymore."

"Sure." I rested my hand on my knee, trying to move as little as possible to not disturb her. She didn't let go of me though. And as I kept reading, her hand trailed down my arm, little by little. I thought she was falling asleep, but right when I decided she must be out, she took my hand.

It stopped me short for half a second, and then I managed to continue. It must have been something I just read. Fate knew Eva probably needed to hear those words as much as I did. What did I just read, anyway? *Focus, man.* I cleared my throat again, and went back a sentence before continuing on.

"*Every unexpected moment is ripe with unexpected fruit: some sweet, some bitter. Such a moment presents the opportunity to reach out and discover which fruit it will offer. The opportunity alone is enough to pour excitement into the heart of the adventurer.*"

Mercy, Brigid.

I closed the book with my free hand.

Eva looked up, but didn't quite lift her head off my shoulder. "Why'd you stop?"

"Because, Eva, I want to tell you who I am."

She closed her eyes again. "I already know who you are," she said matter-of-factly.

I frowned. Panic and relief fought for a seat in my chest. "You do? How long have you known? How did you find out?"

"I've spent the last two weeks with you. Riskin' our lives together. That's a lot of bondin' time."

"Yeah, but I don't understand how that—"

She opened her eyes and jabbed her finger into my chest. "I know who you are because I know your character. I know where your heart and your loyalties lie. I know the lengths you would go for the people you love. Maybe I don't know certain things *about* you like your real name or where you used to live. But I know who you *are*."

"If all goes well, you'll know the rest of those things by tomorrow night."

"Then let me learn tomorrow. I want to enjoy the time I have with you now." She leaned into my shoulder again, and I moved to wrap my arm around her shoulders.

She allowed me to do so, letting go of my hand, and wrapping her arms around my torso instead. She must have been *really* tired, to be touching me this much, voluntarily. But then again, hadn't she been nearly as close last night—the last few days, even?

You need to make it clear you don't return her affections. Don't forget yourself, Silas.

Roland's words came calling back to me, as well as my own: *This is not the time for romance.*

But what was it Brigid wrote? *Unexpected moments ripe with unexpected fruit: some sweet, some bitter.*

"Eva, knowing those things, my name and where I come from, do you think it's going to change things between us?"

"Doesn't it have to? I can't imagine your friends and family will approve of... I mean, look at us, Silas."

I didn't need to look at us. Every place she and I made contact was holding my every thought captive.

"Eva, if I can be forward for a moment," I paused to give her a chance to say no, but also to gather my courage. She didn't stop me from continuing. "You *are* my dearest friend, but I've grown very fond of you over this last week. What Roland said, before he left... He told me yesterday that I should make it clear that I don't have any affection toward you. But if I were to say that, it would be a lie. And I don't want to lie to you anymore, Eva."

She was quiet a moment, but she didn't let go. She didn't move a muscle.

"Eva?"

"Why are you tellin' me this?" It was only a whisper.

"I..." My heart beat wildly in my chest, and I was sure she could hear it, leaning against me like that. "I guess, I'm trying to ask if you feel the same."

"Of course I feel the same, Silas." She sniffed as her tears soaked into my shirt.

Oh no. "Why are you crying?"

She let go of me to wipe her face. "Because it doesn't matter how I feel. How you feel. It's all goin' to change. Tomorrow night we'll be back in the real world. Not hidin' in the woods."

"Why does that have to change anything?"

"You know why!" Her voice cracked, and I pulled her closer. "You know who I am," she mumbled into my chest.

I held her a moment before I spoke. "I do. And just as you said to me, I know your heart and your character, Eva. You are more than your father's choices and your status. Every day I'm more amazed by you than the last. I can't imagine losing you. I want you—I *need* you in my life. If you mean it, that you feel the same, then we'll find a way to make this work."

"How? I ran from Gratsis because I'm not willin' to be a secret mistress. Even if I care for you, I—" She faltered and took a steadying breath. "My standards will not change."

"Mercy, Eva, that's not what I meant. I would never ask that of you. You are worth far more than that."

She kept her face buried in my chest, and I hardly caught her muffled words: "You're the only person in the world who thinks so."

"Eva," I said softly, her words shattering the last remaining pieces of my heart. I pulled back slightly so I could take her face in my hands and look her in the eyes. "Your lineage does not define your worth."

One last tear slipped down her cheek. "It does, though."

"Not to me."

"Silas—"

"We're technically already married, Eva. It could be as simple as that."

"You know no one will let that count." She pulled away from my hands and flopped back against my chest. "Every detail of that weddin' was illegal, and that will be used against us for all it's worth."

"Well, then, I'll just have to find a way to marry you again." I laughed. "Will you actually kiss me back the second time around?"

She scoffed as she pulled back from me. "I *knew* you were upset about that!"

"It was our *wedding* and you didn't kiss me! Why wouldn't I be upset?"

"It wasn't *real*!"

"But the pirates needed to believe it was real!"

"Oh? Like how Officer Larson needed to believe our *baby* was real?"

"Stars above, forget I said anything."

But she laughed. Mercy, she laughed, and it was the best sound in the world. "Too late. You want to kiss me. That's very indecent of you to so openly admit."

"Perhaps, but you avoided the question. Which, if I've learned anything about you, means you don't want to admit the answer. So tell me, will you kiss me back the second time around?"

She considered me a moment, then smiled, her hazel eyes glinting. "There's only one way to find out."

I smiled back. "Good." I pulled her to my chest. "I'll look forward to it."

She huffed. "For all the indirect ways the upper class talk, you sure aren't very good at takin' a hint."

I looked down at her. "What do you mean?"

She gazed up at me. "I just told you to kiss me."

"Oh."

She blinked. "So ... are you goin' to, or has the mome—"

And I did. Before she was even done speaking, I did.

And she kissed me back.

And for a moment, nothing existed except me and her, and that kiss.

And then I heard Roland shout, "*What* on the face of Breslin's seven kingdoms, is *this*?"

45

LOVE AND DUTY TURN OUT TO BE VERY COMPLICATED THINGS

Alastair

Eva jumped and pulled away from me at Roland's voice, but I didn't let go of her hand.

"Roland! You're back early." I was pleased at how nonchalant my tone came out.

I could practically see the rage rolling off him.

"We had a deal, Silas," he growled. "You promised me nothing would happen between you two."

"Yes, and I made that promise in good faith, but it turns out, I was wrong."

"You two are going to be the death of me!"

"Would you relax, Roland? This doesn't change anything about what happens tomorrow.

"I'm not worried about how this affects *tomorrow*."

The intensity of his glare and his tone finally convinced me to let go of Eva's hands. She immediately stood, eager to put distance between us.

Hang the moon.

"Do you and I need to go have a discussion?" I asked.

"No, Evangeline is leaving. You and I can talk when she's gone."

"What?" Eva asked, the first thing she'd said since Roland returned.

"You can't kick her out of the group when we're so close to the end!"

"I'm not *kicking her out*. If you'll remember, the reason you two were alone for so long was because I went to scout things out."

I folded my arms across my chest, not in the mood for his attitude. Though it was clear he wasn't in the mood for mine either.

"And while I was there," he continued, "risking life and limb, I was able to get a glimpse of the royals."

My heart practically leaped out of my chest. "How were they?"

Roland went quiet, looking from me to Eva. "We need to get them out as soon as possible. They're scheduled for another interrogation at midnight. We need to get there before then. Which is why Evangeline needs to leave *right now*."

My stomach dropped. There was something he wasn't telling me. Something *bad*. Perhaps he couldn't in front of Eva.

Roland handed her the map of the caves. She took it and immediately began to ready Port.

"Since time is of the essence, Silas and I won't be able to wait for you to return before we enter the prison. It should take you about forty-five minutes to get to Irimen. We'll leave shortly after you get there. Our rendezvous doesn't have to line up precisely, but it would be ideal for you to be ready for us when we come out with the royals."

"Understood." She studied the map. "Where's our rendezvous?"

"Two mountains north, there's an outcropping of rock. Silas and I will leave all our belongings there when we go in. You can see the entrance of the prison from there. It's not an actual building. It looks like every other cave from the outside."

He pointed it out to her, and she nodded, though I didn't know how she thought that was a good enough direction.

"We should go there, see it all together."

"No time." Roland insisted. "It's here." He pointed again to the spot on the map in Eva's hand. "If we aren't there by morning, assume the worst."

"Lovely parting words, Roland," Eva muttered.

"Clearly you can go to Silas for those."

I glared at him, but my nerves were quickly shifting to pure dread. It felt as though something sinister was creeping into my bones.

I didn't want Eva to leave. I knew she had to. We would need the doctor. But I couldn't send her off like this. It wasn't enough. It didn't feel right. And if we didn't make it out of that prison by morning...

"It's East at the fork to get to Irimen," I reminded her. We should have drawn it on the map.

"I know," she said. "Don't worry about me."

I picked up the book so I could dig through my pack without further upsetting Roland. As I set the book securely inside my pack, I grabbed the ring I'd been charged to keep hidden, concealing it in my hand as I approached Eva.

She hoisted herself up into the saddle, and I hurried over to her before she could leave. I kept my voice low, not wanting Roland to overhear what I was about to say.

"Take this with you." I reached up to take her hand so it appeared as though I was merely squeezing it to say goodbye and good luck. But while her hand was in mine, I dropped my ring into her palm.

"This is Alastair's," I whispered. "Use it to prove your case. Use it as a bribe if it comes to it."

Her brows furrowed. "You think I'll need a bribe?"

"I don't know. But I have a bad feeling, and it's more than just nerves." My stomach was roiling even as I said it. "Be careful, please."

"I will. But I'm in far less danger than you'll be in. You be careful too."

"I will be." I actually did squeeze her hand now, and hoped my smile looked reassuring. "I'll see you soon."

I let go and she immediately took off.

My throat tightened with every step that carried Eva away—for more reasons than one. Of course, I was worried about her going out alone—even if her assignment was significantly less dangerous than what Roland and I were about to do. But I was also worried about being alone with Roland after what he just saw.

Once she disappeared from view, the interrogation began. "Tell me you don't actually have feelings for her, and that was merely a rash, impulsive moment brought on by stress-induced delusions."

"If I tell you that, will it end this conversation?"

"Alastair, you have to think about your future."

"That's *all* I've ever done! *Especially* this last month."

"And you decided today of all days to stop?"

"No. I just—she said—" I stammered. Why was I bothering trying to explain this to him, when there were real issues to deal with? "No, nevermind. I am not having this conversation with you."

"She said, what?" Roland pressed.

"I don't want to talk about this."

"Neither do I. But it's been done so we *must* talk about it."

I groaned. "You said we're leaving shortly after Eva arrives at Irimen? That's nearly an hour. You tell me what's going on in the prison, and then I'll tell you about Eva in the remaining time."

Roland pinched the bridge of his nose. "Fine."

"So when you went in the prison, you saw my parents?"

"I told you I did."

"How were they?"

"Bad. I told you that as well."

"But *how* were they bad? We were expecting them to be in poor health. What's so wrong that has you rushing everything?"

He shook his head. "I don't think you should know that any sooner than you need to."

"They're *my* parents! I'm going to see them in a few minutes."

"And then you'll know why I didn't give you details."

The blood drained from my face. Was it really *that* bad?

"I thought you didn't want to say anything in front of Eva."

"Why? She's tougher than you."

"I—" I stopped, taken aback by his answer. "I know. I didn't know *you* knew that."

"You don't live as an orphaned leech for nineteen years unless you have thick skin and an inordinate amount of resolve."

"You don't travel the kingdom with someone as rude as *you* unless you have thick skin and an inordinate amount of resolve, you mean."

Roland shrugged. "Regardless, I didn't say anything for *your* sake, not Evangeline's."

"Did my parents see you?"

"No, I don't believe so. Though, that's for the best, considering the part I was playing in there."

I nodded. That was for the best. "How many guards are there?"

"Eight, from what I could tell. I'm confident we can handle it."

I let out a long breath. If circumstances didn't allow Roland to use his pistol, most of the fighting would fall to me. "So, how long until we can leave?"

"It hasn't even been five minutes."

I groaned.

"So..." He checked his watch for no other reason than dramatic effect. "That leaves about fifty minutes for you to tell me about *Eva*."

The groan that escaped me that time was visceral. It came from the very depths of my soul.

"You proposed the deal," he reminded me.

"Fine. But only if we approach this like one of your strategy problems, and not like I'm a huge disappointment."

Roland stared at me a moment. "I'll do my best."

I tried to search for the words to tell him how torn I was inside, but I opted for a different angle for now. "Have you ever been in love before, Roland?"

"In *love*? Don't tell me that's what this is, Alastair. You've known the girl, what, two weeks? I thought this was you being stupid and reckless again. Pretending that you're a pauper and having fun. Don't tell me you *love* her!"

I raised a hand in defense. "I didn't say I did. But ... I think I could, eventually. Roland, I'd do anything for her."

He cursed. "That's the mindset that will ruin you. Ruin your *family*. We came all this way to restore your family, restore the throne, and now you want to throw that all away for a lee—"

"Don't you dare call her that anymore."

Roland fumed, but obeyed. He clenched his jaw a few times as he pondered what to say next, as he did in a strategy lesson. He really was trying, although it was insulting how difficult the effort was for him. Finally, he looked up. "You remember I told you I was betrothed once?"

"Of course."

"Why do you think I didn't marry her?"

"Because you didn't like her?"

"I *loved* her."

"Then why didn't you marry? Did she die?"

His eyes widened briefly before he resumed his lecturing demeanor. "No, she didn't *die*. I was hired to be your tutor."

"Why should that stop anything? You're allowed to be married, are you not?"

"It wasn't my choice to call off the engagement. We were in Iridescence, and her father wouldn't let her move so far away. Besides, taking a job at the palace was going to significantly elevate my status. Marrying Magdelena after taking the position could be construed as something scandalous."

Hearing the woman's name was a shock. Some part of me hadn't fully believed Roland up until now. I'd never seen him as much more than a tutor. It was all I'd ever known him to be: smart and calculating. But this story didn't sound like either of those things.

"Who would have possibly found that scandalous? If you were previously betrothed, what difference would it make?"

"I wasn't just an academic anymore, Alastair. I had entered the political realm. Every decision suddenly had dozens of layers to it. You know how that is."

I swallowed. "Then you shouldn't have taken the position."

"When the king and queen ask something of you, you don't have the luxury of saying no."

"So you gave up not only a proper academic life, but also the love of your life, to come teach a toddler?"

Roland nodded.

"And you don't resent me or my parents for that?"

"No, I did at first. Of course I did. But being the royal tutor has many perks. All the academic texts I could ever desire at my fingertips. I don't have to scrape up coppers to further my learning anymore. I was a prodigy, yes, but I was *poor*. Most academics aren't respected until after they die. Not unless they discover something extraordinarily revolutionary. What good does praise do a dead man? At least now, I am respected. I have everything I could desire."

"Except a wife."

"I have had plenty of opportunity for a wife these last fifteen years, should I have wanted one. I've found love distracts from duty."

"So, I'm supposed to just ... forget everything I feel toward Eva?"

"Yes. You have to."

"That's hardly fair."

"*Life* isn't fair. Did you not learn that from your philosophers? You have a duty to uphold, Alastair. And I trust you will do what is right."

I nodded, though his words sounded closer to a threat than trust. In fact, for the first time in my life, upholding duty and doing what was right didn't feel synonymous.

46

I Am the Stupidest Girl in All of Breslin

Evangeline

I held the small object in my hand for a while after I got moving. Silas clearly didn't want Roland to know what he gave me, so I didn't open my hand until I knew Roland wouldn't notice me looking at it. It was well enough, because I was alone in the saddle for the first time and had Port moving at a quicker pace than usual, so it took me a moment to adjust to his trot.

Once I was acclimated and far enough away, I slowly opened my hand, careful that the object wouldn't fall out.

It was exactly what I guessed it was based on the feel of it, though I could hardly believe it was actually Alastair's.

At the center of my palm, a gold ring with the largest sapphire I'd ever seen glinted in the sun. Little diamonds surrounded the gem, adding greatly to its shine and value. How many dozen horses could *this* buy? And I was holding it in *my* hand? And Silas was giving me permission to give it *away* if I had to?

I frowned, a new realization troubling me. If Alastair was captured at the palace, and Silas had fled from his own house, how did he come to be in possession of the prince's ring?

The number of questions I had were going to drive me mad. I slipped the ring onto my thumb so I wouldn't lose it, but—although I'd broken plenty of clothing laws in the last few weeks—wearing the prince's ring *felt* like a crime. I moved the ring to the pouch on my belt, trying to tuck my questions away along with it.

But I couldn't stop wondering what the relationship between Silas and Alastair was actually like. How Silas had cried when he said he hoped Alastair would be a good king. What exactly did that mean? Was he afraid he wouldn't be? Was Alastiar more like Roland than like him?

Surely, he had to be like Silas. If all of Silas's friends were as arrogant as Roland, there was no conceivable way that Silas would be so kind to me. That he would trust me.

That he would *kiss* me.

Granted, we had technically kissed before on the pirate ship. Well, he had kissed me, anyway. But he didn't know who I really was at that point. And we were trying not to die, or lose a hand at the very least.

This kiss had been *quite* different.

And it was all doomed.

Silas said he'd find a way to make it work. Said he would *marry me again*. But that wasn't likely. I never should have let myself get so attached. The odds of him still caring about me when this was all over and he returned to his *noble* life with his *real* friend *the prince*, were next to none. Maybe he didn't even mean what he said to me in that cave. Maybe he was lying again.

But it had certainly felt like he meant it. Which was what caused me to lose all rational thought in the first place. But even if he *had* meant it, there were still laws that would prevent us from a legally binding marriage.

Though, he had an in with the king-to-be. I was sure King Esmond would never allow such a change, but perhaps Alastair would grant such a kindness. Afterall, it was the least he could do to return Silas the favor of saving his life and restoring his family to their rightful place. He had to. Hadn't Silas said the upper class was built upon favors?

We'd just have to wait until Prince Alastair married and assumed the throne. He'd turned eighteen recently, hadn't he? Only a few months ago. Surely he was betrothed already? I suddenly wished I had paid more attention to politics. Would the return to the throne hasten the wedding? Or would the Cathmoores want to stabilize under King Esmond's rule once more before the prince took over?

I shook my head. What was I thinking? *Me? Married?* That was impossible. And there was no use dwelling on impossibilities. Besides, I didn't join Silas's adventure so I could marry him. I did it to save the Cathmoores and, hopefully, find some sort of future for myself—a future that did *not* include a second illegal wedding.

I needed to focus on the original plan now: saving the Cathmoores.

A fork appeared in the road ahead, and I slowed Port until we came to a stop in the middle of the crossroad.

Was it east at the fork? West? Stars above. Left or right?

I pulled the map from the satchel hooked to the saddle, but it didn't help me much. The curving road and my wandering thoughts did no favors in orienting myself. The only marked dot was the cave where the royals were being kept. There were words written on the map—instructions for Roland, I assumed.

I still couldn't read to save my life. But it seemed I would have to give it a try to save the Royal Cathmoores' lives. I stared at the signpost in front of me, trying to make sense of the letters carved on it.

The town was called Irimen. I sounded it out slowly: *Ee-r-ih-meh-n*. It started with an *ee* sound, like my name. I looked for an 'E' on the signpost. The sign pointing east had an 'E' toward the end of the word. I said the town name slowly again. *Ee-r-ih-meh-n*. No, no *ee* sound near the end.

The sign pointing west did have an 'E' at the beginning, but following the E-word, there was a letter I didn't remember from what Silas taught me, and then two more words. Perhaps there were multiple towns in that direction?

I groaned. I shouldn't have let myself get so distracted. Silas and Roland were counting on me. The Royal Cathmoores were counting on me. How could I forget something so important?

Kissing men must make one dumb. Whatever brilliance Silas thought I had had abandoned me nearly an hour ago.

I surveyed the land on either side of me, but the view was obscured by curving mountain paths on either side. I couldn't see a town in either direction. My memory utterly failed me, and I was left taking what I hoped was a somewhat-educated guess.

I turned west.

47

I Am, Undoubtedly, an Idiot

Alastair

After perhaps thirty minutes, Roland offered to fill our waterskins, saying my parents would need any help we could offer them. This was not a helpful thing for *me*, however, as it only reminded me just how dire I didn't know their situation was.

"Let me go with you," I pleaded.

"No. Because then you'll beg to go all the way to the cave. And we have to give Evangeline some more time."

"Fine." I threw my waterskin at him, harder than necessary.

I opened my book again while he was gone, hoping to distract myself or find some encouragement as Eva had mentioned. But instead, I started thinking about Eva, and the mess I'd gotten us both in. Roland would do anything to prevent me from marrying her. If not for the sake of my reputation, he'd do it simply because he didn't like her. And my mother would be just as against the idea, I imagined. My father would side with her.

Stars above. I should never have let things go that far between us. I meant what I'd said. But so much about the future was unknown. Who was I to make claims about what could be?

Nausea churned in my stomach, a feeling that had become far too familiar these last few days. I returned the book to my pack once again, then lay back and closed my eyes, counting down from one hundred. Roland returned when I reached twelve.

"Can we go now?" I asked.

"We're ahead of schedule," Roland said, handing me my waterskin. "Take a sip of water and calm down a moment. You look as though you're on the verge of hysteria."

"I'm fine, Roland." I tucked the waterskin into my pack to prove my point. "As long as we can get moving."

"Fine, then, a toast before we leave."

I glared at him, but he'd had years of practice glaring back.

"Be quick about it," I said as I pulled my waterskin back out of my pack.

"To our swift success tonight and a quick revolution. May Wenterly's true leaders reclaim what is theirs."

"Here, here."

We drank. The water had a slight tang to it.

"I thought mountain water was supposed to be the purest kind."

Roland nodded. "It is."

I took another sip. "Your water doesn't taste strange?"

"No." He took my water skin and took a sip. "Same as mine. Perfectly normal." He handed it back to me. "Are you sure you're alright, Al?"

"All things considered, yes, I'm fine. Can we leave?"

He pulled out his watch. "Ten minutes."

I groaned. "The wait is going to kill me."

"You aren't the only one having a hard time, Alastair. But you are making it a *harder* time for both of us. Lie down and close your eyes. I'll tell you when it's time to go."

"I was doing that before you returned with the water."

He pinched the bridge of his nose. "Would you prefer to make sure Starboard is ready?"

"Yes." I immediately took my waterskin and pack over to the horse. Roland laid down at the mouth of the cave and closed his eyes, apparently taking his own recommendation.

Roland already had his sword. I removed mine from Starboard's saddle and attached the scabbard to my belt. I picked up my pack to secure it opposite Roland's and paused.

Why was I breathing so heavily?

I set my pack on top of the saddle as I took a moment to slow my breaths, nervous I was on the verge of losing it, exactly as Roland said.

I pulled out my waterskin and took a swig before continuing to pack our things. I started sweating. *Really* sweating. It was late afternoon, but not very hot. I couldn't make sense of it.

I took another drink. Took some more slow breaths.

My heart was beating as if I'd finished a run or a long sword drill session. My mouth was dry, and my head was pounding.

"Roland..."

"Five more minutes."

"No, Roland. I don't..." The world tipped, or maybe I was falling. I bent over, resting my hands on my knees, and lowered my head, eyes closed, until the feeling passed. "Something's wrong," I finally managed to get out. I drank some more water.

"Woah, easy, Alastair." He took the water skin from me. "What's going on?"

"I think I—" My vision blurred, and the world tipped again.

I was vaguely aware of Roland's hands on my shoulders. He cursed, but it sounded muffled, as if cotton was stuffed in my ears. I was hot and cold at the same time, and sweat dripped down the back of my neck.

"Did you drink half of this already?"

I tried to tell him I did. That it didn't help. All I could do was gasp instead.

He cursed again. Said something too muffled for me to comprehend.

I was going to vomit.

But before I could, my legs gave out, and all the awful feelings finally stopped.

Because I lost consciousness.

48

WHAT DOES IT TAKE FOR A GIRL TO GET A DOCTOR THESE DAYS?

Evangeline

After over an hour of riding, I knew I'd gone the wrong way.

I should have reached Irimen long before now. I should have turned back, but what good would that do now? I was so far behind schedule, I might as well try to find whatever town the signpost had indicated was ahead. It had to be closer than going all the way back. I decided to keep going until I rounded the next bend in the road. If I still didn't see anything from there, I'd turn back. The shadows were starting to lengthen. I didn't have time for this kind of mistake.

The last time I had gone to fetch a doctor, my mother had ended up dying anyway. Perhaps this time around my efforts would be in vain too, but I had to at least *find* a doctor before I gave up.

I rounded the bend and nearly cried out in relief as a building finally came into view. I prodded Port forward, no time to waste.

But as we got closer, I saw it wasn't a building at all. It was a wall, stretching from one end of the valley to the other, a bridge between mountains. It looked like a fortress. What could the people behind it be so afraid of? The mountains seemed safe enough. What area of Ordelune had I wound up in?

I slowed Port. I could now see that there were people standing at the top of the wall.

This *definitely* wasn't right.

But I certainly couldn't turn back now. I had to at least see if these people could help me.

I continued with my cautious approach to the wall—or perhaps it was a gate. Massive doors were shut across the road.

"Halt!" a man called from the top of the gate. "State your business."

"I need—" My voice came out far too quiet, so I cleared my throat and tried again. "I need a doctor. It's urgent."

"Then why have you come t' us? Surely the mountain villages have doctors?"

The man's accent was not one I was used to. Perhaps the dialect was different in Ordelune, seeing as most of the mountains were a part of Eliston. "It was my understandin' that this is a mountain village. I was sent to find the doctor in Irimen. Though, I gather I've lost my way."

"Irimen is seven miles back the way you came."

Seven miles? How many had it taken me to get here? Port stamped his hooves, as impatient as I was. I doubted he would make it back to Irimen any quicker than if I were to walk myself.

"Please. I don't have time to go back. Is there anyone you have who can help me? It's a matter of life and death."

"We are not responsible for New Glastor's citizens."

"Aren't you—" I started to ask, then stopped short. *Of course.* I was at the border of Eliston and Wenterly. But Eliston didn't sound like it started with an 'E' sound, and that was what the signpost had shown. It must be one of those *other* rules Roland had convinced us to skip. When I got back, truce or not, I was going to give him a piece of my mind.

A truce.

Roland said there was no use in going to Eliston until after we rescued King Esmond. That the alliance didn't mean anything without a living king. But maybe he was wrong.

He *had* to be wrong.

"What about Wenterly's leaders?"

The man tilted his head slightly before answering, and the other men on the wall, who I now realized were actual Elistonian soldiers, nocked arrows into their bows at that question. "We have no official alliance with King Harland," he finally said. "He can return t' Glastor should he find himself in need of medical attention."

"Not Harland. Queen Adeena and King Esmond. Prince Alastair."

"Are dead," the man concluded.

"No. Not yet. Not if you can send me a doctor. They've been held prisoner here in the mountains. I have a map of the cave they're in, and the prince's ring." I held the items up, though I doubted they could see them very well from way up there. "My friends are on their way to the cave now to rescue them. They need someone who can help them when they return. One of them was able to scout it out, and he *saw* the royals, alive. But he said their condition is worse than we feared. They need help!"

The man who was speaking to me waved a soldier over. They spoke for a moment, though I didn't hear any of the words.

The other soldiers didn't stop aiming their arrows at me.

Please. Please. Please.

"We will open the gate for you," the man said. "You will present your case and then we will decide if we will help you."

"I just presented my case!"

"You will do so formally."

I could have screamed. "There is no time for that!"

"I understand your urgency, should your story be true. We will make our decision quickly. But you are welcome t' turn around and try your luck in Irimen, should you prefer."

I nearly did scream that time. This felt like Narim all over again. I had the illusion of a choice, but what could I actually do except agree and go along with someone else's plan?

But Narim had still worked out for us. Reeves turned out to be a good man.

Fate's mercy.

"I'll speak with you," I said.

"Please dismount from your horse and discard any weapons there on the road. Then we will open the gate for you."

I got off Port and pulled the dagger Reeves had given me from my belt. I tossed it on the ground. Once that was done, I heard the clinking of chains for several seconds, and finally the large wooden doors opened. There were six men in the gateway, three of them pointing arrows at me, two with their hands on the hilt of their swords.

As I approached, I was relieved to see that the arrows were not pointed at me, but beyond me, in case anyone was going to rush in now that the gate was open.

"I came alone." I assured them.

"It's a precaution, miss. I'm sure you understand." It was the same man who spoke to me from atop the gate. He was a little older than Roland, I guessed, putting him in his mid-thirties. He spoke with a great deal of confidence and authority, likely meaning he'd been a leader of these soldiers for years. "Motley will take your horse."

I gave Motley the reins without hesitation. As soon as he had the horse, another man stepped forward and searched me for any more weapons. There was no point resisting. Either I had already failed in my task, or these men would offer me a miracle. All I could do now was find out which was the case.

While that was happening, the man in charge introduced himself. "I'm Casimir, Second in Command of Eliston's Army and Chief Advisor t' King Heston. You are about t' cross into Elistonian borders. That means our laws now apply t' you. Is that understood?"

I swallowed. Of all the people to run in to, I ended up with Eliston's Second in Command? Perhaps I should have minded my manners more when I was busy making demands. "Yes, sire."

Another soldier went to fetch my dagger and gave it to the commander. He briefly examined it, then tucked it into his belt. Satisfied that I wasn't an immediate threat, he asked for my map and ring. He didn't care much for the map, but he was very interested in Alastair's ring.

"Where did you get this?"

"My ... friend gave it to me, right before I left to find help."

"And who's your friend?"

"Sil—uh..."

The commander turned his attention from the ring to me, eyebrows raised at my sudden hesitation.

I stammered while trying to find an explanation that didn't sound as though I was making it up. "Er, I don't know his real name, sire. But he is close friends with the prince. He's a Wenter noble. But he's been in hidin' since Harland took over because of his close association with the Royal Cathmoores."

"So, you're telling me, this friend of yours trusts you enough t' give you Alastair's ring, but not enough t' confide his real name?"

I could throttle myself. Hadn't he tried to tell me his real name mere hours ago? And I had so thoughtfully said *no, I already know who you are*. Mercy, romance *did* make me stupid.

"I know it sounds difficult to believe, but the last several *weeks* for us have been difficult to believe. Please, all I'm askin' for is a doctor."

The commander turned his attention back to the ring, his brow furrowed. He finally looked back up at me. "First, we must see King Heston. Close the gate," he ordered, then turned without another word.

I hurried after him as the gate lowered, trapping me in the wrong kingdom. "Please, I don't have time to travel all the way to the king."

He turned back to face me. "You can't walk thirty steps? Should I retrieve your horse?"

I stepped out from under the gate, and he pointed to a tent just off the road.

"I believe Fate has smiled on us both. The odds of the king being here the night such news comes t' us are so slim, it's difficult t' believe. You are right. Many unbelievable things have happened these last few weeks. The greatest of which may be that finally the surprises seem t' have turned in our favor."

49

The Worst News in the World

Alastair

I couldn't open my eyes. A cocoon of muffled noise encased my consciousness. That was all there was. The sounds, so far and distant. I wanted to know what the sounds were. I wanted to—

I sunk down into nothingness, only to rise again. It seemed I rode that wave for an eternity. I felt like I was half asleep, but it was impossible to actually wake up. My eyes wouldn't open. But the sounds were becoming more distinct each time I rose to semi-consciousness. I could pick them out from one another now.

Men's voices. I didn't know what they were saying.

A woman's voice. She was singing. It was a familiar tune.

It was my mom.

Someone was touching me. A hand on my face. Someone holding my hand, too.

I tried to open my eyes again, and this time I succeeded. Though it hardly made a difference. The only light was from a lantern yards away. I was only seeing shadows.

The hand that was resting against my cheek moved to brush through my hair. The singing stopped. "Al, my boy, what has happened to you?"

Was it really her?

"Mo—" I tried to call to her, but my voice caught in my throat. I coughed. But I couldn't move. Couldn't raise my arms or roll onto my side.

"It's me, Alastair. I'm here." My mother waited for me to catch my breath, still holding my face and my hand.

"Where are we?" I finally got out.

"A cave. I assume in Ordelune, but I don't know for certain."

"Stars," I cursed, and she immediately scolded me, as if my vocabulary was something that mattered right now.

I had hoped Roland got them out and I missed it all. What had happened anyway? Last I knew, Roland and I were at the camp. Eva had just left.

"Ordelune is correct," I told her. "Roland and I came to get you."

"Roland betrayed you." The anger in her voice was foreign to me. My mother was an expert at controlling her tone.

I whispered, though my voice was already so quiet I doubted any guards nearby would hear me anyway. "He's pretending. It's part of the plan."

"Was it part of the plan for him to poison you, too?"

"Poison?" I thought my psyche had finally snapped under the pressure.

"Hummel-poisoning. I heard the guards talking about it. You were shaking and seizing. Everyone was yelling. They thought you were going to die."

"Don't tell me the guards saved my life only so they could kill me on their own terms."

"As far as I can tell, they didn't do anything themselves to save you. You vomited a ghastly number of times. Which seemed to calm things down. The guards brought you over here. Truly the only humane thing they've done."

I tried to sit up, but I felt as though my bones were replaced with weights. My head still pounded, and my stomach was definitely unsettled.

"How long have I been here?" I asked.

"In my cell only a handful of minutes, but you arrived at the cave perhaps an hour ago."

I wished I could make out the expression on her face. Actually see that my mother was alive and here with me. "Is Father nearby?"

She shook her head.

Fear spiked in my veins. "Where is he?"

"He's gone, Alastair." I could hardly hear her. "It's just you and me now."

No.

No. We'd come so far. Come all this way.

"How long ago?"

It took a moment for her to answer. "It's difficult to tell time here. Maybe four days ago? I don't know for sure."

"But it was recently."

"Yes."

We were too late. Shortcuts and horses and we were still too late. If I hadn't chased down Eva, if it hadn't been for me getting us captured and arrested and delayed a week, we would have gotten here on time.

But now, my father was dead.

And it was my fault we didn't save him.

50

The Most Frustrating Interrogation Yet

Evangeline

Waiting for the commander to speak to King Heston just so I could have permission to plead my own case was torturous. The soldiers who brought me through the gate stood around me, keeping me from barging into the tent myself.

A month ago, I never thought I'd find myself in the presence of royalty. Of course, I now hoped to see Wenterly's royals before sundown, which I still hadn't quite wrapped my mind around either. But seeing the Royal Cathmoores after a rescue mission was much different from having an audience with the king of a kingdom I didn't even belong to. People like me didn't ask for favors from royalty. We got what we were given and that was that.

Yet, here I was, acting as some sort of ambassador. The last hope for the Cathmoores and all of Wenterly.

I readjusted the white hair-scarf Reeves's wife had given me. I hardly knew the proper protocol for seeking an audience with a king, but hopefully my appearance was presentable enough. Though, after a week or so of travel on horseback, I was asking a lot of a green dress and white cloth. Surely King Heston wouldn't want to meet with someone in my state. And if he did, would he ask for my lineage? Would he deny the royals help based on the status of their messenger? And if he denied me, what would I do? Go all the way back to Irimen?

The sky was beginning to change colors, and my hopes were preparing to sink along with the sun.

I was nearing tears when a man exited the tent, followed closely by the commander.

The man appeared about the same age as the commander, and while he stood only a few inches taller than me, it was clear from the way he carried himself that he was King Heston. His dark blue shirt had sleeves that puffed and cinched in all the right places, trimmed with embroidery of golden thread. It was a well-made garment befitting only royalty. One made for fashion, not function, like that of the soldiers.

He took a good look at me, and I hurried to curtsy. I'd never done a proper curtsy before. I'd never met someone important enough to need to. A simple lowering of my gaze and bowing of my head had always sufficed for the company I kept.

I didn't know if I was supposed to speak first or wait for King Heston to address me. I glanced at the commander to see if he was going to offer me any guidance.

"This is Alastair's ring?" King Heston asked. No introduction. No formalities.

"Yes, Your Highness."

"You swear on your life?"

"Yes, sire."

"And you got it from a man you don't know the name of?"

I winced. "Yes. But I've traveled with him the last two weeks across Wenterly. We've risked our lives together. I trust him with my life. He wouldn't lie to me about this."

The king nodded, his expression blank. There was no way to know what he was thinking. "Come inside. We can discuss this away from gawking eyes."

I expected the tent to be filled with finery, or at least weapons or something, considering the number of soldiers I'd seen. But it was quite empty. A cot in one corner. A small table and chair on the other end. There was a book and some parchment on the table, but not much else. It was clearly a temporary set-up.

There was another man already in the tent, but the king instructed him to stand at the opening to the tent and keep away prying ears. Then he sat in the chair and held the ring against the lantern light. The commander stood closer to King Heston than I did, constantly flicking his eyes between us. I felt awkward, unsure how to properly posture myself. I decided to simply fold my hands in front of myself and stand still. If I fidgeted too much, they may think I was impatient.

Which I was, but I also needed these people to like me.

"We've determined the stones are legitimate," Heston finally said. "If this isn't the prince's ring, it's quite a convincing counterfeit. Did your friend tell you how he acquired it?"

"Not exactly. He's good friends with Prince Alastair. That's all I know, sire, er, Your Majesty."

King Heston nodded. "Your story is terrible and hardly convincing. *So* terrible in fact, it actually compels me t' believe you. Someone sent t' trick us would have a stronger case. So, either you're mentally unfit, or you're telling the truth."

I swallowed. "If anythin' I've spoken to either of you is a lie, I swear on my life I don't know it."

King Heston turned to his commander. "This could be good. If the royals are still alive, we finally have reason t' declare war on Harland."

"I agree. But we cannot let hope cloud our judgment."

I couldn't stand here and listen to these two men go back and forth about what was true or not while everything I'd given up my life for was at stake. "The ring is real. I've told you what I know. So will you help me or not?"

The men immediately snapped their heads in my direction, and I wished I could sink right into the ground. These people were not Silas and Roland, and not a pair of commoners. Clearly, I couldn't afford to forget that.

"What family do you belong to, Lady…" The king looked to the commander to answer on my behalf, but he never asked for my name.

The commander shook his head, and I waited for the king to look back at me before speaking this time. "I'm not a Lady. Just a commoner. Forgive me, Your Majesty, I'm afraid I'm a bit out of practice in proper etiquette."

"Clearly," King Heston grunted, sounding more amused than offended. "Your name, then, miss?"

"Evangeline."

"Evangeline, who?"

I cast my gaze to the ground. "Evangeline of Welven, sir."

There was no response, so I looked up to gauge their reaction. King Heston turned to the commander with his eyebrows lowered, clearly confused at my answer. "Is she mentally unfit, afterall? Am I not making myself clear?"

The commander frowned, but offered an answer. "Wenterly will not give a family name to a child whose father is unknown, sire. Usually such children have mothers who worked in brothels or a similar profession. Is that correct, miss?"

"My mother was an upstandin' woman. My father was a pirate, and she was unlucky enough to conceive after his abuse. But yes, because my father's identity is unknown, I do not have a family name."

The men blinked at me. I bit my tongue. Perhaps admitting the worst part of my lineage was not a good strategy. I didn't have *time* for this.

Finally, King Heston spoke. "My apologies. I didn't realize Wenterly still held t' such traditions." He squared his shoulders and returned to the subject at hand. "We have been looking for a worthy cause to attack Harland since we received word he had taken over. I'm sure you know that every alliance dies with the king. It must be renewed with each transition of power. King Harland had an alliance with Wenterly, and he broke it. He has now offered t' extend an alliance to Eliston. But, naturally, I do not trust him t' uphold his end of the bargain. I have not agreed to it, but I have also refrained from showing any signs of hostility, as Harland has not threatened us yet either. Just because our previous alliance is over, does not necessarily mean the new king is *our* enemy."

I wasn't sure why he was telling me all this. I didn't *care* about his history or his political alliances. All I wanted was a doctor!

But the fact he was still speaking to me at all, let alone explaining the complications of his position, was a good sign. I had to keep humoring him. I couldn't mess this up again.

"I understand you are in a difficult position," I said, "but just because Harland failed to uphold his alliance does not mean we should all throw out our loyalties."

King Heston shook his head. "There's no use proving loyalty t' a dead man."

"But King Esmond isn't dead!"

"How do you know? When did you last see King Esmond?"

I fell silent. I had *never* seen King Esmond. "I haven't seen him myself," I admitted. "But Roland has."

"And who is Roland, that we should trust his word?"

Relief flooded my body. I actually had an answer for this. "He was Prince Alastair's tutor. On occasion, he also taught the nobleman who gave me the ring. Roland has been servin' the Cathmoores for years, as I understand it."

"The royal tutor?" the commander asked. "How is it you're aware of his identity but not the noble's?"

I forced myself to hold back a sigh. "I don't know how to explain it to you. The last two weeks have been very complicated. I've been arrested because people recognized Silas. But Roland is less sought after. Less recognizable, I suppose. And less of a threat to Harland." There was no point explaining Roland's false allegiance to Harland. That would only further muddy the waters, and things were murky enough as it was.

"And Master Roland saw King Esmond alive?"

"Only a few hours ago. But it sounds like he doesn't have much time left. Please, I just want a doctor."

King Heston raised a hand to silence my pleas. "It's not just a doctor, though. Not for me. And not for Harland. Any aid I provide you puts my entire kingdom at risk."

Politics. The more I learned about it, the more I hated it.

"But as long as King Esmond lives, you have a duty to him, yes?"

"Assuming you are telling the truth about that, yes, it does give us reason t' go, as I said a moment ago. But you need t' understand that marching uninvited into Wenterly for the sake of the Royal Cathmoores will start a war with King Harland, regardless of what we find in the cave on your map. And if we start a war and you are *wrong* about the Cathmoores, or you are lying to us and this is a trap, your head will be the first t' roll."

I couldn't guarantee that King Esmond would still be alive by the time we reached them at the rendezvous. But at least I knew I wasn't lying.

Besides, if we failed tonight, and the Cathmoores didn't make it out, or Silas didn't make it out, there wasn't anything more life could offer me. Even if we *succeeded*, I didn't know what more life could offer me. So, I could risk my life for this. I had *been* risking my life for this.

What was one more time?

But can I risk the wellbeing of a whole other kingdom?

I pushed the question away. I had a responsibility to Silas and the royals. Eliston was not mine to worry about. Their king could blame me for the ensuing war, but it was ultimately his decision. I would uphold my loyalties. He would decide where his lay.

"I have told many lies in my life, Your Majesty, but I assure you, this is not one of them."

"Alright. Then it's settled." He turned to the commander. "How soon can the soldiers be ready?"

"I have a squad ready now. I can have a section ready in ten minutes or less."

"Call the section, and we will go. Have Draven bring my armor, and send a second section after us as soon as they are ready. Have Motley prepare a battalion for my beckoning and send a messenger out t' the rest of my army. If this is a trap, we need t' be ready with backup."

"Yes, sire." He hurried away, immediately carrying out the king's orders.

"Battle is no place for a woman," King Heston said to me. "We have your map. You will stay here. Should we succeed, we will promptly reunite you with your friends. But should we fail, I will personally deal with you accordingly."

"I'd like to go with you. Please. You can put me in shackles if you don't trust me. But I can't just wait here. I *won't* wait here."

The king studied me a long while, then, surprisingly, smiled. "You've got spirit, miss, I'll give you that. Tell you what. Seeing as this battle takes place in Wenterly and you're Wenter, once you cross that border, Eliston's laws don't apply t' you anymore. So, I will relinquish my authority over the decision of your location tonight, but neither will I offer you any special protection. And should you interfere with *our* protection, that will be the *end* of your time with us."

"I agree to your terms."

King Heston nodded. "Good. They are the only terms you will get."

51

EVA WAS RIGHT

Alastair

"Why do you think they gave me to you?" I finally managed to ask.

"To shut me up, I assume. But it also probably means something terrible is coming. This is the calm before the storm."

What sort of nightmare was this place where me almost dying, and my father already dead, was the *calm*? I wanted to get up, to fight my way out. But I couldn't even lift a finger. I was stuck on my back like a dying turtle, and it seemed Fate was content to simply spin me like a top instead of helping me right myself.

Maybe Roland was right to not give me any details about what he saw here.

Roland. He had said he saw my parents. Plural. But if my father had been gone for days...

"Father's body. Is it..."

She shook her head.

"What hap—"

"Another time," she whispered.

I swallowed. "Did you see Roland earlier today? A few hours ago?"

"I heard his voice, but thought I must have been imagining it," she answered. "I assumed it was a new guard who sounded similar. They were talking about you and—"

"He's awake!" a guard yelled, cutting her off.

Footsteps pounded and I managed to turn my head enough to see someone approaching our cell. The guard was carrying a lantern, the red and yellow sash of Harland's colors across his chest.

"And here's the storm." My mother squeezed my hand. "Most of their questions are nonsense, but do not give them anything. No matter what, Alastair. Do not bargain with them. Our duty is to Wenterly above all else."

I barely nodded. I doubted she would have seen it even if it wasn't so dark.

The guard reached our cell, the lantern light finally illuminating my mother's features.

I almost wished it hadn't.

Her eyes were sunken, cheeks hollow. Her dark hair was matted and tangled. It looked as though she hadn't eaten—or slept, for that matter—since the throne fell. Her skin was more bruised than not, with a large bump on her forehead and a long cut on her cheek.

I closed my eyes.

"Family reunion in the arena," the guard sneered, unlocking our cell door. "Alastair comes out first."

I didn't move. Not because I was trying to revolt, but because I was still too weak to get up.

The guard kicked my foot. "Don't start your time here by trying my patience."

"I can't." My voice was still raspy and soft.

"He nearly died a few moments ago," my mother scolded. "He can't get up on his own."

I expected the man to tell her to carry me then, but he didn't. He came in and picked me up himself, hauling me over his shoulder as if I was little more than a sack of laundry.

I wished I could die right then. Whatever torture was about to come couldn't compare to how humiliating this was.

The motion of him lifting me made me nauseous all over again, and I reactively clenched my jaw. I wasn't sure if I could physically throw up again, but I wasn't about to find out now.

I could barely flex my muscles, let alone actually move my limbs. My leg muscles tremored, utterly useless. I hoped the guard didn't expect me to stand on my own once we got to the arena.

We went deeper into the cave, light glowing around a corner. This cave was far deeper than the one Eva and I had waited in this afternoon. I wondered if someone had carved out these rooms, or if this was all natural. The guard turned, and I blinked against the brightness.

He dropped me, not bothering to bend down so it was less of a fall.

With no reflexes to catch myself, I landed on my left arm, and my head smacked against the stone floor. I hissed at the impact, tried to lift myself up, and failed once again.

My headache turned from a pounding to a crushing feeling. As though my skull was trying to strangle my brain. Maybe it was the light. I closed my eyes again, but it didn't dull the brightness or the pain.

More footsteps sounded, and I opened my eyes again to see my mother enter the room, escorted by two other guards. Somehow, she looked worse in this lighting than before. She could hardly hold herself up. She must have been nearly as weak as me.

"Put her there," the guard who carried me directed.

My mother stood on the left side of the room, swaying on her feet.

Where is Roland?

As if the guard could read my mind—or had I said that out loud?—he said, "Roland, please introduce yourself."

Roland entered the room, Harland's ugly sash slung across his chest.

Please let this be part of the plan.

"Roland?" I meant to say more, to ask what was going on, what he was doing in that sash, and how we got in this mess. But nothing else came out.

"Stand up, Alastair," he ordered. "I taught you better than that."

"I'd love to." I managed to push myself off my face and rolled onto my back—a major improvement in muscle control. "But I'm so comfortable here."

Roland cursed and turned to the guard who had carried me in. "Graven, I thought you were going to give him some water. This is pathetic."

Graven lifted me to my feet, leaning me against the back of the cave wall. The movement emphasized the crushing pain in my skull. I closed my eyes, grimacing.

"Roland, what is this?" my mother asked.

I opened my eyes, and she was now leaning against the cave wall herself, clinging to it as though it was the only thing that could possibly keep her from collapsing.

Roland turned to the other guards, as though getting permission to speak to her. One of them nodded.

"I've been offered a position at the New Glastor palace. I'm turning Alastair over to finalize my loyalty to the king."

"*He* is your king!" my mother yelled, pointing a shaking finger at me.

Mercy. I was the king now. Or would be. Or should be.

"No." Roland's tone was almost nonchalant. "He's not. And he never will be. A new king has called me for employment. And when the king asks for me, how can I say no?"

What game was Roland playing here? Which one of us was he lying to? I shut my eyes, wincing from the pain that suddenly magnified in my head. I gasped. This hummel poisoning was no joke.

"Did you poison me?" I asked. It took all my strength to keep from slumping back to the floor.

"Yes. Although, you weren't supposed to drink that much. We wanted you sedated, not incapacitated."

I scoffed. "What difference does it make?"

"It's easy to kill a man who looks like he's already dead," Graven enlightened me. "It's harder to kill a man when he's looking at you begging fer his life."

I cracked an eye open. "So you really were a traitor, this whole time?"

Roland paused. Swallowed. Pulled his pistol from its holster. "I play for the winning team, Al." He raised the weapon, pointing it right at me. "Would you like to have any last words? Choose them wisely."

I had quite a few choice words for him. But my mother started speaking first, begging the guards not to let Roland kill me.

It was all a trap. Get Roland to kill me to prove his loyalty. Kill me in front of my mother so she'd say anything to spare my life. And once they got the information they wanted—whatever that was—we were all dead anyway.

I was already dead. Better to get it over with quickly, then.

My legs shook, but I did my best to stand tall, to raise my chin at the very least.

"You are despicable, Roland." I spat. "Eva was right. We should have abandoned you when we had the chance."

It worked like a charm. Roland cocked the gun and shot without missing a beat. The blast was deafening, and it echoed off the stone walls.

I crumpled to the ground.

52

I Forgot: The Worst Can Always Happen

Evangeline

The horse Casimir brought me was *much* faster than Port. Plus, we were running—or galloping, I supposed—instead of the little trot I had going on my way here. As the wind whipped my hair out of my braid and into my face, I couldn't deny that these were horses bred for battle. For war.

Which was what we were about to start one way or another.

I held on for dear life, knowing I'd certainly be left behind if I admitted I was not an experienced rider.

Our company took up the full width of the winding dirt road, dust clouds rising in our wake. King Heston, the commander, and I were in the middle of the group of horses and soldiers. I assumed that was to keep the two men safe, and to keep me from causing them trouble.

We reached the shallow cave where Roland had left Silas and I. I gave it a passing glance.

And my heart nearly stopped.

Silas's pack was lying at the mouth of the cave. *Most* of the packs were still at the mouth of the cave, actually.

"Stop!" I called out, halting my horse as the soldiers accompanying me stopped a few seconds later, confusion clear on their faces.

I dismounted and ran to the cave. Silas's pack was tipped over, and his book had fallen open, the pages bent, face down on the ground.

My chest tightened as I picked it up. "Somethin' isn't right."

"How so?" King Heston asked, riding up to me.

"Silas would never have left his pack here, or his book like this." I picked it up, trying to smooth out the crumpled pages before I closed it and picked up his pack. "They were supposed to leave all their things at the rendezvous point. This wouldn't have happened unless somethin' went wrong."

"May I see the book, Miss Evangeline?"

I handed it to him.

He read the cover and scanned the first few pages. "You said this book belonged to the noble who was friends with Prince Alastair?"

"Yes."

King Heston called the commander over. "This belonged to the young *noble* Evangeline has been traveling with, the friend of Alastair," he repeated, handing him the book with the cover still open.

The commander studied the first page a moment, just as King Heston had, then flipped through the pages briefly, noting all the markings Silas had left. "The Philosopher Prince," he said quietly, amusement at the edge of his voice.

He handed the book back to King Heston, then King Heston gave it back to me. "We'll continue on to the rendezvous point and see what information we can gather from there. But that was a good find for you t' notice, Evangeline. It's helped your case more than you know."

I put the book in Silas's pack and slung it over my shoulders. My own pack had stayed back in Eliston with Port.

I wasn't sure how the book had convinced them to help me, but I wasn't about to ask questions. Not while things were working in my favor.

Though, the fact that the book was there to be found at all did not feel like a good thing.

I pointed out the mountain Roland had chosen as the rendezvous point, and we rode to it.

When we arrived, there was nothing there. Not Silas or Roland. Not the Cathmoores. Not even Starboard.

If we aren't there by morning, assume the worst.

But what was I to do if *nothing* was there? If something had gone wrong before they even made it to the cave?

Had a guard followed Roland to where they were waiting? Did they suspect that his loyalty to Harland was a sham?

There was no way I was going to sit and wait for morning.

I urged my horse forward. "Roland said we could see the mouth of the prison cave from here."

The commander blocked my path. "That means the guards can see *us*."

"The Cathmoores are still in there. We have to go after them—"

"How do you know?" King Heston asked. "The escape could have gone differently than they planned, and they had t' find an alternative route."

I clenched my fists. "They didn't."

"You don't know that."

I dismounted once again and marched over to the outcropping. It wasn't hard to find the Prison Cave. Torches burned on either side of the mouth, and a lone soldier stood watch.

I turned back to King Heston. "There's still a guard there. If Roland and Silas escaped with the royals, don't you think every single one of Harland's men would be chasin' after them? And if I know Silas, he'll die before he leaves that cave without the Cathmoores."

King Heston and the commander shared a look.

"Your call, Your Majesty," the commander said.

King Heston turned back to me. "How many are inside we need to get out?"

"Five. The three royals. Plus Silas. And Roland."

King Heston turned to his men. "King Esmond and Prince Alastair are priority number one. Then the queen. Then the other two. No one working for Harland is t' survive, under any circumstances. Understood? With no one t' escape and report what happens, we can buy enough time t' gather the rest of the army."

"Yes, sire," the men chorused.

"The horses stay here. We go in on foot. No guns unless absolutely necessary."

"Yes, sire."

I nodded. "May I have my dagger now, Commander?" Although King Heston had allowed me to ride unrestrained, he had not allowed me to have my weapon back. It was still sheathed in the commander's belt.

"You're not coming *in* with us." King Heston answered, but not as a command like I had expected. It was genuine surprise.

"You thought I wanted to come all this way to stand here and wait? If that's all I wanted to do, I would have done it in Eliston."

The other soldiers looked from King Heston to me with wide eyes, as if I wasn't already aware how I toed out of line. I didn't care.

"You will get in the way," he insisted.

"I know what your priority is. I'm ensurin' my priority is taken care of, too."

King Heston shook his head, "As I said, battle is no place for a lady."

"Well, I'm not a lady. I'm a leech. So hand me my dagger, or I will run into that cave with nothin' but my teeth bared."

Bang!

The sound echoed over to us, immediately followed by a scream.

I stepped forward to see the lone guard disappear inside the cave.

I took off running without my dagger, the king and his men at my heels.

53

I Can't Even Die Properly

Alastair

My ears were ringing so loudly I could barely hear my mother screaming. She was also on the ground, crawling toward me. A guard stood there, watching her, but he didn't bother to restrain her. She was no threat.

I looked to Roland. He was pointing at the gun and arguing with one of the guards. Blood soaked the left side of my shirt.

But I wasn't dead.

How was I not dead?

Through the foggy cocoon, I could barely register a tingling sensation in my upper left arm. Was that where he'd hit me? Why couldn't I feel it? Was the hummel poisoning really that strong?

The gun must have misfired. Or maybe I made him too angry to take the extra second to aim properly. He'd been only an inch or so off from his mark.

I couldn't even die easily. How much crueler did my existence have to be?

My mother reached me. "Alastair, my boy."

I could hear her better now, the ringing no longer the primary sound. But my attention was drawn back to Roland and the guards.

"Miss again, an' you die with him," Graven said to Roland. He and the other officers had their own guns aimed—but at Roland, not me.

"It was a misfire! I will need to clean and examine the barrel to ensure it doesn't happen again."

"Very well, then. Kill Alastair with your sword an' then you can fix your useless gun."

"I was never a skilled swordsman. Let me borrow your pistol."

Graven ripped Roland's gun from his hands and tossed it aside. He pulled back the hammer on his own pistol, but aimed it at Roland instead of giving it to him. "Then it's a good thing you don't need to be skilled in these circumstances. The boy can't even sit up."

I hated that it was true. Any other day, I could beat Roland in a duel with one hand tied behind my back. But this wasn't any other day. It was turning out to be, undoubtedly, the worst day of my life. By a landslide.

I heard another scream, but not my mother's this time. The scream was distant, and my mother was close to my side, pressing her skirt to my bleeding arm, as if that could stop me from bleeding out.

The scream rattled around in my head, tugging at strings of familiarity. But why would a scream sound familiar?

"Did you hear that?" one of the guards asked.

"Probably Wilcox doing his job."

"But if he saw someone outside the cave—"

Some men shouted from down the tunnel, followed by the clang of sword blades crossing and more shouting.

Everyone turned to the doorway, but since the room was off a curve in the tunnel, they couldn't see anything but the cave wall opposite us.

"Scott, see what that's all about," Graven ordered, not lowering his gun from Roland.

A man ran out of the room and disappeared briefly around the corner.

Roland slowly unsheathed his sword. He seemed uncertain if he was supposed to carry on or wait for Scott to return with his report.

Someone cried out down the tunnel. I hoped it was Scott.

Graven cursed. "This can wait. All of you, get out there an' see what's going on."

The three other guards hurried out of the room, two of them taking lanterns with them.

Roland moved to leave with them, but Graven stopped him. "You haven't proven yourself yet. We will wait for everyone to return. Harland requires two witnesses."

"As you wish," Roland grumbled as he sheathed his sword. But I knew he was relieved. Roland's father wanted him to become a soldier, but he didn't have the stomach for battle. It was his initial motivation to excel at school. If he had a brilliant mind, he wouldn't have to fight.

It was a shame he hadn't dedicated himself to learning anything about loyalty.

We heard the three guards shout and the clash of swords—closer than when Scott screamed. Whoever was out there, they'd reach us soon.

Graven sighed, as if this was all just an inconvenience. "Am I the only one in this place who can do anything properly?"

He ordered Roland to stay put and watch us before he stormed out of the room, as if we could go anywhere.

Once Graven disappeared around the bend, my mother asked, "Do you know what's going on out there?"

Although two lanterns had been removed from the room, the light once again was searing bright. I grimaced and closed my eyes.

"It's nothing we had planned," I finally answered. But, then again, *this* wasn't anything I'd planned either.

"Who is that girl you mentioned?" she asked. "Eva?"

Eva. Had she found help in Irimen? Was the commotion in the cave because of her?

I didn't know how to begin explaining her to my mother, nor did I have the strength to do so even if I did. But I could sum it up easily enough.

"Eva's the best."

54

I Guess Battle Is No Place for a Leech Either

Evangeline

By the time I reached the mouth of the cave, the guard had returned to his post. He put his hand on the hilt of his sword when he saw me, but made a mistake in not drawing his weapon.

I stopped suddenly, skidding along the rocky ground.

"Sorry, sir. I didn't realize there were other people in the area. I'm just out for a walk." I grimaced at the lie. Surely he'd see right through it.

"Looked more like running," he said in his Glastorian accent. "Is everything alright, miss? It ain't safe fer a woman to be out alone."

"Yes, well, unfortunately, I don't have any handsome soldiers like you at my command to protect me." I walked past the guard, hoping to draw his attention away from the king and soldiers who would appear around the bend behind me in a few seconds.

It worked, and he turned to me, his back to the others. "Where are you comin' from?" It wasn't an interrogating question. He was curious. "I haven't come across anyone around here before."

"In truth, I stayed out a bit later than I was supposed to. I'm taking a shortcut I don't often take, just tryin' to get back to my village before people will start to miss me."

Behind the guard, the commander came into view, his hand poised on the hilt of his sword. He gave me a nod, so I continued distracting the man. I pointed behind me, directing the guard's gaze in the opposite direction from the Elistonian soldiers.

"My village is a half mile out. Over there." I turned to smile at him. "Perhaps you'd like to visit some—"

I stopped short as the commander snapped the guard's neck.

The man immediately crumpled to the ground, and I screamed. My hands flew to cover my mouth, as if I knew well enough to muffle my own scream, but not enough to simply *not* scream.

"There goes our element of surprise," he said as he handed me my dagger. "I was about t' congratulate you on the distraction."

"Sorry, I—" I forced myself to look up from the dead man. "I knew it was comin', I just..." I took a steadying breath. "I wasn't fully prepared, I suppose."

King Heston unsheathed his sword, glancing over at me. "Perhaps next time you'll believe me when I say battle isn't the place for a woman."

I hurried to tuck the sheath of my dagger into my belt as two of Harland's guards emerged from the cave, and four of the king's soldiers immediately engaged them. Harland's guards shouted for backup, then met their own end. I gasped as they fell, still not able to wrap my mind around this being a battleground. Silas and I had managed to evade violence on so many occasions, I must have thought we'd somehow manage to do it again here.

Four other soldiers led the way into the cave followed by the commander and King Heston. I grabbed the torch from the sconce next to me and hurried to fall in after them. The rest of the soldiers followed us.

It was a long winding stretch of tunnel, with a few alcoves that may have served as other rooms. Two more of Harland's men approached, calling again for others to join them.

As the four soldiers in front engaged Harland's guards, I pushed forward, looking for signs of any prisoners. Of Silas.

Where is everyone?

I rounded a bend and ran straight into a guard. I panicked, my natural reflexes causing me to thrust the torch forward, instead of my dagger.

The man cried out as the flame seared his chest. I dropped the torch in surprise, and ran past him, quick to switch my dagger to my dominant hand. I heard the man cry out again behind me as someone finished him off.

Light grew brighter from around the next bend. I could hear voices up ahead, approaching. I crouched, pressing myself against the rock wall as best I could. I hoped the shadows would hide me, but I held my dagger ready, in the likely event that they didn't.

Three guards rounded the bend and collided with King Heston and the commander right next to me. The path was big enough to fit two people walking side-by-side, but it was not wide enough for a proper sword fight. King Heston quickly dropped the first guard, but the second one was on him immediately. The king blocked his strike, but as the guard threw back his arm to attack Heston again, his blade swiped across my arm.

I gasped at the hit, alerting him to my hiding spot. He turned, surprised to find me, but Heston struck him down while he was distracted. The commander pushed past us and engaged the third guard.

The third guard was ready and pushed him back, giving me just enough room to escape further down the tunnel.

I ran into *another* guard as he rounded the bend. I instinctively lifted my hands to push myself away from him, the dagger in my hand clattering against the metal weapon in his own hands.

A pistol.

The man grabbed me by the throat. "A *girl*?" A sinister smile replaced his initial surprise. "Am I to presume you're Evangeline?"

His eyes flicked to something behind me, and he flung me aside, clearly more concerned about the other soldiers than he was with me. I ducked around the bend, happy to be forgotten, though my heart was about to jump right out of my mouth.

I squinted against the brightness of the next room. A man stood a few feet in front of me, silhouetted in the light. But there was nowhere else to go. I clutched my dagger and ran in.

For the first time in my life, I was relieved to see the man standing in front of me was Roland. He seemed to think differently, swearing when he saw me. "What are *you* doing here?"

But then a much more welcoming voice addressed me. "Eva?"

I turned to the left, where two people were crumpled on the ground. "Silas!"

I ran to him, my heart sinking the closer I got. He was shockingly pale, his hair damp and his shirt blood-soaked and covered in... Was that vomit? What *happened* while I was gone?

I paid no heed to the woman next to him. I crouched on his other side, touched his face. He was burning. "Silas? What's happened?"

He didn't say anything, didn't even reach for me. Tears rolled down his cheeks.

He looked like he was dying.

I grabbed his right hand. Was he in shock? I glanced at the woman pressing her bloodstained skirt to his left arm, but she didn't offer any explanation for his condition. Honestly, she looked a breath away from death herself. I returned my attention to Silas, speaking through a sudden barrage of tears. "I brought King Heston and some of his soldiers. They'll be here any moment. We're goin' to get you out of here, and take you all back to Eliston."

His fingers curled around mine, the grip weak, but at least it was something.

"How did you end up in Eliston?" Roland asked, making his way over to us. "Irimen is the opposite direction."

"Don't take a step closer, you traitorous scum!" the woman across from me shrieked.

"No, I'm on your side!" Roland protested, throwing off his red sash. "I never strayed. I—"

King Heston and the commander ran into the room, spattered in blood. They quickly surveyed us.

"Fate's mercy, Adeena," King Heston gasped. "That can't be you."

He was looking past me, at the ghost of a woman on the other side of Silas.

A curse nearly escaped my own lips. *This* was Queen Adeena? It hadn't even crossed my mind that she could be the *queen*.

Though, in my defense, she looked far closer to a corpse than royalty.

"How fortunate you're here!" Roland said, offering a bow. "What is the status on Harland's guards?"

"Dead," Casimir answered. "I have five soldiers at the mouth of the cave making sure no one else arrives. Five more are checking the remaining tunnels and the rest—" Four men rounded the corner and entered the room. "Are right here," he finished.

"Arrest Roland," Queen Adeena demanded.

"Wait. Please! I know how this appears, but my loyalties have never wavered! It was all part of the plan!"

"You poisoned and *shot* me," Silas croaked.

That was all it took for the Elistonian soldiers to turn on Roland. They surrounded him with their swords, and he slowly lifted his hands in surrender.

I looked over to Silas.

Poisoned?

Roland shot him?

"As I said before, the poisoning was not supposed to be so serious. And I missed the shot on purpose!" He didn't even deny it. *Unbelievable.*

"You could have missed by a little more!" Queen Adeena retorted, still pressing her skirt to Silas's arm, a murderous look in her eye.

"Do you want him killed?" the commander asked.

"No! Please—" Roland started begging.

King Heston turned to me, and talked over him. "This is the Roland you said helped you and your friend?"

I nodded.

"Then his loyalties are more complicated, it seems." He turned to Silas. "I would recommend a trial for his case, but it's your call."

Silas grimaced. "I don't care. Just get him out of my sight."

King Heston nodded to his commander, who sheathed his sword and bound Roland's arms and wrists behind his back. He handed Roland's sword to another soldier. Then he picked up the sash Roland had been wearing moments before and gagged him with it.

The commander then handed him off to three of the four soldiers, ordering them to kill him without hesitation if he tried to make a run for it.

They led him out as Heston asked, "Queen Adeena, where is King Esmond?"

The queen shook her head, fresh tears streaking down her face.

No.

King Heston knelt beside her. "I'm so sorry. Do you know where his body is?"

"There isn't one," she whispered.

He closed his eyes as he steeled himself. "I hate t' ask you this, but you're certain? There's no chance he's alive somewhere else?"

"I'm certain," she whispered, the horror still fresh in her voice.

King Heston nodded. "Can you two make it out of here on your own feet? We have horses outside."

A small whimper escaped Adeena's throat. She squeezed her eyes shut and spoke slowly, as though every word threatened to bring her to tears. "Alastair can't even lift his head. He'll have to be carried."

Where *was* the prince? I hadn't seen any other signs of prisoners as we went through the tunnel. All the rooms we passed had appeared empty. And this room was a dead end.

"Where is he?" I asked as the commander and King Heston began helping Queen Adeena to her feet.

The queen furrowed her brow in response. The two men shared a look before King Heston nodded slightly, not in answer to my question, but as if I had answered one of his.

I looked to Silas and asked again, sure he, at least, would understand me. "Where is Alastair?"

Silas closed his eyes and squeezed my hand a little tighter. "You're looking at him, Eva."

55

ALASTAIR, IN ALL HIS GLORY

Alastair

"You're lyin'," she said, after the longest pause of my life.

"Not this time."

"But—" Eva stopped short, and I opened my eyes to see her.

This was not how I had imagined telling her. I thought it would be a victorious revelation. Roland and I running to meet her with my parents. The doctor would look them over, and I would thank her and tell her I was Alastair all along. Or earlier today, in a quiet moment, a sign of trust between us. But instead, here I was, lying on the floor of a torture arena, covered in filth and blood, not even strong enough to sit up.

The Crown Prince, in all his glory.

In my imaginings of the scenario, I also never pictured Eva looking so horrified at the news. She let go of my hand, her eyes wide, flicking between me and my mother.

I wanted to reach back out for her, but I couldn't. Her own sleeve was bloodstained, though she paid it no mind. I wanted to ask how she was, but now wasn't the time.

King Heston cleared his throat. "Am I understanding correctly, Miss Evangeline, that Alastair here is the other man you wanted us t' rescue—Silas?"

She didn't say anything. She just stared at me.

"Yes," I answered for her. "One and the same."

"Very good," King Heston said. He nodded for the last remaining soldier to take the commander's place in helping to walk my mother out.

The soldier hurried over, and the commander waited for them to leave the room before addressing me. "How much pain are you in?"

"Truthfully, not much. But I assume that has to do with the poisoning."

"Stars," he cursed. "What kind?"

"Hummel, I'm told."

He cursed again, louder this time. "No time t' waste then."

He adjusted my legs, lifting me over his shoulder in one fluid motion. It was a little more graceful than when Graven had lifted me, but it was just as awful the second time around. With Eva watching in place of my mother. Not to mention the room spun as I rose. I groaned.

"Grab a lantern on your way out, Miss Evangeline," the commander ordered. "I'll have you lead the way."

"Yes, sire." She scurried out of my line of sight.

"Stay with me, Alastair. The doctor is right outside."

We evacuated the cave and regrouped at the outcropping where we were originally supposed to rendezvous with Eva and the Irimen doctor. The three soldiers who had arrested Roland had already started their way back to Eliston. A second section had already arrived, half of them going back right away with the commander, and half remaining to help dress wounds.

Somehow, I was in the worst shape of any of us. Thankfully, none of King Heston's soldiers had died, and they could manage their own injuries.

King Heston kept my mother company while the doctor examined me. I'd only met Heston a few times, but I'd always liked him. There had never been a question in my mind on renewing the alliance between Wenterly and Eliston when I assumed the throne. Seeing him sit there with my mother solidified that decision even more. He was a good man. Someone I'd be proud to partner with.

It seemed to me that my mother just needed to regain her strength. She was weak and traumatized, but with some food and time, she should survive this ordeal.

Meanwhile, I was on the verge of death.

The doctor had cut away half my shirt to examine my bullet wound.

"The bullet is still in your arm," he said. "I believe it will be best if we remove it."

"Brilliant."

"With the effects of the hummel poisoning, you might not feel it at all. But, all the same, do your best t' relax and hold still for me."

"I couldn't move if I wanted to, so no worries there."

I turned my head away from the doctor's work—the one movement I was capable of—and caught sight of Eva. She was sitting off by herself, tying a strip of fabric around her arm as best she could.

"Will you check on Evangeline when you're done with me and my mother?" I asked. "She was injured too."

"Of course, sire."

I watched as Eva slowly surveyed the group. She watched King Heston and my mother for a while, then looked over the other soldiers. Finally, her gaze fell on me, but when our eyes met, she glanced away.

What on earth could she be thinking right now? She was so relieved to find me in the cave. Worried, too, obviously. But even in front of King Heston and my mother, she'd been the same as she'd always been around me. It was as soon as she found out *my* title that her familiarity disappeared.

A wave of exhaustion hit me. I needed to sleep. Whatever was going on with Eva would have to wait until I could think more clearly.

The doctor stood, his work finished. He was right, I had hardly felt a thing.

"When we get back t' the camp I'll have you eat some charcoal. It's likely too late for it t' do much good, but seeing as you're still heavily under the hummel's effects, we'll take every precaution we can."

"Are you saying I could still die from this?"

"The fact you're still breathing gives me confidence you'll recover. T' be in a condition as severe as yours… I believe if this were going t' prove fatal, it would have done so by now."

I couldn't tell if the doctor actually believed that, or if he only meant to soothe my worries. I almost pitied him. Trying to decide how honest to be with a patient near death could not be an easy task. But more than I felt sorry for him, I felt sorry for myself.

However unlikely the doctor claimed it to be, I could still die tonight. We'd made it out of the cave, but the rescue wasn't enough to guarantee my survival. I tried to rouse myself. I needed to talk to Eva, talk to my mother, but the exhaustion tugged me down harder.

"Eva," I called, but it came out much quieter than I intended.

The doctor nodded. "I'll check on the young lady. But you need t' drink all of this before we leave for Eliston." He set a waterskin next to me and called a soldier over to help me drink. "It should dilute the hummel that's still in your body."

"No, that's not—" but he didn't hear me. He was already gone.

I hate this.

King Heston came over and knelt to talk to me while the doctor tended to my mother.

"I believe this is yours." He showed me the ring I had given Eva. I nodded and he put it on my finger.

"What's the story with the young woman? Your mother says she's never seen her before."

"I met her on the way here. She's been a faithful friend, and given up everything to help me. She should be treated as such."

"Yes, of course." He paused to look over at her. "Though, if I may, the fact that she was unaware of your identity, along with her status, raises a few questions."

I was too tired to talk about this. "I think we all have bigger things to worry about right now than Evangeline's status." My voice was growing weaker, no longer rasping, just a whisper. I tried to clear my throat, but it made no difference. "If she hadn't found you, I would definitely be dead by now. She told you where we were. People are deemed heroes for such things. She deserves the same respect."

"Undoubtedly. Are you aware of whose care she's under?"

I cursed under my breath. Did we have to go through all this right *now*? Did Eva have to deal with this every time she met new people? Fate's mercy—

"She's with me. That's all that matters for now." My tone was meant to be stern. In different circumstances, I would have looked down on the king, making it clear my word on this was final. But there I was, lying on the ground, half-dressed, my voice barely audible. Any authority my words carried were from my title only. A title I wasn't even sure I could still claim.

But hopefully, it was enough.

56

Whether or Not Fate Hates Me, I Sure Hate Fate

Evangeline

I tried to tell the doctor not to bother with me. That it was a minor cut, and I'd be fine. But he said Prince Alastair insisted.

I couldn't reject the wishes of a royal, I supposed.

The doctor unwrapped my one-handed attempt at a bandage. He said it needed stitches.

Brilliant.

I gritted my teeth at the tug of the thread. It seemed every moment of this evening was intent on being unpleasant.

As soon as the doctor finished his examination, he left with the royals and most of the soldiers. I stayed behind with a handful from the second section to gather Roland's and Silas's things.

We didn't talk. I wouldn't have wanted to anyway. My exhaustion was pressing on me with a nearly tangible weight, and it took all my energy to keep myself from tears. I didn't know how to even begin processing the events of the day, let alone surrounded by Elistonian soldiers.

So I tried to pull every thought out of my mind, focusing only on gathering supplies, getting in the saddle, and listening to the horses' hooves as we all made our way back to Eliston.

Along the way, one of the soldiers spotted Starboard and retrieved her at my request. I *did* cry then, my general overwhelm making me far too relieved that she and Port wouldn't have to be without one another.

But once we were traveling again, and there was nothing left to do but ride, my thoughts kept turning back to *him*, no matter how hard I tried to think on other things.

I directed my horse closer to one of the soldiers. "Are you familiar with hummel-poisonin'? How serious do you think the prince's condition is?"

The soldier glanced over at me, seemingly surprised that I'd engage him in conversation. But he obliged me. "Hummel is potent. I don't know how much he ingested, and I'm not a doctor, so I can't rightly say. But a few of the flowers can kill a child or dog. The root is worse."

"That's what I thought," I muttered. "I was hopin' what I'd heard about it was an exaggeration."

"Not a lot of hummel in Wenterly?"

"Not enough that it's ever been an issue for me."

"It's quite common in Eliston." He shrugged. "Do you know when the prince was poisoned?"

My chest tightened. "He was fine when I left him. We spent most of the day together." My face flushed at the memory of how we'd spent that time. "He said that Roland poisoned him, but it must have been after I left, because I'm fine."

"Perhaps Roland had no reason t' harm you."

The notion that Roland would dare to poison him, but not me, sent my stomach twisting and lit a fire in my chest. "He had far more reason to poison me than ... him." I couldn't quite bring myself to call him by his rightful name. Not yet. I wasn't ready to accept it as the truth.

The soldier glanced over at me again, mild concern evident in his frown. "Hummel acts quickly. A few minutes, and that can be that. Alastair's a fortunate man."

The sentiment was so surprising, I laughed before I could stop myself.

"Why's that funny?"

"My last two weeks with him have been anythin' but fortunate. The number of times things went wrong and we nearly died was absurd."

"And yet, it all worked out, save for the king, rest him. So if you ask me, facing failure time after time and still surviving sounds a lot like fortune. Fate's on your side."

Fate. There it was again. Could anything be done without its guiding hand?

"But King Esmond is dead. King Heston risked comin' here for the sake of an alliance that no longer exists. What does that mean?"

The man shrugged. "War." It was matter of fact. Unemotional. I supposed war had to be for a soldier.

"But when? And where? And what does it mean for Prince Alastair and Queen Adeena?"

"I don't worry about matters above my rank." He looked at me again, this time with a pointed stare instead of a passing glance. "I imagine they're above yours, too, though I don't really understand your involvement in all of this."

I sighed. "That makes two of us."

We rode in silence the rest of the way to Eliston. Maybe Fate was on our side, like everyone kept telling me, but *maybe* Fate had been punishing us for my involvement in matters above my rank, as the soldier had put it. Silas—Alastair—never mentioned any problems in his mission when it was only him and Roland. But once he met me? It was just one disaster after another.

Or, perhaps our *mis*fortune wasn't outright punishment, but rather that my presence was an obstacle Fate was constantly having to work around to have its way—for Alastair to live and take the throne back. What if, somehow, King Esmond was dead now because of me?

I shook the thought from my head. That assumed that my lowly life was somehow tied to the king's. I didn't know much about the threads of Fate, but I was confident that King Esmond's and mine never crossed paths in life's tapestry.

As the gate at the Elistonian border came into view, I couldn't help but wonder if Heston would follow through on his threats to me. I hadn't lied to him, but I was still wrong about King Esmond being alive.

I doubted he would consider the mission successful. Yes, two of the three Cathmoores made it out of the prison. But would Alistair make it through the rest of the night? And if he did, was a war across three kingdoms a price worth paying to get Harland off the Cathmoore's throne?

The soldier was right; it was best not to worry about such questions. Which likely meant that my involvement in this mission was over. I'd wait to see if the prince lived or died, and then, if King Heston didn't kill me for the way this night had gone, I'd be off to find yet another future.

The soldier I'd spoken to helped me take Roland's and Silas's things to the commander. Or, more likely, I helped him.

The commander dismissed the soldier, and once he and I were alone in the tent, he asked the question I'd been dreading.

"Miss Evangeline, who's care are you under?"

I leaned back on my heels, looking for a way around the question. I should have thought about how I would answer this on the ride back instead of all that Fate nonsense.

At my hesitation, he clarified, "Alastair has requested you remain here for now. And, theoretically, he has the right as a royal t' speak for you for a short period of time. You aren't being sent away. But, a woman being involved in these kinds of affairs requires a notice t' her guardian, let alone when such affairs reside across kingdom borders."

"You said Alastair can *theoretically* speak for me. Why only theoretically?"

"Were King Esmond on the throne when he died, Alastair would automatically be King. However, since Harland was on the throne at the time, Alastair's authority is not *technically* valid."

"But he's the rightful ruler."

"But that's not the same as *being* the ruler."

"Well, my guardian certainly won't be lookin' for me here, if that's what concerns you."

The man was quiet a moment, and I got the sense he was holding back an exasperated sigh. "Regardless of where he looks for you, sooner or later, he is sure t' find out that you were involved in instigating a war and that we failed t' alert him that you crossed kingdom borders. That is at least one problem we're hoping t' avoid."

One problem. Because I had already provided a whole sea of problems for them tonight. "I understand that I have very little room to negotiate right now—"

"That is correct," the commander affirmed.

I tried not to glare at him. "But, if Fate has any kindness left for me, my guardian will never see me again." I could see the man was getting ready to push further, so with a deep breath, I steeled myself to tell him the difficulty of my situation. "This isn't me rebellin', sire. I truly don't think I'd be safe if he were to find me."

He blinked. "I'm sensing that there is more t' this than I realized." He cleared his throat. "Regardless, we've agreed t' honor Alastair's request for now. Were you a citizen of Eliston, you would be under obligation to immediately disclose such information t' me, but as it stands, perhaps Fate will indeed show you more kindness, Miss Evangeline."

"Thank you, sire." I meant it. I didn't have the energy to fight this battle right now. To keep minding my manners while I did so.

"You may call me Casimir."

I raised my eyebrows. Was the commander too tired for protocol's nonsense too? Or was he trying to build trust so I'd spill my secrets for him?

"If you'd like."

"I much prefer it."

I nodded. "Where will I be stayin'?"

"The women here all sleep in the same tent. However, because of what you have done tonight, you've earned a private tent, should you desire it. You're welcome wherever you will be most comfortable."

I'd earned a private tent? For starting a war?

I fidgeted with the fabric of my skirt. "How many women are here?"

"About a dozen."

I wasn't keen on being alone with my thoughts, but a dozen women peppering me with questions about who I was and how I ended up in this army camp did not sound the least bit comfortable.

"I'll take the private tent, and, if it's not too much to ask, I'd appreciate a bath."

"It is a delicate thing, to trust another. Yet, I have never had a stronger foundation than when I took up such vulnerability."

Brigid, *Duty to My Fellow Man*

57

The Pain of Living

Alastair

I woke in soft light as the morning sun filtered through the tent.

I was alive—I knew that because I woke to pulsing pain in my left arm and my head. And a general ache throughout my bones. If I was dead, I wouldn't hurt like this.

And not just physically.

King Heston's aid saved my and my mother's lives. But not my father's. Which meant, when we restored the throne, I would have to rule without his guidance. Whatever kingly advice my father had yet to offer me was gone.

Hopefully the lessons I'd learned from him in the time we had would be enough.

It also meant that Heston had involved himself in my family's war. As soon as Harland found out what had happened, he would come for Eliston.

But even after learning of my father's death, Heston had helped us. Brought us back here and had us cared for. That was a good sign.

I hoped.

A man entered my tent. He startled when he saw me awake.

"Alastair, forgive me, I only stepped out for a moment. I'm glad t' see you're awake. How are you feeling?" He stepped further in, but maintained a respectful distance. I started to sit up, but he quickly told me to stay put. "I'm the doctor King Heston sent for. I took over for the other one a few hours ago. Please, rest there."

"Are you also caring for my mother?"

"Yes, sire. That was why I stepped out."

"How is she?"

"It seems she's suffered a few cracked ribs and trauma to the head. But nothing physical that cannot be mended."

I closed my eyes a moment. That was good news, though I didn't miss his clarifying use of the word 'physical.'

"What's the verdict for me?"

"Let's find out, shall we?"

He asked again how I felt. Which wasn't great. But that was actually a good thing, he confirmed. It meant the hummel wasn't affecting me any more. He handed me a cup and told me to drink as much water as I could today.

"Drinking water is what nearly killed me," I tried to joke.

"If the water is bitter, don't drink it. That's my advice."

I frowned. "I'll remember that."

The doctor demanded I stay in bed for two days. It would have been alright, if I wasn't left alone the whole time. The doctor brought me meals, gave me regular check-ins, and the commander—Casimir, he'd told me to call him—would also check on me every so often. But King Heston was in no hurry to meet with me it seemed, and my mother was confined to her bed as well.

The evening of the first day, Casimir arrived to tell me how my father died.

Harland knew that if news of my parents' actual deaths reached me, I'd never be lured into his hands. But once it was clear my parents' lives weren't of any further worth to Harland, he wasn't willing to spend his resources to keep them both alive.

It was quick, at least. They'd beheaded him. Then burned his body—a pauper's funeral.

I wept as soon as Casimir left my tent.

I slept most of the next day, since in my waking hours, I only had three reasonable trails of thought: worrying of what the future held, grieving my father's death, and wondering what had happened with Roland.

None of those topics were pleasant, though, so I welcomed how frequently my thoughts strayed to Eva.

What I would give to see her. To lean my head on her shoulder, so I could at least think about all of this with her at my side.

Where was she? *How* was she?

I had been afraid to ask. If she had left, or Heston had sent her away… I couldn't handle that right now.

On the second day, Casimir brought my dinner, which was a welcome change of pace.

I greeted him enthusiastically. "Do you come with news, or just food?"

"As a matter of fact, Heston would like t' meet with you and your mother tomorrow. There is much t' discuss regarding our next steps."

"Certainly. Where will we meet him?"

"In his tent. I will come t' get you, since you don't know your way around the camp, though it won't be difficult t' get there."

"Where is my mother?"

"In the tent next t' Heston's." He handed me my tray of food. "You're across the path from her."

Casimir was more likely than the doctor to know anything about Eva, and I forced out the question before I could change my mind. "May I inquire about Eva?"

He frowned. "Who?"

I tried to tell my heart not to race. "Miss Evangeline," I corrected. Had I ever called her 'Miss' before? "She's still here, isn't she?"

"Oh, her, yes. She's been very enthusiastic about helping the other women, doing laundry and mending the soldiers' uniforms."

I nodded. She was always trying to make herself useful to Roland and me. Of course she would do the same here. "She likes to stay busy."

Casimir laughed. "So it would seem, sire."

"Just Alastair, please." I hardly knew what my title was these days, and based on the state Casimir and Heston and found me in, we were well past formalities. "Has she asked to see me?" I pressed.

"I'm afraid I don't know. If she has, I haven't heard about it."

"Does she *know* she can see me?"

"No one should have told her otherwise."

"But has anyone told her she *can*?"

Casimir's eyebrows furrowed. "I'm afraid I don't know, s—Alastair."

My jaw tensed. "Would you send for her? Or have someone send for her?"

"Of course. When would you prefer her t' stop by?"

"As soon as possible."

He nodded. "I'll go fetch her."

"Was there anything else you and I needed to discuss?"

He smiled slightly. "No. We'll have plenty t' talk about tomorrow."

58

I'm Full of Nothing but Dread and Grief

Evangeline

I dunked a shirt into the washtub, trying not to let the woman's story of how she met her husband cut through me like a knife.

I had heard no news of Alastair's wellbeing that first morning in Eliston, and decided to take it as good news. I assumed I would hear about it if he died, if by no other means than getting thrown back to Wenterly because Alastiar didn't have authority over my whereabouts from the grave.

So, I stuck to the lesson I'd learned long ago: be useful or be a ghost.

I got involved with the laundry right away. By late afternoon, the wash tub was a good place to be. The cool water was welcome in the heat, though the mountains were certainly cooler than my summers in Welven. And, I had to admit, the company wasn't half bad. The women were curious about me and my adventure with royalty, but hadn't forced me to tell them anything. And I didn't. Just that I'd been through a lot the last few weeks, and needed some time to sort it all out. Which was all true.

I worked quietly and let the women introduce themselves and tell me about how they got involved with the army camp. Most were dull stories, or at least dull in the way they told them. But it was better than being left alone with my thoughts.

As such, the private tent I'd been granted was both a blessing and a curse. I didn't have to play a part in front of anyone, but my worries were relentless, and I had nothing to keep them at bay. While my body craved rest, I'd spent the last two nights tossing and turning for what must have been hours.

I should have been able to calm my thoughts enough for sleep. Everyone seemed to think that since Alastair had survived the first night, he would make a full recovery.

But were they still treating him? And where was he? Here? Or had they taken him to a city with more doctors?

The commander had assured me I could come to him if I needed anything, but I hadn't dared to ask him any of those things. I doubted he would let me demand answers when I wasn't willing to answer his questions. I was well aware I was walking a narrow line, and I didn't want to push my luck any further than I already had.

Even so, I had to repeatedly beat down the urge to go find Alastiar and see how he was doing for myself. He needed to rest. *I* needed to rest.

Besides, I didn't really want to visit *Alastair*. I wanted to see Silas: the one I'd joked around with; the one I had escaped pirates and jail with; the one I had insulted and argued with.

The one I had kissed.

I couldn't do any of those things with Alastair. The prince. The rightful *King* of Wenterly.

But I had, hadn't I? So what did that mean? For me? For him? For *us*?

Was there even an 'us'?

Roland had warned me, hadn't he? *The chasm between you is wider than you can imagine.*

Somehow, he was right.

There was no future with me and Silas. Because *Silas* didn't exist. Yes, technically, the man I'd spent the last few weeks with lived, but as far as I was concerned, Silas had died in the prison. Every favor I thought the prince might have granted the two of us would certainly never be possible now.

I knew those things he said to me before we kissed were little more than hopeful words, but I didn't think they were outright *lies*. Had he manipulated me? Knowingly? Or did all that time hiding in the woods make him forget for a moment the reality we lived in?

Perhaps it was for the best that I didn't know where he was. If the hummel poisoning didn't kill him, I had half a mind to for the way he'd led me on, making me think I ever had a chance of being more than what I was.

I had trusted him.

And this was where trust had gotten me.

I wrung out the shirt and grabbed another, while the woman droned on about the stew she prepared for her husband the night he asked for her hand.

Everything had been so much easier when I was just a seamstress in Welven and that was all I would ever be. That was *still* all I would ever be. It had never changed. I had just forgotten.

I nearly got up then and there to set out again for a new life and leave this whole mess behind me. But I only had to think as far as "how to leave the army camp" to remember we were indeed on the brink of war. A war I knew next to nothing about. So where could I go when the whole world was about to be thrown into chaos again?

The only place I wanted to go was dead to me now.

"So I was five years into my work at th' inn," the woman explained. "And I thought t' myself—"

"Forgive me for interrupting. I'm here for Miss Evangeline."

I lifted my head at Casimir's voice. The women stood upon noticing him, and I hurried to join them.

He held a letter in his hands. My stomach dropped. Was it time for me to go? Were they alerting Gratsis of my whereabouts?

"Yes, sir. How can I be of service?" It didn't feel right to call him by name, not here. I hoped he'd accept the less formal 'sir' in place of it.

His voice was nothing but polite and formal, but his gaze held far more curiosity than usual. "Alastair has requested your presence. I will escort you."

I nearly sighed in relief, though a summons from Alastair stirred up a different kind of anxiety. "Right this moment?" I was elbow-deep in wet clothes mere seconds ago.

"Yes, miss."

I apologized to the other women, who assured me they'd manage just fine while I was gone. I dried my hands on my apron as Casimir led me away.

"Do you know what he would like to see me about?" I asked.

"No, miss."

I indicated the letter. "He didn't say in his note?"

Casimir glanced down at it, as though he forgot he was holding it. "Oh, no. This isn't Alastair's. I spoke with him personally about you, miss." He tucked the letter into his vest pocket.

"You don't have to call me 'miss.'"

He lifted his eyebrows. "It seemed t' me you were more comfortable with formality."

"I'm not." I scoffed, as if I needed to prove the point. "But everythin' is strange here and I'm tryin' not to stand out."

He laughed quietly. "Then you ought t' call me Casimir. Everyone does."

"Even people like me?"

"Everyone means everyone, Evangeline."

I pressed my lips together, but let the issue go.

"Alastair is t' remain in bed for the sake of his recovery," Casimir explained, content to change the subject. "It's clear you two have ... some things t' sort out, but do your best not t' upset him, if you can help it."

"Because he's royalty?"

He looked back at me with something akin to a glare. "Because he's suffering."

My stomach dropped. "I'll be sure to watch my tongue, Casimir."

59

THIS IS NOT A REUNION

Alastair

It took Casimir an eternity to find Evangeline. I nearly got up and searched for her myself, but if I was out looking for her when she finally arrived, and we missed each other, I'd be even more frustrated—and in trouble for getting out of bed.

So, I mindlessly flipped through *The Meaning of Shadows* as I waited. Casimir had delivered it the morning after we arrived here. He told me the book was the reason Evangeline knew something had gone wrong with Roland and me, and how it had also convinced King Heston to follow her into the prison.

I opened to the first page and read my handwritten note from when I bound the book three years ago.

Bound by Alastair Cathmoore
in the 126th year of the Gilded Age

I'd nearly forgotten it was there, an insignificant note for myself so I could keep track of my progress with the skill.

And it turned out to be a note that very well saved my life.

I attempted to further smooth the wrinkled pages, but they would never look as well-kept again. Granted, they were already worn from getting covered in my own annotations, but now they were also crinkled and bent. It was poetic. It was metaphorical. I could write the literary equivalent of *The Meaning of Shadows*. A philosophy on pain with the allusions found in paper and ink rather than the celestial heavens. I was the Philosopher Prince, after all. I could—

I snapped the book shut. What was taking Eva so long?

Right as I was about to call for someone else to look for her, Casimir's voice called from outside my tent, "I have Evangeline here t' see you, Alastair."

"Send her in, please," I practically yelled in relief.

I set the book aside as Eva walked in. She was dressed in new clothes, similar in style to what she was wearing when we first met, though not in color. A simple brown skirt and a tan linen shirt, a lighter brown corset over the top. The colors befitting her status. Her hair was tucked into a scarf (unbleached cotton, of course). She nervously brushed her hands on the sides of her skirt.

Casimir stood awkwardly in the entrance, unsure if he was supposed to leave or not.

I was quick to clarify. "Thank you, Casimir. You may go. I'm sure you have more pressing matters to attend to."

I worried he was about to protest, but he decided to nod and leave, much to my relief.

The tent flap closed, but Eva simply stood there, her hands still fidgeting at her side, as though she wasn't sure what to do with herself. Her uncertainty made me hesitate.

"Eva, I'm glad to see you." It sounded as awkward as I felt. I wanted a reunion. Not ... whatever this was.

"Yes, it's good to see that you're well."

What was that?

"Eva." I tried to laugh, but failed. "That is *not* how we talk."

"Sorry." She attempted to tuck a stand of hair that wasn't even there behind her ear. "I'm realizin' I'm not really sure what proper protocol is around here."

"No, that's—" I tried to cut her off, but I was too late.

She'd already dropped to a curtsy, her head bowed. "The pleasure is all mine, Your Highness."

"*Absolutely* not!" I was out of bed so quickly I didn't have a chance to wince from the pain the sudden movement caused until I'd already reached her.

She stood, rigid. "Casimir said you're to remain in bed."

I ignored her and took her by the shoulders. "That's not how *we* talk. You and me. *Us*."

"Not anymore." She pulled back, and though it broke my heart, I let her.

"Why? I'm still me."

"Are you?"

I faltered. Did she truly doubt that? After everything she'd said to me before about knowing who I was?

"I'm still me, Eva," I repeated.

She frowned. "And I'm still *me*."

"Eva—"

"I'm not sure you should call me that anymore."

My heart fell right out of my chest. I nearly took a step back. There was no playfulness in her tone. Not like the way we had argued before.

"What's gotten into you?"

"Reality, Silas!" Her eyes widened, the name itself forming a rift between us. Eva folded her hands in front of her and spoke again, quieter this time, with her eyes carefully focused on the ground. "Reality, Prince Alastair."

"Just Alastair is fine. Preferred, actually."

"Was there somethin' you wanted to see me about?" she asked, blatantly ignoring every attempt I'd made at familiarity.

"No. I just wanted to see you."

She held her arms out slightly. "Here I am."

"No, I don't think you are."

She furrowed her brow. "Excuse me?"

"This"—I gestured to her—"is not the person you have *ever* been as long as I've known you."

She gestured to her clothes. "*This* is who I've always been. I told you that. Or did you think I was still lyin' about my identity too?"

It would have hurt less if she'd stabbed me.

She scoffed. "Besides, you've only known me two and a half weeks."

"And they were the best two and a half weeks of my life."

A short laugh burst from her mouth. "You've almost died *at least* three times since we met."

"*Okay*, yes, in that sense, they were beyond awful. But you made them a lot less awful than they could have been."

She didn't say anything. Didn't even look at me. She was still looking at the ground.

"Eva, I called you here because I wanted—I *need*—to see you. The normal you. I need Eva who'll tell me I look awful, or tell me I'm wrong—"

"You *are* wrong. You made me think it was okay to treat you that way. To be familiar with you. But it's not. It wasn't then, and it certainly isn't now."

I shut my mouth.

"We're not alone in the woods anymore, *Alastair*." She emphasized my name, as if that alone proved her point. "There are boundaries put in place for people like us. Rules we have to follow. Yes, at one point, you made me think maybe there was a way to get around those rules. But *now*? Now, the rules matter more than ever. If you had just told me you were the prince from the beginnin'—"

Tears stung my eyes as regret sunk into my chest. All those times I had wanted to tell her and hadn't, because *Roland* had convinced me it wasn't safe to tell anyone... How different might things have ended up if I had confessed—

She cursed as a tear rolled down my cheek. "I'm sorry. I didn't intend to come here and yell at you. I—"

I blinked away the rest of my tears and did my best to keep my voice soft, not wanting anyone outside the tent to overhear our conversation. "Eva, all my life I've had people treat me the way you are trying to now. Distanced and placating. Do you have any idea how nice it is to have someone treat you like their equal for once?"

She inhaled a shaky breath. "Yes."

Our past conversation from a late-night watch came flooding back to me. When she told me she never had any real friends. Until me.

"Eva, I loved our time together."

She looked up, and though she had tears welling up in her own eyes, she glared at me. Which, ironically, was an improvement. "No, you didn't."

"The first few days, I wasn't thrilled," I admitted. "But then I realized that you're actually a decent woman. And you were easy to talk to. Because I didn't have an image to uphold with you, and you didn't care about upholding an image with me. The last few weeks with you have been some of the most honest weeks of my life—even with all the lying and the hiding. Because I could be myself around you."

"You couldn't though. You were never fully honest about who you were."

"I tried to tell you—"

"Three days ago! That's too late, Alastair." She shook her head. "I should go," she said, but a tear slipped down her cheek before she could turn around.

I caught her wrist. "Please stay," I whispered. Any louder and my voice would have broken. Though I held onto her gently, she didn't pull away. "I'm sorry, Eva. I thought I was doing the right thing. If I knew the truth would hurt you like this, I never would have kept it from you."

"I know," she whispered, once again looking down at the ground.

"I asked you to come here because I wanted to make sure you were okay. And because I don't know how to handle any of this. I need someone who can sit by my side through that, telling me the fact I'm barely keeping it together isn't a weakness, but just part of being human."

She finally gazed up at me, tears trailing down her face. "I can't be that person for you anymore."

I let go of her. "Can't, or won't?"

She sniffed and wiped her tears with her sleeve.

"Talk to me. I want to fix this."

"You can't fix the way the world works."

"What if you're the world to me?"

"Don't," she whispered, then burst into tears.

My heart ripped itself to shreds. I stepped to pull her into a hug, but then hesitated. That might make things worse.

But to my relief, she closed the rest of the gap between us. I wrapped my arms around her, cradling her head against my shoulder as she cried. She leaned against me a few seconds, then finally hugged me back.

I nearly started crying with her. I'd missed her so much. More than I had realized. As I held her, her tears soaking my shirt, there was a bittersweet ache in my chest, and I realized this *must* be love.

I didn't say anything, content to hold her as long as she needed. Like she had done for me a few nights ago. She cried quietly, perhaps concerned, as I had been, of people overhearing her. It was a shame that the only time we'd had real privacy was on the pirate ship, when we practically despised each other.

After she calmed, she still didn't lift her head from my shoulder. "All of this is so complicated. Even more than I realized."

"But *I* knew how complicated it was."

She lifted her head. "Yes, that's why I'm mad at you!" But she didn't entirely pull away. Her arms were still wrapped around me.

"Because I lied about who I was?"

"Because you knew nothin' could ever happen between us, and you let me think it could! It's one thing to lie to me about your name. It's another to lie to me about my own future. I already lost all my plans for my life—because of you, if you recall. So when you said there could be—that you *wanted*—a future with me, of course I hoped you meant it."

"I did mean it. Every word. I still do. We'll find a way to make it work. I don't want things to change between us just because you know my real name and where I used to live. If you feel the same, then I'll find a way to marry you again. That's a promise."

She let go of me, taking a step back to put more space between us. She opened her mouth, then closed it again.

My heartbeat pounded in my ears. "Do you not feel the same?"

"I don't know what to feel."

I swallowed. "How come?"

"Because I'm not supposed to receive a betrothal. From *anyone*. Let alone someone like you. You're promisin' somethin' that's impossible."

"Harland isn't *supposed* to be sitting on Wenterly's throne, and that didn't make it impossible for him."

"But now an entire *army* is plottin' to get him off of it."

I sighed. "Fine, so it's a bad analogy."

"I think it's a perfect analogy."

I dragged a hand down my face. "If none of these rules and statuses and expectations existed—if we lived in a world where everyone was equal and we could do whatever we wanted—*would you feel the same?*"

"That's a complete fantasy!"

"Please, just answer the question."

She huffed, looked at me, looked away, looked at me again. "Maybe," she finally said.

"*Maybe?*"

"I have to think about this!"

"It's not a thinking question, it's a feeling question!"

She held up a hand as she began to tear up again. *Fate's mercy.* "I've already lost the few people I've been close to in my life, and if losin' you is inevitable too, then I'd rather be done with it now. Can you promise me all of this isn't just another lie? That once you're on the throne again, you'll still feel the same way?"

I stepped forward and held her tear-streaked face in my hands. "Eva, I can't bear the thought of losing you. I'm sorry I lied to you. I really am. If I could take it back, I would. You deserve so many more apologies than I can give. I'm sorry that I interfered with what you wanted for your life. But, selfishly, I'm also glad that I did. You've taught me so much. About the world and myself, and how *little* I know about everything. But I love you, Eva. I can't imagine moving forward in this mess without you at my side, and—Eva?" I brushed my thumb across her cheek. Her eyes were wide, and she'd grown so still, I wasn't sure she was still breathing. "Eva, I feel like I lost you somewhere."

She blinked. "You love me?"

I tried not to frown. Was that not implied in 'I want to marry you whatever it takes' and 'do you feel the same?' It shouldn't have been *that* shocking of a conclusion for her.

"Yes, I love you."

She held onto my wrists and closed her eyes a moment, and I nearly leaned down to kiss her. But her brow furrowed, and she suddenly pulled my left hand away from her face and stared at the ring on my finger.

Was it my imagination, or had she grown pale?

"Are you alright?" I asked. "You look like you're going to faint."

"I need some air." She broke away from me and stepped toward the tent flap.

"Eva?"

"I'll be fine." But her tone was far too cheery to sound genuine.

"Will you come back?"

"I don't know."

And she was gone.

60

People in Eliston Sure Love to Talk About Running

Evangeline

I couldn't breathe.

The last time I'd heard those three words said to me was seven years ago. From my *mom*. I never thought—never imagined—I'd hear them again from anyone, let alone *royalty*! And he looked at me so sincerely when he said it, and it was all *wrong*.

All of this was wrong.

I hurried back to the laundry tub, then changed direction to go back to my tent. I needed a moment alone. If I had known the conversation with Alastair would have included a marriage proposal and a proclamation of love, I never would have gone with Casimir in the first place.

My eyes began to blur with tears, and I ran around the corner, hoping I could get some privacy before I completely lost my composure.

But of course, I ran straight into someone.

I apologized and stepped away without looking to see who it was, but he caught my arm before I could run off.

"Evangeline, are you alright?" Casimir asked.

Why, of all the people in this camp, did it have to be *him*?

"I'm fine."

"You can't be running around an army camp."

I sniffed, trying to keep it together. "I'm sorry. I won't do it again."

He didn't loosen his grip on me. "Did something happen with Alastair that I should know about?"

Definitely not.

"It's just difficult. Everythin' he's been through."

His frowned. "Don't lie t' me. If there is something concerning about Alastair, it's my job t' know about it."

"Casimir, please, let me go. This has nothin' to do with politics."

He did let go of me, but the way he continued to search my eyes kept me from walking away. "Let me say one more thing, and then I'll let you make your own choices: Running from your problems is not the same thing as solving them. And running from people who care about you is going t' do more harm than it'll do you good."

I took a shuddering breath. "Why are you tellin' me this? You don't know me."

"I know *people*, Evangeline. Last I checked, you were one of those."

I picked up the first bit of cloth I saw and began scrubbing the moment I reached the wash tub.

The women gave me curious glances, but wisely refrained from asking me anything.

I scrubbed away, my thoughts shifting too quickly for me to sort through anything. Alastair, Casimir, the war, *love*. It was too much to think about, too much to—

"That one's clean, Evangeline." The woman next to me put a hand out to stop me. "Are you alright? You're breathing like you ran t' Westol and back."

"I don't know where that is."

"Doesn't matter." She took the shirt from me. "I know you're only here t' keep yourself busy so you don't have t' think about what all you've been through. But something has you *really* riled up, and you can't run from the world forever."

What was with these people? Did everyone in Eliston share the same mind?

"Thank you for your concern, but I don't need a lecture right now. I'm fine."

"A handful of minutes ago Casimir took you t' see the Wenter Prince. Is this all about that?"

"I can't talk about it." I picked up another shirt from the pile and dunked it into the tub.

"Did the prince mistreat you in some way?"

"No." I scrubbed at the shirt. "*That* I would be able to handle."

She snatched the shirt from me.

"Can I just do one thing I'm supposed to do!" I snapped.

The woman was unbothered by my outburst. "I think right now, you're supposed t' work out whatever has your feathers so ruffled. You can take this out on me all you want, but I'll not sit here and watch you beat the daylight out of these shirts while mumbling like a madwoman."

I glanced around at the other women, who were suddenly *very* focused on their own washing. "Fine." I stood and stormed off to my tent.

But sitting alone in my tent was excruciating. I needed to talk through all of this. And the only person I wanted to do that with was the very person I was currently avoiding. Guilt and conviction ate away at me.

You can't keep running.

It was absurd that everyone here seemed to think they knew so much about me. But then again, all I'd done for the last month was run: run away from Gratsis; run away from the pirates; run from the officers; and run from Alastair. Maybe my patterns were just easy to read.

I took a deep breath and walked the trail back to Alastiar's tent before I could talk myself out of it. The sun would start to set in the next hour. It wouldn't be appropriate for me to visit him after dark, and it would be too cruel of me to make him wait until morning.

As his tent came into view, I realized I wasn't sure how to go about entering. Did I just walk in? Did I announce myself? Surely Alastiar wouldn't care. But there were plenty outside who would see me, and if someone else was already inside his tent...

I stopped at the opening. "Um, Alastair? This is Ev—"

The tent flap whipped open, and Alastair stood before me, eyes wide and red-rimmed, hair a mess. Whatever guilt I'd felt before was nothing compared to what I felt now.

"You came back."

I nodded.

He didn't move.

"Can I come in?"

He sidestepped and dropped the flap once I entered. He stood at the entrance, eyes still wide, staring at me like I might disappear if he blinked. I supposed I deserved that kind of welcome.

"I'm sorry I left like that," I started. "I'm learnin' I tend to run from my problems."

"Is that what I am, then?" he asked, his voice strained. "A problem?"

I shook my head. "I know you want a simple answer, and I know you deserve one. But the best I can do is explain everythin' that's goin' on in my head right now. Can we start with that?"

He nodded. "Of course. Whatever you need."

My chest tightened. Mercy, how was he so understanding about all this? How was it he cared at all about what I needed?

"You should sit."

"I've been in bed all day."

"Very well, then." I steeled my nerves and cleared my throat. "My lineage makes everythin' complicated. Legally, I shouldn't even be here. They've only let me stay because you demanded it. And your authority won't keep me here forever. I can't cross kingdom borders without consent from my guardian."

He nodded.

"Because of that, I suspect one wrong move from me and King Heston will be more than happy to send me away. He's already declared war on King Harland because of me. He's not about to risk a legal dispute on my account."

"You think Gratsis will actually come for you? How does he know where you are?"

"He doesn't know. Even if the Narim officers told him I'm still alive, he'll never guess that I'm here now, but that doesn't matter. My existence in Eliston without his approval makes me a liability."

"But do you want to stay?"

"Where else would I go? There's nothin' for me anywhere else." I took a deep breath. "At least here I have you."

He blinked at my last sentence, but didn't directly acknowledge it. "Then I'll keep refusing them sending you away. You saved my life. They have to honor that."

"They *have*. But I don't know how much longer they'll put up with it. Your own authority isn't really clear, you know. No one knows what to call you. The prince? The king? Just Alastair?"

He stepped toward me. "My title doesn't matter for this. As far as I'm concerned, you can be under my care. How do you think our pirate wedding would hold up in court against Gratsis?"

I pressed my palms to my eyes. "That's what I'm tryin' to tell you. No one can find out about that. Not your mother. Not Heston. No one. If I'm to stay here, I need to be invisible. That means there can't be *anythin'* between us."

"But you said—"

"I'm not done."

He nodded for me to continue.

"We are in the middle of an army camp for soldiers who fight for someone else. King Heston has been a good man so far, but his people come first for him. If he doesn't think he can trust you to be the king *he* needs you to be, that could be the end of his kindness."

Alastair smiled and shook his head, which did not at all fit the warning I'd just given him.

"What's so funny about that? I'm serious, Alastair."

"I know. I never expected to have to listen to you lecture me about politics."

"I'm lecturin' you about *survival*. Playin' the game so you can see another day."

"I have no intent to do anything that would turn Heston on me or my mother. I owe a huge debt to him. I know that."

I took a deep breath. This was the hard part. I lowered my voice, ensuring that any passerby wouldn't catch my words. "But don't you understand that any fondness you have for me might be the thing that ruins all of this? If anyone gets the slightest suspicion that there's somethin' between us, even if they still decide to help you reclaim the throne, they'll probably send me away."

"So, what I'm hearing is, there *is* something between us?"

"Alastiar. Please. I'm serious about this."

"Yes, you've made your point. For your safety and the future of Wenterly, we can't give anyone any reason to turn against us. I'm hoping there's a second part to this lecture. About how I should act around *you*?"

I sighed. "It's not the answer you want to hear."

"You decided, then." It wasn't a question. His tone was flat, an acknowledgment. "You're saying no."

"No, I haven't decided anythin' yet. That's why I can't give you the answer you're lookin' for. I *do* care about you, Alastair. Very much. You're the dearest person in my life."

He blinked. "But?"

"But the whole world is about to turn upside down again! I can't make you any promises in these circumstances. And you shouldn't make me any either. I don't want to lose you. I do know that much. But I can't promise to be anythin' more than your friend right now. Once everythin' with Harland gets settled, then I can consider somethin' different."

He let out a long breath.

What was I doing? Crushing him like this after everything he'd already been through at the Caves? But it was insanity to even *consider* something beyond friendship with him, now or in the future. Friendship alone was insane enough.

"I'm sorry," I added, though it would hardly soften my rejection.

"No, you're right. I hate it, but you're right." He sat on the edge of his cot, shoulders slumped in defeat. "There's a lot going on politically right now. I don't need to rush whatever is going on—or isn't going on—" he hurried to add, "romantically."

I slowly approached him, unsure if he would want me to stay or not. "I'm sorry," I repeated. "I know it's not fair to make you wait. But somethin' like this... I need time to sort it out."

He took my hand and squeezed it briefly before letting go. "Something like this is worth waiting for."

61

Maybe the Prince Isn't So Bad After All

Evangeline

The short silence between us wasn't awkward, but it certainly was heavy. It didn't feel right to leave so soon, so I sat on his left, careful that I wasn't close enough that our shoulders would brush.

"So, you're blond?" I finally asked. It was a stupid question. But nothing else felt like an approachable topic right now.

He laughed. "Usually."

I studied him. Would I have recognized him if he hadn't dyed his hair? I tried to recall the last portrait I'd seen of the Cathmoores and compare the memory, but everything I'd ever assumed about nobles and royals from their portraits was nothing like the person sitting next to me.

"Would you believe me if I told you I had already guessed you were the prince, and your hair color was the one thing holdin' me back?"

He leaned forward as he smiled, resting his right elbow on his knee. "Not for a second. I know how to tell when you're lying now."

"Oh? What gives it away?"

"Nice try. But I'm not giving up that information so easily." He smiled, the teasing glint in his blue eyes making my stomach flutter a moment. It'd been too long since I'd seen that look.

"Why should it matter? I thought we weren't goin' to have any lies between us anymore."

He raised his eyebrows. "Which is why it shouldn't matter that I'm not going to tell you."

I shook my head, but I couldn't help but smile. "Fair enough."

"How are you doing?" he asked suddenly. "You were injured at the caves."

I shrugged. "Some stitches. Nothin' serious."

"Me too. In my arm."

I laughed, though I probably shouldn't have. "I know. Mine is from a far less excitin' injury, though. I was just crouched in the wrong place at the wrong time. I should be askin' how you're doin'."

His smile dropped a moment before he forced it back in place. "I'd rather you didn't."

I almost pushed him to answer, then decided better of it. "Do you think Roland actually betrayed you?"

He groaned, falling over onto his side. "Do you have any easier questions for now?"

"How easy?"

"Ask me again if I'm blond."

"Hmm, how about this." I angled toward him. "Can I keep learnin' how to fight?"

He sat up. "I thought you were going to say 'read.' When did you start to care about fighting? Didn't you decide it was useless for you to learn?"

"In reference to my life as a seamstress, it *was*. But as I ran to that cave without so much as a dagger, I realized that even if I had a weapon, I still wouldn't know how to use it. So it wouldn't have made much difference anyway."

"You weren't even armed?" he yelled.

"Shush, I got my dagger once they realized I was serious."

He groaned as he dragged a hand down his face. "Dare I ask if this realization was prompted by anything other than you running *unarmed* into an enemy prison?"

"I distracted a guard so Casimir could sneak up and..." The image of the guard dying in front of me flashed before my eyes. "So Casimir could..."

"Dispose of him?" Alastair offered.

"Yes." I took a deep breath. "I screamed. I knew it was comin', so I don't know what I was expectin', but still..."

"There's no glory in battle," he agreed. "There may be in coming home victorious. But never in the actual fight."

We both fell silent a moment.

"Not that I'm against you learning," he started again, "but are you planning on running into *more* battles?"

"That depends on if you need me to rescue you again."

He smiled, but it faded before it could reach his eyes. We both knew the coming days held war, and survival was impossible to guarantee.

"How soon will you be fightin' in the war against Harland?" I asked. "I assume you'll need to recover fully from your injuries first?"

He nodded. "At this point, it's difficult to say what the battles will look like. I'm meeting with Heston tomorrow to discuss that matter. The mobility of my left arm will be limited for a while, but I can't sit back and ask someone else to fight my battles. I'll be among the army one way or another."

I suspected there were plenty of kings who demanded their battles be fought for them, but Alastair didn't strike me as one of them. He *would* be a good king. Although the thought of him in battle still scared me to death.

I risked nudging his forearm. "I'm goin' to have to get used to worryin' about you, aren't I?" I meant it to come off as a joke, but he didn't seem to take it that way.

He took my hand in his. "I'm sorry—"

"Don't apologize. It's not your fault the world is in chaos."

"Isn't it though?"

I frowned.

"You're mad at me because I didn't tell you who I am. Heston is trying to figure out how to avoid a war because I'm alive instead of my father, who died because—"

"You can't—"

"—I didn't get to the caves in time, which only happened because I lost a week from deciding to try to recruit you. And—"

"Alastair." I held his face in my hands, sure that was the only thing that would convince him to stop talking.

He instantly stilled.

"Everythin' you think is your fault, I've already blamed myself for. So you can sit here and make yourself feel so guilty that you can't bear to do anythin' more for fear of makin' another mistake. Or, you can decide that there is no changin' the past, and all you can worry about is what to do right now to make things right."

His expression softened, so I let go of his face. He caught my hands before they were out of reach. "What can I do for you? Do you want to stay with the army? Or, do you want to wait somewhere else until the war is over?"

"I want to stay wherever you are," I answered without hesitation.

He smiled, then quickly let go of me and looked away. "I'll see if they can train you to fight. No better teachers than soldiers, right?"

"You think they'd train me? King Heston was very insistent that battle was no place for a woman."

"I could play the angle that it's better to include you in the battle plans than risk you running in and deciding to help however *you* have deemed best. Clearly, he already knows that much is true."

I winced. "I'm not sure remindin' him I'm a liability is goin' to help my case in stayin' with you all."

He nodded. "I'll work on it."

"Thank you."

"And what about us?" he asked. "I know you need time, but when we're alone, how distant should I—"

"I'm sure the times we're alone will be *quite* rare for the foreseeable future. But, in private, we're friends for now."

"Dearest friends?" he teased.

I rolled my eyes. "I suppose since I'm not robbin' the prince of that title from *his* dearest friend, Silas, I can accept that."

"Good." He smiled. "I can work with that."

I stood to leave, but turned back, not confident he fully grasped what our relationship had to look like now. "But publicly, I'm just the girl who helped you. We have to mind our statuses. There can't be any familiarity between us," I reiterated.

"We traveled across Wenterly together, people will expect familiarity."

"No fondness, then."

"You saved my life. At least twice."

I glared at him. "You know what I mean."

"Yes," he muttered. "I understand."

"Are you sure? You have to let things be weird between us. You have to let me bow and call you sire and—"

"I will *definitely* not let you bow."

I huffed. "Alastair!"

"I will only allow you to *curtsy*." He smirked.

I stared him down, deadpan, for all of two seconds before breaking into a smile of my own. "So, we're good?"

He nodded and stood. "We're good."

"Then, I bid you a good night, Your Highness." I offered a deep curtsy.

"Hm." He frowned. "That needs some work."

"I'll be sure to practice for next time."

"Please do."

"I will."

"Good."

We stood there a moment, looking at each other.

"Goodnight," I said, and hurried out of his tent.

This was a *royal* mess I'd gotten myself into.

And worse, I realized, I was smiling about it.

62

WELCOME BACK TO ROYALTY

Alastair

Casimir arrived early in the morning—far earlier than I expected him, to collect me for the meeting with King Heston. He brought me proper clothes and stepped out while I changed.

It was odd, dressing myself in things made for beauty after a month of dressing for practicality. Granted, the blue shirt and gold embroidered vest were hardly *impractical* compared to some of the things I'd worn in the past, but still, it was the first time in a month I'd dressed according to my actual title. Would seeing me this way affect how Evangeline perceived me even more?

You have to let things be weird between us.

So be it. Besides, the clothes didn't make the man. Surely, Eva knew that better than anyone as a seamstress.

I stepped outside my tent, and Casimir nodded in approval. Elistonian soldiers stopped as they passed to nod respectfully at us.

I never thought of all the attention much before. The extent to which people paused what they were doing just because I was in the room. I had grown up with it. That was always how it was.

It was strange how quickly everything could change.

"This way," Casimir said. "Heston will have the meeting over breakfast."

We crossed the path, passed one tent—my mother's, if I guessed correctly—and entered the next one.

King Heston stood as we entered. When I reached him, I offered him a small bow.

"I'm glad t' see you up and about, Alastair. You look far more lively than I saw you last."

"I feel far more lively. I can't thank you enough for all you're doing for my family and Wenterly."

"Of course, Alastair. But don't thank me yet. We still have much t' discuss on that front."

I nodded. "Most certainly."

He clapped me on my good shoulder. "Have you seen your mother yet?"

"Not since the caves, sire."

"I'd like her t' join us as well, if she is feeling up to it. I thought the invitation coming from you might allow her a more honest assessment of her well-being. And please, take a moment with her, if you'd like."

I found my mother propped up in bed—a real bed, unlike the cot I'd been sleeping on.

"Alastair! You look so much better!"

I closed the distance between us. She hugged me, but not with her usual strength. I was careful not to squeeze her either, due to her cracked ribs. "I feel much better. Almost good as new."

"Good. The future of Wenterly needs to be strong."

I frowned. "So does its present. How are you feeling?"

"Much better now that I've seen you."

I rolled my eyes. "Mom, I'm serious."

"As am I."

She patted the bed, and I sat on the edge of the mattress. The bruises on her face had changed color since I'd last seen her. The purple blotches were now closer to yellow, and while she still appeared weak, she at least looked as though she'd been able to sleep.

"I would have seen you sooner, but the doctor wouldn't let me get out of bed until today."

She waved my words away. "We've both been on bedrest. Terrible timing with the war coming."

"Heston would like to speak to us about that this morning. Are you well enough for such a discussion now? I can request he come over here if that would help—"

"We will be making next to no requests from Heston. He is already doing more than we can repay him for."

"He's a good man. I don't think a change of location is going to try his patience with us."

"Nor will we risk it." She began to move out of bed, wincing as she went.

"We don't have to go right now. He said we could have a few minutes alone."

"I'd rather you and I catch up *after* whatever Heston wants to discuss."

"If you wish," I relented.

We left her tent, her tight grip on my arm the only indication of any pain or uneasiness in her steps.

My mother and Heston exchanged pleasantries. He invited both of us to sit with him at the table, which bore a modest selection of fruit and biscuits for our breakfast. Casimir stood at the entrance of the tent. There was no one else; this meeting was highly confidential.

"Before we begin the more complex matters," Heston started, "Roland has sent a letter for you, Alastair. As a prisoner in my kingdom, he is not warranted t' privacy in his correspondence, so Casimir has already read the letter for matters of security."

Casimir held the folded paper out to me.

"How long ago did he send this?" I asked.

"We received it yesterday," he informed me. "It seems he wrote it as soon as he reached the prison. Under the doctor's recommendations, it was decided it was best not t' trouble you with it until you had proven a recovery."

"That was wise." I held up the still-folded paper. "Did you find any security concerns in this, Casimir?"

"No, sir."

"Good." Without opening it, I promptly tore the letter in two, then tore those pieces again for good measure. "What else do we need to discuss?"

Heston cleared his throat in an attempt not to smile. But as his eyes flicked from me to my mother, a more somber look overcame him. "First, I'd like t' make it clear that I am very sorry for the loss of Esmond. He was a fine king, and a good man from what I knew of him. I know these coming weeks will be difficult in their own right, so if you want t' hold a service for him, I'm sure my men can arrange that. But it would have t' be soon, in the next day or two, as there is much t' do in Wenterly."

My mother nodded, and she wiped a few tears from her cheeks, but she spoke without letting on to any emotion. "That is very kind of you, Heston. But please, don't trouble yourself. We will have a proper service for him in Wenterly when this is all over. His people deserve to grieve him as well."

Heston looked to me for confirmation. How long would it be before the service my mother wanted came to be? How long would I have to pause my grief? But I couldn't contradict her. Not on this. My mother was right, in order to get what we really needed from Heston, we couldn't ask much of him.

I nodded my agreement.

"If that is what you wish," Heston said. "Then, I apologize for the quick turn in conversation, but every minute that passes is another minute for Harland t' uncover what happened at the Caves and make the first move. Forgive me for being blunt the remainder of our time, but I believe that is what this matter calls for."

"Certainly, Heston. By all means, you can speak freely to us."

"Very well. I have spoken with a few of my advisors. We are still willing t' aid you in reclaiming the throne. The long-term benefits of having friends in Wenterly outweighs my concerns of war. Harland will bring us t' battle one way or another. I need you"—he turned his attention fully on me—"to issue a full alliance with Eliston, both this morning, and officially when you reclaim the throne. No addendums or exceptions. If we call for your aid in the future, you will answer."

"Without question. Wenterly is in your debt. However, I do have a proposal for one addendum to such an alliance."

My mother pinched my forearm under the table.

Heston raised his eyebrows. "What might that be?"

"Once Harland is removed, Glastor will have no leader, and while his kingdom would ordinarily fall to me, I would like it to go to you."

My mother squeezed my arm.

Heston folded his hands. "Are you worried his people will revolt against a new leader as Wenterly will soon revolt against him?"

"No, sir. If the way he's ruled Wenterly is any indication, I think his people will be relieved to have a new king. But I am inexperienced, and will have to assure my own kingdom I am worthy to govern them. I believe you would have a more effective approach in providing Glastor with a transition of leadership than I would."

Heston looked to Casimir, but if Casimir gave any kind of answer, it was too subtle for me to notice.

Heston lowered his gaze, clearly still pondering the offer.

"We don't have to come to a conclusion right now," I clarified, "but I wanted to make it known that that is my wish."

He nodded. "Let us see how the war progresses. If you still believe that is best at the end of it, we can discuss it then as a separate arrangement. But if you have no other objections t' the alliance, we'll sign it now so we can begin strategizing."

My mother and I agreed. Heston pulled the contract from a folder on the table. I failed to see what else was in the folder. How much planning had he done in the last two days?

"I'll give you a moment t' look over everything."

After scanning its contents, everything seemed in order to me. A full alliance. We would come to Eliston's aid no matter the cost to us, and Eliston would do the same. We would be kingdoms in partnership, practically co-rulers in the eyes of the other kingdoms. A risky level of trust, but a great strength when done with the right people. Of course, the alliance would only last as long as Heston and I both ruled. But his son was still young, which meant we would have quite a long partnership, assuming we both survived the next few weeks.

I waited for my mother's nod of approval.

When she gave it, I reached for a quill.

"I'm happy to sign," I said. "But we have no signet ring for the seal."

"Yours will do for now. You'll be resigning it when you are officially king anyway."

I nearly laughed. The prince's ring would leave no indentation in the wax that meant anything. But then again, I wasn't actually king yet, so what authority did I have to make such an agreement with Heston in the first place? Did any of it *really* mean anything, outside of our own good intentions?

I signed my name, then Heston signed his. Casimir poured the wax, and we pressed our rings into it.

I held my breath. This was my first act as Wenterly's leader. I never imagined it would be like this.

We pulled our hands away, the agreement made.

"Now, Alastair, you have all of Eliston behind you. But you need Wenterly behind you as well. In two days, we'll send you t' Hallen. Your people need t' know firsthand that you're alive.

"I have already sent two ships of soldiers toward Glastor. They will sail t' Wenterly's eastern border and hold off any Glastorian soldiers who try to enter Wenterly. As far as we know, Harland still knows nothing of your rescue, but that could change at any moment. I'm sure he kept regular correspondence with his men there, and a few days of silence will certainly be cause for concern. My men will reach the other side of Wenterly the same day that you make your appearance in Hallen."

"It seems you already have most of this in order." I leaned forward. "What do you need from me?"

63

SHOCKING NEWS: I AGREE TO ANOTHER STUPID PLAN

Evangeline

Today, we were working on mending at the laundry. I offered a quiet apology when I first arrived, and the women carried on as if nothing had happened the day prior. I kept to myself, as usual, trying to make decisions about a future that could go a thousand different ways.

It wasn't long before my thoughts were interrupted by the *last* voice I expected to hear. "Miss Evangeline, may I take you from your duties for a moment?"

I turned to face Alastair, all the ladies standing with me as they had for Casimir yesterday. So much for my lay-low-and-work-hard strategy.

I nearly gasped when I saw him, because I saw him, for the first time, as he should be. A deep blue shirt with a gold embroidered vest. The fabrics were crisp, well dyed, *expensive*. Yesterday I knew he was a royal, but today, he *looked* like one.

"I need to speak with you in private," he added when I failed to respond.

I couldn't refuse him without causing a scene. But what good reason did he actually have to meet with me *alone*?

"Yes, sire." I panicked for a moment. Did I curtsy before I approached? Once I reached him? Should I take off my apron?

So many rules, and I didn't know any of them. I would have to ask the ladies for some lessons in protocol if I was going to stay with the army.

I was so flustered, I ended up walking right to him, no curtsies at any point, and not removing my apron.

"Sorry for the interruption, ladies," he apologized. "I won't keep her long."

He turned and led me away from them, and once we were out of their view, he turned to me. "Which way to your tent?"

I blinked. "*My* tent? Wouldn't it be more proper to go to yours?"

He shook his head. "It's too close to Heston and my mother. If you get upset and yell at me, I don't want them to overhear it." The gleam in his eyes assured me he was teasing, but it hardly stopped the uneasiness rising in my chest.

"Oh?" I pushed myself forward to lead the way to my tent. "Have you done somethin' stupid again?"

"Not yet. It depends how this conversation goes."

Brilliant.

"Are you sure this isn't a conversation we can have out in the open?"

"You'll rather we didn't."

I took a steadying breath as too many concerns arose for me to handle.

I hurried my pace to my tent and unceremoniously flung the flap open for him.

He walked straight in. I looked out at the bustling camp—no one paying us any mind—took a deep breath, and stepped in after him.

"It's been a big morning," he started.

"It looks like it." I nodded to his clothes.

He rolled his eyes. "I never realized how uncomfortable these collars were." As if he needed to prove his point, he unfastened the clasps at his throat.

I fought the natural response to blush at such an action. Alastair hadn't worn a collared vest in the entire time I'd known him. But the action itself was immodest enough in its own right.

"What is this about?" I asked. I couldn't think of how a morning that involved him dressing as a king could have anything to rightly do with me. Unless... "Are they sendin' me back to Wenterly?"

"Yes and no." He took a deep breath. "We're going to Hallen in two days, and you'll be coming with us so that Heston isn't liable for you anymore."

I waited. Obviously there was more. He wouldn't risk meeting me alone just to tell me that. Right?

"When we're in Hallen, I have an idea for how to win over the people to help us fight against Harland. And it involves you."

"Oh, brilliant," I deadpanned.

"Let me finish!" He glared at me. "It was well thought out. Your status is—"

"Worthless," I finished for him.

He glared again. "*Valuable.* At the end of the day, you are the reason my mother and I are still alive. The least in the kingdom of Wenterly, and you're the one who was willing to risk everything to save it. You are living proof of the significance of the Common Man."

"I'm *below* the common man."

"All the more my point! If we want this revolt against Harland to be over quickly, we need every citizen to know that their actions matter. They don't have to have a certain level of skill or education to help. They only have to care. No one can convince them of that better than you."

"This feels like a back-handed compliment, I'm not goin' to lie."

He looked up to the roof of my tent. "I'm trying to be practical about this." He lowered his gaze to mine again. "You know I think the world of you."

The sincerity in his eyes forced me to look away. "So what does this idea of yours require of me?"

"Talking to people. Mostly one-on-one, but maybe a short speech here and there."

"I don't know the first thing about that."

"You talk plenty."

"Not diplomatically!"

He laughed. "I wouldn't want you to. The point is that you're yourself. The Common People will see themselves in you."

I scoffed. "I highly doubt that."

"Do you trust me?"

Of course I did. But this was about far more than a matter of trust. "What happened to me knowin' more about the common world than you? Don't you think I have a better grasp on how people behave around me than you do?"

"In ordinary times, yes. But this is a political matter, so my experiences trump yours."

"Is that so?"

He raised his eyebrows. "Would you like to make a bet?"

I squinted at him in disapproval. "And if you make me this public figure, how will that affect things with Heston? Will he lose faith in you for treatin' someone of my status with such favor?"

"That's why I came to talk to you. I'm sure he'll see the value in the idea, but again, your status makes the whole thing—"

"Ineffective."

He grabbed my face so suddenly and spoke with such intensity that I nearly forgot how to breathe. "Eva, I'm begging you, when it comes to the topic of who you are and what you matter, please, for once, shut your pretty little mouth and listen to me."

I swallowed. Nodded. And kept my mouth shut, as requested.

He sighed and let go of me, but I could have sworn I heard him say "I love you" again in that sigh.

"Your status makes things *complicated*. Only because in order for us to officially and publicly use you in the war, we would need to alert your guardian."

I closed my eyes. *That* was why we were speaking alone. "Have you already sent word to him?"

He took my hands, and I looked up at him, that intensity I heard in his voice now present in his eyes. "I haven't told anyone who your guardian is yet. I haven't told anyone *any* of this yet. You deserve to decide what we do. It's your life."

Was it? Every time I'd tried to take charge of my own life, Fate seemed to intervene with its own plans.

I took a deep breath. "I don't know what Gratsis would say."

"You told Captain Mothway it would be more trouble to get you back than you were worth."

"And I was lyin' through my teeth!"

"You think Gratsis would actually take you back to Welven with him?"

I bit my lip. The thought of it terrified me. "I don't know. A year ago, I wouldn't think so, but a year ago I never would have imagined him gettin' me in this situation to begin with. I don't know what kind of man he really is. Which version of him was the real one." A tear slipped down my cheek, and I hurried to wipe it away.

He hugged me, allowing far more intimacy than he should.

But I didn't pull away as I should have either.

"That's how I feel about Roland," he muttered.

Roland. I still hardly knew what had happened between the two of them.

"I guess all our lyin' is finally catchin' up to us," I said.

"Well, I'm done lying. Especially to you." I felt the vibration of his voice in his chest as he held me close. "Which is why I have another idea. The stupid one you might yell at me for."

I pulled away. "None of *these* ideas were your stupid ones?"

He crossed his arms and frowned.

I lifted a brow. "What is it?"

"We could transfer your guardianship."

I stepped back as a laugh burst from my mouth. "And who do you think would want me?"

"I do!"

"We *just* agreed we were puttin' an ongoin' pause on marriage discussions—"

"I'm not talking about marriage." He smirked. "Though if you prefer that route, it's fine by me."

I brought a hand to my forehead. The man was relentless. "What's the alternative?"

"In certain cases, such as the safety and wellbeing of a person, guardianship can be transferred from one man to another. We just pay him some money and send him a letter, and it's done."

"Wouldn't such a thing have to go to court?"

"Not if the proposed redemption price is satisfactory. He would simply sign that he agrees and walk away a very rich man."

"But if it would ruin his reputation, he might not agree—regardless of how much money you bribe him with."

"Luckily, in our case, I'm not some random commoner blackmailing him. I'm the Crown Prince, and I have need of your services. I *could* demand your presence and neither of you would have a choice in the matter, but I'm *so* gracious that I'm also offering to permanently take you off his hands *and* pay him for the privilege."

"That's—This is—I mean—" I stammered a while, the entire situation too outlandish to wrap my mind around. "This is not what I had in mind when I said things needed to be weird between us."

"I know, but—" he stopped himself, then began again. "What do you think is best?"

I sat down on my cot and considered it all for a moment. "What if I didn't do this 'public figure' thing? Would Gratsis being my guardian still pose a potential problem for you?"

"Potentially, yes. Besides, if you don't plan on ever returning to Gratsis, then he will have to be dealt with sooner or later. And if you don't know how he'll respond, I think it would be better we make the first move rather than wait for him to make demands."

I sighed. "And you honestly think Wenterly is goin' to rally for you because of me?"

He nodded. "You'll give the people hope that they can make a difference. That their ordinary lives will matter under my rule. It could be monumental for the revolution."

"I think you may be overestimatin' how inspirin' I am."

He smiled. "I'm willing to take my chances."

I paused a moment to think, but, truthfully, I'd already made my decision. "I'll agree, *if* you can do it in a way that won't be detrimental to your cause should it turn out that no one cares a whit about me."

"Done. And your guardianship?"

I studied him a moment, his blue eyes brilliant and hopeful. This was probably the best chance I had to get out from under Gratsis's authority. "Transfer it."

He grinned, pulling me back into his arms. "Thank you." He kissed the top of my head—*definitely* an intimacy far more than he should allow himself.

I closed my eyes as I gently pushed him away. "Alastair. We talked about this. We're friends for now. You said you could be okay with that."

He stepped back but protested all the same. "I think it's the fact that you keep adding 'for now' onto that statement that makes it a little difficult to stick in my mind."

"Oh? And how do you know the 'for now' doesn't mean I'm plannin' on ditchin' you the second you officially ascend back to your throne?"

He offered a sly smile. "I just do."

I frowned. "Arrogance is not a good look on you."

"I'd call it confidence."

"You need to keep your focus on what's in front of you."

"I am!"

I whacked his good arm. "*Politically*, Alastair. Not physically."

He laughed.

"You are insufferable," I added under my breath.

"I learned it from you."

I gave him a playful shove. "Anythin' else you needed to talk to me about?"

"No, I suppose that's all. Though, I don't know when I'll get a chance to see you again."

"In Hallen, I'm sure."

"That's *two days* away."

"Oh, Fate forbid, Alastair! You've gone your whole life without me, and now two days is too long?"

"Yes, Eva. *Fate forbid* I miss your company." He gave me an exaggerated glare and mumbled, "Though sometimes, I wonder why."

I shook my head. "I should get back."

"I'll walk you there."

"You will *not*. I am tryin' to keep a low profile with those women, and you askin' for me two days in a row is ruinin' that."

"How does walking you back make a difference in that?"

I frowned. "Your status ... makes things *complicated*."

He nodded. "Well then, until Hallen, I suppose." He held the tent flap open for me. "Someone will let you know the details once we settle them."

"Great." I stepped past him, but he cleared his throat before I could get far. "Yes?"

"You're supposed to curtsy before we part ways," he whispered.

Right. *Protocol.*

I bid him good day with all the platitudes I could muster. Then I took my time walking back to the laundry. Despite a war still on the horizon, for the first time in weeks, I felt a little less fearful of the future.

64

My Mother Gives Me Financial Advice

Alastair

I took my time walking back to Heston's tent. While my conversation with Eva went as well as I had hoped, this next one was going to be far more difficult.

I barely remembered to refasten my collar before I reentered the tent.

The three of them stared at me, eyes wide and expectant. I had left somewhat abruptly. Heston had merely asked if I knew who Eva's guardian was, and I had then excused myself.

"I spoke with Eva." I winced. Cleared my throat. "Miss Evangeline."

"And what of it?" my mother prodded. She was furious. Understandable. I doubted what I was about to say would make her feel any better.

"I think she could be useful. In Hallen. For winning over Wenterly's citizens."

She raised her eyebrows. "Our family has led these people for generations. You are your father's son. Esmond led our people well. Harland has not. You do not think that is enough?"

"I can't be sure about anyone's loyalty these days."

"These people have no reason to question *your* loyalty to them."

"That doesn't mean they can't." I sat at the table. "Do you want to hear my idea or not?"

My mother frowned. "What is it?"

I swallowed. I could not let my emotions get the best of me in this conversation. "One thing my time with Evangeline has taught me is that the Common People are wary of the upper class—royalty especially. We *need* the people to rally for us, but the trouble is, we live different lives from them, and they know it. Why should any of them believe I can provide them a better life than Harland has?"

"Because Esmond did!"

"But I'm not him. Some people may think it's easier to let Harland keep ruling than to have to readjust their lives once more under my reign." She started to interrupt, but I kept going. "*So*, if one of their own can vouch for us, it could make a world of difference."

"Is Miss Evangeline willin' to be that voice?" Heston interjected, preventing my mother from further argument.

"She is. And I know that requires we contact Gratsis—er, her guardian—all the more, but she has a ... complicated past with him."

"How do you mean?"

I clenched my jaw. I wasn't sure what was my place to tell.

To my surprise, Casimir said, "She ran away from him. From the little I gathered, he mistreated her in some way."

I nodded. "Which gives us grounds to transfer her guardianship, in addition to a request to serve the king."

"And who would become her guardian?" Heston asked.

"I will." But I wasn't the only one who said it.

My eyes locked on Casimir, the surprise on my face mirrored on his.

"She's not a citizen of Eliston," I said.

"No," Casimir said slowly. "But I understand her value. If you are willing and think it *wise* to transfer the guardianship over t' yourself, don't let me complicate the matter. But should you think the difference in your statuses may prove problematic down the line, I am willing." He focused on me with an earnestness that reminded me of Reeves. He was trying to tell me something without the others catching on. What in Breslin's seven—

"Transferring her citizenship is a whole other process," Heston said. "For the sake of time and resources, Alastair should do it. He can always transfer the guardianship again should it become a problem."

"Have you promised Evangeline anything else, Alastiar?" my mother asked. "If she continues to aid us, will she expect further reward?"

"Freeing her from the fear of a man who wronged her is hardly a reward, Mother. She saved our lives. *Your* life."

"I am not arguing that. I am asking if she has *expectations* of us. Have you promised anything to her in return for her help?"

I'd made promises all right. But never as rewards or motivators. "No. Roland did promise her money. I said we might be able to help her find employment again. But I've made no promises of rewards."

My mother sighed, wincing at the deep breath. "Very well. I'll allow it, if we all agree that's what's best."

Heston nodded.

Casimir locked eyes with me once more, then gave me a subtle nod. A *knowing* nod. I would definitely have to investigate that further.

"Should I send the notice to Gratsis today? Or after our appearance in Hallen?"

"After," Heston said. "If you explain that we need her for the revolution, and the letter gets intercepted by Harland's men before the revolution even begins, that will do us little good."

My mother brought a hand to her side. "I apologize, my lords, but this morning has worn me terribly. I'm afraid I must excuse myself."

Heston and Casimir stood, and my mother reached out for me to assist her. I slowly led her out of the tent. Once we reached her own, she sat on the bed but lectured me with all the strength of a healthy woman. "You are out of your mind, Alastair. What has gotten into you?"

"I had hoped you would be proud of me for standing up for a girl left at the mercy of the world."

"I'm not just talking about that. The alliance? Offering Heston jurisdiction of Glastor? Don't you want to grow your kingdom?"

I scoffed. "This is the modern world, Mother. Harland's betrayal was such a blow because we are not meant to be fighting over territories any longer. I am far less concerned about expanding our borders as I am with taking care of the people currently inside of them."

"Glastor's resources would help you take care of them."

"Do you doubt my ability to make decisions for our people?"

Her expression softened slightly. "I know you are doing your best. And when you are King Proper, I will gladly be the first to pledge my allegiance to you. But until you marry, you and I are co-rulers. You cannot be making decisions without consulting me."

Ah. That was what this was about. "I'm sorry. I did not intend to pass over you. But there's been no opportunity to see you, and—"

"You have opportunity now. What's your plan with Miss Evangeline?"

"Precisely what I told you in Heston's tent. We'll be speaking to the common people in Hallen, and she's one of their own. If they see that she matters to us, they'll trust that *they* matter to us."

"*Is* she one of their own, Alastair? She is below the common people. Only criminals are lower than she. And I've heard rumor that she's *worse* than illegitimate. Is it true her father was a pirate?"

"Yes." I crossed my arms. "But doesn't that emphasize the point? *Every* citizen matters to the Cathmoores. Every person has worth in our kingdom."

She pursed her lips. "You have to be careful with statements like that. People may interpret it to mean they have *equality* with us. It's all well and good that the people know they matter to us. But it also matters that each person is in their place. Especially where traitors and criminals are involved. You need to write this speech with the utmost care."

"*Evangeline* isn't a traitor or a criminal."

"Nevertheless, every person is best in their place," she repeated.

"All our citizens have value. How are we to assign that from one person to another?"

She clicked her tongue, clearly disappointed. "I can hold a copper and a gold in each of my hands. Both will buy me a loaf of bread, but only one will purchase a horse."

I bowed my head to suppress a laugh. If a single gold could buy a good horse, our lives would have been a lot easier on the road.

"The value of the gold does not negate the value of the copper," she continued, "but not even a fool would confuse one with the other."

I glanced up, trying to find the proper response. Failing. "You think Eva is a copper."

"The people out in Hallen are copper, Alastair. *Miss Evangeline* is a peb."

"She is the reason you and I are alive to have this conversation!"

"And for that, she has proven her value, and I am grateful. A peb is still *useful*, my son. But it is still a peb."

I clenched my jaw. "I understand, Mother."

But I certainly didn't agree.

65

My Stupidity Almost Gets Me Killed

Evangeline

I woke sweaty and gasping for breath. The nightmare replayed in my mind as I opened my eyes: Alastair and I in Hallen, preparing for our speeches. I look out over the platform, and when I turn back to him, an officer comes up behind him and snaps his neck, just as Casimir had done to the guard at the cave.

It was only a dream, I reminded myself.

But the man who'd died at the cave was real. And the coming war was real. It would begin tomorrow.

What if it's not just a dream? What if it's a warning?

I got off my cot.

Don't be stupid.

I sat back down.

But I couldn't stop envisioning him dying from my dream, and then I thought of him lying on that cave floor, bleeding out and poisoned in *real* life—that memory hardly an improvement from the nightmare. And I thought—not for the first time since I'd been here—about how if I hadn't made that wrong turn and found the Elistonian soldiers, that dream could have been reality. My dearest friend, the rightful *King of Wenterly*, dead in a cave hidden in the mountains, with no one the wiser.

I'd never been so thankful I didn't know how to read.

I lay back down, attempting to return to sleep, but the visions from my dreams blended and mingled with what I really saw in that cave.

I saw him, and saw myself finding him, in half-asleep dreams, reliving the moment over and over again. Eventually, I had enough of it. I stood up, threw on an overdress, and rushed out of my tent, not bothering to search for my shoes in the dark.

It was quiet in the army camp, though I could hear activity toward the gate from the soldiers still on duty. I slipped down the paths quickly and quietly, careful not to be seen by anyone I heard nearby.

I reached his tent, and I tried—I *really* tried—to talk myself out of it. It was just a dream, after all.

But the fear, dread, and grief still sat in my chest, and I knew he was the only one who could set me at ease.

I looked around quickly for witnesses, and seeing none, stepped inside.

It was nearly pitch-black inside his tent, and I had to wait a few seconds for my eyes to adjust to the darkness. I could barely see anything more than the outline of his cot.

I took a step closer to him. "Alastair," I whispered.

Of course, he didn't wake up. He was a heavy sleeper. I'd learned that on watches. Not as heavy as Roland, but heavy enough that a simple whisper was never enough.

I took two steps closer to him before I realized the absurdity of what I was doing. It hit me as though I myself had only just woken up. I'd been lecturing Alastair about things being different between us, and yet here I was, sneaking into his tent and waking him up in the middle of the night, for ... what, exactly?

I turned around, changing my mind just in time. I could sneak back out and no one would ever know I was so foolish.

My foot collided with leather. I couldn't help but yelp in surprise as I fell face down into the grass, my bones jarring at the sudden impact. I winced, holding back the groan I would have let out had I not been sneaking around.

I heard the movement of fabric above me, and I froze.

"Is someone there?"

I held my breath.

Please, please don't see me here. Go back to sleep, Alastair. Please.

But instead I heard the cot creak with more movement. "I could have sworn—" He cut off his own sentence as he stepped on my calf.

He lifted his foot off me just as quickly as he stepped on me, and I rolled over onto my back. I expected him to shout for guards or demand I identify myself. My heart jumped into my throat. I couldn't get a word out even if he'd asked, but a second passed where nothing happened.

And then he attacked.

In only a second, he pulled my leg toward him with one hand, and grabbed my arm with his other. He turned me around so I was sitting with my back against his chest, my left arm pinned behind my back. For a split second, I was reminded of when he so effortlessly flipped me onto my back the night we first met. He was a trained fighter. I needed to do a better job remembering that.

Cold metal touched my cheek, the flat of a blade pressed to my skin. "Tell me what you're doing in my tent or—Eva?"

"Yes, it's me!" I squeaked.

He cursed, quickly moving the knife away from my face. "Mercy, Eva, what are you doing here?"

Embarrassment heated my face. "I'd rather not say."

He stood, pulling me to my feet with him. "I almost killed you."

My heartbeat pounded in my ears. "I noticed."

His hands didn't leave my shoulders. "Why didn't you identify yourself sooner?" he whispered. "Or come in here like a normal person?"

"I was hopin' you would go back to sleep. Why didn't *you* call for help?"

He released me and took a step back. "What are you doing here, Eva?"

I crossed my arms, suddenly cold at the absence of his touch. "I couldn't sleep."

"And you thought the ground of my tent was a better place to try? I don't have to tell *you* how that would have gone over had someone seen you."

"I *know*, Alastair, so save the lecture. I was tryin' to leave when I tripped over somethin'. What do you have lyin' on the ground in the middle of the tent—"

"My shoes."

"How did I miss them when I came in, but not on the way out?" I mumbled.

"Eva?" He set his hands on my shoulders again. "Are you going to tell me what you were doing here in the first place, or keep avoiding it?"

"I told you, I couldn't sleep."

"And that brought you here?"

"Yes."

"Why?"

I huffed. "Why do you think?"

He lifted his hands in surrender. "I don't want to be presumptuous. You might call me arrogant again, and I'm trying very hard to look good in front of you."

I could hear the smile in his voice, could almost see the teasing glint in his eye despite the darkness. When we first met, not being able to see him compromised my ability to read him. Now, it was hardly an impairment.

"I had a nightmare," I whispered.

"What about?"

"You."

A beat passed. "Well, I certainly hope there's more that made it a nightmare than just *me*."

I may have laughed if I wasn't still fighting off embarrassment. "I should go. I'm sorry I woke you."

"Wait, Eva. It's okay. What do you need?"

"I just needed to see you. To remind myself that you're alright."

"I'm alright."

"I know."

He moved, and I thought he was going to hug me, but instead he slid past me and sat on his cot. "I haven't been sleeping well either since the Caves."

"You didn't sleep well before them."

He laughed, but it sounded bitter. "It's not been an ideal month for sleep."

"I don't think the next month will be much better."

He sighed. "Everything keeps changing, so much and so quickly. I just want some stability."

"I know."

Silence fell on us, and I registered that this was the right time to leave. But for the first time since arriving in Eliston, things between us felt the way they had before. It was the littlest bit of normalcy, but I grasped it while I could.

I sat next to him. "I'm really glad you're okay. I don't think I ever said that to you."

"You didn't need to."

"But you should know. I've never been so happy to not read a sign correctly. If I hadn't ended up here..."

"I know. Good thing I'm not a very good teacher, huh?"

"I'd still pick you over Roland any day. What happened with him, anyway?"

"He nearly killed me twice." I thought it was all he was willing to say. But then he took a deep breath and continued. "I've been replaying it all in my mind. Trying to decide if he intended to kill me or only make it look like he did. But why would he actually poison me if he was on our side? And I keep going back to when you found us. Right before you came in, he was alone with my mother and me, and he didn't do anything to help us. And when he saw you, he seemed so surprised, beyond the fact that you weren't supposed to follow us in." Another pause. "I think he'd been planning to betray me all along. And I can't help but think you were never supposed to make it out of Irimen."

I reached for his hand. The news was a lot to take in. "I get why Roland might have wanted me out of the picture, but why would he betray you?"

"Power. Politics. Harland offered him a better future than my family did."

My brows lowered. "That doesn't make any sense to me."

"Only because you're a better person than most, Eva."

My heart fluttered. He truly believed I was a good person? After all the horrible things I'd said to him when we first met? *Mercy.*

I quietly cleared my throat to refocus my thoughts. "And right now Roland is imprisoned, right?"

"Yes. He'll stay there until we can give him a trial."

"Does he deserve one?"

"Now that he's been arrested, he has to have one if we're going to punish him. But, unless some miraculous evidence proves Harland's men forced his hand, his end is guaranteed at this point."

"I'm sorry." I took his hand. As many questions as I had about Roland, he was the last thing I wanted to talk about. "Alastair, I also came here because I'm afraid of what could happen in Hallen. In the war."

"So am I."

"Then why go back? After everythin' your family has suffered, why stir up more hardship? Wouldn't it be easier to retire to a quiet life and let Harland have his way?"

He paused a moment before answering. "Ruling isn't just a job, Eva. It's our life. It's all we've ever known. I don't think my mother would know how to live a quiet life. And we especially couldn't with Harland ruining the kingdom by pulling young people from their families and demanding more taxes than the people can afford. It's not about us moving back into the palace. It's about making King Heston's trouble in rescuing us worth it. It's about saving our people. Harland is evil. Maybe not for wanting to expand his kingdom, but for the way he did it. For the things he ordered be done to my parents. For the way he's oppressing Wenterly's people as we speak. It's about justice and responsibility."

I nodded. "I'm sorry. It's hard for me to remember how much you matter, I guess. My world has always been so small, I can't grasp havin' a life that affects the whole kingdom."

"Would you want to? Have a life that affects the whole kingdom?"

I slouched forward, resting my elbows on my knees. "I don't know. All my life, I've wanted to matter. To mean somethin'. But on that big of a scale ... that's terrifyin'."

It struck me then why he may have been asking. If I were to accept his marriage proposal, I'd have that kind of effect. Up until this moment, I'd still thought of agreeing to marry Alastair as us living a hidden life in the woods, or in a little village outside of Arten. But that wasn't how it would work, was it? Marrying him wouldn't just require me to become a wife. It would require me to become a *queen*.

Stars above.

"Here's the thing, Eva." He reached over to take my hands in his. "I think, in your own way, you already do affect the whole kingdom. Because you seem to have a profound effect on me." He paused, but continued before I could gather my thoughts enough to respond. "Are you ready for tomorrow? You know what to say and everything?"

I was nearly as disappointed in the change of subject as I was relieved for it. "Yes. I'll stay back with Casimir to address the women." I had practiced my speech with the commander all afternoon.

He squeezed my hands. "Do you trust Casimir?"

The question surprised me. "Of course. Why do you ask?"

"When I brought up transferring your guardianship two days ago, he volunteered to do it."

"He *what*?"

"You don't know why he would do that?"

"Not a clue."

He sighed. "I think he was trying to tell me something, without alerting Heston and my mother to it. But I don't know what. I haven't had an opportunity to ask him."

"I can try to find out while I'm with him tomorrow."

"Be careful about it. I think his motives are genuine, but..."

"It's hard to trust people these days," I finished.

"Right."

I leaned my head on his shoulder. Just when I thought I had a grasp on things, some new development left me questioning.

"I'm sure it's nothing to worry about. But I wanted you to know."

"Thank you." I squeezed his hand.

"Get as close to the platform as you can tomorrow. I'll call you up when it's time."

"What if I get nervous in front of everyone?"

"You? Nervous? The way you talk to royalty, Eva, I don't think you should be nervous in front of commoners."

I bit my lip. "I should go. Big day tomorrow."

"I suppose so." He let go of my hand. "Don't trip on my shoes on your way out."

66

LONG LIVE OUR KING

Evangeline

"The king is here!" I yelled down the streets, stopping every passerby I saw. "The king is here! He's headin' to the square to give an address."

"What's she yellin' about?" a woman asked.

"Harland is here in the square. He's goin' to make an address."

"Fate's mercy, he's *here*?"

I kept going down the street, not bothering to correct them. No one matched my joy, their reactions more akin to fear than excitement. But we expected that. Fear would bring them just as effectively.

I finished running my assigned block and made my way back to the square.

It was packed. I skirted along the edge of the crowd as long as I could and then weaseled my way up to the platform. The crowd gave way for me more easily than I expected. Apparently no one was overly keen on being in the front row.

A group of officers entered the square, confused as ever. Surely Harland would have let them know if he was visiting, if for nothing more than to manage the crowd.

I scanned the group for men in green vests—Elistonian soldiers. Sure enough, they were everywhere, scattered throughout the square, keeping careful watch of the officers.

People kept filling the square, overflowing into the streets.

Casimir stepped onto the platform. "Good people of Wenterly!"

The crowd's clamoring turned to silence.

A woman next to me whispered, "That slip is sure to cost him."

I'd been so far removed from normal life these last few weeks, I hadn't even noticed. But this wasn't Wenterly anymore. It was New Glastor.

Seeming to read the crowd's mind, Casimir repeated himself. "People of *Wenterly*, it is my pleasure, on behalf of King Heston of Eliston, to present to you, your rightful rulers!"

The carriage entered the square right on cue, and people shifted and murmured as it made its way to the platform. It was an old carriage—not one befitting royalty.

I eyed the officers, but they didn't look alarmed yet, just confused.

"Harland took over your kingdom by way of a powerful lie," Casimir said. "And he has continued t' rule over you based on lies. But today, the spider is caught in a web of his own making. Two of the Cathmoores live yet!"

The carriage came to a stop at the back of the platform, and Alastair stepped out. As he turned to assist his mother, the crowd let out a collective gasp. Queen Adeena stepped onto the platform, and the crowd burst into a cacophony of murmurs, applause, and shouts.

I looked for the officers again, but now the crowd was pressing around me, everyone trying to get a better look at the royals, wanting to see if they were being lied to once again. I would have to trust that the Elistonian soldiers were doing their job.

"My good people!" Queen Adeena raised her hands as Casimir stepped back, blending into the background. The crowd fell silent at the sound of her voice. "Today, you are witnesses of the truth. You have been duped, just as my family and I were. Harland is a man made up of deceit, and as such, is not fit to rule over any person—let alone the beloved people of Wenterly!"

The people shouted and clapped in agreement. This was going better than I had anticipated.

"In the short time that Harland has tried to claim you as his own, he has robbed you, oppressed you, and lied to you. My family and I have suffered the same from him. Your faithful King Esmond was killed at the hands of Harland a mere week ago." Her voice cracked. "We have all been betrayed by Harland's promises of peace and a better world."

She paused. The crowd would likely interpret it as dramatic effect, or perhaps a moment to collect herself after announcing her husband's death. But I knew she was still physically weak. She was catching her breath.

"I know Harland has eyes in this city," she began again. "Eyes that are preparing to tell him of this even now. And to those, I say, give him this message." She paused again, planting herself firmly in the center of the platform. "If Harland does not surrender at the gate of the Wenter palace by noon overmorrow, he will bring war upon himself. And Wenterly does not fight alone."

She paused again, and Alastiar approached her. She nodded and stepped back, allowing him to take over.

"Good people, I now have a message for each of you."

I'd never seen the Cathmoores give an address. Only heard about it second or third-hand. But I realized that the stories never exaggerated. Both Adeena and Alastair exuded confidence, heads held high, words ringing loud and true. They did indeed charm the crowd. But it was genuine, not just for show. They truly loved their people.

"If you want to rid yourselves of Harland, the Lying Oppressor, you must aid us. Tell everyone you can that my mother and I are alive and well. I implore your able-bodied men to fight with us. I fear that you will fight one way or another, so choose your sides wisely. If you want to return to the life you once knew, a life of harmony and peace, bow down to Harland no longer. Take back your lives with me and all of Eliston at your side!"

The crowd murmured, and only a few cheers rose. The reality of a revolt was not nearly as exciting as simply saying Harland was a snake.

The response didn't seem to bother Alastair, though. He scanned the crowd, his smile growing even bigger when his eyes fell on me.

"Perhaps some of you are thinking to yourselves, what do I have to offer in this revolution? I cannot fight. I am not well-educated. I am poor. I want each of you to know that none of those things disqualify you from making a difference. If you care about the future of Wenterly—about *your* future—you still have the power to bring about change." He walked to the very edge of the platform, directly in front of where I stood. "One of your own is the very reason the Cathmoores stand before you today."

He held out his hand to help me on the platform. The people next to me gasped, and the woman who had whispered to me earlier reached out and touched him, as though she was ensuring that he was real. He ignored her, his eyes only on me. "Miss Evangeline, please join me."

I took his hand and stepped up on to the platform. This was the moment of truth. I would either solidify the people's support or make no difference in the matter. But what if I made things *worse*?

Alastair walked me back to the center of the platform. He let go of me and turned to the crowd. I looked out at them, and despite Alastair's assurances last night, I was instilled with a fear I'd never known before. There were *thousands* of people in the square. The whole town was here. I fought the urge to run.

"This woman is a humble seamstress. Uneducated. Illiterate. Not more than a peb to her name when I met her. And yet I tell you today, she has fought for me—for all of Wenterly—with intelligence, bravery, and strength unlike any soldier I've trained alongside."

I desperately wished I could take his hand back. Have him hold me steady as all these people openly stared at me. I'd spent my life working hard to stay invisible.

But I certainly was not invisible now.

"Each of you has unique skills, unique perspectives," he continued. "Use those to your advantage. You can defy Harland in every aspect of your lives—not only on a battlefield. Your support may be the very thing that turns the tides."

Casimir stepped up to us. "Sire, I'm afraid it's time t' move," he said quietly.

While the majority of the crowd hung on Alastair's every word, fights were starting to break out at the edges of the square. A few shouts, a few thrown punches. The Elistonian soldiers were there in the blink of an eye, working to keep things from getting out of hand.

"Miss Evangeline will speak to the women and those unable to fight. Those of you who would like to join the ranks, follow Casimir's instructions. It is a pleasure to be with you once again, beloved people of Wenterly," Alastair concluded.

The Cathmoores raised their hands, one last wave to their people, before Casimir ushered them into the carriage.

"Long live the king!" someone shouted.

"Long live the true king," I said to myself, echoing the words Reeves spoke to me in Narim a lifetime ago.

But the woman I'd been standing next to in the front row must have heard me, because she repeated, much louder, "Long live the true king!"

The crowd went wild, yelling and chanting "Long live the true king," as the carriage pulled away.

Casimir turned to the crowd and quieted them. "Those of you who would like t' fight, report to the Law Office. Harland's officers are being removed from your city as we speak. You'll find Elistonian soldiers there, eager t' equip you in the fight for your own kingdom. Those of you who cannot fight but would like t' know how you can help, you can stay here, and Miss Evangeline will speak with you momentarily."

The people shouted and shuffled around, trying to leave the square all at once. I was to wait until the people had organized their next steps to speak, and no one was paying us any mind yet.

I turned to Casimir. "Alastair told me you volunteered to be my guardian."

He turned, surprise on his face. "Did he tell you why I did so?"

"He didn't know. But he felt you had a reason beyond the one you gave in front of King Heston and Queen Adeena."

He nodded. "Roland wrote a letter. Alastair refused t' read it, but I had. It was the worst plea of innocence I'd ever read. The first half was full of excuses for his crimes, and the second half full of threats t' blackmail Alastair, mostly with his ... *affiliation* with you."

The blood drained from my face. "What exactly do you mean?"

Casimir glanced at the crowd clamoring around us. "We shouldn't discuss the details here. But suffice it t' say, if you hope t' have a future at his side, it may be beneficial to be under the care of a third party when the time comes."

Hang the moon. He knew. Casimir *knew*.

"Have you told Heston? The things Roland said about us?"

"No. Nothing in the letter compromised Alastair's integrity in my eyes. There was nothing that needed t' be shared."

"Casimir—"

"We can discuss it later. Right now, you have an audience to address, Miss Evangeline."

I looked over to the front of the platform, wondering how long I had to re-gather my thoughts before the women started coming. But I gasped at the sight. I had expected maybe a handful of curious souls, intrigued by what I could possibly offer them. But women were elbowing their way forward, dozens of them in every direction. There was an eagerness in their movement that went far beyond curiosity. They *wanted* to see me. To hear from me.

"They're actually comin' over here," I breathed.

"Of course they are. Alastair just made you the face of the Common Man's revolution. These people trust him. And so, they trust you."

"What if I say somethin' wrong? I haven't had a chance to run all my ideas past him. What if my ideas for defyin' Harland aren't in line with what Alastair wants?"

"Miss Evangeline, he trusts you t' make those decisions on your own." He smiled. "If anyone knows how t' defy authority, it's you."

"Are you insultin' me, Casimir?"

"Merely making an observation."

I took in the growing crowd of women. It had tripled in size since I'd last looked. My heart pounded. "I don't know if I can speak in front of all these people."

"You have to give it a try, at least this once. Alastair promised you would speak. If you don't, it would make him a liar, and we can't have that."

"He started off as a liar when I met him, yet I'm still fightin' for him."

Casimir smiled. "Perhaps. But you seem a bit more resilient than most, Evangeline."

67

Eva Really Has a Way with Words

Alastair

I opened the bag I'd thrown into the carriage and pulled off my jacket. I told the carriage driver to pull into an alley, slipped on the commoner's tunic and hat I'd packed, and opened the carriage door.

My mother's look of confusion finally solidified into a scolding. "Where do you think you're going? We're to meet the men at the law office."

"And I will. But I want to hear what Evangeline says first."

"Alastair, you can't seriously—"

"I'll be careful. See you in a moment." I hopped out, shut the door, and made my way back to the square.

I then realized that only those who weren't able to fight were instructed to listen to Eva, and I certainly was not a woman. *Should I limp?*

It didn't matter. I lingered toward the back of the crowd. It was probably better if she didn't see me, anyway. I didn't want to make her more nervous.

She and Casimir spoke together, and then he gestured for her to move up to the front of the platform.

"Good women of Wenterly," Eva began.

I moved closer. I could barely hear her from where I was.

"And good men of Wenterly," she added after a moment, realizing she might be addressing the men at the edges of the group too.

"I am not good at speeches, so forgive me for lackin' a stronger voice or a more dynamic way of speakin'. I am just a seamstress from Welven, and I have no titles or wealth. I never thought I'd be anythin' but a seamstress.

I never thought my life would matter much to anyone at all. But that didn't stop the Royal Cathmoores from seein' somethin' worthwhile in me." She looked down at the people crowding the platform, then sat—c*rosslegged*, not even kneeling—in front of everyone.

"Can you all still hear me alright?" she asked, adjusting her skirt to maintain some semblance of modesty. People nodded and shouted yeses.

"I'm not going to pretend to be someone I'm not. I'm not a political leader. I'm not a revolutionary. I'm *certainly* not a war strategist. But I do know that the people we surround ourselves with make all the difference in what we're able to accomplish. Your husbands, your friends, your brothers, are goin' to go and fight for a better future. They will go to fight for your sake, as well as their own. It is your job between now and then to remind them that they also need to *win* for your sake.

"I have been in one battle, and it was indeed one too many for me. There was—" She shook her head, deciding against whatever she was about to say. "The battle I faced was over quite quickly, and we had the advantage of surprise. This war won't be like that. So when the battle gets tough, you need to remind your men it's not enough for them to die for their kingdom, they need to live for it. If all our good men die, what good is victory goin' to bring us?"

I understood her point, but I also wished she would stop talking about death so much. Obviously that came with the territory of war and revolution, but she was going to scare the people away.

"It's your job to remind your loved ones what they'll be comin' home to," she continued. "What they have to look forward to in the bright future under the Royal Cathmoores' rule." She took a deep breath. "When I was a girl, my mother would tell me a story whenever I had a nightmare. Though it may seem silly, I still tell myself that story when I feel afraid or upset. Even King Alastair has a book he turns to in times of crisis." She took a deep breath. "What I mean is, whether the least in the kingdom, like me, or the highest in the kingdom, like him, we draw strength from the words of those we love."

I wondered if Eva knew what she had just said was only half-true. I *did* love that book, but it wasn't Brigid's words I drew strength from during our journey. It was hers. It was always hers.

"Before your loved ones leave to fight, give them letters to carry with them. A story or the reasons you love them. You know what will encourage them most to remember in the heat of battle. I know most of us here can't write ourselves, but you can recite it for your soldier to write down. Then he won't only have the words to read, but also the memory of your voice. All the better, in my opinion.

"And when they go off to fight and you are still here, live as citizens of Wenterly, not as citizens of New Glastor. You don't have to pay dues to a tyrant. You don't have to tear apart your lives and your families for a man who has never understood the value of such a thing. We are people of a better kingdom, and we will see it come again."

A few people clapped, but a lady near the front raised her hand. "Miss, I'm not understandin' how a letter is goin' to make a difference in anythin'."

"Oh, er, let me see how to better explain it." She thought of it fairly quickly, which I was pleased to see. "Have any of you spun wool before? Or woven it into fabric?" She waited for a few nods. "Some might say that only Fate can spin and weave the threads of our lives. And that may be, but I believe we decide how to weave Fate's threads together once they're off its spinnin' wheel. The love letters you give to your soldiers are reminders that they are not lone threads goin' to war. Their lives are interwoven with yours. Fate may spin the threads, but we weave ourselves together."

I nearly laughed. I wasn't sure I agreed with her on that, as I could only account for us being together the last few weeks because Fate had refused to let us separate when we had wanted to. But she *was* a philosopher. A philosopher with analogies of fabric and thread. She was brilliant. She was beautiful.

"We are stronger together." Eva pulled the scarf off her head, and I smiled at her complete disregard for public protocol. But that was exactly why I knew she'd be so good at this. She asked Casimir to hold the fabric taut for her, and he, though clearly confused, obliged.

"A lone thread is easily severed." She used her pendant to cut off one of the strings on the edge of the fabric. "But when many threads are woven together"—she attempted to cut the fabric with her pendant, but it made no damage—"they are able to survive the blade."

She raised her pendant. "Harland is powerful, yes. But he has few friends."

She raised the fabric. "If we all work together, he will be no match for us."

The women cheered, and the men clapped. My heart burst with pride. Eva was *beyond* brilliant. She would be a marvelous queen, if she decided to accept the position.

But even if she did, we'd still have to convince the rest of the world she was worthy of it. And if we couldn't do that? What would become of me? My heart was woven helplessly around hers.

I shuddered at the thought that it might yet unravel.

HAVERLAY, ISLE OF GLASTOR

Podge held his breath as he entered the pub and approached his captain. He didn't need to read the letter in his hand to know it would not be well-received. He sat next to the Pirate King at the bar and passed the envelope over. "From yer favorite partner."

The captain scoffed. "This had better be a letter expressin' his gratitude and nothin' more."

"If only."

The captain ripped the letter from the envelope as Morrison, the barkeep, handed Podge a full pint. He sipped cautiously, knowing any moment the captain would have an outburst, and he wasn't keen on sloshing good ale onto a new shirt.

He expected a curse, a fist on the table top, or some other normal response. But after a solid two minutes of silence, something happened that actually scared him.

The Pirate King laughed.

Podge shifted on the stool, unaccustomed to being caught off guard, let alone by his captain. "Don't tell me he actually only wanted to express his thanks."

The captain choked down another laugh. "Hardly. Harland seems to have lost his favorite pet. Master Roland failed to kill the kid, and now he and Heston are startin' a revolution in New Glastor. Serves the moron right for disobeyin' orders and leavin' the Cathmoores alive in the first place."

"Roland double crossed him?"

"Must have. Once a traitor, always a traitor." The captain took a hearty swig of ale. "Harland also wants us to provide aid for the revolution. As if he didn't get himself in this position."

The captain passed the letter back over to Podge. "Forward this to the Gray Dagger. Baxley owes me. He may have saved me the trouble of killin' Mothway for his incompetence, but he still failed to bring me the kids. If he wants to prove he's worth his salt as a captain, his orders are to investigate our Cathmoores' revolution and find out the whereabouts of Roland, if the fool is even still alive. If he is, Baxley is to bring him to me."

Podge tucked the letter into his vest. Roland was a dead man, regardless of if his heart was currently beating. "And what of Harland's request fer aid?"

"Ignore it. Harland has forgotten his place. He wanted to play games. He can deal with the risk of losin'." The captain downed the remaining half a glass of ale in two swallows and stood. "On second thought, why don't you write back to Harland and tell him we'll be there, startin' with the Elistonian soldiers at the border of Glastor."

"I take it we have no intention of following through?"

"Not at all. I didn't become king of the seas to answer to the wishes of men on land." The captain turned, then added one last amendment. "Regardin' the Grey Dagger's *capture of Roland, do remind them that dead men tell no tales. If there are witnesses to his capture, they are to leave one survivor to spread the news." With that, the Pirate King stormed out of the pub.*

Morrison took the captain's empty glass. "Almost wish I was on the mainland to see it all go down."

Podge laughed. "You've got the best seat in Breslin right here. All you'll see from the mainland is a slow an' pointless revolution."

"You know who'll win then?"

"It don't matter. Captain's decision is made. Neither one of 'em can outrun The Reaper's Shadow.*"*

Acknowledgements

Maybe it takes a village to save a kingdom, but it also takes a village to publish a novel.

Thank you to the indie authors who have not only gone before and done the hard thing, but who have taken the time to one-on-one answer my questions and encourage me in my next steps, namely Alissa J. Zavalianos, Erin Phillips, and Candice Pedraza Yamnitz.

Thank you to my editors: Olivia Jarmusch from The Glory Writers and Caitlin Miller. Olivia, your insight into these characters and pushing me to dig deeper into their motivations has made this story come alive. Caitlin, your encouraging notes and attention to detail has made this story shine.

Thank you to my proofreader, Teri Sammon. Your flexibility and willingness to make this happen was an immense blessing in the midst of everything else going on at the time.

Thank you Emilie Haney for creating the cover of my dreams.

Thank you to the ladies of SubClub for your wisdom, input, and friendship.

Thank you to my parents, my sisters, and Rachel for encouraging me to write (and tolerating me talking about all the stories I make up) since grade school. I finally did it, and this is just the start. Thank you for helping me get here.

To my newsletter fam: Some of you have been with me since I started writing the first draft of *The Webs We Weave*. All of you have been a monthly reminder of why I write what I write. Thank you for cheering me on.

To my alpha readers: Mom, Staci, and Rachel, you read the absolute worst version of this story and still believed in it. Thank you for getting me where I am today.

To my beta readers: Kat, Elisabeth, Sarah, Laura, Erin, Ian, Miriam, Brinley, Abigail, and my mom, you all blew me away with your insight (and delight) in this story. You have encouraged me more than you will ever know. Sorry about your favorite pirate captain.

Thank you to my street team Pirates and Politicians. You are all amazing. Having your support as I worked on and released this book was a game-changer. You have encouraged me beyond my wildest dreams. I am so thankful for you.

To Staci and Laura who have willingly endured more of my questions and info dumps in the last year than anyone else on this earth, you guys are unreal. I love you forever.

Thank you to those who supported the Hope & Wonder fundraiser and *especially* thank you to my family members who believed in this book so much they financially supported it when I lost my job. Mom, Grandma and Grandpa, and Aunt Shelly, this book would have released an entire year later without you. Thank you for believing in me as much as I believe in this story.

To Jesus. Almost three years ago to the date of this book's release you told me you called me to write. I'm sorry I (metaphorically) laughed in your face and told you I needed a stable career first. It is clear now that you had the last laugh. Thank you for your kindness to me in my resistance to the call, and thank you for making all my dreams come true in this regard anyway. You are so good, and I am grateful to call you my God and my friend.

And finally, thank *you* dear reader, for taking a chance on a debut novel. This book in your hands is simultaneously the last step of a life-long dream, and the beginning of a new one. Thank you for reading.

About the Author

Cassandra Grace has been writing fantastical stories and sad poetry since childhood. She reads an average of four books at a time while wishing she could go on an epic adventure of her own—until she remembers she's a homebody. Cassandra has dreamed of being a published author since second grade. She is now a multi-genre author, encouraging weary hearts that life is a gift despite its hardships. You can keep up with her latest shenanigans on social media @cassandraspocket. For monthly updates and insight into her next writing projects, join her newsletter at cassandraspocket.net/newsletter

www.ingramcontent.com/pod-product-compliance
Lightning Source LLC
LaVergne TN
LVHW091655070526
838199LV00050B/2176